Falcon Dreams

Stephan & Melodi Grundy

TLS

ISBN13: 978-1-959350-03-3

Set in: Georgia 11pt/Concetta Kalvani 27pt, Farmhouse 36pt

©The Three Little Sisters
USA/CANADA

Chapter One

Margerite arose before dawn on Easter Sunday, shivering in the cold air as she slid from beneath her coverlets. Her serving-maid Gertrude had not yet come in to light the tallow candles and kindle the fire in the stove that served the chamber for heat, so that Margerite had to fumble in the dark for the clothes that had been laid out neatly on her chair the previous night. The light woolen shift was unaccustomedly chill and a little damp against her skin: Gertrude usually lay her clothes over the stove to warm them in the morning before Margerite got up. Hurriedly she drew the thick wool gown over the shift, then climbed back into bed to warm herself before her maidservant came. It would not do for Gertrude to see her shivering, though Margerite's single castle chamber, even with the hangings covering the damp stone walls and the floor heaped high with fresh rushes and dried strewing-herbs, was colder than the crowded buildings of wood around the castle foot where most of the servants lived.

The servant's knock on the door was light, barely more than a brushing of knuckles. At once Margerite rose, drawing her cloak around herself, and went silently to open the door.

Gertrude hurried in, her shoes whispering soft over the worn rugs on the stone floor. "Mistress," she said as she set her basket of firewood down and began to walk about with her taper, "the first light of dawn is showing. You told me..."

Margerite nodded as she bent to tie her shoes on, then brushed back her long fall of ash-blond hair with the back of her hand - Gertrude could see to it later. What mattered now was reaching Maria's Well before the first edge of the sun showed over the horizon, so that she could wash her eyes in the holy water and see whatever vision the Virgin granted her.

A vision of my husband-to-be...please, Mother Maria, show me a man young and kind. Trembling as much from excitement as from the cold, Margerite made her way hurriedly down the uneven stone steps and through the kitchen. The Paschal lamb, slaughtered yesterday, hung skinned, gutted, and beheaded from one of the great iron wall-hooks, little pools of dried blood on the stones beneath it; the scullery maid and pot-boy still snored beside the last ash-furred coals in the hearth. On another morning, she would have stopped to wake them, but she knew that she must not speak until she had come back from the Well, lest the enchantment of her prayers be broken.

Gertrude had been slower-footed than she should have, or else slept longer: the dawning sky was already grey, the rocky path down into the woods clear before Margerite. She went as quickly as she could, her cheeks reddening with warmth beneath the sting of the cold breeze. The first birds were singing, their clear voices calling through the green tracery of budding leaves above; it would not be too long before the deeper song of the Easter bell answered from the village's church. A sweet scent rose up from beneath Margerite's feet as she turned from the main road down a smaller trail, a trail overgrown with wood-master and wild strawberries. The white-flowering brambles at the sides of the pathway caught at her cloak, as if to snare her and hold her back, but she pulled the garment more tightly about herself and hurried on.

The grey sky had already lightened to blue by the time Margerite broke through into the clearing where Maria's Well stood - a small circle of rough stones heaped to the height of her waist, with a rope running down from the well-tree into the dark water below. Hastily she hauled the bucket up, hand over hand. It came out dripping, tendrils of green moss streamingfrom the oaken sides.

Maria, she prayed silently. Show me - am I to marry this year? Or will I still be here next Easter, the spinster daughter of a poor knight, still with little dowry and my father's land only held in fief? And if I am to marry, will he be...?

But Margerite could not go on longer, for the brutal truth was as clear to her as to anyone. Since her childhood betrothed Joachim had died in the return of the plague, she had known that she would be married to whoever her father could find for her, another knight like himself if she was lucky, perhaps a burgher with enough money to make his breeding acceptable if she were not. And as for the chance that he would be young, or handsome, or treat his wife as well as horse or hound...she knew the likelihood of that as well.

Yet I will see! Margerite said fiercely to herself. She dipped her left hand into the bucket, forcing her eyelids to stay open as the icy water spashed over her face. It stung sharply in her eyes, blurring her sight to rippled glass as she looked upward at the blue sky.

As she blinked the water from her eyes, a small gray turtledove fluttered overhead, its cooing call soft through the rustling of the leaves and the higher songs of the other birds. Margerite's heart sank in disappointment. A gray bird, a spinster - the quiet life of a nun, perhaps? Surely it was no vision of a husband, unless perhaps her father married her off to a soft-handed city clerk.

Then, so suddenly that she had no time to blink or cry out, the great shape flashed down like a dark arrow cleaving through the brightness above. The eagle's scream of triumph scraped rough against Margerite's ears as his talons struck the turtledove, a few drops of blood spraying out red. The eagle's wings beat, lifting him high above the treetops again, and he was gone with his prey, leaving only three small grey feathers tumbling slowly to earth on the morning breeze.

Margerite stretched out her hand to catch the falling feathers - soft as thistledown, yet the delicate brushing against her palm almost made her faint. Though she was not sobbing, her eyes were hot and her cheeks wet, her heart thudding furiously against her ribs. The first ring of the deep iron bell sounded from the valley below the castle, its clanging rising loud through the forest: the sun was rising, heralding Christ's rising from the tomb, and the time of vision was over.

I wanted to see - and I saw. But what? A raptor, a RaubRitter or highwayman? Yet the eagle had been so noble, so powerful, that he had taken her breath away even as he struck it from the turtledove's body; but Margerite knew that she could not dare to think the best. If there had been any doubt in her heart that all hopes must someday be dashed beneath the doom of mortality, she would have lost it two years ago, when the great plague that had spared her a year after her birth circled back through the Rhineland in 1361. Then, though she and her father still lived, Margerite had seen her mother and her little sister crying for water, the tender flesh of armpits and necks and groin-hollows swelling agonizingly with the grim black buboes; and she had lain out their bodies and sewn the shrouds herself, knowing that though God's mercy must serve for the afterworld, it could have little place on earth.

And I could not fly such a bird from my wrist, Margerite thought. For all the years that I have lifted hawk and falcon into the air, he would be too much for me. Better for each to hold what is fitting to their station: as the English book says, the merlin for the noblewoman, the gyrfalcon for the king, and the eagle - for the Kaiser alone. Few heed that in their hawking, but does it not show how the orders of nature are ranked and set as those of men?

And still Margerite held the feathers tenderly, fingers closed over palm as if she feared to crush them; and held them like that all the way back to the castle, where she brushed past the rousing kitchen-folk without a word and hurried up to her own room. Only when she had tucked them away safely inside the carven chest where her best linens lay did she pay any heed to the presence of her maid, or to Gertrude's quiet question, "Did you see?"

Margerite sat down on her bed, letting her breath out in a great sigh and wiping the last dampness from her face with the trailing hem of a woolen sleeve. "Yes...I saw. But do not ask me what."

"Ah...well." Gertrude took up Margerite's little silver comb from her table. "The Easter bells are ringing, and your hair is still tangled. And what will your father do to me if you come uncombed to Mass?"

"Nothing, for you are my servant and not his," said Margerite, gritting her jaw against the little tugging pains of Gertrude's swift strokes. "Simply pull it back and tie it. My hood will cover it anyway, and you can braid it properly later on."

Gertrude sighed with annoyance, but did as she was bid. Although she was two years younger than Margerite, she often seemed to think that her peasant birth had somehow gifted her with twice the knowledge of the world that a knight's daughter had, for all Margerite had been chatelaine of her father's castle since she herself was fifteen.

In the low wooden building that served Ritter Martin von Hirschenberg and the people of his village as a chapel, Margerite barely heard the words of the Easter Mass, the familiar sonority of the Latin washing over her like water over a stone - a soft clear plashing over the solid weight of the question, Who will he be?

Although the chapel was dim, lit only by the smoky torches around the walls and the two beeswax candles on the altar, her eyes were still dazzled by the sight she had seen at Maria's Well, and though she sat proudly beside her father, she had to hide the trembling of her hands in the woolen fold of her cloak. Even when she went up to take her bite of Communion bread, the sweet taste was faraway in her mouth, hardly more than a memory on her tongue.

Afterwards, however, there was little time for her to sit and think. Although the keep of Hirschenberg was small, there was still an Easter feast to hold. She had a hall to be swept clean and strewn again with fresh rushes and the first fronds of meadowsweet and woodmaster; bread had to be baked, children had to be sent to fetch dried onions, dig leeks, and gather the young leaves of sorrel and rocket and fresh nettle shoots. The scent of the roasting lamb wafted up through the castle, so that Margerite could smell it where-ever she went, the savoury aroma making her mouth water - after the forty days' fast of Lent, with little more than fish, bread, and cheese on the table, the promise of rich fresh meat was almost sinfully intoxicating.

More than once, on her frequent trips to the kitchen, she saw the boy who turned the spit snatching his fingers away from the trickles of fat that glistened down the lamb's browning sides to wipe them hastily on his stained grey trousers, and a few smears of stolen drippings shone about his mouth. Yet she could not bring herself to chide him, for he might well get little more than the bits left on a marrowbone, and it would be cruel to grudge him a taste of the roast he tended.

At last the sun was setting, and the long table down the middle of the hall readied. The Ritter Martin's seat, and Margerite's at his right, were lit with fat beeswax candles; the poorer folk farther down had to make do with tallow lights. As well as the lamb, now lying in a steaming heap of roasted joints, several chickens had been slaughtered; they shone golden as fabulous phoenixes in the candlelight, though their gilding was only a brushing of egg-yolks.

Margerite had read of how the tables of the great might be adorned with swans or peacocks, their claws and beaks glittering with gold-leaf and their feathers stuck back in so that it almost seemed as if the living bird sat regal before the assembly, but she was very proud of her chickens: she had brushed the gilding on herself, and watched carefully to make sure that they were taken from the fire before the glaze turned from rich gold to plain brown.

In honour of Easter, baskets of painted eggs were set along the table, decorated by those who would sit in each place so that they could be given to friends and dear ones. One bore a declaration of love - Margerite had been asked to write it, scribing in a careful hand, and knew she would likely be asked to read the message to the girl who received it. Other painted eggs, their contents blown out for use in the Easter baking, hung from flowering branches like an early ripening of bright fruit.

It was, Margerite thought as she surveyed the hall, the meats and braided rings of bread and pots of stewed greens beneath the egg-trees, as fine a feast as the little Hirschenberg castle had ever set before its people, and would not have shamed them if Kaiser Karl himself had stopped in unexpectedly, as he was said to do at times in his many travels throughout his great realm.

Freshly clad and brushed, with all the grime scrubbed from their faces and hands, the Hirschenberg folk began to wander in by twos and threes. Fighting men, of less than knightly rank, but still well-tutored from an early age in handling their halberds and swords; the tall, lean figure of Michael Falconer, who kept the castle's mews; Johannes, who trained their horses and oversaw the stables...the warriors and the highest-ranking of the servants would be there, together with a few of their wives, some thirty-five or forty folk in all. They knew their own places, seating themselves accordingly, as they had done for years; but Margerite stood by herself at the head of the table, waiting for her father.

And yet the Ritter Martin did not come. Margerite's mood of expectation was beginning to change swiftly to irritation, then to annoyance. The faint chiming of metal from her side warned her that she was fidgeting like a child, twiddling the small bunch of keys that hung from her belt. More irritated, she pulled her hand away - the keys were the sign of her adulthood, her chatelaincy, not a jingling toy to distract her - and folded her fingers carefully, letting the long edges of her sleeve drape across each other.

The voices of the gathered folk were getting louder: though no one would set to eating until Martin arrived in his hall, they were not so shy of drinking. The flushed faces of some of the men-at-arms told Margerite that they, at least, had started the celebration early, and already Gertrude had refilled three of the pitchers on the table from the oak barrel in the corner of the hall.

Half the guests would be sliding under the table by the time the feast began, if her father did not get there soon, Margerite thought. And she could see the food chilling before her very eyes: the steam rising from the meats and stewpots into the cold air of the hall was already thinning like mist beneath the sun. Soon it would be gone, the outer portions cool as yesterday's leftovers - and why was her father not in his hall?

Her anger died within her, drowned out by an icy wave of fear. Martin had been well when she had seen him that afternoon, striding about his duties as Margerite went about hers, but there were many things that might happen to a man in a scant two hours - seeming health was no guarantee of life. Gertrude was halfway to the wine barrel, another empty pitcher in her hand, but she caught Margerite's gesture at the corner of her eye, swerving over to her mistress' side.

"Go find my father," Margerite said softly. "Quickly - make sure no ill has befallen him. If there is need, come back to me at once, and do not give any alarm unless I command it, do you understand?"

Gertrude's round cheeks paled as she saw her mistress' face. She nodded once, her long brown braid swinging like a horse's plaited tail, and turned to scurry from the hall.

But even as the serving-maid lifted her hand to the iron-bound oaken door, it swung open, nearly knocking her over. She leapt back, regaining her balance with a dainty half-step, even as Margerite sighed silently in relief.

The man who entered first, however, was not the Ritter Martin, but a taller and slimmer figure, a dark-haired man in a yellow doublet and blue hose, wearing a blue-trimmed cloak with yellow edging. Margerite did not know him, but she recognised the livery of her father's liege-lord, the Graf von Hohenfels. At once she grasped the pitcher of wine from the table in front of her, turning to curtsey low before the man who - whatever word he brought - could only be treated as an honoured guest in their hall, then treading forward with her pitcher ready to fill the silver goblet that hung on a strand of gold braid from his wide belt.

Behind the Graf's messenger bulked the low, broad-shouldered shape of the Ritter Martin. A smile opened in the gray bush of his beard as his guest undid the goblet's tie and lifted it to be filled.

"You are most welcome in the hall of Hirschenberg, my lord," Margerite said, taking care to keep her voice low and musical, as that of a maiden of good birth ought to be. Though the messenger might or might not be nobly-born himself, it was best to address him so, for the sake of the one whose commands he bore. "Be greeted in Jesu's name this holy day, and take this seat, if you will." She gestured the messenger to her own chair, the place of honour at her father's right, and moved to stand at the left of Martin's seat: Gertrude would fetch another chair for her.

"I thank you for your greeting, noble maiden," the man answered. His voice was high and strong - the trained voice of a herald, if Margerite did not mistake it. He proceeded to the seat, Martin following behind him. The Ritter did not sit at once, but stood looking down the table, at the faces of his men and their feast-bedecked wives.

"The fast is over," Martin said, the words rumbling loud from his deep chest. "Good folk, let the feast begin!" He drew the knife from his belt, plunging it into the roasted lamb. The crackling-brown skin split, sending up a wave of fresh scent, and his men cheered, waving cups and tankards in the air before reaching, at last, for the food set in front of them.

By the time her father had carved the first of the joints for their end of the table, Margerite had settled herself at his left, and sat sipping at her own goblet of wine. She could see the letter in his belt, the ends of parchment crinkled beneath the broad strip of leather, and only her awareness of her position kept her from grasping for it to read it then and there. Yet she thought that her father would not speak of the matter until their guest's first hunger had been sated, and so she held herself quiet, only nodding and smiling graciously as Martin said to the messenger, "Sir, this is my daughter Margerite, chatelaine of this castle since my wife's death. Whatever you find on this table that pleases you is her work."

The Graf's man inclined his head towards Margerite. He was well-favoured, she noticed, his smooth, regular features marred only by a straight scar across his left cheekbone, such as might have been left by a grazing arrow or blade-edge. "Frowe, you are capable, as well as beautiful," he said. "Your father is fortunate to have such a daughter: even the strongest tree is bettered by a fair flower." He spread his hands out, as though to lighten the weight of his words. He wore but two rings: on the one hand, a gold wedding-ring, on the other hand, a thick band of silver engraved deeply with black writing. Margerite could just make out the letters, ...BRAE LUX. Something about light...

She could not keep the blush from tinging her face, for she was not used to such words. Most of her father's fighting men had known her since childhood, and still patted her cheeks or ruffled her hair occasionally, while the youths of the village would never have dared to speak words that might be misread. Though she knew the speech was no more than courtesy, it still warmed her in an unfamiliar way.

"I thank you for your kindness," she murmured, lowering her gaze.

Her father laughed and patted Margerite lightly on the back, the tap of his big hand gentle against her shoulder-blade. "She is, indeed, the jewel of my castle, and the joy of my old age. And she is educated, as well: she can read and write both Latin and German, far better than I can. You see..."

Martin pulled the letter from his belt, giving it over to Margerite. Her fingers shook slightly as she unfolded the parchment, smoothing the wrinkles from it.

The letter was written in a good hand, the Latin characters smooth and rounded. Margerite translated easily as she read aloud.

"To Ritter Martin von Hirschenberg, from his liege lord Graf Günther von Hohenfels, greetings. I send you the good news that my friend, Graf Ruprecht von Falkenstein, has given me the joy of his company over this Easter week. He, and a small troop of his men, will soon be passing through your lands on the way back to his own castle. I therefore ask you, by the love and faithfulness you have always shown to me, to guest them well before they pass on. In trust and honour, Günther von Hohenfels."

Margerite drew in a deep breath, her head whirling with the unexpected news. Steadying beneath her sudden excitement, however, like a slab of thick-buttered bread after the first rush of a quickly emptied winecup, were the more practical thoughts that came to her mind at once. The Graf and his men would need food, at least one welcoming feast, and fitting lodgings as well - how many? For how long? And how much time did they have to get ready before their noble guest and his following descended upon them?

The same thoughts must have been in her father's mind as well, for his hand tugged at the tangle of beard spreading across his wide chest even as he smiled broadly. "This is indeed a great honour, for the Graf Günther von Hohenfels to find us worthy of guesting his friend. Tell me, sir, when may we expect their coming?"

"Some three or four days hence," the Graf's man answered. "Graf Ruprecht von Falkenstein's troop is not large: a mere thirty men, only enough to make his way safe, for the journey from the edge of the Schwarzwald can be a chancy one. And I think he will not stay more than a night, since he will have some way to travel yet."

Three days? Margerite thought. And how many of the troop would be knights like her father, expecting the full courtesy of equals? Even for one night, they could not be billeted in the stables, or told to lay their bedrolls upon the floor of the hall. And the Graf himself: they had a chamber for noble guests, but it had not been used in some time, and was heaped to the ceiling with bedlinens and bales of cloth.

They would have to hurry, to take the wooden shutters from the windows and air the mustiness away, then carry up a stove and keep it going, to take the chill from the stones. No, they must at least take away all the stored fabrics, warm it and get the bed freshly made now, for von Hohenfels' messenger would have to sleep there tonight. The good beeswax candles - how many had they left? She would have to arrange for more, to see that all the bedding in the castle was gathered and washed and dried: God send them fair weather for the next three days!

Though the lamb was succulent, sweetly flavoured with rosemary and the first sprigs of mint, Margerite hardly tasted it. First she had to send Gertrude scampering to ready the guest-chamber for the Graf's man; then her mind was too busy turning over all that needed to be done, struggling with the problem of sleeping and tending to thirty men decently in their little fortress on such short notice, to spare any attention to the meat. Her wine sat nearly untasted until her father tapped his fingernail against the bronze goblet's figured rim.

"Drink, my girl!" Martin said. "You've earned this feast better than any, and we have good news to celebrate." Though his words were not slurred, the Ritter's cheeks and nose were very red above his beard: he had not stinted his own cup. Yet Margerite knew that, however much he drank tonight, her father would be out of his bed at dawn the next day, giving his orders and getting his men to work. So she lifted her goblet and took a deep swallow, hoping that the strength thrumming beneath the wine's cool sweetness would calm her racing nerves.

Instead, the drink seemed to rise to Margerite's head at once, the fumes dizzying her thoughts so that the well-ordered rows of plans and contingencies, assigned bedding-spaces and measures of food, fell about like a child's army of wooden dolls disarranged by a careless hand. Struggling to keep her composure, she glanced across her father to the Graf's man, who sat twirling his silver goblet slowly by the stem, looking cooly about the hall. It must seem very small and poor to him, she thought.

Was he wondering why Ritter Martin von Hirschenberg had been chosen for the honour of guesting Graf Ruprecht, when so many of Graf Günther's knights were richer and better housed?

"Of your courtesy, my lord," Margerite said to him, "would you tell me more of Graf Ruprecht von Falkenstein and his troop, that we may be better ready to receive them as is fitting to their ranks and expectations?" She hoped she did not sound as breathless as she felt, though her voice sounded high and girlish to her own ears.

The messenger's eyes fixed upon her own. They were very blue and clear, drawing her gaze like a candle-flame flaring in darkness for a moment - a brightness that seemed to brush against the inside of her skull. Then his lips curved into a small smile.

"You need not fear that his men will overwhelm your holding," he answered kindly. The tips of Margerite's ears burned, for it seemed to her almost as if he had read her thoughts with that single penetrating glance. "Graf Ruprecht has brought only his own house-troops with him, so that there are no other noblemen for whom you must care. They are soldiers, and used to the hardship of the road. The Graf himself..."

Again the messenger smiled, but his bright eyes seemed somehow shuttered against Margerite's glance, as though he had closed himself away for a moment to make a private little joke. "I think you will find him a welcome guest. He is a young man, skilled in arms and experienced in battle, as befits his noble birth. Like you, he reads and writes well, and I have heard that he keeps a library with many books. His chief joy, though, is hunting, and if you, sir," he said, nodding to Martin, "can show him the way to good hunting here, he will surely be your friend forever."

"I am sure we can find him a chase," Martin answered. "There are deer and a few boar, and, if nothing else, we have good hawks. Is he interested in falconry?" Her father did not ask this without good reason, Margerite knew. Though their mews was small, those birds they had were of the finest quality - Hirschenberg's one extravagance - and Michael Falconer could have found service in a greater court on any day he chose to. Her mother had loved riding out with a falcon upon her wrist; indeed, Michael Falconer had come from her own family's holding so that she could pursue her passion to the fullest, and had stayed after her death out of loyalty, not only to the hawks who were used to their tending, but to Margerite, who had inherited all her mother's pleasure in the sport.

"Graf Ruprecht finds all kinds of hunting to his taste. If you have fine hawks, he will be glad to fly them with you."

"What of his frowe wife?" Margerite enquired. "Has she come with him?" The Gräfin would surely need a chamber of her own, as well. It would have to be Margerite's own, it would not be fitting to house her in the room that had been the chamber of Martin's wife...

The face of the Graf's man did not change, the smooth planes of his face still, almost too still, as if he chose to hide...sorrow? amusement? Whatever his thoughts might be, Margerite could not tell. His voice was cool and light as a cup of wine fresh-drawn from the barrel as he said, "Graf Ruprecht's frowe wife is two years in her grave. He lost her when the Death returned, and has not married again."

"As I..." Martin murmured, his soft words echoing empty as stones dropped into a deep well. Margerite reached out, pressing her father's hand for a moment in sympathy. He would not marry again while he lived, she knew. She had spoken of it to him once, after his year of formal mourning was done, and he had answered only, "Geese mate for life." After she was gone, he would be alone - Margerite had often wondered if that had slowed him in searching for a husband for her, and if sometimes the thought had angered her, she was more often grateful that he had not already sold her to a man of his own generation.

But as she lay alone in her bed that night, the warm coverlets pulled up about her head against the swiftly chilling air, the messenger's words came back to Margerite again and again, like nagging fleabites that would not let her get to sleep. If the Graf Ruprecht were young, and single - could he look with favour upon her?

Surely not, for men of his rank did not marry for beauty, or charm, or even skill in managing a castle. If Ruprecht meant to marry again, he would look among his own.

Thus thinking, Margerite turned over, pulling the covers tightly around her ears as if to shut out the sound of her own thoughts. She would have to rise early tomorrow, for there was much work to do.

The Graf's messenger bade them farewell the next morning, and went on his way. From the castle door, Margerite watched him riding down the path to the river, her gaze following the shrinking figure until he had rounded a bend at the foot of the next hill and she could see him no longer.

"That was a handsome man," Gertrude said with a little giggle when her mistress turned back inside. "And well-mannered, too: I brought him food and wine all evening, and he did not slap or pinch me once."

"Is that your measure of manners?" Margerite asked, amused and annoyed at once. "We had best hope that he will bring a good report back to his lord, at any rate. But you must hurry to work now. There are a few spots on my best gown that will take some work to get out, and it must be clean and dry within three days. And be sure all the tarnish is scrubbed from my silver chain and bracelets, for I must look my best, to uphold the honour of Hirschenberg."

"You will need to sleep better, to look your best," Gertrude answered. "From the circles under your eyes, I think you hardly went to sleep at all last night. Perhaps you should go back to bed for a little time, my lady, while I bear your orders to the others."

Margerite's hand lifted to slap Gertrude across the cheek, but she forced herself to drop it again. The serving-maid was telling nothing but the truth, and there was real concern beneath her impudent words.

"What would my father say, if I spent the day in bed like a slattern? Still, when you have finished washing my dress, you may tell old Bertha the herbwife that I shall want one of her possets tonight before I go to sleep."

Gertrude nodded, flashing a crooked-toothed smile at her. "I will do that, my lady." She cocked her head to the side, looking mischievously up at Margerite like a little wren. "Now I wonder...the Graf's messenger is a very handsome man, after all. Did his blue eyes have anything to do with your sleeplessness last night?"

"No!" Even as she spoke, a little shudder ran down Margerite's back, remembering that strange piercing glance. "If you speak so again," she added severely, seeing the glimmer of glee lighting Gertrude's brown eyes, "I shall beat you, and you will know you have earned it, too."

Gertrude's smile flattened, and she dropped her gaze. "Of course, my lady," she answered, her voice more subdued. "I shall go wash your dress now." She hurried off, and Margerite quickened her own steps, making for the kitchen. If she ordered a pig slaughtered now, and hung in the cool air of the cellar for two days, it would be perfect for roasting upon the day of Ruprecht's arrival.

Margerite wondered if Graf Ruprecht's fondness for hunting meant that he would prefer game meat on the table, but after a moment's thought, she decided that, if the messenger's account was correct, the Graf was likely to eat game more often than not, and he might well be happier with the dainty meat of a young pig than the tough flesh of a boar. As for hinds, only a barren doe could be taken now, and while a young buck might be good eating, the time of grease, when the stags were in their summer fatness, had not yet begun.

When Margerite arose on the morning of the third day, she dressed quickly and hurried down the stairs. If the weather was good, and Graf Ruprecht arrived early enough, she would be able to go out on the hawking expedition; if rain were falling, her father would go into the woods with him, leaving her behind to wait.

But the sky was dazzling blue above the last tatters of river-mist, the sun shining fair and unclouded as a great yellow gem in a setting of burnished silver. Margerite sighed deeply, unclenching her hands. Only when she saw how white her fingers were, and felt the little prickles of pain where her nails had driven into her palms, did she realize how afraid she had been - And for what?

"You are a silly girl," she said severely to herself. There was more to worry about: what if the Graf came that day, but too late to start the pig roasting? What would they do for an evening meal then? It would have to be fowl, or fish if they had caught enough - she would send some of the boys down to the river, for, properly cooked, pike or trout would make a fine enough dinner for anyone.

Margerite fretted and paced all through the morning. She could barely sit still long enough for Gertrude to do her hair, brushing the ash-blond mass out and plaiting the sides into two thin braids that were tied with a twist of silver wire at the nape of her neck to hold the rest of her shining fall in place.

Once properly coiffed, Margerite walked up and down the castle stairs to make sure of this thing or that - was the guest chamber properly turned out, with fresh linens tucked upon the bed; were the corners of the hall swept; had full barrels of wine and beer been brought up from the cellars?

Gertrude had laid out her lady's finest clothing upon her chair, the long shift of close-woven linen and the pale blue linen overdress that Margerite had embroidered herself with flowers and vines twining about throat and cuffs, with the woven silver chain, hammered bracelets, and flower-worked girdle-buckle glittering in a neat heap upon the dress' empty lap, but Margerite did not want to put her good clothes on until the last moment, for fear of soiling them before the Graf ever arrived.

At last Margerite went down to the castle mews, where Michael the Falconer sat staring into the glittering eye of a large goshawk. She stood quietly, not wishing to disturb him, for she knew that he must not be the first to look away. Although she could see the long lines of his lean back taut against his tattered brown tunic, the sinews of his neck standing out beneath his cropped gray hair, there was something so quiet, so assured, in the way he sat perched upon his wooden stool that Margerite felt her own heart quieting as well.

Accustomed to hawks as she was, even Margerite could not tell when the shift came, when Michael's eyes had moved from challenging the bird's gaze to mastering it. But he lifted his head, nodding to her. "Good day, frowe." His voice was deep and soft, comfortingly familiar to her. The same gentle tones had guided Margerite when, as a child, she had walked among the perches in the mews, reaching up to stroke the sleek feathered sides.

Michael had fitted the first hawking-gauntlet to her hand, setting a little merlin upon it, and soothed her startlement at once when the bird had bated, rising and flapping his wings. He had told her of the intricate mysteries of hawks, their lives and loves, and how he must sit up nights matching gazes with those yet untamed, so that they might know themselves mastered, and at last take the meat he gave them.

"Good day, Michael. That is the new hawk?"

"The one your father brought in two weeks ago, yes. She promises well, though, as you know, the birds will all start their moulting soon, and after that it will take some training before she is ready for you to fly her."

"I shall look forward to it. Michael, you know that we may be hawking this afternoon, if Graf Ruprecht comes timely."

"The thought was in my mind when I saw the sky this morning." Michael smiled, a strangely soft expression on the lean angles of his face. "Enide, Kriemhilt, and Gawan are ready to fly today, if you wish them." He gestured towards the three falcons, the pride of the mews.

Kriemhilt shifted on her perch, the bells of her jesses chiming softly. Enide's eyes were closed, as if in disdain, but Gawan's sharp black glance followed the movement of Michael's hand avidly: he had not been flown for a week, so far as Margerite knew, and would be more than eager to take to the air again. As if to confirm her thoughts, he rose on his toes and bated, the little bells of his jesses ringing clear through the sound of his beating wings.

"Oh, yes. I…"

The sound of a trumpet, faint but clear through the walls of the mews, cut off Margerite's words.

"Go on," Michael said, but Margerite was already out the door, shouting for Gertrude as she raced towards her room to dress.

Margerite was a little breathless, but otherwise, she hoped, calm and well-arrayed as she descended the castle stairs again, a pitcher of the best wine in one hand and the castle's silver-bound guest-cup in the other. The oaken door was flung wide, her father's shadow breaking the sunlight that streamed across the stones. As she walked down, the shadow bent before the light: Martin was bowing, his sonorous deep tones echoing through the stairwell as he said, "You are most welcome to our hall, Graf Ruprecht von Falkenstein, for your own sake and for the love and trust we bear for our liege, Graf Günther von Hohenfels. Enter, and may you find delight in the time you while here."

The Ritter stepped aside, making a sweeping gesture with his hand. Margerite had reached the bottom of the stairs; now she stopped, staring at the man who stepped in through the bright door. Graf Ruprecht's shoulder-length hair burned gold in the sunlight, so that a halo of light seemed to glimmer about his head. His face was high-boned and noble, the fair skin deeply tanned, with a lighter shadow across forehead, eyes, and chin where the metal of a helm would protect his face from the sun; he wore no beard, though, unshaven for two days on the road, the sharp line of his jaw glittered with hair-prickles like a sprinkling of gold dust.

Graf Ruprecht stood a handspan taller than Margerite, and the figured cut of his red velvet doublet showed the breadth of his shoulders and heavy muscles of his chest tapering down to a narrow waist and slender hips; the muscles of his thighs and calves stood out clearly under his tight cream-coloured hose.

His deep blue shoes were pointed at the toes, but not elongated or curled upwards: he was clearly a man who preferred action to fashion. The impression was borne out by his square tanned hands, adorned only by a single large ring on the left forefinger - an amethyst set in smooth gold, with tiny lettering around the shining purple dome of the stone. But it was his eyes that drew Margarite's sight most of all.

They were a very light blue, glowing like aquamarines in full sunlight, with a piercing intensity that reminded her for a fleeting second of the peculiarly sharp gaze of von Hohenfels' messenger. Yet where that had unsettled her, Graf Ruprecht's look sent an odd thrill through her, more of a tingling than a shudder. So angels, Margerite thought, may walk among us unawares...Her head was spinning, and she felt suddenly dizzy: she realized that she had been holding her breath, and let it out in a long silent sigh as she filled the cup and proffered it to him.

"I thank you for your hospitality, Ritter Martin von Hirschenberg," Graf Ruprecht answered, nodding to her father. His light baritone voice was mellow and clear, like the sound of a wire harpstring through the warm spring air.

Graf Ruprecht turned his gaze back to Margerite, taking the filled cup from her hand. His fingertips grazed hers on the cup's smooth bronze curve; she almost jerked her arm back in startlement, but mastered herself just in time to withdraw smoothly. "And greetings to you, fair and noble frowe. I drink to your health, and to that of your father - for you must be Margerite von Hirschenberg, of whom Günther has spoken often to me."

Margerite could feel the blush mounting to her face, her head pounding. It is only courtesy, she reminded herself sharply: Graf Günther had not seen her since she was thirteen, a gawky child just on the brink of womanhood.

"You are discerning, my lord," she said. "I am, indeed, Margerite."

Graf Ruprecht nodded slowly. For a moment Margerite felt disconcerted, as though something had taken place that she did not quite understand - as though, unknown to her and quite by chance, she had spoken a secret password to admit herself to a strange place.

But she pressed on, her training as lady of the castle bearing up her desire that their noble guest look well upon her. "You and your men must be hungry and thirsty after your journey, my lord. Follow me, if you will. A light repast has been laid out for you in our hall - " and if it has not, there will be sore backs in the kitchen tonight, Margerite promised herself - "and after you have refreshed yourself, if it is your pleasure, we should like to invite you to an afternoon of falconry."

The Graf smiled at her, the smooth whiteness of his teeth a pleasant contrast to the snaggle-toothed grin beaming from the depths of her father's gray-brown beard. "Falconry is always a pleasure for me, frowe," he replied. "And Günther has told me, as well, that the castle Hirschenberg is known for its fine hawks. Will you be riding with us?"

"If you wish, my lord, I should be delighted to."

Mindful of her dignity, Margerite kept her light tread slow and measured as she and her father led the Graf and his troop through to the castle's great hall, though it would have been easier for her feet to skip like a peasant girl's. It is only courtesy, she told herself again, though she fancied that she could feel Graf Ruprecht's gaze warm on the back of her head.

The kitchen staff, to Margerite's relief, had been as prompt as she could have wished. Braided loaves of bread lay on the table already, together with three wheels of white cheese and a large ham on a round wooden platter, its translucent pink flesh neatly sliced and arranged in heaps about the joint. The glazed clay plates had been laid out in rows along the table, some forty in all - better too many than too few - and pitchers of wine and beer brimmed between them.

Gertrude, too, had changed her clothes hastily: now clad neatly in a clean dress of deep blue wool with a narrow band of embroidery at wrists and cuffs - her best dress, one that Margerite had outgrown a year ago - she stood quietly behind Margerite's chair, ready to serve.

Throughout the meal, Graf Ruprecht spoke lightly of his visit to von Hohenfels. "Yes, it was good hunting up there," he said, his handsome features lighting with pleasure. "We went out for boar on Easter Sunday - and there he was, waiting for us just inside the forest."

"On Easter Sunday?" Margerite said, surprised and a little shocked. "But..." She shut her mouth quickly, even before her father's glare could light on her face. Yet Graf Ruprecht only laughed.

"I have heard priests going on about Sunday hunting before. But as for me - well, God may keep his Heaven, so long as I may hunt in the woods. And this was one of the biggest and fiercest boars I have ever seen. An old one he was, with tusks like Saracen sabers, and angry as well. Someone had wounded him a few days before, not too deeply, just a long gash along his side, but he was out for revenge on the human race. He came charging out of the bushes when he heard the baying of the hounds, snout low and eyes rolling in rage. I got from my horse, for I had liefer hunt boars on foot, and set my spear just in time to meet his charge: he knew my weapon was destined for him, and meant to take me if he might.

I was well-braced and struck true, but he nearly knocked me over all the same. And that would have been the end of me, for he was fighting even with the spear through his chest, ready to spit himself even deeper upon it, if it only meant he could get to me - I feared he would break the shaft, stout as it was, and be free. But Günther's alaunts held tightly to his limbs, and his great heart and all his strength failed before my spear did, and he fell at last. That was a hunt!"

"A fine hunt indeed," Martin rumbled, and Margerite nodded quickly in agreement, eager for Ruprecht to forget her hasty outburst. And he seemed to have, for soon he was asking her about the hawks they would be flying that afternoon.

When they had finished lunch, Martin, Margerite, and Ruprecht went out into the courtyard, waiting for their horses and hawks to be brought to them. Graf Ruprecht's steed was, as befitted his rank, clearly a fine warhorse: glossy grey-black with deep black mane and tail, powerful-bodied, his muscular neck arching gracefully as he surveyed the horses one of the young grooms was leading out of the stables. The man holding him was not Graf Ruprecht's Knappe Wolfram, the young squire who did the Graf personal service in return for his teachings in the arts of war and chivalry; he was an older man, who had sat by Graf Ruprecht's right side at dinner, and the Graf had introduced him as the captain of his guard...what was his name? Bertram, that was it.

Standing like this, Margerite could see how tall he was, a good half-head above Ruprecht's height, and broad-shouldered in proportion. Bertram's long hair and bushy beard were jet-black, and his mouth was set in a suspicious scowl as though, even here, he were watching for an enemy. There was something about him that unnerved Margerite, and she was glad when his hazel eyes turned away from her. Margerite wondered where Graf Ruprecht had come by such a man, who seemed too common and hard-bitten to hold a position of trust like the one the Graf had given him.

Graf Ruprecht should not trust him, she thought with a sudden shiver. For looking at the two of them, the grim dark man holding the horse and the fair-haired lord reaching out for the reins, Margerite was suddenly reminded of an illumination she had seen for that old poem, the Nibelungenlied. Hagen holding Sigfrit's reins, before the young hero mounted to ride out on the hunt that would be his last - the hunt ending with Hagen's spear through Sigfrit's body.

For that moment, she seemed to know somehow, as utterly sure as she was of blue sky above and green earth below, that Bertram would someday betray his lord. I should warn Graf Ruprecht, Margerite thought. But with that, her sureness drained away like spilt beer soaking into dry ground. What could she say that was more than a girl's silly fancy - as surely it had been? She was no prophetess or holy woman. And now Michael and his apprentice were coming with the three falcons, and it was time for Margerite to mount up on her bay mare Rosalind, and let Michael hand up glove and bird to her. She would fly Gawan that day, leaving the larger female falcons - almost twice the male's size - for the two men.

The road down to the river was an easy ride, the horses stepping lightly over the rocky path. The cool breeze had brought a bright tinge of colour to Graf Ruprecht's fair cheeks, and he smiled as he spoke, complimenting Martin on his lands. The road wound around the foothills, until they turned off into a meadow, its green stretch starred by drifts of white daisies and golden dandelions. Margerite could feel Gawan almost quivering with eagerness through the thick leather glove on her arm, his head turning as his shining dark gaze darted from place to place. The bells of his jesses tinkled, soft as far-off elf-bells.

"Soon you shall fly, Gawan," she whispered. "A hare, or a partridge - or perhaps a pigeon, if that is what you chance to catch. My fair one, my fierce one, my hero and prince..."

The soft jingling of another set of bells at her elbow alerted Margerite, so that she stopped speaking to the falcon and glanced up. It was not her father by her side, but Graf Ruprecht. Margerite was a little embarassed to think he had heard her words to Gawan, but he smiled kindly, as if to put her at ease.

Yet even as he spoke, his light blue gaze was roaming out over the meadow. He did not stare at any one spot, but seemed to keep up a constant, restless scanning; and yet, though his horse was still walking, he hardly seemed to move at all - no nervous blinks or twitches, no playing with his reins. Nothing, Margerite thought, would be able to escape his sight or startled by his movements: if she had not known before that Graf Ruprecht was a great hunter, watching him now would have told her.

"You love your hunting birds," he said softly, "and that is well, for man and falcon always do best when they are glad together. Wait - there is something moving on the far side of the meadow there. A hare, I would guess. Will your bird take it?" For a moment Graf Ruprecht looked straight into Margerite's eyes. She felt suddenly transparent, open as a window whose shutters had fallen away beneath the stormwind.

"Yours first, my lord," Margerite answered. A little nervous giggle nearly escaped her lips. She clamped her mouth tight upon it, calming herself for a breath. "This is your hunt, after all."

"So it is - but I would see you have first kill."

"As you wish."

Margerite lifted her hand, so that Gawan stretched up on his toes. The wind of his bating fanned Margerite's cheeks as she slipped his jesses. He rose up, beating the air hard, then suddenly arrowed across the meadow, sweeping down upon the sudden rustle in the grass. Margerite heard the shrill squeal as his claws struck, then silence.

"Well done!" Graf Ruprecht applauded as they kneed their horses into a canter. Margerite stopped and dismounted shortly before she reached the falcon and the body of his kill, handing her reins to her father and scooping a few pieces of meat from the falconing-bag at her waist.

"Bold Gawan, fine Gawan," she said as she squatted down beside the falcon. "Here, it is hard work to break into a fat hare, take this meat instead."

Gawan, used to having his prey ransomed like this, snatched a lump of meat from the ground and retreated a few steps, tearing at it ravenously. Margerite quickly moved the hare aside, hiding it from the bird behind her skirts.

She had always been used to butchering her own hawk's kills, and, mindful of her clothes as she had to be, it did not take her long to slit through the hare's skin and stomach muscles, cutting its warm bowels free below, then reaching in above the stomach to tug the esophagus loose.

The fleas were already crawling from the hare's brown fur, but Margerite paid them no attention: they were nothing like so bothersome as chicken mites, which always left her scratching at her scalp for hours whenever she had to take a hand in slaughtering or plucking fowl.

"Here you are, my brave bird," Margerite told Gawan as she laid the slippery mass of guts on the grass before him. "This is your share: I know you won't grudge me the rest." She carefully eased out the hare's liver, slicing the gall bladder free with a couple of neat strokes and flicking it away. The heart and lungs she pulled out for Gawan, then she pushed the liver back into the body cavity - it would be needed for the sauce when the hare had been soaked and simmered in wine.

Margerite cleaned her dagger and sheathed it, then wiped her bloodied hands off on the long grass as best she could. I should have brought the cloth from my saddlebag, she thought; but, as often, she had been so anxious to get to Gawan before he broke into his kill and began to feed in earnest that she had thought of nothing beyond the hawk's needs.

Lifting the hare by its hind legs, holding it carefully at arm's length, she carried it over to her horse and dropped it into the bag of loose cloth hanging behind her saddle before taking the damp cloth for her hands and turning back to watch her feeding falcon. Only then, as Margerite waited for Gawan to finish his meal, did it dawn on her how she must look to Graf Ruprecht - squatting on the ground like a peasant woman pissing, up to the wrist in the hare's quivering guts. I should have stayed indoors with my tapestry, or at least asked my father to tend to the kill for me.

She wanted to glance up sideways, to see if the Graf's face was really turned away from her, but Gawan's crop was filling quickly. Margerite pulled on her hawking-gauntlet again, calling him with a low whistle. The falcon's head hung, and he gave the remains of his meal a last mournful look, but he hopped up onto her fist. At once Margerite bent for the rest of the meat, feeding it to him bit by bit, until she could feel that his crop had stretched nearly as full as it ought to be. Then she slipped the hood over his head and let him nibble a few more bites before he was done.

"A good kill," Martin said, beaming proudly at his daughter and her falcon. "Graf Ruprecht, it was gracious of you to let Margerite have the first quarry."

The Graf smiled, his glance passing quickly from Martin to Margerite. "It was a pleasure to see that she is as accomplished in deed as speech. Even to butchering her own kill - not every woman who hawks has the strength of heart do that. My own wife..." He set his teeth hard against the words, and, for a moment, the brightness seemed to go out behind his blue eyes, the darkness at their centres empty as the frame of a wind-snuffed lantern.

As the sudden chill shivered over Margerite, it seemed to her that the warm afternoon light had drained away in a heartbeat, leaving a faint gray frost over green field and blue heavens. Is it his sorrow I feel? she thought, her limbs surprisingly weak with confusion. It is a week and a half till my moon-bleeding: that cannot be disordering my mind.

But Graf Ruprecht laughed, and the coldness shattered as if it had never been. "The crown of the day belongs to you, good frowe." He glanced out past Margerite's shoulders, over the green meadow and the woods beyond. "Though it is still April, I think the poet Walther had words for such a day. 'May brings her wonders to us all - what is so fair, whate'er befall, as her loveworthy light? And we let all the flowers stand, and gaze but on the maiden bright.'" He blinked, shaking himself a little, as though his thoughts had rapt him away for a moment. "I do not think we men will have such luck in the hunt as you have had...but let us ride on, for our hawks are hungry too."

He tightened his knees on his horse, shifting his seat a little, and the grey-black steed began to walk again.

The sun was setting when the three falconers made their way back to the castle, the long shadows of the hills rippling dark over the river. Enide, flying from Graf Ruprecht's wrist, had brought down a wood-pigeon, but Kriemhilt had missed her quarry and sat sulking upon Martin's glove. Once they were within the walls, Michael and his apprentice took the hawks back, while Gertrude delivered the game to the kitchen. When she hastened back, the serving maid whispered in her mistress' ear.

"Graf Ruprecht, our dinner will be ready soon, but there is time for you to rest and refresh yourself as you please." The Graf's golden hair, Margerite noticed, was wind-blown and disheveled, with a streak of blood on one side where he had pushed it out of his face while gutting his pigeon. He would surely want to wash face and hands; she would see to it that a basin of warm water was sent to his room straightaway.

"Your man -" she gestured to the young servant of Ruprecht's who had appeared as soon as their horses entered the courtyard, and now stood by ready to hear his master's commands - "can show you to your chamber, and our servants will fetch whatever you require."

"You are most gracious, frowe," Graf Ruprecht said with a slight bow towards Margerite. "I thank the two of you for a good afternoon's hawking, and look forward to seeing you at dinner."

The hem of Graf Ruprecht's red cloak brushed against the backs of his muscular calves as he followed his man into the castle. Margerite watched him until the door closed, then turned to Gertrude.

"Now, Gertrude, is this dress as clean as it ought to be? Are there any stains upon it?" She turned around slowly so that the maid could see all of the garment clearly.

"Your dress is as neat as it was this morning," Gertrude answered. Then she giggled. "But your hair is a mess, and your face is very pink from the sun. The dress should change its wearer, not the wearer her dress."

"You are impudent," Margerite said, but there was no heat in her tones. "Hurry, then. Get warm water - send one bowl to the Graf's room, and bring one up to mine. And a cooling cloth for my face, so that it does not burn any further."

"As you wish, my mistress."

Though she had not long to wait, Margerite was already twitching with impatience by the time she heard Gertrude's light tap at her door. Margerite suffered the girl's chatter for a little while, while Gertrude patted her warm cheeks gently with the cool damp cloth, then bent to scrub the blood and dirt from beneath her mistress' nails. But by the time Gertrude began to comb her hair, teasing the worst tangles gently free with her fingers, Margerite could hold her thoughts back no longer.

"What do you think of Graf Ruprecht?" she asked.

Margerite had expected some giggling answer, some remark about golden hair or blue eyes or the muscular legs filling the Graf's hose. But instead, Gertrude pursed her mouth, her wide brown eyes narrowing. "He is a nobleman of wealth and good breeding," the maidservant said slowly. "He knows what he wants, and he will have it. If he were to call me to his bed tonight..."

"Gertrude!" Margerite cried. The comb lodged in her hair, whipping to the side as she pulled her head away from Gertrude's hand. "How dare you?"

"Forgive me, mistress," Gertrude answered in a low voice. "But there are some things I cannot afford not to know. I have been warned many times since I came here: of how, though I may dress in your old clothes, I must not forget that I was born to wear gray wool and hempen sandals - and of how things may go for a peasant girl who serves in a castle. My lady, you are not too young to know that noblemen may do as they please with women of lower station, though your father's virtue has kept you from seeing that happen here. But perhaps you are too young to think..."

"To think what?" Margerite answered. The words were tight in her throat, and she realized that her fists were crushing wrinkles into the pale blue linen of her overdress.

"Some greater noblemen," Gertrude said carefully, "may not always realize how much difference lies between a peasant maid and the daughter of a simple Ritter, though one be born to serve and the other free and noble by blood.

Nor do all men, whatever their station in life, honour maidenhead or marriage. Now I clearly saw the way Graf Ruprecht was looking at you, and the way you were looking at him as well. I know that he finds you fair - and if he does not mean to marry you, then you had best keep your distance from him while he is in this castle."

Gertrude stood braced as though she expected a slap; her round cheeks were as red as if Margerite had slapped her already and her hands were wringing at the end of her belt, but her brown eyes did not blink nor falter. "I would not have said this to you, frowe," she added hastily, "but your father charged me to tend your virtue, and you did ask me, and it has always been my way to answer truthfully."

"Does he not trust me to tend my own virtue?" Margerite snapped. But that was of little matter, for what else should a father ask his daughter's maid to do? "As for Graf Ruprecht, I think you are deluded. He is the most courtly of men, gracious and well-spoken. He would no more try to seduce a daughter under her father's roof than...than..." Margerite could not think of anything to compare the act to, and gave it up before she began to splutter.

"Forgive me, mistress," Gertrude said steadfastly. "But I have not kept my maidenhead this late by knowing nothing of the ways of men when they want what they want. If you smile and flutter your eyelashes and seem to return his interest tonight, he will be sure that he can lure you to him - if you are cold to him, it will make him all the keener for you, like a ferret kept hungry before it is set to the warren."

"Then what is it you think I should do?"

"Trust in God and agree to nothing. Drink little wine, and come back here to your chamber when dinner is over, and do not leave it again until the morning. If he cannot find you, he cannot seduce you, and you cannot anger him by refusing him."

"I think you have an ill view of a good man," said Margerite, and then, the words coming to her mouth before she could stop them, "and that is clearly because you are a peasant, with no knowledge of chivalry or courtliness."

"That may be so, mistress," Gertrude answered cheerfully as she set to combing Margerite's hair again. "And I can tell you this: whatever poetry is stored in Graf Ruprecht's head; whatever arts of war his arm has been schooled to, or whatever vows of knighthood may be engraved on his heart, there is a part of his body that cares not a whit for any of those things. And when it comes to what men do - not what they say, or believe, or promise, but do - that is a stouter rod whipping them on than any other may be. That is the truth, mistress: the noblest stallion will behave like any other when he scents a mare."

Margerite said nothing more, but her heart was all the more troubled when she came to the dining hall to see that the feast was properly laid out, and found that the chairs had been set so that she would sit, not at her father's left, but at Ruprecht's right. Martin was in his seat already, and smiled as she came in.

"You see where you will sit," he said. "That will do honour to our guest, and make it easier for you to speak with him, for he seems to think well of your conversation."

Looking at her father's face, craggy and thick-browed above his brush of beard, Margerite could not bring herself to speak of the misgivings that Gertrude had set in her mind like an adder in her bosom - how could she, without slandering Graf Ruprecht or proving her own thoughts unchaste, or else accusing Gertrude...wretched, vile, jealous maidservant, Margerite thought, but she knew that was untrue. So she merely took her place, but she could not keep herself from starting every time she heard the door swing open.

Ruprecht's men had cleaned and refreshed themselves while their master was out, and came in groups of three or four to sit about the table according, Margerite assumed, to their own rank within his company; the Knappe Wolfram stood behind the Graf's chair, ready to spring to his command. Only Bertram - glowering, to her annoyance, in the chair at her father's left - did not seem to have combed his hair and beard.

The thick tangles hid most of his face, but she could see that he was still scowling, and the candlelight caught baleful glints of green from his hazel eyes. *If Graf Ruprecht takes this man to other courts with him often, why is he not more civilized?* Margerite thought. *For all that hair, he might almost be wearing a wood-wosel's mask. He must be amazingly ugly beneath it.*

Just then, Bertram glanced across at Margerite, meeting her eyes before she could look away. His scowl deepened, and a sudden lance of terror struck into Margerite's heart, her legs quivering like those of a hind caught in the sudden luminous fierceness of a wolf's gaze.

Yet he did not speak, and, to Margerite's great relief, the door opened again, and Graf Ruprecht came striding through. His golden hair, now smooth and neatly combed, fell in a shining sheet about his shoulders; his face and hands were clean again, the pale brightness of his skin marred only by the tanned helm-shadow.

"Greetings and good eventide, Ritter Martin, frowe Margerite," Ruprecht said, sweeping his red velvet cloak to the side and sinking gracefully into the chair between them. He looked down the length of the table, nodding as if pleased. "You have set a fair feast. I am greatly honoured."

Margerite inclined her head graciously, warmed inside by his words. The roast pig held pride of place before them, sizzling drips of fat still oozing down its crackling brown sides. The hall was lit, not with tallow candles, but the good beeswax, their flame warm and mellow as the glow of polished gold, and Margerite had ordered that it be adorned with flowers and green branches as finely as it had been for the Easter feast.

Though their cook had not had time to make up any of her finer subtleties - no whole fowl stuffed with other whole fowl inside them, no confections of pastry disguised as meat or meat as pastry - the loaves of bread on the table were in the shapes of wreaths and animals of the chase, stag and boar, wolf and bear, hare and fox.

"It is only what is fitting, my lord," she murmured. "I know Hirschenberg is but a small castle, and you are used to better…"

Graf Ruprecht shook his head. "I have been a guest in - if you will forgive me - many larger castles than this, sitting at the tables of men of higher rank, and not been offered so fine a feast, nor entertained so pleasantly as I was this afternoon. Gold unpolished is still gold, and a knight dressed in homespun is still a knight. Ritter Martin, of your courtesy…" He gestured to the roast pig, and Martin rose to carve it.

The Graf ate neatly, dipping his fingers often in the little washing-bowl by his plate. Watching him, Margerite strove even harder to cut her meat fine and nibble it in dainty bites, careful that no drop of grease should fall upon her dress or drip down her chin. She noted with approval that her father was doing likewise, though Martin was not usually the most careful of eaters. To her surprise, when she glanced across the table, expecting more cause for scorn, Bertram also ate like one who had been well-reared, with only the occasional dropped crumb or lost dripping…although, she thought, he could hide a whole herd of swine in that beard.

"Indeed, your falcons are fine," Graf Ruprecht was saying to Martin. "I think you could easily advise me in that noble art."

Martin waved a hand deprecatingly. "I am not highly skilled in it, my lord," he rumbled. "It is my daughter, like her mother before her, who is the true falconer in my family."

"Ah." Graf Ruprecht stroked his chin lightly, as though smoothing down a small beard. He would not look unhandsome bearded, thought Margerite, though she thought she preferred him without…With an effort, she brought her mind back to what he was saying.

"...had a fine ruddy peregrine, very like your own. She was trained to the heron, as well, and would often take three or four on a good day. But she was free in temper, and one day..." Ruprecht paused to look Margerite in the eyes, the blue light of his gaze holding her entranced for a moment..."I was careless, I fear. She was not long out of moult, and, as you know, falcons in moult are tender creatures, prone to wildness and odd fancies. Though I had thought her thoroughly manned, when I set her loose at her quarry, she pulled up halfway through the stoop and settled herself in the top of a tree. I tried everything I could to get her down - I whistled until my lips would purse no more, I lifted up meat and called to her, and tried her with the swing-lure, but she would not come. I was back in the woods before dawn the next day and the next, courting her as sweetly as I could, and yet she had no eye for me, and each day she was deeper and deeper in the forest." Again Ruprecht's eyes met Margerite's, and as he shifted in his chair, she felt his thigh just brush against the edge of her skirt. It seemed that the intensity of his gaze was searing through her, even as his voice softened.

He cannot be flirting, she scolded herself. You are a vain and silly girl...he is only asking about a hawk.

"I asked a better falconer than I, what should I do? He advised me to seek out a less fine bird, suitable to my skills, but I would not give her up. The second man I asked knew less than I, for he told me to trap her with a net, which might have damaged her wings. At last I took a heart, still bloody and warm, and tied that to the end of the lure, swinging it up for her. And for the first time she stooped to me...and struck the heart, bearing it away in her talons on her flight. I never saw her again. So tell me, what should I have done?"

Graf Ruprecht laid his hand on the table - near enough to Margerite's own that she could almost feel his touch tingling through her fingertips, yet far enough away that she could not be sure he had thought of touching her.

"That was a cruel and wild hawk," Margerite said distantly. She could not meet his eyes again; she was sure he would read her feelings in the rising pink of her cheeks.

"A well-manned bird..." the phrase made her blush more deeply..."and well-trained, should have come down to you when she struck the lure. A warm heart makes a most tempting lure to a falcon: I am sure it would have drawn any of ours back to the fist."

Graf Ruprecht's smile was very bright, but behind his head, Margerite saw Gertrude frowning. "I have also heard," she added carefully, "that if one offers a wax image of a lost bird to the Virgin, she may sometimes take pity and help."

Ruprecht did not lose his smile, but it seemed to Margerite that she could see a shadow of sadness softening his features. "I have heard that also," he said, "but I put little store by it." He lifted his winecup, tilting his head back, the sinews of his throat rippling as he swallowed the last drops. Margerite reached to refill it at once.

For the rest of the evening, Graf Ruprecht spoke mostly to Martin, though now and again he would turn to address a question or remark to Margerite. Still unsettled by their conversation, she sat quietly, torn between her fear of drawing his attention too closely - for what should I do, if Gertrude were right? - and her wish to be again, for a moment, the center of his regard.

At last, full-fed, they had washed the last crumbs of sticky honey-cakes from their fingers, and dried their hands. Graf Ruprecht was still deep in conversation with Margerite's father, and Margerite wondered if she dared to stay. Yet even as the Graf had quoted Walter von der Vogelweide earlier, more of the poet's words came to her now. As I so wondrously, was cast in dreams foreby - then day dawned, and I must wake.

She rose to her feet, and the men broke off their talk. "My lord," Margerite said to Ruprecht, "and my father, I pray you will forgive me. I should go to bed now, for I am wearied by the day."

"I also," said Graf Ruprecht smoothly, rising from his own chair. "I have ridden far, and have a farther ride to make tomorrow, so I will bid you both goodnight."

Margerite's heart hammered against her ribs, and she could feel her palms beginning to sweat. Though the Graf did not glance back at her as he strode lightly from the hall, it almost felt to her as though his warm gaze were still considering her.

"Goodnight, father," she said hastily, leaning down to brush her lips lightly against Martin's bearded cheek.

"Goodnight, Margerite. Sleep well, and rise early, for Graf Ruprecht will surely wish you to bid farewell to him."

Margerite glanced sharply at her father, wondering if there were more guile beneath his words than it seemed. Did he think...had he noticed..? And a darker thought came to her as well: for all Gertrude thought her innocent, she knew well enough that men had bartered their daughter's maidenheads for the favour of the powerful before. But that must be her own wickedness thinking ill; she could not doubt her father's love, nor believe for the most fleeting heartbeat that he would barter her honour so.

"I will be sure to arise early, and see to it that our guest and his men are well-fed before they set out," Margerite answered.

"You are a credit to your mother's memory," murmured Martin. He turned his goblet about in his thick fingers for a moment, as though seeking more words within its depths. "Well, off you go to bed, then."

"Come, Gertrude," Margerite called. Her maidservant trailing behind her with a candle, she made her way out of the hall and up the stairs towards her chamber.

Above, she could see a warm glow on the stone walls, a single light shining in the darkness. The shadow on the wall was huge, distorted like the shape of a tree in faint moonlight, but she could still make out the figure of a man crouching, then standing - a tall man in a cloak. Behind her, Gertrude's breath hissed out faintly.

Graf Ruprecht was standing by the door of Margerite's chamber, regarding her calmly as she walked up the stairs. Margerite could feel her own breath coming swiftly, her heart beating harder, as though, instead of ascending the staircase at a dignified pace, she had dashed up it in a few moments.

"Graf Ruprecht," she said, trying to calm the breathlessness in her voice. "Your chamber is above."

"Of course," the Graf said, bowing slightly. "I had merely dropped something on the way up - but I have found it. A good night to you, frowe, and I hope to see you in the morning before I leave."

Ruprecht continued on his way up. Margerite did not quite run into her chamber, but she sank onto her bed in relief as Gertrude followed her in and closed the door.

"Was I not right?" Gertrude muttered softly.

"No!" Margerite answered. "Not in the least. You are too eager to think the worst."

"Perhaps so - but I would wager a silver brooch against a copper penny that Graf Ruprecht never lost the falcon he was speaking of."

"The best of falconers may lose a bird."

Gertrude laughed. "And lure her back with a heart on the end of a string? The silly poets you read would scorn to be so plain about their meaning."

"You know nothing of hawking, and should be quiet about it," Margerite told her. "But if you are so fearful, I will make sure that my door is locked tonight. Be sure that you call loudly enough to wake me up in the morning, and call me before dawn, that I may make ready to bid the Graf farewell."

Margerite yawned loudly. Though she had thought a few minutes before that she would get no sleep at all that night, suddenly she was so tired that it was a struggle to stay awake while Gertrude helped her to undress, and she had to fumble with her key in the lock before blowing out the candle and dropping into bed.

Margerite did not notice passing into sleep, but suddenly it seemed to her that she was sitting on a high place, the wind rushing about her. The sky was starry, Iring's Way shining milky above the countless white glints winking through the blackness. Beneath, the river coiled about its hilly banks, moonlight rippling pale off the dark waters. Exhilarated by the night, she cast her head back to call out, and the scream of a peregrine ripped through her throat. Now she could feel the air rushing through her feathers; now she leaped, beating her wings and letting the wind bear her aloft.

But falcons do not fly after sunset...The cool air swept the thought away quickly, for Margerite was circling higher and higher. Each feather on her body felt alive, tingling under the soft touch of the wind; her muscles tightened and loosened rhythmically, answering the subtle pressures of the air she rode. Her sight seemed almost unbearably keen, gazing down upon the meadows and woodlands below, the pale pink blossoms of the apple orchards and the ghostly white shapes of wild cherries in bloom shimmering against dark grass and dark trees.

And it seemed to her that she could see other shapes moving there as well, figures from dreams and childhood stories - woodwose and bilwisse creeping through the forests, the curve of white breast and back above a flashing fishtail in the river, a ring of half-misted shapes glowing faintly like err-lights in the grassy field where Gawan had brought down his hare...

Yet far below and further on, a single light shone, and Margerite found that she was flying towards it, her long wings bearing her on at a steady pace. She could see the gleaming golden hair, the upturned face, white in the moonlight - and the dark thing whirling on the end of the lure-lead, a single trail of sweet scent from it wafting upward to her. With a single cry, she dropped, the wind of her falling howling about her as she plummeted down to grasp it in her claws.

As Margerite struck, the man cried out as if in pain, but he kept tight hold of the lead. The heart Margerite held beat still within her talons, its warmth rising through her body as he reeled her in.

"Come to my hand, my falcon," he murmured. Gloved hand between her feathered legs, he was easing the bloodied heart away from her, letting her claws tighten upon the hard leather glove as his other hand stroked her breast. She beat her wings, bating wildly upside-down for a moment, but he had already grasped her jesses, binding her to him. Slowly Margerite calmed, clambering about his arm to right herself. The brightness of his pale blue eyes nearly blinded her, gazing into her own; she felt herself captive, and clung all the more tightly to him.

"Hush, my falcon," he whispered. "Now I have you; now you are mine, to dwell with me and fly for me..."

The soft leather touch of the hood closed over her head, its sudden rush of blackness blotting out her sight. For a moment Margerite could feel only the strength of the arm she rode on, hear nothing but the muffled voice of the falconer whispering to her and the beating of her own heart, growing louder and louder like...

Gertrude knocking on the door. Margerite opened her eyes, blinking dizzily against the darkness of her room. Gertrude was calling, her shrill voice only stilled a little by the door's thickness. "Wake up, Mistress! It is nearly dawn... wake up!"

Margerite climbed groggily from her bed, feeling about until her fingertips met the cold metal of her keyring. Although she had drunk little the night before, her head was pounding and she felt oddly dizzy. Seized by a sudden horror, she pressed her fingers hard into the side of her neck, then beneath her arms, to make sure there was no trace of swelling or soreness.

I arose too quickly from a sound sleep. It will pass off, Margerite told herself, and opened the door.

Gertrude was out of breath, her brown hair straggling over her plump shoulders. "Mistress, we must make haste," she said. "Your father and Graf Ruprecht are already in the great hall, and your father has said that they would see you at once."

"See me?" Margerite gasped. "Why?"

Gertrude shook her head. "They did not say, frowe. But it seems to me that something must have happened in the night."

The serving-maid's eyes narrowed, and Margerite grasped her by the shoulders, shaking her until the water slapped over the sides of the washing-bowl she held and droplets of hot tallow scattered from her candle. "Do not even think it!" she cried. "Hurry now...light the candles and get me clad, for whatever it is, I must be fit to see our noble guest."

It seemed to take forever for Gertrude to ease the close-fitting gown over Margerite's upraised arms, then pull it down over her hips and smooth the wrinkles from her back before clasping her girdle. Margerite grabbed the mirror from her chest, staring into it. Even the candlelight showed that her hair was disheveled from sleep, her left cheek still bearing the faint white creases of the pillow. Impatient, she snatched the comb from Gertrude's hand, dragging it through her hair, then slapped a few bent strands down with a sprinkling of water from the wash-bowl. Drawing herself up to her full height, she said, "I am ready now," and strode down the stairs.

New candles had been set in the sconces and candleholders, so that the hall blazed with light as if at a feast. Martin and Ruprecht sat together at the head of the table, a pitcher of wine between them, and as she walked in, Martin was filling both cups so full that a few pale drops spilled over the metal rims, trickling down like drips of rain on a helmet.

Surely it is good news, Margerite said to herself. But the answering thought fell over her like night after day: or else bad, if they are drinking like this before dawn.

"I am here," Margerite said.

The two men turned to look at her. Graf Ruprecht's face was very serious as he rose to his feet and walked over to her. Then, to Margerite's surprise, he went down on one knee before her, taking her right hand in both of his own. His touch was gentle, but very strong: Margerite felt that she could not have broken away from the light grasp of his sword-calloused fingers. "Frowe Margerite," he said, "I have spoken to your father, and he has given his consent to our wedding, if you will have me."

Margerite could only stare down at him, open-mouthed. "Our...wedding?" she managed to squeak.

"It is my wish," Graf Ruprecht went on, "that you come to Burg Falkenstein by this St. Walpurga's Eve, and on that night become my wife, the Gräfin von Falkenstein."

It seemed to Margerite that she could see nothing in the room except the man who looked up at her - the golden hair falling about his shoulders, the finely chiseled mouth, lips slightly open, the fair arches of his brows above those palely brilliant eyes. Kneeling thus, gazing into her face, Ruprecht could have been posing for an illumination of a Minnesänger singing to his goddess Love; it almost seemed, though she knew it could not be so, as though he were pleading with her. And she was dizzy: this had come too quickly for her thoughts to prepare, like a thunderstorm rolling in to drench her before she could get to shelter.

Even if she had guessed that Graf Ruprecht might seek to marry her, she would have expected letters, visits, time to be sure that all her possessions and the affairs of the castle were in order...this Walpurga's Eve? A year hence would not have been too long for a betrothal.

"Will you consent, Margerite?"

"I will," she said, her voice choking in her throat. "I will gladly."

Ruprecht rose gracefully, still holding her hand in one of his. Now she saw the two rings of emerald-set gold in his other palm, a greater and a smaller: their betrothal rings. Margerite let him set one upon her hand. The smooth gold, still warm from his skin, clasped her finger softly. It will always feel as though he is holding me, she thought. In turn, she took the other ring up, sliding it over Ruprecht's finger. He bent his head down - his breath was sweet, as though he had chewed upon fresh herbs that morning - and Margerite tilted her own face up towards him.

Ruprecht's lips were soft upon hers, a tingling caress that seemed to spread down through her body. She wished that he could embrace her more closely; she wanted to feel him pressing against her, stroking her hair...When Ruprecht stepped away, Margerite felt a little disheveled, as though they had truly done more than touching lips for a moment. But her father was beaming in delight as he watched them, his wine-cup in his hand.

"To the betrothal!" Martin said. He waited to drink until Ruprecht had picked up his cup, touching it first to his own lips, then to Margerite's. She sipped the sweet wine gladly, letting it trickle down her throat. It was so strange to have a cup held for her like that, held by a man...this man who would soon be her husband!

Ruprecht had already written out the betrothal contract, and he and her father had signed it, the young man's fine writing graceful beside the older man's heavy scrawl. It only remained for Margerite to sign her own consent, and then it was done.

"Seven days' ride, from here to Falkenstein," Ruprecht said. "You will have a little time to prepare before the wedding. But I must go and be sure my men are ready to ride, for we, too, have a great deal to do before my castle is ready to receive you. Margerite..."

Ruprecht gazed long into her eyes, and Margerite thought that he would come forward to embrace her. But he said only, "Keep yourself well, my betrothed. Be sure that I will be longing for the sight of you, and awaiting our wedding-night with the greatest joy."

"As shall I," Margerite answered. "Travel safely...my betrothed."

"Until we meet again." Ruprecht bowed to her, then to Martin, and left the hall.

Margerite turned to her father. The letters of the contract blurred on the table before her; only the thought that Ruprecht might still be within earshot, and her new dignity as a woman soon to be wedded, kept her from letting out the shriek of delight that had been building in her since she first heard Ruprecht's words. But she hugged Martin hard about the shoulders, and his deep chest shook with joyous laughter.

"Well-done, my daughter!" he said. "Oh, well-done!"

"I did nothing," said Margerite, bewildered. "Only went hawking with him, and spoke a little at table..."

"And yet you have won for yourself a better husband than I could have hoped to find for you. And so swiftly..."

"So swiftly," Margerite echoed. "As if in a courtly tale."

Martin laughed again, and it seemed to Margerite that, behind his graying beard and the deep lines carved into his craggy face, she could see the young man he had been, in those bright days before the Death's shadow fell over the land. "No tale, my daughter, but a great deal of work to be done in a very short time, for the Graf made it quite clear to me that we must be at his court by St. Walpurga's Eve, and that leaves us a scant three days to ready ourselves for your wedding."

"Yes," Margerite said, the tears of joy blurring in her eyes. "My wedding."

Gertrude stood before the door of her mistress' chamber, holding something in her hand. The girl looked dazed, as though someone had struck her a heavy blow; the pupils of her eyes were wide and dark, almost swallowing the brown irises in black. She started as Margerite came up the stairs.

"Frowe," Gertrude said, her voice a hushed whisper, "Graf Ruprecht gave me this for you, just a few moments ago. I do not know..."

Margerite took the piece of folded parchment from her maidservant's hand. The creases were neat and sharp: Gertrude had not tried to look at it. And why should she, when she cannot read? Margerite asked herself. She gestured the maid into her chamber, closed the door after.

"Well, Gertrude, what do you think this might be?" she asked.

"I think...forgive me, mistress, but I warned you about him. I think it is something unseemly."

"Let us see." Margerite could barely hold back her smile. It was a little cruel of her, perhaps, to torment Gertrude so; but it was fair return for her suspicions of Graf Ruprecht - simply Ruprecht, he would be to her hereafter, save when she was Gräfin Margerite!

She recognised Ruprecht's fine, graceful hand at once, the neat lines of his writing gracing the pale parchment like bands of dark-stained ornament standing out from white limewood. Slowly she began to read aloud, savouring each word.

"The falcon circles high through spring-bright skies,
And gazing down, knows herself most fair.
Her single glance blinds the love-filled eyes,
Of him, who seeks the powers of the air.
Through leaf-brown wood and mead I've followed on
The proud-antlered stag, the grim low-tusked boar,
The barking hounds, horn's sweet lingering song,
Each joy promising ten thousand more.

And yet above you soared, too high to see,
O, huntress above, as I hunt here below,
Cast your gaze down now, to look on me,
Whose tears at your gold beauty freely flow.
I never guessed I would be quarry or prey,
Or transfixed so by gaze of raptor-queen,
Yet your first strike tore my heart full away,
With joy and love, your talons keen.
Though never bound with jesses, or falcon's hood,
Come to me now, swoop down to my glove,
Together we'll hunt in green-leafed wood,
This quarry alone: our own spring love."

Margerite smiled dreamily, folding the parchment up.

"That is indecent, my mistress!" Gertrude said. Red spots burned high upon her cheeks; her brown eyes were bright and furious. She reached for the parchment, and Margerite whisked it away from her grasp.

"Not from a husband to his wife," she said. "Or rather, betrothed to betrothed."

Gertrude's mouth opened. She stared at her mistress blankly for a moment, as though the first shock of the news had stunned her dumb. "You can't mean...he is not..."

Margerite grinned. "He proposed to me this morning."

Gertrude stood a moment more, then flung her arms around Margerite with a shrill shriek of joy. "Oh, my mistress! When?"

"We must be at Burg Falkenstein by St. Walburga's Eve. That leaves us little time. You must see to it that all my clothes are packed, my linens, my...everything."

"So sudden!" Gertrude squealed. "How could he - so quickly?"

"I do not know," Margerite confessed. "I do not know why, or how. But the Devil himself could not keep me from being at Burg Falkenstein on my wedding day, and nor will the sloth of one maidservant who speaks ill of her betters."

"Sloth!" Gertrude said indignantly. "You have never had cause to accuse me of sloth, I hope, nor will you ever."

"But you did speak badly about Graf...about my Ruprecht, you must admit it."

Gertrude hung her head, scratching at the flagstones with the toe of one battered shoe. "I did," she said. Then, looking up with a smile, "But what was I to think, when I saw the way he looked at you, and you at him? How could I have guessed that he meant to marry you?"

"You could not," Margerite admitted. She patted her maid on the shoulder. "And you have rarely been slothful, either. Go rouse the women, and set them to washing my linens - everything must be perfect for my wedding night."

The next three days passed in a blurred haze for Margerite, a fever dream of dizzied preparation and packing, of writing out lists and instructions for Burg Hirschenberg's new steward, her father's old retainer Nicholas. She had little time to sit and think about her wedding or the man she would be marrying: there was too much to be done, and her time too short.

Still, she carried Ruprecht's poem in her belt pouch, and would reach in now and then to feel the smoothness and sharp-creased edges of the parchment; and every so often, as she was folding linens or gathering her possessions for Gertrude to pack - it seemed as though she would be taking all the chests in Burg Hirschenberg - she would catch sight of the gold betrothal ring on her finger, still surprising and new, and its gleam would bring a blur of joy to her eyes.

The horses were saddled by sunrise on the day of their departure; the canopied wagon bearing all of Margerite's wedding goods had been loaded by torchlight under the first glimmers of dawn. Gertrude sat in the wain beside the driver, Schwarze Jürgen.

Margerite had mockingly warned her maidservant about the dangers to her chastity on the road if the driver were young and handsome, but Schwarze Jürgen was a man of her father's age, bald and black-bearded with a bear's pelt of hair growing over his arms and sticking tufted from the neck of his tunic, and his ugly face was scarred from many battles:it was unlikely that he would seduce Gertrude on the way.

All the men who rode with them - most of Martin's company of fighters, with only a skeleton guard left at the castle - were fully armed and armoured already, for Martin guarded the farthest march of Graf Günther's land. They would no longer be under his protection when they had passed beyond their own borders, and then there would be many dangers on the road, from RaubRitter and legitimate noble alike.

Only Michael the Falconer wore no armour save for a thick leather cap, and even he had a sword girded at his side. He had insisted on coming to watch over Enide and Gawan through the long journey, leaving his two apprentices to tend the mews while he was gone; he, too, would ride in the wagon with the lid-sealed and hooded falcons.

Margerite's father came up to her, his chain-mail jingling under the soft clanking of the iron plate he wore. He was bare-headed, his helmet hanging over his shoulder on a strap; if the clear skies promised truly, it would be too hot for him to wear it riding all day. Around his neck was a small signal horn.

"Are you ready to go, my daughter?" Martin asked her. "Is everything packed and loaded?"

"It is. I am ready to go."

The words sent a nervous thrill of excitement through Margerite's belly, even as her eyes began to sting. She had kept herself from walking the halls and stairways of Burg Hirschenberg one last time, as if to say farewell to each stone, each room, fixing them in her memory like a glowing illumination in a book: that was only silliness.

She could no more forget the passageways and chambers that she had trodden since she could walk than she could forget her father's face; and she would be back to visit Martin, God willing, many times before either of them died. Yet, looking up at the little castle rising square and stony against the sunrise, Margerite felt oddly guilty, as though she were abandoning it. Like a sparrowhawk, left sitting on its perch when the peregrines were taken out to fly...

But every bird must leave its nest, Margerite told herself, the simple commonplace calming her heart, even as Martin patted her on the shoulder.

"It will be lonely without you here," her father said. "But you need not worry: Nicholas knows his duties well now, and the castle will not fall apart." He glanced up at the sun, now half a handspan above the horizon. "Mount up, my daughter, for we have a long way to go to meet your husband."

Courteously Martin made a stirrup of his hands for Margerite to step into, lifting her up and onto the back of her brown mare Mathilde. Once she was settled in the saddle, he leapt onto his roan gelding - a little more stiffly than he had a year or two ago, but with no less show of strength and balance. Martin steadied his horse for a moment, then lifted his signal horn, blowing one high, clear note that hung quivering in the sudden stillness of the courtyard for a moment.

"Form up!" Martin bellowed. "Ride out!"

The men-at-arms were mounted and reining their steeds into place within heartbeats, surrounding Margerite and the wagon. Martin nudged his horse into a walk; behind her, Margerite heard Schwarze Jürgen clucking to the horses pulling the wain, and tapped her own heels against Mathilde's side. The brown mare moved into her easy amble at once, following the others, and they were on their way.

The journey to Falkenstein was an easy one, for the weather held good and there were no attacks on the train. Mindful of her fair skin, Margerite spent most of the trip inside the wagon, although now and again she could not resist mounting her horse and riding alongside her father. As they travelled south, the mountains grew taller and thicker with forest, peaks shadowed black with pines looming up ahead of them.

Margerite was sorry that their way did not take them through Freiburg, which Ruprecht had said was only three or four days' ride from his castle; but there was no time for even a short detour. Perhaps after we are wedded, he will take me there.

I will need better clothes if I am to sit at his side as Gräfin, fine stuffs such as they sell in the cities...It was the seventh day on the road, and Margerite was beginning to grow anxious, when a sudden turn in the path showed the castle standing high on a hill above them, a wooded island of darkness in the middle of a gently rolling sea of green grain.

Even from far away, Margerite could tell that it was much bigger than Burg Hirschenberg, its crest rising tall above an assortment of buildings ringed about by a thick wall of stone. A banner flew from the top of the tower, flapping gently in the cool wind: Margerite stood up, straining her eyes, and could just make out the white bird of prey on its deep red field.

"It is his castle!" Margerite said to Gertrude. "We are almost there."

Gertrude bounced from her own seat, bracing her hand against the wall of the wagon as she peered up at the tower. "O my mistress, we are, and tonight is your wedding night. Do you think you are ready?"

Gertrude's words set up a swift fluttering in Margerite's breast. Her knees going weak beneath her, she sat down hard. The wedding, Ruprecht - all her dreams had become too real to her, as though, standing on the battlements of a castle with her arms outspread and the wind in her hair, she had suddenly looked down to find her feet at the edge of the drop and realize the depth of the dizzying fall below.

"I must be, mustn't I?" she said, dazed. The sun had already just passed her noonday height: there would be barely time, when they arrived, for her to wash the dust of travel from her body and get dressed before her wedding.

"Why did he want it done so quickly?" Margerite wondered, as she had many times before on the journey. "Why not wait a month, or even a week? Most betrothals last for years…"

"Perhaps St. Walburga is his patron?" Gertrude suggested. "Or perhaps he wishes to have it done before the rest of his family can object."

"His father must be dead," Margerite mused slowly. "Or have given over his lands and title early, though that is unlikely. His mother…"

"A mother-in-law can often be a dreadful trial," Gertrude said, a little self-satisfaction in her voice. "My older sister is always complaining of hers, since she can do nothing to please the old hag. Perhaps Ruprecht's mother is like that. If she is, you will have to take great care to keep out of her way, since a man will never hear a word against the one who bore him, especially if she is an aged harridan."

"Or he could have brothers - no, he mentioned to my father that all his sibs had died in childhood, leaving him to inherit alone. We shall see. Anyway, there is some water in that skin there: get out a cloth so I can wash my face, and then you shall do my hair, so I do not look like a wild wood-wight when I meet my betrothed again."

"Or like a woman who has been travelling for a week?" Gertrude said, but she began rummaging in one of Margerite's chests at once.

As they drew closer, Margerite heard a distant fanfare, calling clear as a hunter's horn through the dark trees. She could see Martin straightening upon his horse, the other men riding more closely in formation. She forced herself to sit quietly, hands in her lap, as Martin raised his own horn and blew an answering note.

Ruprecht and a small band were waiting on horseback for them at the edge of the woods, banners uplifted. They were all dressed festively, armed only with the swords at their sides, but Ruprecht outshone his men like a falcon in a flock of starlings.

His golden hair spilled over the deep green velvet of his tunic; bands of gold trim glittered about his sleeves as he raised a hand in greeting, and the little gold horn hanging around his neck glowed so dazzlingly in the sunlight that Margerite could see it burning behind her eyelids when she blinked.

She suddenly felt very small and drab, dusty from the long journey, and wished dreadfully for a moment that Ruprecht had sent someone else out to meet them, and stayed away himself until she had gotten a chance to wash more thoroughly and change her clothes.

"Hail and welcome!" Ruprecht called. He swept out an arm in a grand gesture, taking in castle and fields and woodlands. "My betrothed, behold your new home!"

"It is most fair," Margerite answered, pitching her voice to carry to the front of the train. At Martin's signal, the horses parted, stepping to either side, and the wagon drew up between them, stopping before Ruprecht. The Graf dismounted, courteously offering Margerite his arm as she got down.

"Ritter Martin," he said to Margerite's father, "may I offer your daughter a seat upon my horse as we ride to Burg Falkenstein?"

"Of course you may," Martin answered, beaming down at him. "Are you not betrothed?"

"Come, my darling," Ruprecht murmured to Margerite. He gripped her about the waist, lifting her up into the air. Shocked by the strength that held her up so effortlessly, Margerite barely gathered herself in time to swing one leg over the big grey-black gelding's back and balance herself in the saddle before Ruprecht was leaping up behind her. His thighs tightened against her own as he nudged the horse into a walk.

"Are you comfortable thus?" Ruprecht enquired, shifting slightly.

"I am...thank you," Margerite said breathlessly. Her seat on the saddle was a little uneasy, for she was not used to sitting in front of a rider. But stranger to her, and more disturbing, was his closeness - closeness with a man such as she had never felt. Ruprecht's arms held her lightly as he guided the horse, the deep green velvet of his sleeves brushing against her own wrists.

His broad chest was warm against her back; his thighs pressed against the backs of her own, and her buttocks were almost nestled in the fork of his legs. It was almost indecent, to be riding like this with the horse's slow pace jostling them gently against each other. Though the breeze from the mountains was very cool, crisp with the scent of pines, Margerite could feel the little droplets of sweat beading on her hot brow.

Then she flushed even more deeply, for she could feel the stirring of Ruprecht's body against hers, the growing hardness in his groin. She knew quite well what was happening: she had seen stallions with mares, and Gertrude, careful of her maidenhood as she might be, had taken great pleasure in repeating what they both knew about the ways of men with women. Almost as if we were in our wedding bed already...Margerite thought. O Maria, let anyone who looks at me think I am only flushed by the sun!

She was torn between wanting to pull away in fright...and to nestle closer to her betrothed, to feel more thoroughly the certain assurance of his body's power against hers. Yet, trapped on the horse's back with the eyes of her father's band and Ruprecht's men on her as they followed the road through the fields, seeing the doors of the little wooden houses open as they passed and curious heads sticking out to gaze at the new arrivals, she could do neither. And surely it is not wanton of me to be eager for my wedding bed, when the marriage is this night and my betrothed is beside me?

The hill on which Burg Falkenstein stood was steep: the land fell off in a sharp ravine behind the castle, before rising again to a rocky, pine-darkened crag; the road that wound up between the neat rows of grapevines was graven with deep ditches. Thick wooden plank-bridges made the crossing easy now, but Margerite knew that those bridges could easily be taken up in times of siege, leaving the attackers to make their own way across as well as they could under fire from the castle walls. This would be a safer place than her father's keep: that was little more than a glorified watchtower on the edge of a great lord's lands, while this was a Graf's last refuge in battle as well as his court and home.

The huge oaken gates at the top of the hill were wide open, the pikes of the sentries who stood between them ornamented with leafy garlands. As Ruprecht's horse bore them in, a dazzling torrent of petals showered down from the walls, like the hot oil and molten lead of a castle's defense transformed, by a miracle, into a blessing of flowers. Their scent rose up around Margerite, dizzyingly sweet and strong; the cheering sounded distant in her ears, like the rushing of a faraway river.

"Behold my bride!" Ruprecht said to the folk gathered there. Margerite blinked her eyes clear, looking about herself. Everyone in the castle had clearly been told to turn out in their best, the higher-ranking servants in livery, the lower ones in clean tunics and gowns of gray and brown wool. Each of them held something - a blossom, a green branch, a brimming cup - which they lifted to wave at her as they cheered.

I will be happy here, Margerite thought mistily. She did not know whether the folk of Burg Falkenstein cheered because they loved their lord and rejoiced at his marriage, or whether Ruprecht had merely ordered them to reflect his own happiness: but he must have arranged this for her welcome, and meant her to know how gladly she was received.

Ruprecht leapt down from behind Margerite, then lifted her carefully off the horse, his strong arm steadying her until she had found her footing on the uneven paving-stones of the courtyard. She looked up into his face, meeting the warmth of his blue gaze with her own.

"Does Falkenstein please you, my frowe?" he asked.

"It does. It does...very much."

Catching her breath, Margerite looked about herself. The castle seemed even grander from within the walls, now that she could look up and see the full daunting height of the tower and the size of the stone buildings that surrounded it. Trestle-tables, their bare plank tops adorned with flowers and leafy branches, had already been set up in the inner courtyard, and to one side, a bullock turned on a great spit above a roaring fire: Ruprecht must mean to have all the folk of the nearest village to the wedding feast.

Stable-boys, as scrubbed and neat as the other servants, were approaching the men as they dismounted, taking the horses' reins and leading them to the long stables in the outer courtyard; other manservants appeared out of the throng when the wagon rode in, standing ready to unload it as soon as the command was given.

Ruprecht turned to Martin, bowing slightly. "Good knight, and gracious frowe. You must be tired from your journey, and in need of refreshment." He raised his hand, clicking his fingers, and two more servants appeared, a liveried youth and an aged woman in a long, shapeless black dress. "These two will show you to your chambers, and my men will bring your belongings up to you shortly.

"When shall you wish to see us again?" Martin asked.

"In the castle's chapel, where the wedding shall take place, a little before sunset- I would wish you to be well-rested for this glad occasion."

"A kind and noble thought," said Martin.

"Indeed it is," Margerite agreed. She turned around to look for Gertrude. The peasant girl was busy supervising the unloading of the wain, her voice sharp as she pointed to the different chests.

"That holds my frowe's clothes - over here, we will take it with us. Bedlinens there, and there..."

"Come, Gertrude," Margerite called. Gertrude hurried to her mistress' side. The two of them moved to follow the old woman, but Ruprecht caught Margerite's arm, his grip warm and light about her wrist.

"Until this evening," he said, his voice low.

Ruprecht bent down to kiss her hand, then turn it over, brushing his lips softly against the palm. The gentle caress against her sensitive skin seemed almost more than Margerite could bear, an overwhelming, tantalizing pleasure. She clasped his hand in hers, as if to hold the moment of his touch just a few heartbeats longer, then let him go.

A faint smile moved his lips; his blue eyes met hers for a second, as if they were secret lovers in the middle of the courtyard, and then they turned away from each other again. The castle was cool and shady after the heat of the sun; Margerite could feel the sheen of sweat chilling on her skin as she passed through the great doors, and blinked several times before she could see anything but the scattered afterimages of the sunlight outdoors against the shadows.

"This way," the old woman said. Her voice was remarkably clear and high, the voice of a maiden coming unexpectedly out of the wrinkled, sunken lips. She glanced up at Margerite, a sudden dark glimmer beneath her hooded eyelids, then gestured them onwards. Oddly unsettled, Margerite stood where she was, straightening her dress for a few breaths. She might be young, and strange to this place, but she knew that if the old servants once thought they could run over her, she would never be able to manage them.

"What is your name, woman?" she asked cooly.

The old woman's face did not change - she was remarkably ugly, Margerite noticed: her skin so deeply crevassed with age that she might have been scarred by heavy sword-blows, a large black wen on the side of her jaw, her nose a narrow, deformed beak.

The longer Margerite looked at her, the stranger her sweet voice sounded as she answered, "The lord calls me Cundrîê."

An odd whim of Ruprecht's, Margerite thought as she and Gertrude climbed the stairs behind Cundrîê. Or perhaps not so odd: an ugly, wild-looking creature, yet a trusted servant and helper - why should she not bear the name of the woman from Wolfram's poem? And Cundrîê must stand high indeed among the castle servants, for now that she could see more clearly, Margerite could tell that the old woman's black dress, worn and often-mended as it was, was made out of silk.

Some long-ago castoff, a gift from Ruprecht's mother or grandmother to a favoured maid? Or was Cundrîê perhaps an aged relative, taken in by Ruprecht out of charity and given the best position she could hold? There was no way of telling, or of asking without offending the old woman, but Margerite determined herself to find out as soon as she could.

The chamber was more than twice the size of the one she had slept in at home. Its floor was covered with soft woven rugs, its walls with tapestries of hunting scenes, and a warm fire burned in the stove at the centre of the room. The fine embroidered linens on the bed would make those Margerite had inherited from her mother look like a peasant's musty blankets by comparison - well, adornment could always be added, and the bedstuffs she had brought would do for second-best.

Of course Ruprecht had not worried much about her having time to pack her wedding-things, when his castle was already equipped with much better than the best Hirschenberg could afford! The thought was relieving and irritating at the same time: relieving, because Ruprecht clearly expected to provide for all her needs; irritating because he had judged her father's possessions and means so quickly, and found them wanting.

But not too badly wanting, Margerite thought. She smiled. For he chose to marry me.

As Ruprecht had promised, food and drink were laid out upon a small table of highly polished dark wood - smoked ham and cheese; a little tub of butter beside a loaf of fine white bread; a pitcher of cooled wine, the droplets of condensation beading and running down the shiny sides of the bronze vessel.

The table was set nicely in an alcove spreading out from one of the windows overlooking the rocky fall of the ravine below, so that it would get light when the sun was in the right position: she could sit and embroider there, perhaps, or do the castle's accounts, as she had always done for her father.

A large enameled basin of water sat on top of the stove, just beginning to steam gently: Margerite sighed in anticipation of the warm wash, stretching luxuriously before she called Gertrude to help her undress. The light through the window was reddening when Margerite heard the knock on the door.

She rose from her seat, ready to open it, but Gertrude reached it first. Cundrîê stood there, the lighted candle in her hand throwing her maze of wrinkles into deep relief so that her face looked like a carved Fastnacht-mask.

"It is time for you to come to the chapel," she said. She stood waiting, clearly expecting Margerite to follow her at once.

"I shall be out in a moment," Margerite replied, nodding at Gertrude to close the door.

Suddenly Margerite's legs gave way beneath her and she sank down on the bed, the fine goose-down comforter puffing up on either side of her. A strange terror was coming over her: she could feel her heart clutching irregularly beneath her ribs, and her hands were shaking like leaves in a storm.

"O, Gertrude," she breathed. "Can I really go through with this?"

"You can and must," Gertrude replied stolidly. "What are you afraid of, my frowe?"

Margerite cast about desperately in her mind, but could find no answer. She was not afraid of Ruprecht, for he would not mistreat her; this castle was grand, but the basic mechanisms of running it would be little different from those she had grown up with at Hirschenburg, she was sure.

Perhaps it was the goblin-faced old woman who stood outside - no, there was no need for her to fear a servant. She did not know what she feared, and yet she was as terrified as if she had felt the first fever-shaking of plague in her own body, or felt its soreness swelling in her armpits. She wanted to run, to burst past Cundrîê and flee into the woods like a hind with the hounds snapping at her heels. Yet this was her wedding, her day of joy: how could she be so terrified of it?

Gertrude sat down on the bed beside Margerite, patting her shoulder. "All brides are nervous," Gertrude told her. "Why should you not be, when you are leaving your father's house to dwell with a stranger for the rest of your life? And yet you were glad enough when Graf Ruprecht made his proposal, and I did not notice you struggling when he lifted you up to ride before him. Come: as my aunt says, a marriage is quickly made, and it only hurts the first time." Gertrude put the wine-goblet in Margerite's hand, and Margerite had to force her fingers to steady, lest she spill its contents upon her dress. She drank deeply, as though the sweet coolness flowed from a holy well and she sought blessing from it.

"Up, now," Gertrude told her, taking the goblet from her again. "Walk proudly, and be brave, my mistress. Once he has spoken the words, you will be the mistress of this castle and all these lands, with none over you save the Graf himself and the Kaiser."

Margerite straightened her shoulders and stood. The shaking in her legs had passed off, though she was still trembling and knew she must be pale. She pinched her cheeks to bring the brightness back to them, and the slight pain seemed to steady her.

"Here is your crown," Cundrîê said when she opened the door. The old woman lifted up a woven garland of linden-branches and wild roses, the long stems held together by a twist of gold wire. Its beauty shone incongruous against the withered claw that held it; though she was loath for Cundrîê to touch her, Margerite lowered her head and let the hag place the leafy crown upon her hair.

A day early, she thought, but I am the May-Queen. A sudden pang flashed through Margerite as she remembered the May-day festivities of last year, sitting upon the green throne by the river with the flowers twined in her braid, her father's men standing about her as the Queen's guard, while the folk of their village danced about the bonfire singing, "Old Winter's dead, and Summer's green - hail to May, the holy queen." She would never sit there again, never see the familiar faces that had ringed her since childhood flushed with delight and beer and the new spring sun as they celebrated the winter's end...

There is better ahead, and you are wasting time, she reminded herself. She waved Cundrîê on, following the old woman down the stairs and out into the courtyard.

The Falkenstein chapel was a small building, not even as large as the one at Hirschenberg. But it was bright with beeswax candles, sweet with the costly smell of frankincense; though Margerite was the bride, she saw several women there who were better-dressed than she, and her father's finest clothes looked simple and rough beside the fur-trimmed cloaks and velvets of some of Ruprecht's men.

Though she tried not to show it, the sight daunted her: she knew that they would think her dowdy and poor, wonder why the Graf was doing this...But Ruprecht, standing before the door, looked up and smiled at her, and with that sight a wave of joy rushed across Margerite's heart, for he had chosen her. With the best dignity she could, she walked down to stand before him.

He had changed his clothes as well, she noticed: now he was wearing a long robe, of silk so deep blue that it almost seemed black until he moved and the blue glimmers of the fabric caught the candlelight, embroidered with running silver stags at hem and sleeve-bands and collar.

His fine-boned face was beautifully ageless in the warm glow of the candles; it seemed to her that she could feel the strength radiating out from him, the power of his body coupled to the quiet knowledge that he was lord of the land, and best of those gathered there.

"Now," Ruprecht said when the rustling of whispers had quieted, "may all those gathered here be witnesses, that I, Graf Ruprecht von Falkenstein, take Margerite the daughter of Ritter Martin von Hirschenberg, as my lawful wife. Margerite, do you consent to this?"

"I consent," Margerite answered. Trying to speak loudly enough for her voice to be heard throughout the room, to her horror, she felt the words breaking into a squeak. But no one laughed, or even sniggered. Ruprecht lifted up her hand, sliding a ring onto her wedding-finger and placing another in her palm. She set it upon his hand in turn; he drew her to him and kissed her. Margerite closed her eyes, lost in the silken warmth of his embrace until he let her go.

"Do you witness this, Father Hans, Ritter Martin?" Ruprecht demanded

"I witness it," answered the old priest from behind the altar. Margerite's father echoed his words.

"Then it is done," Ruprecht said. "Let us go out to feast, in honour of my new bride." He took Margerite's hand, leading her out into the courtyard and seating her at one of the two great wooden chairs that stood at the head of the largest table. A serving-boy was there at once with two goblets of wine; Ruprecht lifted his towards her. "I drink to you, my beloved bride. May all our nights together be as happy as this."

"And I to you - my beloved husband," Margerite answered. They drank, and Ruprecht leaned over to kiss her again. Yet a thought was nagging at her mind, and she could not quite catch it...there!

"My husband," Margerite said. "Ruprecht...will there be no Mass this evening?"

Ruprecht's fair brows furrowed, then he laughed. "A wedding Mass? What need? Sunday comes soon enough, and our feast is ready for eating."

Martin was walking towards them, steady enough on his feet, but moving with a care that suggested that he had already drunk well in anticipation of the wedding. He grinned at the new-married couple, and the matter of the Mass left Margerite's mind.

"Congratulations!" Margerite's father said to them, settling himself easily in the chair at Ruprecht's right hand. "Now, Graf Ruprecht, you have won a treasure such as Sigfrit never dreamed of."

"That is so," Ruprecht answered, smiling. "For his marriage brought him pain and an early death, whereas I think that mine will bring me many years of joy. I would not trade, even if all the Nibelungs' horde were thrown into the bargain."

"A wise man," Martin said, nodding and reaching for the goblet in front of him.

Afterwards, Margerite only vaguely remembered the feast - the flickering torches, the plates of tender calf-flesh smothered in cream, and the sweetness of the wine. It was Ruprecht's voice that stayed in her memory, his smooth baritone a soft counterpoint to the laughing and singing around them; the golden gleam of his hair and the soft glimmers of deep blue silk as he moved drew her eyes away from the flickering torchlight around the courtyard.

She heard her name raised in toasts again and again - "To the Graf's bride! To the Gräfin Margerite!" - and found herself blushing each time: as Martin's daughter, she was used to being hailed at feasts, but that was by men who had seen her as a stumbling toddler, who might have been kindly uncles or older brothers, not by strangers who knew her only now as woman and wife.

At last their plates were empty, and Ruprecht rose to his feet, taking Margerite by the hand. Candles and torches glimmered around them, and the voices of the merrymakers rose higher. A few people were singing an old song about stallion and mare, ram and ewe.

More took it up as Ruprecht led Margerite across the courtyard, the song's chorus echoing through the stone hallways of the castle, and other voices called out rough wedding-advice. Margerite ducked her head, suddenly embarassed, but Ruprecht smoothed her hair beneath the leafy crown, and his touch reminded her that she must carry herself proudly.

Her chamber had been bedecked with roses while she was gone, the sweet scent of their petals filling the room as if it were a bower beneath the stars. Margerite saw her father and Gertrude watching from the doorway, their faces the only clear ones among the blurred strange ovals staring at her as Ruprecht gently lifted the crown from her head. The door closed: although Margerite could still hear the singing outside, she and Ruprecht were quite alone in their wedding-chamber.

Ruprecht sat down on the bed, patting the coverlet beside him. "Come, my wife," he said gently. "You need not be afraid."

"I am not afraid," Margerite insisted, but she knew that she lied. Again, she felt her body tensing as if to flee, but she walked over to the bed and sat down beside her husband.

Ruprecht kissed her softly for a long time, the warmth of his embrace seeping through her like good wine. His hands stroked her back, strong fingers kneading all the muscles knotted from days on the road, soothing away pains she had not even known she felt. Margerite felt as though she were melting beneath his touch, like iron softening under the caress of the flame.

Now and again his fingers would brush lightly down the braids that hung to either side of her face, caressing her breasts as softly as a falconer smoothing his charges' feathers; and when his touch passed over her tightening nipples, a shimmer of pleasure rippled over her body. After a time, Margerite felt her overdress loosening about her sides. Ruprecht was undoing the laces, taking his time with each knot and stroking her between. Yet his face seemed pensive, almost worried.

He fears to frighten me, or hurt me, Margerite realized. And I am here willingly: I ought to show him so. And so she reached down to lift her skirt, letting Ruprecht take it from her and pull the dress off over her head to leave her in her shift. His blue eyes were very bright in the candlelight; his gaze never left her as he rose, unfastening his swordbelt and laying it to one side before he stripped off his silken robe, standing before her in only his tight cream hose. Looking at him, Margerite caught her breath.

She had seen her father's men training bare-chested on hot summer days before, their hairy bodies welted with blows from the blunt practise-swords. But no swelling belly marred the smoothly muscled lines of Ruprecht's chest and stomach; only a thin line of fair hair grew along his middle, a glittering gold swirl outlining each small pink nipple. She reached out to stroke the firm low curves of his breast, marvelling at the warm hardness beneath her fingers.

His eyes still on Margerite, Ruprecht pulled down his hose, kicking them away to puddle pale on the floor. To Margerite's eyes, his spear seemed huge, jutting low and heavy from the shadows of his groin. Determinedly, she grasped the hem of her shift, tugging the garment off to sit naked before her husband. She did not know what she should do next, but Ruprecht was beside her again, his skin hot and soft against her own as he held her to him. Again his hand caressed her breasts; this time his fingers lingered on one nipple, tugging softly at the hardening bud.

Margerite gasped at the sudden stab of pleasure that went through her, and Ruprecht smiled, bending to kiss her again as his palm curved over her breast, stroking her belly and slipping at last between her legs. She felt her thighs moving open as he caressed them, easing the tight muscles; his tongue circled her mouth, dipped to lick at the soft flesh of her throat. Ruprecht's hand curved over her groin, his fingers pressing lightly, and she gasped at the intensity of the flare burning through her body, as though she were tinder to his spark.

"My bride," Ruprecht said, his voice quiet with wondering delight, "shall I come to you?"

"Yes," Margerite whispered, half-laughing, half-sobbing. "Oh, yes!"

Carefully Ruprecht's strong hands grasped her shoulder and buttock, moving her to lie full-length on the bed. He eased himself over Margerite, looking down into her face. Supporting himself on one elbow, he reached down between them. Margerite felt herself moving to his caress between her legs, to the soft prodding growing harder and more insistent.

Suddenly a burst of pain stabbed up through Margerite's body. Her breath hissed out and she bit her lip. Ruprecht's gentle movement stopped, but he did not pull away from her. He was still within her, held deep in her embrace; and the ache where he had stabbed in was already starting to subside.

"I am through your maidenhead," he murmured. "Let us wait a little: the pain should pass."

"It is passing," Margerite answered, but then, as he began to move within her again, she had to say, "Not quite yet." Ruprecht stopped, embracing her quietly with his cheek - smooth-shaven, but still nearly rough enough to rasp - nestled against hers. She thought of Gertrude's warnings, of how the man would take what he wanted with force and the woman could only bear the pain until she became used to it. From all she had heard, Margerite had expected no better, and for a moment she thanked Maria with all her soul that she had been wedded to Ruprecht.

The pain within her had settled to a dim warm throbbing; and, almost without noticing, Margerite found that her hips were moving slightly against it, rocking against Ruprecht's body. He began to thrust slowly again, his body following hers like a horse answering the shifts of a skillful rider.

The throbbing between Margerite's legs was growing stronger, but now it urged her on, welling up from within her like a stream bubbling from the depths of the earth, until at last her back arched and she cried out, then moaned again and again as her inner convulsions ground her against Ruprecht's thrusts.

He groaned softly above her, his hips spasming tight, and she held tightly to his muscular back, pulling him down onto her. Margerite was content, then, to lie like that, feeling their heartbeats slowing and softening together, listening to her husband's warm breath against her ear.

"My beloved wife," Ruprecht whispered, turning to lay a line of light kisses along the edge of Margerite's jaw until he came to her mouth. His tongue was sweet with wine and cream and honey; Margerite circled it with her own, as if to shape silent words of her delight.

"Beloved husband," she murmured back, and there was no more that needed to be said.

In spite of stove and fair weather, the chamber was growing chill in the night air. Ruprecht pulled the comforter up, folding it over them. Margerite nestled closely into him, her head resting on the broad muscles of his chest. His warmth lulled her easily into drowsiness, then into sleep.

Chapter Two

Margerite awoke slowly, drowsing in contentment, lulled by the soft mouse-rustles of Gertrude busying herself about the chamber. If she opened her eyes, she thought, the dream might vanish, and she be back at Burg Hirschenberg, a maiden and alone...But the slight ache of her thighs, like the strain of long riding on an unaccustomed horse, and the lingering, almost pleasant soreness between her legs were certain proof that she had not dreamed, that she was Graf Ruprecht's wedded wife.

She rolled over, stretching out a hand fondly towards the hollow where Ruprecht had lain as if she thought to find him still beside her - and touched something warm and soft, that moved beneath her fingers. Startled, Margerite's eyes flew open. There on the bed was a black tomcat, a huge, long-furred beast with a thick mane and slanting golden eyes, sitting lordly upon the coverlet as if he had a right to be there.

"Prrrow," said the cat, ducking his head to rub against Margerite's hand, so that she found herself caressing his soft ears even as she sharply said, "Gertrude, what is a cat doing in here?"

"My frowe?" Gertrude said, turning from the chest in which she was rummaging. She started back, brown eyes wide. "My frowe, it was not here a moment ago. I don't know how it got in...I'll take it away at once."

The cat purred loudly and rolled over, nuzzling Margerite's fingers in ecstasy, and she found herself smiling. "Leave him be for now. He is doing no harm."

"Tomcats have dirty habits, frowe. Best I get him out before he pisses on the linens."

But Margerite sat up and lifted the cat into her lap. He was a heavy beast, long-legged and with ears tufted like a lynx's, and his coat was black without a single white hair. Although the musky odour of a tomcat wafted from him as he rubbed his broad head against Margerite's thigh, there was no tattering about his ears, and she could feel no lumpy scars beneath his glossy hide.

"You are a fine beast," she said to him, and his golden eyes gazed up lovingly into her own. "Are you the kitchen's mousecatcher? Or are you..." she laughed, remembering something her nurse had said, when she caught the woman setting out a little plate of bread and milk beside Burg Hirschenberg's door... "are you this castle's kobolt, whom we must feed for luck?"

The cat only purred louder, settling himself against her. "No, I suppose that is a peasant's superstition, with no place in a Christian castle. Still, I think I shall call you Kobolt, until someone tells me your name. Now, Kobolt, will you get off my lap and let me dress?"

"Your wedding-night must not have been so bad," Gertrude murmured tartly, "if you are prattling so to a cat."

"It was..." Margerite felt the blush spreading warm across the face, even as her lips parted in a smile. Gertrude nodded wisely.

"Well, your husband is a fine courtier, and he has been married before. It is only to be expected. Now, your washing-water is hot, and the sun is well-risen, and I would be surprised if the men have not gathered in the hall already. Tell me," she added, her voice suddenly soft, "are you sore in your womanly parts? My mother taught me to make a soothing salve for it."

"A little," Margerite admitted. "But I need no salve. It is... someday, I pray to Mother Maria, you will have a husband of your own, and know something of this joy!"

"Ah, well, the priests would not rave against the pleasures of the flesh as a sin if there were no pleasure in it. But I am glad that Ruprecht has dealt well with you. Still - " Gertrude lifted a plump finger - "my mother warned me of this also, and all my old aunts - if matters are ill on the wedding night, they may improve, for some men can learn; but if they go well, you must not think that everything will be honey and blossoms forever after because of that. He is only a man, after all, and some nights he will lose his temper, and some nights come drunk to bed, or unwashed and smelling like a boar hog in rut."

Margerite laughed. "You are a silly girl, and become an old aunt yourself before your time. Gertrude, I must find you a husband here, or you will dry your own brains up with your nonsense."

"I have more sense than you, my frowe," Gertrude sniffed. "Now, I had your silver comb right here yesterday...where did I put it? I hope none of the other servants here have been meddling with your things, but if they have, I shall set them to rights straight away, for Ruprecht may be a fine Graf, but his folk do not know what you need and I do. Ah, there it is, and someone has indeed been in here, for it was not polished this brightly yesterday."

As Margerite walked out of her chamber, she caught the scent of greenery and flowers, and looked up to see the pale leaves of a birch-branch fixed above her door, intertwined with woven ropes of sweet woodruff and violets: Ruprecht had sent her a May-day love-token. She kissed the tips of her fingers, reached up to brush them against the leaves. She had never thought to be courted so - and the less by her own wedded husband; it nearly brought tears of joy to her eyes.

Kobolt followed Margerite down the winding staircase to the great hall, the sound of his tufted paws muffled against the narrow oaken steps. Shafts of sunlight spilled in through the broad windows above and the narrower ones below, illuminating the motes of dust dancing in the air and gilding the disordered heaps of reeds and strewing-herbs on the floor.

Ruprecht was seated at the table already, with Ritter Martin beside him, the two of them helping themselves to bread and sliced sausage from a gilded platter. At either side of his crimson-cushioned chair sat a pair of great gray mastiffs, their pointed ears pricking up as their heads swiveled to look at Margerite.

"Greetings, my wife," Ruprecht called cheerfully. "It seems you have slept well. Will you come and break your fast with us?"

Margerite crossed the length of the hall, settling herself beside her husband. By the time she had reached her place, a servant had already set a silver goblet before her. At a motion from her hand, he filled it half with water and half with pale wine, the two mingling to gild the inside of the bowl with glittering brightness.

Ruprecht caught Margerite's hand as she reached for the bread, raising it to kiss her fingers softly. His lips brushed against the gold of her wedding ring; she met his eyes above it, and it was as if, in the warmth of his blue gaze, she could feel his tender caress upon her breasts and thighs again. The breath of his silent sigh grazed her cheek like a kiss, and her heart seemed to melt within her in a flood of warmth. Later, she thought, there would be time to speak of their feelings and their wedding-night; with her father there, they could say no close words to each other, but the glance they exchanged was enough.

"I have been telling your father of the pleasures to be had here, if he is minded to stay with us a while," Ruprecht said. "My woods have some of the finest hunting in the Empire: there are plenty of deer and boar, and even bears. Or we could go hawking for roebucks - yes, I have a pair of eagles, which Johann our falconer has trained to hunt roe!"

Margerite's eyes widened in surprise, but she had made up her mind not to be overwhelmed by anything Ruprecht's castle might offer, however much it might be grander than what it was used to. "That would be a fine hunt, and one I would gladly see."

But Martin shook his grizzled head. "I am not the falconer to ride out with eagles; that is far past my skill. Do not let me stand in the way of your pleasure, though. You two go if you wish, and leave an old man to rest his bones, for it has been a long journey here. And I must not linger, lest my keep be unguarded too long. Though there has been no trouble of late, these are uncertain times."

"What do you say, my wife?" asked Ruprecht.

Margerite could not answer for a moment. The thought of seeing the eagle circling, to stoop on a buck as a falcon would on a hare, entranced her, as did the lure of riding out beside her husband in the sunlight. But she knew it would be discourteous to leave her father behind, the more so if he would not stay long...and she had not seen half of the castle and its grounds herself yet.

She was about to answer when a sudden rustling in the rushes behind her was pierced by a shrill squeak. A moment later, Kobolt leapt onto the table, swishing his thick black tail. The mouse that dangled bloody from his mouth was still twitching a little, but its head and legs hung down limply. Horrified, Margerite reached to shoo him away. He dropped the mouse at once, like a well-trained falcon relinquishing its prey, and leaned in to nuzzle her hand with a soft chirping purr.

Ruprecht's gale of bright laughter burst over the table. "Your cat has an opinion, I see. Did you bring him with you from Hirschenburg?"

Margerite was about to protest that Kobolt was not her cat, but he had already jumped into her lap, kneading her legs with heavy paws. She gestured feebly; the same servant who had filled her cup was already whisking the mouse from the table and wiping off the stain where it had fallen.

"He was waiting for me when I woke up this morning," she said. "I thought he had come up from mousing in the kitchen."

"Well, he is a fine hunter, wherever he came from. Shall we take his advice?" Ruprecht reached across an mastiff's head to pet the cat; Kobolt laid his ears back, tolerating the touch for a moment, then stood, arching his back in a great stretch before he stepped onto the table again. He sniffed at Margerite's wine before taking a few dainty laps, then leapt to the floor, dashing off into the shadows. The gray mastiffs watched him with interest, but no more: they were trained to chase boar and stag, not to run after small game.

"The hunt would be fair on such a fine day," Margerite answered reluctantly. "But I would not leave my father alone - and I would see more of my new home before we go riding through the woods."

If Ruprecht was disappointed, he hid it well. His smile did not waver as he courteously inclined his head towards Margerite, then Martin. "As you will. There will be fair days enough this summer."

Now that the first rushing excitement of her arrival had ebbed, Margerite was ready to take a better look at Burg Falkenstein. Within the inner courtyard, as well as the castle itself - a great crenellated edifice, angled sharply against the inner wall - stood the lesser buildings: the smithy, its wall abutting the castle, the guard tower housing the chapel, the stables where Ruprecht's finest horses and those of his noble guests were kept, with a mews and small kennel for his favourite hounds; Ruprecht pointed out a larger square tower as holding the chapel and guard headquarters.

Between smithy and chapel was a walled garden: Ruprecht, trailed by his two mastiffs, passed by it as if it were of no importance, but Margerite paused to look beneath the arch of its entrance. Once there had been a small pleasure-garden there, with a seat built around the trunk of a great linden; an unpruned tangle of roses tumbled thorny around the walls, and those flowers that had not died out had run wild, rioting in creamy-white and yellow blossom above their decaying beds.

But the half of the yard that was given over to kitchen and medical herbs was neatly tended, the older plants trimmed back into shape and the new year's seedlings set firmly and tidily in their place. Margerite knew most of them at a glance: salad rocket and sorrel, rosemary and thyme and tansy, comfrey and borage and the other plants needed to flavour the food and tend the hurts of everyone from serf to Kaiser. But many of them were unknown to her, or, like the thin-fingered leaves and spike-rowed purple cowls of monkshood, strange to see in such an assortment.

She made up her mind to ask the cook - for who else would have overseen the kitchen garden, and left the pleasure garden to run wild? - about these herbs, and see to the restoration of the other half, where it would be pleasant to sit doing her needlework, or twining her fingers with Ruprecht's in the warm summer evenings.

"Come, Margerite," her husband called. "There is nothing there worth seeing." She hurried to catch up with Ruprecht and Martin, making their way past the stables to the gate to the outer yard, flanked by a round guard-tower on one side and the castle's outer wall on the other..

Beyond the inner courtyard, Burg Falkenstein's walls encompassed a span of perhaps two acres. Much of it was given over to a larger vegetable garden, its rows sprouting lush green; across from the garden was a larger stables and a long building before which a group of armed men stood in a circle, calling advice to the two who sparred with blunted swords within. Margerite had seen enough of her father's armsmen at their training to know that this was a training bout. She knew Bertram by his height and the black beard bushing over his breastplate; the man he was instructing, holding him at bay with easy, almost leisurely sweeps of his long sword, was almost a full head shorter, and even she could see the awkwardness of his movement in contrast to Bertram's.

"Come on, Eckhardt!" Bertram shouted, his deep voice carrying easily over the cries of the other men. "Now come at me again…lower, boy, who do you think you're fooling?A firmer grasp, damn you, that's not your pizzle you're holding! God's Wounds, how do you think you'll ever kill a man if you can't strike him a solid blow!"

Ruprecht took Margerite's arm, leading her swiftly away. A faint wash of pink stained his high cheekbones, as if he were a boy listening to the speech of men for the first time. "I am sorry, my frowe. Some men will speak so when they are together, and although Bertram is trusty, and a mighty man of his hands, he is more than somewhat rough."

"I have heard men at sword-work before," Margerite said lightly. "Think nothing of it."

Martin averted his eyes, mumbling something into his grizzled beard, and Margerite knew her father was ashamed by her sudden avowal, as though he felt that she should have been able to stay in the gentle company of women through her youth, instead of taking on the duties of chatelaine to what, they all three knew full well, was hardly more than a soldiers' garrison. Quickly she cast about for a way to change the subject, and at once struck upon the thought that had been troubling her since her hurried betrothal, like a boulder standing hard above the rushing waters of a stream.

"How did such a man as Bertram come to be the captain of your guard?" she asked. "He seems…"

"Too rough for such a post?" Ruprecht answered, a slight smile glinting in the corners of his eyes. "Perhaps so, but it is not for his courtesy that I keep him. He came to me highly recommended by a friend whose judgement in such matters I trust, who told me that Bertram was not only a fighter good as any belted knight, but as fine a commander of men as he had seen; and in the year he has been with me, Bertram has proved those words true. But you need have little to do with him, for his place is with my guards and soldiers, not in our hall."

The bitch-mastiff had wandered off as he spoke, sniffing at the hem of a tall warrior who ignored her steadily; now Ruprecht clapped his hands sharply, and she dashed back, sitting down on her haunches and looking up at him with the great brown eyes of a hound hoping that her sin has not been seen.

He petted her broad head, scratching behind one pointed ear. "Good girl, Brangaene. Come along, now…Margerite, did I forget to introduce you to Mark and Brangaene? They are the best pair of mastiffs I have ever hunted with, of good obedience and great worth: fierce as lions when pulling down their quarry, but mild and gentle with men, when so many of their breed seem as ready to turn on their masters as on their prey."

Margerite held out her hand to the hounds for sniffing, glad of her husband's reassurance: the mastiffs were large dogs, their heads nearly as high as her hip, and thick-built through the shoulders, as befitted hounds that must close with boar and bear. Mark rolled his eyes at her, licking her hand, and she ventured to pat him between the ears.

"Mark and Brangaene are a strange couple," Margerite said with a little laugh. "Why not name the bitch after Îsôt, rather than her serving-maid?"

"Mark has been with me the longer," Ruprecht replied, and to Margerite's ears, his voice sounded slightly distant for a moment, almost sad. "He is a faithful creature, who has shared my bedchamber and followed me for two years. I would not see him lose his place to some Tristan when he grows older - and how should I name a good loose-hound, who must follow a quarry and hold it, after a wavering runaway like Îsôt?"

The maid Brangaene had not served King Mark so well either, but Margerite thought it best not to remind Ruprecht of that. "So long as she is not Patient Griselda, I shall not quarrel with your choice of names." Margerite smiled at her husband, and Ruprecht lifted her hand to his lips.

"Do not fear: I know well enough, without any foolish tests, what a good woman I have."

Margerite opened her mouth to answer him, when an unearthly yowl split the air. Ruprecht whirled to stand between her and the sound, his sword leaping bright from its scabbard and his left hand uplifted as if to hold a shield, the sunlight striking a sudden deep purple glow from the amethyst in his ring. Margerite's father drew his own blade as well, stepping forward stolidly. Then a striped gray cat streaked out between the guard-towers, blood scattering from the ribbons of his ear as he tore past, and Kobolt followed on his heels.

The two men sheathed their swords. Ruprecht laughed ruefully as the colour seeped slowly back to his blanched face. "For a new arrival, my love, your cat has distinguished himself this morning. If he keeps going as he has begun, there will be neither mice nor other tomcats within three days' ride of Falkenstein, and every kitten born this year will be tuft-eared and black as the...face of Satan." He laughed again, but his fingers were cold as he took Margerite's hand in his to lead her on.

She tightened her grasp a little, giving him her warmth. How beautiful he was, his gold hair glittering around his finely-chiseled face, the sunlight burning deep in the blue pools of his eyes! Margerite wondered what he had thought in that flickering second as he drew his sword - that the castle was under attack, perhaps? More likely, he had not thought at all, but only reacted as trained warriors would do; she had seen the same reflexes in startled fighting men before. And his first thought was to stand between me and harm...

"If you will not hunt today, Ritter Martin, would simply riding out be to your pleasure, that you may see more of the lands your daughter rules?" Ruprecht asked. "We can easily be down to the village by the Tiefensee and back in time for our midday meal."

At Martin's assent, Ruprecht raised his voice, the mellow baritone carrying easily over the sounds of the men at their training as he shouted for their horses to be saddled at once. Two of the men-at-arms broke off from the circle, hastening into the inner courtyard. It was not long before the three steeds were led before them, ready for mounting. Ruprecht made a cradle of his hands for Margerite's foot to help her up, then leapt lightly onto his own horse's dark back - a leap, Margerite had no doubt, that he was accustomed to making in full armour.

The gate-guards saluted as the three riders went out through the castle gates, passing single-file over the hard-packed dirt embankment that bridged the ditch. Margerite thought fleetingly of words she had read once: In a castle there are three things that are strong, the ditch, the wall, and the keep...what is a ditch, except deep ground which is humility? The spiritual wall is chastity, and as you have this ditch of humility and wall of chastity so must we build the keep of charity...

She nudged Mathilde's sides lightly, urging the mare up beside Ruprecht's horse again, eager to see how those folk lived here who were closely bound to the Graf's chief castle - for they were her folk now, and she would be, at least in part, responsible for their welfare, as she had been for the villagers at home. A few pale blossoms still starred the fresh green leaves of the orchard that stretched down one side of the hill, and the gentle breeze wafted their sweet scent over the three riders. The grapevines were budding out along their neatly terraced rows, unfolding leaves and tendrils beneath the sun's warmth, and the beehives at the edge of the orchard hummed softly.

Out of the corner of her eye, Margerite saw something black flickering: Kobolt's plumed tail, twitching up as the cat stalked between two rows of vines. I could not be happier, she thought suddenly. Had they not been on horseback, and her father beside them, she would have flung her arms around Ruprecht and kissed him from pure delight.

At the foot of the hill, they turned aside from the main road, following a narrower track down to where the river rushed out of the ravine behind the castle, tumbling over the wet rocks in a spray of foam. The river led down through a stretch of alder-trees, their branches reaching low over the road; Ruprecht took the lead again, holding back the black-catkined twigs so that they should not slap Margerite in the face. The path veered sharply to the right at the edge of a low precipice where the water cascaded down, churning up the still waters of the lake below into a froth.

"This is the Tiefensee," Ruprecht told them. "Although it may seem small, no one knows how deep it is...but those who drown in it do not come up again. There is never any lack of fish here, either, so you only need to give the word when you would see it upon our table. Our cook has a good hand with fish."

"That will make Fridays no hardship," Margerite said. And today was Friday, indeed: it would be pike or trout upon the table, or perhaps eel, if there were eels in this river.

Ruprecht blinked, then waved his hand with a little laugh as if to brush her words aside, the amethyst in his ring glinting. "As you will, my wife. Such matters are yours to order as you think best."

The village on the shores of the little lake was a large one, spread over the hills that ringed the water's edge. Its fields were green with sprouting barley and rye; Margerite saw a few children walking among the rows of grain, pulling weeds, but the main work of ploughing and planting was over for now. A cow mooed gently in the distance, the mournful sound of her bell carrying clearly across the water.

The sharp-gabled houses were all adorned with May greenery and flowers; colourful ribbons were tied about the slender birch trees that grew between them, and the lower branches of the linden in the middle of the village square were adorned with ribbons and wreaths of flowers, put there to honour St. Walburga. The village folk had dressed in their best in honour of the saint, as well; though their clothes were mostly the gray and brown of peasant wool, now and again Margerite saw a maiden with a bright hood or a man in a white-bleached tunic.

They did not greet Ruprecht with words of welcome and blessing as their Graf rode through the village, as Martin's folk would have greeted him, but bowed deeply and backed away from the riders, their plain blunt faces frozen into grave masks of respect. For a moment, Margerite felt homesick, thinking of the May-day dancing and singing about Burg Hirschenberg, and the good people who were so proud to crown Ritter Martin's daughter as their May-Queen every year.

But of course, the gap between Ruprecht's villagers and their lord was far greater than that at Hirschenberg, and thus there should be no expecting the same sort of familiarity. Still, it seemed strange to Margerite to see how swift the village folk were to bow and withdraw, without so much as a "God bless you, lord Graf," to their ruler or a branch of May greenery offered him for luck.

I must get used to this, she told herself sternly. I am not a simple knight's daughter any longer, but Gräfin von Falkenstein. Nevertheless, Margerite decided that she would make sure to see what provision the castle made for those around it, whether the leavings from their table were sent down to the sick and hungry, or any care taken to be sure that all went well for the folk outside Burg Falkenstein's gates. As Ruprecht had promised, they were back well before noon, and their meal laid hot before them within a few minutes of the time they sat down.

Margerite ate with a good appetite, now and again passing tidbits to Kobolt, who was rubbing about the legs of her chair and purring, and would stand up to knead her thigh with his great tufted paws if she ignored him too long. She wondered briefly where he had come from: had he been trained, perhaps, by some wandering juggler? But though he followed her about, he showed no sign of doing tricks, or indeed of doing anything other than his own pleasure. Still, he was a charming creature, if not as well-behaved as the mastiffs that gazed devotedly up at each morsel that passed from Ruprecht's plate to his mouth.

After the meal, Martin excused himself, explaining that he must make ready for his journey homewards. Ruprecht turned to Margerite.

"Well, my dear wife, what is your pleasure for the rest of the day?"

"I would see more of the castle," Margerite answered. "I do not even know the name of your seneschal yet, let alone anyone else, and I must learn quickly how things are done here if I am to be a proper wife to you."

Ruprecht cupped her chin in his hand, turning her face up to him for a kiss. "Günther told me that you were a most capable and hardworking maiden, as well as a great beauty. But there is no need for you to trouble yourself too greatly here. Our seneschal, Kai, oversees the running of the castle well enough, and I am sure he can go on doing it now that you are here. But I shall call him in, and any others you desire, so that you may speak with them as you will and give them your orders."

Kai the seneschal, Berthe the head cook, Johann the chief falconer...one by one Margerite greeted those who would serve her and weave her orders into the weft of Burg Falkenstein. But when the last of those who held the posts of governance within the castle had left, Ruprecht leaned his head back and called out two other names.

"Cundrîê!" he shouted, and then, "Clingschor!"

Beneath the warm wool of her shift, Margerite felt an icy shiver ripple across her skin. She did not know why, but those names - both from Parzival, the wild messenger-woman and the evil, castrated wizard - disturbed her more deeply than she knew how to name. *It is only because I was nervous last night, and Cundrîê seemed so strange to me,* she told herself sternly. Nevertheless, her hands gripped hard at the smooth blue linen of her skirt, and she could feel her heart beating fast, her breath whispering swift, as the door of the great hall swung open.

The figure beside Cundrîê was dressed, like her, in an old and often-mended garment of black silk, but the cut was that of a man's robe; yet he had no beard, and his face was a twin to Cundrîê's, deeply wrinkled and beak-nosed, even to the dark wen disfiguring the left side of the jaw. *Twins: is that why their parents named them so oddly?*

Cundrîê and Clingschor bowed together, but it was Clingschor who spoke, his voice a clear, deep bass. "You summoned us, Graf, and we are here. What is your desire?"

"The Gräfin wishes to know the folk of this castle," Ruprecht replied. "The two of you will serve her as you serve me, tending to her wishes and giving her advice at need. Cundrîê, you will tend to her chamber…"

"No!" Margerite broke in. Her voice rang sharp and high in her own ears; she was suddenly aware that she was sitting bolt upright, the sweat beading out on her forehead - as if I were in mortal terror. She drew a deep breath to calm herself, went on more quietly. "I thank you, my husband, for the offer, but my maid Gertrude is more than able enough to care for me, and she does not wish to share her trust; she says that two do only half the work of one in such matters, for they can never agree, and she is used to my needs and ways."

The old woman and the old man listened silently, their ugly faces impassive, but Ruprecht's forehead creased in a frown, his golden brows drawing together. "My beloved wife, I wish you to have your desire in all things, but truly, your maidservant is new to this castle, and it will be some time before she understands how things are here. Let Cundrîê aid her, at least for a while, and you will find that everything goes much more smoothly and well than your maid can possibly manage by herself."

"She will not be happy…" Margerite ventured tentatively.

Ruprecht laughed. "It is hardly her decision to make. No; it is best for Cundrîê to serve in your chamber until your maid is better trained to her new position as the servant of the Gräfin. Or you may decide that you wish a more fitting attendant, who knows how the Gräfin von Falkenstein ought to be tended and dressed."

He stopped there, and Margerite felt her cheeks flushing. Surreptitiously she smoothed down the wrinkles of her skirt - she realized then how it must look, for Ruprecht's wife to be wearing clothes no better than the finest dresses of a poor knight's daughter, and seized upon that to turn her mind from the unnerving thought of Cundrîê creeping quietly into her bedchamber.

"I had meant to speak to you about that, my husband. I know that the clothes I brought with me are not worthy of Burg Falkenstein's mistress, but I have no others."

Ruprecht leaned his chin on his hand, a slight smile on his lips as his gaze gently caressed Margerite. She could see - Maria be thanked - no pity or contempt in his face, only tenderness and delight as he looked at her.

"Something must be done about that at once," he said. "Soon I shall be sending men to Freiburg for various supplies, and you can give orders for material, or even go yourself to deal with a dressmaker if you wish. But until then - Cundrîê, see to it that the Gräfin is able to dress herself properly tomorrow, and on every day following."

"As you wish it, Herr Graf," Cundrîê answered, bowing again.

"You are dismissed."

Margerite did not feel at ease until the iron-bound door had swung closed behind the strange pair. Only then did she realize that her legs were cramped with tension, her shoulders and arms aching as if she had been straining against something with all her might, and the sweat-soaked wool of her shift was growing cold against her back.

"Who are they?" she asked her husband. "They are so..."

"They are old and faithful servants," Ruprecht answered. "And they are very wise. If they give you advice, I ask you to take it, for your own good...and as you trust me. Will you promise?"

He took Margerite's hands between his own, his touch warm on her chilled skin, and gazed deeply into her eyes, his handsome face very grave and earnest. Margerite felt that she was being asked something she did not understand, though she could not guess what. Yet to argue or question would be as if she were telling Ruprecht that she did not trust him, and she did trust her husband, even as she loved him and was grateful to him.

"I promise," she said reluctantly, wishing that she could call the words back even as they left her mouth. But Ruprecht lifted her hand to his lips, kissing it, and Margerite was greatly relieved that the moment of strain had passed.

"And you have not been properly introduced to my Knappe, either," Ruprecht said. He raised his voice. "Wolfram!"

The squire was there almost before the echoes of Ruprecht's voice had died away. "You called, Graf?" He smiled charmingly down at his lord and Margerite. Ruprecht's Knappe was a tall, heavily-built youth, dark-haired and blue-eyed, with the stubbly shadow of a beard thick upon his square jaw; it seemed to Margerite that there was something familiar about him, but she could not place him.

"Margerite, I believe you saw Wolfram at your father's castle. He is the son of one of Graf Günther's knights, Ritter Wenzel von Obenheim."

Margerite drew in her breath sharply. Once or twice, her father had mentioned that Ritter Wenzel had a son of an age to marry her - if Ruprecht had not chosen me, I might have been wedded to this boy!

Wolfram bowed over her hand in a courtly manner. "Frowe Gräfin, it is the delight of my day to find myself in your presence. My father spoke often of the chivalry and courtesy of your father, and of his prowess in battle. It joys me greatly that you have come to cast your light upon this castle, and that you are wedded to a lord whose greatness is the match of your own noble soul."

"You are a kind and well-spoken squire," Margerite answered, smiling back at him. "If your bravery matches your courtesy, I am sure you will win your spurs soon."

"The fear of death is as nothing when measured against a glance of approval from such radiant eyes," Wolfram declared.

Ruprecht coughed into his hand, and Wolfram abruptly flushed, dropping his eyes. "Herr Graf, if I have offended…"

Ruprecht shook his head, smiling. "I am sure the Gräfin is delighted to know that she has such a dedicated servant. But you have work to do: I am sure that you have not finished going over my armour yet."

"At once, Herr Graf," Wolfram replied, trotting briskly from the hall. Ruprecht waited until the door had closed behind him to laugh.

"Wolfram is very young, and very well-read, and has many ideas," he explained. "You need not fear that he will behave improperly to you in any way, but I fear he has fixed upon you as the ideal of his chaste and courtly devotion."

"I am flattered." Margerite was, though she could feel the warmth burning in her cheeks.

"He may, however, be useful to you. If you want anything from the library, for instance, you have only to ask Wolfram: he knows where every book is, better than I do myself. He is talented enough upon the lute and the small harp, though his voice is somewhat rough, and if you can get him to think of anything other than being your Minnesinger, you will find his conversation interesting."

When Margerite went to her bedchamber to tidy herself for the evening meal, she found Gertrude pacing angrily about the room. The maid's round cheeks were pink with anger, and wisps of brown hair had escaped her braid to curl disarrayed about her face.

"What is the matter, Gertrude?" she asked, although she already suspected the answer.

"That…that woman! That old hag! She came in here and began to go through your chest, and took several of the dresses. When I asked her what she was doing, she said that your care had been commanded to her, and that I did not know enough to serve you. Can you imagine! As if I had not been with you for years, seeing to your every need!"

Margerite sighed. "The Graf wants her to assist you," she said calmly. "And you must admit, Gertrude, that neither of us has had much to do with life in castles greater than Burg Hirschenberg. It cannot hurt to have the help of one of the old servants, who has doubtless been here since before either of us was born, and served Ruprecht's mother and his first wife."

"But she has not," Gertrude protested. "I was talking to one of the women in the kitchen, and she said that Cundrîê and her brother - some odd name, that I cannot remember - only came to Falkenstein after the death of Gräfin Radegund, when the Pest came again in thirteen sixty-one. She said when she saw them first, she thought she must be about to die, for she was sure that they were Plague and Death themselves." Gertrude crossed herself rapidly, three times, and Margerite realized that she was making the same gesture herself, and that her other hand was touching the loop of garnet prayer-beads at her belt. Still, she steeled herself, making her face as stern as she could.

"There will be no such foolish talk from you," she snapped. "Ruprecht said they are old and faithful servants; perhaps they came here from one of his lesser castles. I cannot order you to like Cundrîê, but I can tell you not to make any trouble with her, for the Graf himself seems to think very highly of her and Clingschor."

"Then he is the only one who does," Gertrude muttered, subsiding into angry silence as she combed Margerite's hair. For the silence, Margerite was grateful, if not for the sharp yanks of the silver comb. At last, she had to say, "Enough, Gertrude. I would sooner be groomed by Kobolt's claws."

At the sound of his name, the cat, who had followed Margerite in and curled on the bed, stood and arched into a stretch, digging those same claws deeply into the comforter.

"That cat will destroy everything in this castle if you let it," Gertrude complained. "Shall I toss it out, frowe? It stares at me as if it were the master here."

"Leave him be," Margerite answered absently.

"Cats and damned old hags," Gertrude grumbled. "Such creatures to live in a Graf's castle."

Margerite grasped her servant's wrist and slapped her sharply on the back of the hand. "You may not swear, Gertrude! The less so now that we are here. Ruprecht will allow me much, but I do not think that he would hesitate to send you off if he thought that you were really an unfit servant for a Gräfin."

"As you wish, Frowe Gräfin," Gertrude answered, her lower lip pouching out sullenly. She returned to her task, not speaking for a while. Suddenly she burst out, "You would not let him send me away, would you, frowe?"

"Not if I could help it," Margerite replied. "But…I do not know yet how much power I really have here. If the Graf… if Ruprecht chose to do something like that, I do not know if I could stand against him, even in such a matter as the ordering of my own chamber. It would be best if we never had to find out, for I love my husband and do not wish to quarrel with him. Though," she added, "you may be sure that I would, if the question were one of sending you away."

"Thank you, frowe," Gertrude choked. Although she was not weeping, her face was blotched pale and pink as if she had cried for hours.

Margerite patted the maid's hand gently. "There, I understand. You miss home already, do you not?"

"Yes, frowe," Gertrude admitted. "This castle is so big, and so strange, and the other servants are dressed far better than I and look down their noses at me as if I had just come in from the pigsty with sloppy shit all over my shoes."

"Gertrude," Margerite murmured warningly, but there was no heat behind it, for although none of the castle folk had let it show before Ruprecht, she knew full well what they must be thinking of her, and if they felt belittled by the Graf choosing a bride so far beneath his station, it was Gertrude who would bear the brunt of their discomfiture. "I shall see to it that you are clothed fittingly for your rank as the Gräfin's personal maid, never fear. Indeed, choose a dress of mine that you can alter to fit yourself tonight, since they have all been deemed unsuitable for me, but should do very nicely for you."

"Thank you, frowe," Gertrude said, her voice still subdued. Then she looked straight into Margerite's eyes again, and the blood rushed back into her cheeks. "And do you know what else I found out in the kitchen? I meant to tell you straight off, but I was so angry…They are cooking veal for dinner tonight, and it a Friday! I asked the cook why, and she told me to mind my own business, and not eat it if I didn't like it."

Margerite rose abruptly to her feet, gathering the heavy mass of her hair in her hands and tossing it back over her shoulders. "That is not as it should be, and I shall set it to rights."

The kitchen was nearly three times the size of the one at Burg Hirschenberg, with narrow slit-windows letting light in between the fireplaces and two wider windows in the wall on the side overlooking the ravine. Only two of the four fireplaces were burning, but their heat and that of the ovens struck Margerite hard in the face as she stepped into the room, looking around for Berthe the cook. The big woman was standing over one of the fireplaces, stirring something in a long-handled pan, and Margerite could smell the rich scent of meat in a heavy sauce.

"Berthe," she said. The cook did not turn around, and she raised her voice. "Berthe, look at me." Something in her tone must have cut through the other woman's concentration, for Berthe whirled at once, bobbing a clumsy curtsey.

"Forgive me, Gräfin! I did not know you were here."

"Berthe, today is Friday. Why are you not cooking fish?"

The cook's heavy face, already red and shiny from the heat, grew redder yet, and a drop of sweat trickled down her nose as her gaze dropped to the floor.

"Gräfin, the Graf said that he wanted veal. Perhaps he forgot...It is not my place to tell him what he wishes to eat."

Margerite stared at her for a long moment. The truthfulness of Gertrude, or the truthfulness of a woman who had just been told to obey a new mistress, no more sure than Margerite herself of just how much power the new Gräfin could actually wield: there was no doubt in Margerite's mind as to which she could trust. Nevertheless, she would gain nothing from bandying words with the cook, and much from making her will known early and firmly.

"Tonight, and hereafter," she ordered, "you will serve fish on Fridays and other days of abstinence, for it is a sin to do otherwise. And you must make confession to Father Hans, and ask him for a penance, for your role in leading others into sin."

"As you will, Gräfin. But there is no fish in the castle now, and scarcely time to send a fisherman down to the lake, let alone be sure of what he will catch."

"Do it, for maybe God will provide. If not, I am sure you can make something fit to eat on a Friday, or else Burg Falkenstein stands badly in need of a new cook."

Berthe curtsied again. "You will have a good dinner tonight, Gräfin."

"See that we do, for this is my father's last night here." Margerite turned on her heel and left, climbing the stairs back to her chamber. She was pleased with herself, for she felt that she had handled the matter well, but something about it still made her uneasy.

Perhaps it was seeing with her own eyes how little Ruprecht cared for holy days, though he had spoken of his Easter Sunday boar-hunt; it was one thing to hear shocking words from a handsome man during light talk at table, another to see red meat being prepared for dinner on a Friday in her own kitchens. Still, she had put things to rights, and he had told her that she might do that: if she had to be a little more vigilant to look after her husband's soul for him, that was a small price for all he had given her.

Despite the cook's doubt, there was a fine eel on the table that night, its wine-seethed flesh turned inside out around its backbone and spread with spices and honey. When all the remains of the dinner had been cleared away, Margerite, Ruprecht, and Martin sat talking and sipping at Falkenstein's sweet wine for a while, but at last Martin rose to his feet.

"I crave your pardon, Graf Ruprecht," he said, "but I must leave early tomorrow, and I would speak alone with my daughter for a little time, if I may."

Ruprecht smiled, inclining his head graciously. "Of course. I will bid you goodnight and good dreams, then."

He left the hall quietly, his deep red velvet shoes almost silent against the flagstones. Martin looked at his daughter for a little time, and Margerite could see the grave sadness in his blunt features. "My daughter, it is not easy for me to leave you so," Martin said, his gruff voice very quiet. "I never thought that you would come to dwell so far from our home, nor in such grandeur. And...I know not why, for there is no sense to it, but I am almost afraid to leave you alone. Perhaps it is because you are the last of our family, and though your wedding is a happy parting, and one I knew must come, it is still a parting, and I shall still miss you."

Margerite embraced her father, the tears stinging in her eyes even as they shone like dewdrops in Ritter Martin's beard. "You need have no fear for me, dear father. I shall miss you as well. But I know we will travel back to Hirschenberg now and again, for I think Ruprecht goes regularly to visit Graf Günther, and he would not deny me the pleasure of seeing you."

"Still…I am sure that all will be well here. But be careful, Margerite. I have taught you as well as I could, but this castle is both great and strange, and a young woman, even one of intelligence and capability, may easily be wrongly led. If anything ill happened to you, it would be the final breaking of my heart - and you know what the limits of my power to help you are."

Yes: if anything went wrong between herself and Ruprecht, Margerite knew that the Graf could do as he pleased with her, for her father could never match his might against her husband's.

"I know," Margerite said softly. "But be of good heart, for, God and Maria and Christ willing, no ill will befall me here. Ruprecht loves me, and I know that he will protect and care for me as a husband ought."

"Then it is good." Martin embraced his daughter again. "Be happy in your marriage, with my full blessing, and bear the Graf many strong sons and lovely daughters - as, maybe, you have already begun to do."

Margerite blushed and giggled, her face warming as she thought of the pleasure Ruprecht had given her, and her father smiled back at her. "There is more to marriage than love, but I am glad you have learned some of its sweetness already. I shall leave you to go to bed now, for I must rise well before dawn, in order that we may be on the road not long after first light."

Their goodnights said, Margerite made her way back to her chamber. She was hoping that Ruprecht would be waiting there for her, but found only Gertrude, busy ripping and stitching seams on one of her dresses. Another dress was laid out over the back of her chair, and Margerite could tell without even touching it that it was made of rich silken velvet, shimmering darkly in the candlelight - deep red or deep violet, it was hard for her to tell the true colour in the low light; but there was white fur about the collar and at the cuffs of the sleeves. She drew in her breath in a soft gasp: how could something so fine have been found for her so quickly?

"That woman brought it in," Gertrude said, her voice muffled as she bent over her needlework. "I must say it is very nice."

Margerite brushed her fingers against the incredible softness of a sleeve. She would have liked to try it on at once, to see if it fit her - Cundrîê must have taken her old dresses as a pattern - but she managed to bridle her impatience.

"You know as well as I that I have never owned anything as good. The Gräfin von Falkenstein need not be ashamed of her clothes now."

"No. Frowe, do you wish to wash before bed? The water is hot, and I have brought fresh cloths and sponges. That woman left a packet of herbs to be steeped in it, but I would not trust anything she brings to you."

"Let me see it," Margerite ordered. The dried herbs were wrapped in a little square of white linen; she unwrapped it and sniffed at them. She could smell lavender and chammomile and hops, their scents sweet and soothing, but there was something else in the blend as well, something sharper and musty. Woundwort, perhaps, or mugwort, she could not tell.

"I do not think she will do me any ill, and these are good bath-herbs. Put them in."

As the sweet smell rose up from the steaming water on the stove, Kobolt sat up on his hind legs with his paws hanging before his chest like a dancing bear's, sniffing the air. He sneezed sharply, then leapt onto the bed, grabbing one of the pillows and clawing it with fierce ecstatic kicks of his back legs. When Margerite sat down to disentangle him, he rolled onto her lap in a fury of purring, butting his head hard against her hands and licking her fingers.

"What is it you want, cat?" she asked. "If you try to play such games with my dress, you will be skinned and made into a fine fur hood."

Kobolt ignored her words, kneading her legs blissfully with his paws and rasping his tongue along her skin. Margerite petted him for a little while, then stood up so that Gertrude could help her to undress. She wondered if Ruprecht would come in to her that night…but by the time she had bathed and dried, she could barely keep her eyes opened.

Her body felt unstrung and loose, almost as if she were floating. Bath-herbs for sleep, she thought drowsily as she climbed between the fresh linen sheets. Lavender and chammomile and hops and…valerian, to drive cats mad, and…

She was flying in the sunlight, the green earth circling below her as the wind beneath her feathered wings bore her up. Each blade of grass shimmered in her keen sight; she could see each needle upon the dark pines that covered the mountain rising up behind Burg Falkenstein's crenellated crest.

She was not alone in the air: beside her flew a greater bird, his huge eagle's wings outstretched to catch the updrafts. He turned his head to look at her, and his fierce predator's eyes burned blue as the heart of a flame. But the fields below drew her gaze, and she was ravenous, the hunger thrumming through each of her taut muscles.

She did not look down at the village by the sky-mirroring lake, for there was no prey there. Turning, she circled up over the deep ravine, but did not seek within the courtyards of the castle, where no rabbits could come to feed upon the garden or fat partridges shelter in the overgrown half of the herber; and sharp though her eyes were, it seemed as though a heat-shimmer blurred the castle so that she could not look straight at it.

Gladly she turned her gaze instead to the river, the water eddying and foam-edged over the rocks like a spill of clear brown beer. And there, stalking long-legged through the water by the bank, was a heron, its narrow head bobbing up and down as it sought prey of its own.

Margerite folded her wings and dropped like a stone, talons stiffening to strike. But something had frightened the heron: it rose, wings beating frantically, and was above her before she could check her fall. Swooping up again, she circled higher and higher in a dizzying gyration that brought her over the fleeing bird.

Once more she stooped, plunging from her height with a harsh shriek of triumph. Her talons struck with a shock that almost knocked the breath from her body, but her prey crumpled beneath her, falling from the air...

"Frowe," Gertrude called breathlessly. "Frowe, are you all right? I heard you cry out."

Margerite blinked against the darkness, blinked again as the little candle-flame flared from the embers of the open stove.

"It was only a dream," she said, staring dazed at the shimmering light of the candle in Gertrude's hand. "And... not a bad one, I think, though it has already fled from my mind. What time is it?"

"Not long before dawn, I think. I had just opened my own eyes." The maid went about the room, lighting the candles with her taper.

"Hurry, then, for I would bid my father farewell and God's blessing as he sets out on his journey homewards."

After Ritter Martin and his men had ridden off, Margerite and Ruprecht went to the mews together. Although the building was larger than that at Burg Hirschenburg, and the falcon-bath in the middle of finely-carved stone, with proud raptor-heads standing about the rim and figures of their prey - hare and partridge and heron, wood-pigeon and rabbit - carved in low relief on the bowl, there were only six birds in the mews: Enid and Gawan; a goshawk and a sparrowhawk; and, brooding lordly on their high perches, the two eagles of whom Ruprecht had spoken. Johann, a small, broad-built, red-haired man, was sitting cross-legged on the floor, cutting up meat. At the sight of them, he rose to his feet, bowing low.

"Herr Graf, Frowe Gräfin. What is your pleasure this day?"

"We would fly the eagles," Ruprecht declared. But, looking at the huge birds, Margerite was less sure.

"Let me hold one on my arm first," she said. "It may be too heavy for me to carry, and if it is, I will take Enid or Gawan."

"Frowe Gräfin, Gawan's moult is well-begun now. But Enid is moulting very late this year - Ritter Martin's man told me that she is always a late moulter - and is still fit to fly, though she will not be for long."

The eagle's golden eye looked harshly into Margerite's as she lifted her gloved arm to the perch; the great talons shuffled on the rounded wood before it raised its leg at last. Even through the thick leather, she could feel the fearsome strength of its grip, and she knew that she could not hold it up too long.

"This is a bird for a strong man," she stated. "Ruprecht, you must take him, and I shall fly Enid today."

Ruprecht grinned, stretching his arm out so that the eagle might step onto his own glove. He bore the huge bird's weight lightly, and Margerite received Enid with relief.

"We shall go down by the river first," Ruprecht said. "Is she trained for heron?"

"She is," Margerite answered proudly: peregrines did not stoop at herons by nature, and it took a good falconer to train one to it.

They rode down through the orchard, a sleek greyhound bitch pacing beside them. Now and again Margerite saw the black flash of Kobolt's back as he pounced through the long grass, following them in the self-willed way of a cat. The orchard gave way to dark pines, the prepicice of the ravine lowering as they went along the edge, so that at last they rode along a track on the riverbank between two high wooded slopes.

"There is often fine hunting here," Ruprecht told his wife. "Deer and boar come down to drink, and there are many waterfowl."

When Margerite saw the heron picking through the shallows, its long thin beak stabbing down into the water, she almost cried out. Her arm went up; Enid flew free. At the same moment, Ruprecht whistled sharply, and the greyhound dashed forward. The heron's wings unfolded in a desperate flurry of flight even as Enid plummeted towards it, and it slipped out from beneath her talons, beating desperately upriver.

But Enid was circling upward, gathering height for her next stoop; and when she dove through the air again with a harsh shriek, she struck the heron hard and sure.

Its wings buckled, long neck and legs dropping as it fell to the riverbank. The greyhound was there almost in the moment it hit, mouthing the bird's thin neck, but the kill had been clean and sure. Enid circled low, flying back at Margerite's call.

"Well struck!" Ruprecht cried exuberantly. They dismounted, Margerite taking great care for her dress among the slippery reeds of the riverbank, and went to the heron together. Margerite had to cut it up herself, for Ruprecht still held his eagle, and she gave Enid the heart and wing-bone marrow as her reward.

"A good quarry for your last hunt before your moult begins, my darling," she said. Then the memory of the dream she had forgotten flooded back to her: flying beside the eagle, the heron, its loss, pursuit, and death…The blood drained from her head, leaving her dizzy.

Ruprecht's hand was on her arm at once, steadying her. "What is the matter, beloved? Is it the blood?"

Margerite laughed. "I helped train Enid to the heron myself, and you know well that seeing prey cut up does not make me faint. No: it is only that I dreamed so strangely last night, and this morning the dream has come true."

"Will you tell me of it?" Ruprecht asked. His blue eyes were very steady on her own, but the pale helm-shadow on his face stood out starkly against his tan. Margerite could not tell what he was thinking, for he had sunken again into his hunter's easy stillness.

"I dreamed I was a falcon, flying beside an eagle. I flew over the castle, and though outside the walls I could see every blade of grass, within there was a sort of shimmering, so that I could see nothing. Then I stooped upon a heron - here, at the river - and just as it befell a few minutes ago, it flew out from beneath me, and I had to rise and take it on the second stoop. And then I awoke, and Gertrude told me that I had cried out, but I could remember nothing."

With his free hand, careful of the great bird on his left arm, Ruprecht pulled Margerite to himself, embracing her. He kissed her fiercely, so that she could almost taste blood in her mouth. She found that she was trembling, pressing herself hard against his taut-muscled chest; and she did not know whether it was out of desire or the need for comfort that she clung to him.

"My sweet, my love," he murmured, caressing the tight-wound coil of Margerite's braid against her head. "And does this make you afraid?"

"I...I do not know. I do not know what it could mean." For had she not dreamed so, when Ruprecht first came to Burg Hirschenburg and chose her as his own?

"We often dream of what we love, and it may happen that those dreams are true. Cherish that gift, my beloved, and do not be afraid to speak to me of it when it happens." He kissed Margerite again, more gently this time, stroking her until her trembling eased.

They caught nothing further that day, though they rode out again after the midday meal, but Ruprecht did not seem cast down or disappointed when he parted from her before supper. "The hunt has brought us enjoyment and a fine meal, and why should I be greedy of the woodlands when we can hunt again tomorrow?"

Margerite had been dreading this moment, and she could hear the faint quaver in her own voice as she said, "Tomorrow is Sunday, my husband. I shall not hunt."

Ruprecht smiled indulgently at her, patting her hand. "As you wish, my love. If it is your desire to stay in the castle, I shall go after boar, since that hunting is too fierce for a woman." He kissed her mouth, as though to silence any further words, though in truth Margerite had none to say: if he would not force her into breaking the Sabbath, neither had she the power to force him to keep it, and nagging him would do good to neither of them.

But Margerite did not go straight to her rooms to wash up before dinner. Instead she walked towards the castle's chapel. On her way, she paused at the gate to the herber, looking inside. The pale rose-petals glimmered dimly against the stone walls in the twilight, like faint err-lights shining from the dark thorny tangle of their overgrown tendrils, and the linden tree cast a dark shadow over the garden. Beyond, in the herb-bed, a black figure moved. Either Cundrîê or Clingschor, Margerite could not tell which, was bent over tending the plants. She shuddered, passing quickly on. But of course, the bath-herbs last night must have come from this very garden, and why should Cundrîê not care for it, if she was wise in herblore?

A rustling at her feet drew her eye; she looked down, and Kobolt was looking up at her, black amid the shadows. He opened his mouth, the ivory splinters of his teeth glinting in the fading light, and miaowed softly.

"What do you want, cat?" Margerite asked, bending to pet him. He arched to her touch and purred, then suddenly darted off into the courtyard, to sit down and stare at her again. When she came close, he ran a little way and sat down once more, twitching his black-plumed tail as though daring her to come after him. But she had turned aside from her path once, and would not again: she strode resolutely on.

The chapel, on the second floor of the large guard-tower, was dark save for the faint guttering light of a single candle on the altar. Its flickering glimmer shone off the smooth pale wood of the crucifix, darkening the shadows and brightening the arches of Christ's limbs so that his body seemed to twist in agony as it hung, the deep red paint on his wounds shining as if the blood were flowing freshly from them. It was, she noticed now, the only adornment in the place: there were no statues of Maria, nor of any saints.

"Father," Margerite called softly. "Father, are you here?"

A deep snuffling answered her...a burbling snore, rising from a heap she had not seen in the corner. Without thought, she stepped back, drawing her skirts away with hands that shook in sudden fear, even as images of the Death rose in her mind. The black boils in the hollows of her sister's body...the burbling of her mother's lungs...

"Father!" she cried out sharply, before her terror could overwhelm her.

The man in the corner stirred, sitting up with a belch. Now Margerite could see that it was the old priest who had witnessed her marriage, though two days before he had been neatly combed and attired, whereas now his gray hair and beard stuck up in a mat of spikes, and she could smell the old wine and sour flesh beneath the last lingering sweetness of the wedding-night's beeswax and frankincense. *He is ill...* No, she realized as the priest pushed himself unsteadily to his feet, bloodshot eyes cracking to peer at her in the dim light, *he is drunk.* A vast relief washed through her, too great to be dulled by either shock or disgust.

"Frowe Gräfin," the priest croaked. "What do you wish?"

"I wish..." Margerite had wanted to tell him about her dream and what had come to pass with it, to see what counsel he could give her, whether he thought it was a work of God or the Devil, or only a flight of her own mind and Nature's fancy. But this man was not fit to carry out the least of his spiritual charges, let alone to hear and judge such a matter. "I came in only to light a candle for Maria."

The priest stumbled up the stairs, and she heard the banging of him rummaging about above. At last, leaning heavily on the wall, he came down again with a candle in his hand. It was simple tallow, as was the one burning now, but Margerite asked no questions, for she wanted to get out.

This chapel is still consecrated ground, just as the Sacraments are the Sacraments, regardless of the priest who administers them, Margerite reminded herself. She lit the candle from the guttering wick-socket of the candleholder on the altar, sticking the fresh one in over it and genuflecting briefly.

"Mother Maria," she whispered under her breath. "I am confused; please help my confusion, amen."

Although Margerite tried to hide her distress at dinner, she found herself very quiet, and more than once Ruprecht had to ask her a question twice before she could answer it. At last, over dessert, as she stared at the sweet custard settling on her silver plate, he reached over to put a hand on hers and said quietly, "My beloved, what is wrong? Are you still disturbed by your dream?"

"I am...no, that is not it." She gathered her courage: she would have to speak of the matter sooner or later. "I went to the chapel, and our priest was drunk, and had clearly been so since our wedding. Is this proper for the dignity of Burg Falkenstein?"

Ruprecht sighed deeply, settling back in his chair. The warm candlelight smoothed his skin so that he might almost have been a boy of her own age, but the look of resigned sorrow that lay over him like a pall was that of a much older man. "It is not proper for our dignity," he admitted. "But it is proper for the trust we hold. When I was young, we had a very fine priest: a young man, but well-learned, the fourth son of a knight, who could sit at table and talk of weighty matters with the best of men.

But then, when I was ten years old, the Death came. My mother lay in her bed, twisting and moaning in her agony as the stench rose from her and vile black matter dribbled from her body. And she called for our priest to give her the Last Rites...and he ran, leaving her to die unshriven and in mortal terror for her soul." Ruprecht's eyes were wide now, staring into the candleflame as if he were viewing his mother's death again. Margerite reached out to him, wanting to soothe his pain, but the muscles of his shoulder were hard and unyielding beneath her hand, as though she were touching the plates of his armour.

"After the Death had passed," he said softly, "the Church had lost so many priests that they were willing to ordain any who came to them, lettered or not. And my father commanded Hans, who had stayed with us faithfully through that dreadful time, to take ordination and henceforth be priest at Burg Falkenstein, saying that whatever befell, or how well or badly he could do the duties of a priest, at least Hans would never run away when he was needed most. Nor did he, when the Plague came back: he went bravely to the dying, like the warrior he was once. And therefore he may drink as he pleases, and do as he will, for I will not cast him off while he lives."

"I understand," Margerite murmured. "I did not know. I am sorry." And I should have thought before I spoke - is there anyone living today who does not have such sorrows, or any evil in the world which was not magnified an hundredfold by the Death? Ruprecht's wife had died of the same illness: could that not explain the untended pleasure garden, the wooden love-seat left to rot beneath the linden? She would not speak of it to him until she knew more.

"You could not have known," Ruprecht said, the sorrow and weariness heavy in his voice. "Come, my bride. It is growing later, and I would lead you to your chamber."

Hand in hand, Ruprecht holding a candle before to light them, they walked up the spiraling staircase. Gertrude was waiting in Margerite's room, but slipped out without a word when she saw that Ruprecht was with her mistress. They sat down on the bed, and Ruprecht slowly unpinned and unbraided the thick coil of Margerite's hair, running his hands through the shining waves. She nestled more closely to him, stroking his back as if to ease the hard muscles beneath his velvet tunic.

"My love," she murmured. Ruprecht kissed her: his mouth was sweet from the custard, but underneath it seemed to Margerite that she tasted the salt of tears.

"The dress looks well on you," he said softly. "It was my mother's...no," he added swiftly at her start, "all that she touched since she began to sicken was burned; only the clean clothes were kept. I think she would be glad to see one so fair wearing it, though you must have other dresses made that are not after the fashion of twenty years ago. But we shall see to that."

He put his arms around her, slowly undoing her dress and pulling it down together with her shift so that her breasts were bare as a nursing mother's, then cupping one in each hand. Her nipples tightened under his sword-calloused touch; he bent his head to kiss the swelling buds, the caress of his lips sending a tingle of desire through her body. Carefully she reached to undo his belt, laying it aside on the floor, and lifted his tunic until he could shrug it off. Margerite stroked the fair skin of his muscular chest, smoothing down the sparse swirls of golden hair about his pink nipples.

To her surprise, they hardened just as her own did, and she could feel the breath coming faster in his body. Ruprecht drew her close, clinging tightly to her, her breasts soft against his hard chest. Margerite felt as though her loins were melting in the wanton warmth that swelled within her, pressing her hips against the taut muscle of his thigh. He kissed her again, more fiercely; his tongue circled her lips, slipping hot and sweet into her mouth.

She closed her eyes with a little shiver of pleasure as her arms tightened about Ruprecht's bare back. She felt his hands tugging at her dress, and raised herself a little off the bed so that he could pull it down all the way. Gently his finger caressed the golden curls at her groin, the soft touch stirring her desire so that it seemed as if a cauldron seethed within her. She could think of nothing but her husband's spear filling her body; when his hand slipped a little lower, she had to bite back a scream at the wave of intense pleasure that swept through her.

"My husband, my darling," she gasped. Ruprecht's lips closed on one nipple, and it was as if a shock ran from her breast to the place where his fingertip circled at the top of the gateway to her body, the tender flesh between her legs tingling and throbbing to his touch. Margerite could not stifle her soft cry, but as the little spasm passed, she became aware of a deeper and more urgent desire within her. Still caressing her groin, Ruprecht pulled his hose down, letting his manhood spring free.

Margerite reached out to touch him as he was touching her, stroking the soft hood of skin that gathered around the thick crimson head, the satiny shaft hot under her hand. Ruprecht gave a little hoarse moan and eased her back on the bed, his hands going beneath her to grasp her buttocks tightly.

"Yes," she encouraged him, "yes," and spread her legs, pushing up to meet him as he pressed slowly, inexorably into her. Margerite could feel herself tightening about Ruprecht with each steady thrust that filled and emptied her, a pulse of rising pleasure beating through her whole body.

The blood sang in her ears; she could see nothing but the brilliance of his eyes above her, hear nothing but the quickening sound of their breathing and her own hammering heartbeat as he drove into her again and again, until she gripped him with all her strength and cried out in unbearable ecstasy. His last shuddering spasm came a moment later, as the aftershocks slowly ebbed in her flesh. They lay locked together thus for a little while, Margerite feeling him sweetly subside within her.

"It is easier for you now," Ruprecht whispered, "is it not?"

"Oh, yes. It is…" Margerite could not find words for the delight that had possessed her, so she kissed him instead. They stayed intertwined thus until the sweat began to chill on their skin, then crept under the covers. Margerite did not know if their lovemaking had truly lightened Ruprecht's heart at all, for she knew that such sorrows stained like strong dye, fading only slowly with time and use; but for now he seemed easier, the tightness gone from his body and the shadow no longer darkening his eyes.

The pleasures of marriage are good for him, Margerite thought, and with that complacent thought in her mind, it was easy for her to drift off to sleep in his warm arms, with the soft sound of Kobolt's purring in her ears.

Sunday passed quietly in the castle, with Ruprecht and most of his men out hunting boar. Father Hans was barely able to get through the Mass, slurring his words and handling the Sacraments clumsily, but Margerite thought on what Ruprecht had said, and held her peace. The more so, since the old man was clearly ill as well as drunk, his face an unhealthy yellow and the breath wheezing in his lungs: though she pitied him and would murmur a prayer for him, she also knew that it would not be long before Burg Falkenstein was in need of a new priest.

But will Ruprecht send for one? her traitorous mind murmured. There were only five people in the chapel: herself and Gertrude, a maid and a boy whose plain gray wool marked them as among the lowest servants in the castle, and one old man, clearly a retainer of some sort from Ruprecht's father's days. Still, watching Father Hans stagger around the altar, she thought that the folk of the castle could hardly be blamed for sparing themselves the sight, and there were enough people in the world who only went to Mass at Christmas and Easter anyway, without marking Burg Falkenstein as the seat of any special impiety.

Ruprecht came back empty-handed that day, having tracked his boar but not been able to bring it to bay. He was not too ill-humoured, but he was determined to take up the chase again the next day. The fair weather broke at nightfall, black banners of cloud streaming swiftly across the red sunset. Margerite went to sleep to the sound of rain lashing against the windows of her chamber; she awoke to the soft spattering of raindrops and Kobolt nuzzling her face and licking her ear with his rough tongue.

When she went down to the great hall, she found that Ruprecht and his men had already broken their fast and left to go after the boar in his dawn wallows, leaving her to herself. Well, she thought, breaking a piece off the loaf of bread on the table and sipping absently at a silver cup of watered wine, there will doubtless be many days when Ruprecht has his own matters to tend to: I should not expect him to be with me every moment. But what to do? It was not in her nature to sit idle, nor was that a fit repayment for the great kindness Ruprecht had shown her.

She did not want to order the herber set to rights until she had spoken with her husband, but whenever the matter crossed her mind, she had held her tongue, fearing to cause him pain. Kobolt reached up to paw at her skirt, rumpling it; she petted him absently, smoothing down the folds with her other hand, and the touch of the fine soft wool beneath its embroidered adornments reminded her of Ruprecht's words about a visit to Freiburg to buy her new clothing.

I should speak to the seneschal, Margerite told herself. He would be able to give her some idea of the income of the castle and its expenses, that she might better know how much she would be able to spend. And it would be best for her to know these things, for no matter how competent Kai was, it was herself and Ruprecht who would ultimately have to decide the courses of Burg von Falkenstein.

The seneschal's chamber was at the end of one wing of the castle, on the same level as the balcony of the great hall. His door was locked, so that Margerite had to rap sharply on it.

Kai bowed deeply to her. "Frowe Gräfin, be welcome," he said in his deep bass murmur. "What can I do for you this day?" He looked little pleased to see her, but Margerite suspected that he was one of those men who never looked joyful: tall, thin, with the drooping jowls of an old leithund and a straight droop of gray-shot black hair over his ears to complete the resemblance to the scenting hound.

As befitted his age and post, Kai wore a long robe of deep blue linen trimmed with squirrel fur over black soled hose, and there were several large silver rings on his knobbly fingers.

"I would look over the castle accounts," Margerite replied. "Of your courtesy, you will show them to me."

Kai frowned heavily, his thick gray brows drawing together. "Is this the will of the Graf, frowe?"

"It is my will, that I may do my duties as his wife properly. If you have some objection to allowing me to see the accounts, we shall take up the matter with my husband together."

Kai bowed again. "As you wish, Frowe Gräfin. Come in."

The chamber was very large, larger than Margerite's own, with two wide windows looking down on the inner courtyard and arrow-slits on the two walls overlooking the outer one. A dark oaken table stood beneath one of the two wide windows where the most light would fall upon it, with inkpot and neatly trimmed goose-quills laid to one side of a half-written piece of parchment: she had clearly interrupted Kai at his work.

There was a deep alcove in the inner wall, and beside it a relief-carving in the stone, showing St. Hubert beside his stag. It was no surprise to Margerite that the patron saint of hunters should be honoured in Ruprecht's castle, but she would have expected to see his image in the chapel, rather than...there was something about this room that bothered her, but she could not say what. Perhaps it was the size: though the seneschal both slept and worked here, she would have expected such a large room to be put to a different use.

Even in May, with the stove going and a small charcoal brazier beside Kai's writing table, the air was chilly in this room, with the deep stone-cold that only a number of folk close together could ease.

Margerite stalked over to the table, seating herself with the window's light at her back, and waited as Kai unlocked one of his chests and brought out a bundle of parchment. "Here are the accounts for the year past, my frowe." Back straight, he waited beside her chair, staring at her almost rudely as she began to read.

Unhelpful as the seneschal seemed to be, he wrote a fair hand, which Margerite could read with little efforts. The rents of the villagers who worked the castle's fields; the details of the harvest and sale of wine, the salaries paid to the servants, from the least scullery girl or stableboy up to the seneschal himself: those were neatly recorded.

It was in the lists of purchases that Margerite first found difficulty, for there were a number of items paid for, but not named; a quantity of candles 'of the purest and finest virgin beeswax' were listed as being delivered to the chapel at regular intervals, but she knew that only cheap tallow lights burned there when there was not some great occasion taking place; and there were three interspersed sheets, with sums of money written on them and no explanation or date given.

Not small sums of money either: one read "750 marks in gold," one "500 marks in gold," and one "1000 marks in gold."

"What is this?" Margerite broke out, exasperated, holding the third piece of parchment up and shaking it until it rattled. "Where did this come from...or go...and why?"

"Frowe Gräfin," Kai said lugubriously, "I cannot tell you."

"What do you mean, you cannot tell me? Are you not the castle's seneschal? Have you any business holding your post? You can, and must tell me."

"I cannot tell you what I do not know. The Graf set those papers there, and told me to keep them with the rest of the year's accounting."

"And why are there so many withdrawals that have no explanation? How can you know what is needed and what held if you do not keep track of what you pay money out for - or prove that you have not taken it yourself?"

"Frowe Gräfin," Kai rumbled, "you will see that each of those withdrawals has been marked by the Graf himself. If he chooses to take money for his own purposes, and not tell me what it is for, how can I mark it down?"

"You may be sure that I will ask the Graf about this. Then, if you are guilty of any dishonesty or of concealing anything from me, you may well be afraid! I was chatelaine of my father's castle before I came here, and I would have scorned to keep such sloppy accounts. I will not see them kept thus here in Burg Falkenstein, and if any fault or negligence is yours, it is the skin on your back that will pay for it, however long you may have served Graf Ruprecht or his father."

Kai's wrinkled eyelids drooped, and he nodded. "Ask the Graf as you will, frowe. You will find that I have done the best I can."

"And give me a fresh piece of parchment now, for I will make a note of each thing that I am doubtful about, so that they may be entered rightly by noon tomorrow."

The seneschal stooped to rummage about in his chest for a moment, then gave her the parchment that she had asked for - a worn piece, the ink often scraped from the thin hide, but good enough for the sort of notes Margerite wanted to make.

A little before sunset, Margerite was sitting by the window in her room to make use of the greying light in beginning a small piece of embroidery work when she heard the sound of a hunting horn ringing out muffled beneath her. She rose, laying her stitching down, and hurried to the great hall.

Ruprecht and several of his men stood about the bristling black body of a boar, lifting their cups: they were wet and looked tired, and a stain of blood darkened the sleeve of one man's tunic, but they seemed jubilant enough as they cried out toasts to their slain quarry.

A deeper shadow crept out of the darkness as Margerite walked towards them: Kobolt was slinking towards the boar, his tongue showing pink as he licked his chops. Margerite hastened to catch him, but he was already lapping at the blood that dripped from the boar's open belly to the flagstones.

"No, let him have his taste of it," Ruprecht said as Margerite bent down to pick the cat up. "Ah, that was a fine hunt, and well worth the long chase! He is not the biggest boar we have ever brought down, but..." he toed the ivory-tusked head lightly... "he ran and hid cunningly, and put up a strong fight when we brought him to turn and stand at last."

"I am glad that your hunt went well, my husband," Margerite replied. Ruprecht drank a good draught from his cup, then held it to her lips for her to sip at. She admired his prey and listened to his tale of the chase until the serving men came to bear the boar away and lay the table for the evening meal.

It was a little time before she could summon up the courage to say, "Ruprecht, I went to our seneschal today to look over the castle's accounts, and I was much troubled by what I found."

His blue eyes narrowed slightly. "What is wrong with them?"

Margerite unfolded the parchment she had made her notes on from her belt-purse, and began to list her points of question. She was not even half-through before Ruprecht held his hand up, laughing.

"There is nothing to doubt here; my own carelessness is solely to blame. Sometimes I will take money without bothering to tell Kai what it is for - and why should I? He is my servant, not I his. But so long as he knows what we have, and keeps a fair enough count of what is in our stores, there is no need for every small thing to be written down. And such things have never been of interest to me, nor is my brain well-able to grasp them. As a young Knappe, I fear, I spent my time in hunting and fighting, and left the arts of the mind to those who were better suited to such things."

"But these sums here - how could such monies come in or out without being a matter of great note?"

"As for that: those were portions of an inheritance from a cousin who died last year, and hence too well-known to need any marking."

"Then Kai was sullen to me, and insolent, when he would not tell me what they were for."

Ruprecht caressed Margerite's cheek with a finger, smiling at her. "He is not used to having his records questioned, for he takes great pride in his post. I shall speak to him, and tell him to be more civil in future. Now, my beloved, shall I see you to bed this night? I find that a good hunt stirs my passions, and the sight of you beside me stirs them even more, but if you are not willing to receive me..."

"Oh, I am most willing," Margerite answered, a small catch in her throat as she thought of the pleasure Ruprecht had drawn from her body before. If it were not unseemly, she would have asked him to go upstairs with her there and then; as it was, even the least brush of his fingers over the back of her hand tingled through her body, inflaming her desire.

As when he had lain with her before, when Ruprecht was sure that Margerite was asleep, he moved gently from beneath her, tugging a pillow into place beneath her head. The candles were guttering low; he paused for a moment, looking down at her sleeping face in their soft light. Her beauty still amazed him: the ash-blond brows gently curved over her closed eyelids, the short straight nose with its slightly upturned tip, the pale planes of her cheeks and firm little chin...

When Günther had told him that he must marry this woman of seventeen, still unwedded and unbetrothed, he had expected to find a sallow-faced, stringy-haired, lonely girl, not a maiden coming into the full of her beauty. He had been ready to do as he was commanded, and to take the poor wretch into his household and his bed as kindly as he could; but he had not been ready to find himself overwhelmed by a woman who could not only hawk, but skillfully butcher her bird's kill, who came to him as though she had been made solely to be his wife.

Ruprecht shook himself, as though casting a heavy mantle from his shoulders. Why should he not love Margerite? Did the falconer not love his birds, or the master of hounds his dogs? He had seen Joseph weep quietly over a mastiff gutted by a boar, as though it were one of his own children who had been slain; he had heard Johann calling through endless hours for a lost bird, until at last the falconer came voiceless and bereft back to the castle.

He had tested Margerite himself through his night at Burg Hirschenberg...and he had only himself to blame, for letting his tempting words to her become real and luring her in with his own heart. But now the wedding was done and sealed, and she was his; and the real work was yet to begin. First the wedding, then the war: thus Günther had instructed him, and thus it would be done.

Chapter Three

Although Margerite rose early the next day, by the time she had washed herself and dressed, the great hall was already thronged with men. At the head of the table sat Ruprecht, his head close together with those of Kai and Bertram. They might have been planning a stag-hunt, but instead of the dark nubbles of fumes spread out upon the table for the hunters to examine and guess at the quality of the beast that had produced them, Kai was pointing to something on a sheet of parchment, and their faces were grim. Margerite hastened to sit beside her husband, Kobolt leaping onto her lap.

"What has come to pass?" she asked anxiously, stroking the cat's arched back to urge him to lie quietly instead of turning about and rubbing against her.

Ruprecht laid his hand upon hers for a moment. "My wife," he said quietly, "we are soon to be at war."

His words struck Margerite hard, but she was not greatly surprised: the thought had already come to her mind as soon as she saw the gathering in the hall. "With whom?" she asked. "And why?"

"It is our neighbor, Graf Heinrich von Fürstensee. He has always looked ill upon me, for he covets these lands. After the death of my first wife…" Ruprecht's breath choked in his throat. "He was heard to say, and say often, what a wonder it was that the plague passed so swiftly from my lands after she had been laid in the ground. I have been waiting since for a chance to avenge those words upon him, but he is strongly fortified, well-armed and provided with knights and soldiers to protect him. But now I have received word that armed men bearing his device have been seen gathering near the castle of my vassal Ritter Sigmund von Eichenwald, who guards the lands at the border between us, and it seems likely that Heinrich plans to strike against me now."

A small sharp pain pierced Margerite's thigh as she drew in her breath to speak; Kobolt, kneading at her skirt, was digging his claws in hard enough to prick her. Absently she disengaged the cat from her lap and tossed him down, her mind already working. "What do you mean to do, my husband?"

"If it is war he seeks, then war he shall receive!" Ruprecht declared. "But I shall not leave it to him to strike the first blow: he has lost his chance to take me unawares, and if we move with good haste, it will be he, and not I, who is caught by surprise. I have been speaking with Kai about the castle accounts, and by good luck it proves that we have more money than we had thought: enough to buy supplies and hire on more men as we need them. Bertram shall set out for Freiburg tomorrow, and Kai shall go with him..."

"He shall not!" Margerite broke in hotly. "I do not know how the accounts have been kept up to now, but I know how they shall be kept, because I shall see to it henceforth. Today I shall see to the state of our supplies and our needs, and tomorrow I shall ride for Freiburg to oversee the purchasing of more myself."

Ruprecht stared at her, taken aback a moment. Then a bark of laughter broke from his mouth. "Margerite, I had thought to send you on a pleasure-trip to buy clothes, if you wished it, but if it is your will to go on this errand instead, so be it. Indeed, there may still be money left over..."

"For dresses?" she said crisply. "I shall not believe that until I have seen everything else bought that we need in this war: fine clothes will do me no good if there are siege-engines battering at our gate."

"Well-said, my darling!" Ruprecht leaned over to brush his lips swiftly against hers, but as he straightened again, Margerite found herself aware of a chill feeling down her spine. She looked up to see that Bertram was staring at her, his hazel eyes cold as pebbles in the frost. He hates me, she thought, and I do not know why. To cover her discomfiture, she stared back at the big warrior as haughtily as she could.

"Do you find any fault with this plan, Bertram?" she asked, her voice sharp. "You do not seem to be much joyed by it."

"I am not sure that a woman is needed on this ride. Nor, if there is danger to be expected, do I think that the Gräfin should leave the castle."

"The danger is in the opposite direction," Ruprecht told him. "And you and eighty picked warriors will be with her, guarding her with all the strength and skill in your bodies. You may be sure that Margerite has my fullest trust, and that she will acquit herself well."

Bertram lowered his eyes, but Margerite could still see the scowl beneath his tangled black beard. "As you command, Herr Graf," he growled.

Margerite rose. "Come, Kai. If I am to ride out tomorrow, you and I have much work to do today, for I wish to inspect the castle stores as they are - not as they are written down at the moment - and then the two of us will try once more to see if we can make any sense of your accounts."

Kai looked no more cheerful than Bertram at this, but he grumbled, "As you will, Frowe Gräfin," and rose to his feet.

The party of travellers assembled in the castle's outer courtyard at first light, their heads covered against the spatters of rain gusting into their faces. Bertram had tried to insist that Margerite should ride in one of the wagons with Gertrude, but she had argued that if they were attacked on the way and there were no other recourse, she would be better able to flee on horseback than on foot, and Ruprecht had agreed with her.

Now, with the sharp wind blowing the scattered showers against her, Margerite almost wished that she had listened to the captain of the guard, but it was too late to change her mind - and she would not complain in front of Bertram, for he had made it clear that he thought her presence on their journey would be nothing but a foolish hindrance.

The ten wagons were waiting at the foot of the hill, the horses harnessed and ready. Gertrude had already seen to the packing of all the things Margerite would need on the way; she rode in the same wagon as the locked iron chest that held their money. As Margerite reined up her horse to speak with Gertrude, Mathilde jerked suddenly sideways. Kobolt had leapt from the ground to the saddle, and was now clambering up, his strong claws digging deep into the leather, to settle himself before Margerite.

"Is that...that creature to go with us?" Bertram demanded, riding up beside her on his great bay stallion. Margerite had been about to toss the cat down again, but at his words, she straightened her back and looked him angrily in the face.

"And why should he not, if I wish him to?"

"It will be difficult enough bringing two women on such an errand, without having to tend to their pets as well. Before God, Gräfin, have you any sense? Yesterday you seemed willing enough to settle down to the work that must be done, but this...cat would hardly be the creature to take on a pleasure-visit, let alone coming with us when we must travel fast and get our business done slightly."

"Kobolt will not hamper either of us," Margerite answered. She could hear her voice rising and sharpening as she spoke to him. "He comes and goes as he wills, and takes care of himself - be sure, you will not have to feed and comb him."

"And if he runs off and gets lost in the woods, we will not delay for so much as a breath to find him."

Bertram wheeled his horse, shouting at the other men. "Form up! Four abreast, two rows before and behind each wagon; the Gräfin in the middle. Hurry, you laggards, the day is growing no longer while you sit there staring."

The first night, they stayed in one of Ruprecht's lesser castles, held by one Ritter Wolfhart - a young man, only a year or two older than Margerite, who had inherited his place after his father's death in the second wave of the plague.

Wolfhart was well-mannered enough, but Margerite could tell that he was nervous at the visit of his Gräfin, and no matter how often she told him that the food at his table and the chamber that had been hastily prepared for herself and Gertrude were well to her liking, he would not stop apologizing and insisting that if he had known of her arrival beforehand, he would have been able to offer her better.

Kobolt was behaving badly, as well, and every time he leapt up on the table to steal a morsel of pork and she had to lift him down, she could feel Bertram's cold gaze upon her, and read in his scowl, as plainly as if he had spoken, I told you so. It was a relief when she was able to excuse herself for bed at last.

"That boy needs a wife," she said to Gertrude as the maid undressed her. "It is a pity you are not better-born."

Gertrude laughed and tossed her head. "He is too skinny, and he has spots. I would be happy enough with one of the Graf's men-at-arms."

"As may be," Margerite said lightly. "Have you chosen one yet? Bertram, perhaps?"

Gertrude gave an exaggerated shudder. "That man! He is worse than any of your father's soldiers - I would sooner bed a wild boar."

Margerite stiffened. "Has he done you any wrong? If he has, I will see to it that..." Her voice trailed off, for she remembered how Ruprecht had spoken of the captain of his guard, and she did not know what she could do, save try to keep Gertrude out of his way.

"Oh, no. I am sure he looks on me as nothing but a piece of baggage. It is only the way he stares, so grim all the time... and that beard! He must look gruesome beneath it. And he never smiles, have you noticed that."

"I have looked at him as little as I could," Margerite admitted. "I do not like him, and I wish Ruprecht did not trust him so."

"So do I," Gertrude mumbled, looking at the ground. Then she brightened. "Still, Eckhardt says he is nearly the finest warrior in the castle - only the Graf can match him - and all the men at arms seem to admire him greatly, so perhaps there is more to him than meets the eye."

"Eckhardt? Who is Eckhart?"

Gertrude's cheeks flushed so pinkly that Margerite could see their heat even in the light from the single candle. "Eckhardt is one of the Graf's guardsmen. He is not with us, because Bertram chose only experienced fighters, but you may have seen him at drill in the courtyard. He came from the village of Tiefensee, where he was one of the strongest of the young men, and the best with quarterstaff, so that he was taken up as a castle guard last year."

"And how did you learn all this?" Margerite teased. "Have you been dallying with young Eckhardt when you should have been doing your work?"

Gertrude shook her head, her brown braid switching from side to side. "Oh, no, frowe! I only spoke with him for a little time yesterday…I brought him some bread and cheese and small beer from the kitchen, for he helped me with loading your things onto the wagon."

"I see." Margerite smiled. "Well, guard your chastity as diligently as you guarded mine, and we shall see how matters turn out."

The weather was no better the next day, sheets of gray drizzle drifting across the purple-black mountaintops and soaking slow and cold into the riders' heavy wool cloaks. By sunset, when they neared the monastery tucked into a narrow valley between two dark peaks where Bertram had announced they would be stopping that night, they were all sodden and chilled. Even Kobolt had taken up refuge in one of the wagons, only looking out now and again to hiss at the rain.

When they stopped before the monastery gates, Bertram gestured Margerite curtly to ride up beside him. Dismounting, he knocked at the oaken door beneath the stone gate-arch, the booming sound of his blows echoing hollow through the rain.

"Ho!" he called. "Open your door, brothers, for there are travellers who seek shelter for the night with you, and one of them is the Gräfin von Falkenstein."

Margerite heard the sound of thick iron bolts sliding aside, and the door swung open. The monk who stood there was dressed in a black Benedictine habit, with a narrow ring of gray hair around the wet gleam of his tonsured skull. As he looked at Bertram, his eyes narrowed and his lips pressed together.

"Who are you?"

"I am the captain of the guard of Burg Falkenstein, escorting the noble Frowe Gräfin. There are ninety-three of us altogether, soldiers and wagoneers, and I pray you to let us in, for we are cold and hungry."

The monk's broad face hardened as he glanced from Bertram to Margerite, then at the wagons and armed men behind them. For a moment Margerite was not sure that he would not close the door in their faces, but at last he nodded curtly.

"Come in in peace, and in Christ's name," he said at last. "We shall make the hospice ready. How many of your company are women?"

"Two only," Bertram answered before Margerite could speak. "The Gräfin and her maid."

The monk nodded again. "You may set your horses to grass in the outer court, for we have only a few stables. I shall open the gate and tell the Abbot that you are here."

He closed the door again, but the gates opened shortly after. As soon as the wagons had rolled to a stop, Kobolt leapt out, shaking the wetness of the grass from his paws in disgust with each step, and came over to rub up against Margerite's legs. She picked him up, holding him to her, and looked into his golden eyes.

"Behave yourself tonight, cat," she said in a soft undertone. "We cannot have you tormenting the good brothers."

"Prrow," Kobolt answered insolently, butting his head hard against her chin.

"Will I have to lock you in whatever chambers they give us?"

The cat only purred, gazing up at her as innocently as a small kitten, and Margerite was quite sure that she would have to lock him up.

It was not long before the monk who had let them in came back. "Frowe Gräfin, the Abbot wishes to speak with you and your captain. Follow me, please."

Margerite set Kobolt down, but he trailed along as she and Bertram walked through the monastery grounds behind their guide. The monastery was not large, but in the darkening twilight Margerite saw the fruit trees planted between the headstones of its cemetery, the well-tended gardens and the little walled yards where the monks would go for silent contemplation; a wide brook ran quiet through the monastery grounds, with paved paths among its banks and a small mill near the wall where it entered.

The beehives that stood in a neat row beside the cemetery were quiet, but Margerite knew that they would be humming constantly in the warmth of the day, a living example to the monks of the sweetness brought forth by their industry for God's sake. The monk led them past the chapel, the soft deep psalms wafting through the damp air from its windows, and to a larger building where the monks must dwell. Soaked as she was, Margerite was shivering now; it might be a sinful thought, but she hoped that the Abbot was not so free from the need for earthly comfort as to not have a large fire laid in his quarters.

When they came in, Kobolt slipping between Margerite's legs before she could close the door to keep him out, the Abbot was sitting behind a massive oaken table, with a good fire burning in the hearth at his back. He was an old man, but still strong and vigorous, his shoulders broad and bulky beneath the generously cut black wool of his habit and greyish-red hair curling thickly beneath the bare spot of his tonsure.

His bushy eyebrows drew together alarmingly as he looked at the two of them, sparing Margerite barely a glance before he turned the full force of his glare on Bertram.

"We have met before," he stated bluntly. "You seem to be travelling in better company than you were the last time you entered these walls."

"That is so," Bertram acknowledged, a red flush creeping up from the tangle of his beard to darken his cheekbones. "But now I am here as the guard of the Gräfin von Falkenstein, and there is no need to speak of earlier times."

The Abbot stared at him for a long moment, their silence broken only by the crackling of the sweet-scented applewood beneath the flames.

"What is this?" Margerite asked at last. "Is there something which I should know about?"

"There is not!" Bertram snapped, even as the Abbot said, "Well, God's will has brought us together again, and it is not for me to question, so long as you do no harm and accept our hospitality in the spirit of Christ. Frowe Gräfin, I am Joseph, abbot of this monastery, and I bid you welcome here for this night. Supper will be served to you in the guest-hall when we have finished the compline-prayers; should you wish to make Confession, Father Peter will be in the chapel for a little time after that." He paused for a moment, his brows drawing into an unnerving glare again, and Margerite realized that he was looking at Kobolt. "Did you bring that creature with you?"

"He is mine," Margerite admitted.

"It cannot be allowed to roam freely here. It should have been left outside the walls."

"I am sorry, Abbot. I will make sure that he does not disturb the brethren."

"See that you do," the Abbot snapped. "Shut it in your chamber, if you must have it here."

"I thank you for your hospitality in the name of Christ," Margerite replied. She reached into her heavy purse, fumbling among the coins Ruprecht had given her with the order that she must buy something to please herself in Freiburg, and bringing out two gold marks. "Please, good Abbot, accept this gift for the sustenance of the brothers and your good works."

The Abbot did not smile, but his craggy face seemed a little warmer. "Blessings upon your charity," he said, taking the money from her hand.

The room where Margerite and Gertrude were to stay, behind the guest-hall, was not large, but it was very comfortable, with a warm feather-bed and thick coverlets beneath the crucifix on the wall, and Gertrude already tending the fire. Gladly, Margerite shook off her wet cloak, letting Gertrude wring it out into the chamberpot and hang it over the gentle heat of the stove. Kobolt curled up as close to the hearth as he could, looking up from narrowed eyes as though to make it clear that he thought very little of travelling in the rain.

"You are a cat," Margerite said fondly, bending to pet him and scratching behind his ears as he purred for her. "Slothful, greedy, proud, lustful, and no doubt full of the other sins as well, though how a cat can be avaricious I do not know." Kobolt yawned in her face. "You are not coming to supper with us, for the Abbot will not have it, and even if he did not mind you, I do not trust you not to leap on the table, but I shall bring some food back to you."

The Abbot was the only one of the brethren who sat at table with them, though two others served food and drink without speaking. As Margerite might have expected, there was no meat on the table, but the chief dish was fine blue trout in a thick cheese sauce, flavoured temptingly with fennel and dill. The silent cellarer offered Margerite her choice between wine and ale; she chose the ale, and found it rich and warming. The Abbot said little, and that chiefly pleasantries, but now and again she marked that his penetrating stare was fixed on Bertram, and wondered how they had met before.

It could not have been a good meeting, of that she was sure. Was Bertram a runaway monk? Not likely, if he was as skilled a warrior as everyone claimed. And the Abbot had said something implying that he had been among bad men earlier; perhaps he was a bandit of some sort? It would fit well enough with the measure and demeanour of the man. But if so, how could he have come so well-recommended to Ruprecht's hall? The thoughts occupied Margerite's mind through the uneasy meal, until at last the Abbot rose.

"We retire early here, for we rise early and work throughout the day. Ora et labora: praise and work, as the blessed St. Benedict laid down for our Order. Frowe Gräfin, I bid you good night."

"And good night to you, Brother Abbot."

Margerite was ready enough to go to bed, but once she was snuggled down among the warm covers, she found that her tiredness was slipping away from her like butter melting through her fingers. Gertrude had no such trouble: the maidservant was already snoring away on her pallet in the corner.

What could be troubling me? Margerite wondered. I have ridden all day; I ate well, and I am warm. What more could be wrong?

If her trouble was not of the body, it must be of the soul.
Suddenly she thought again of her strange dream and
its consequences, of the conversation she had planned
to have with Father Hans before discovering the priest's
drunkenness. But the men of this monastery were proper
men of Christ, and Abbot Joseph had said that the priest
would be in the chapel for some time after supper. Perhaps
she ought to go and make Confession, to ask for his advice
and receive the penance he would give her.

And if it is a penance you cannot perform now, or ever?
an inner voice jeered at her. Suppose he tells you that you
have unknowingly performed an act of witchcraft, and that
you must walk barefoot to Rome, or even humble yourself by
wearing sackcloth for a week? How will you explain that to
the men you travel with; how can you do your duty to your
husband and his castle if the priest gives you a penance that
is more than the saying of prayers?

For a moment Margerite struggled with herself, but the
restlessness tingled troubling through her limbs, and soon
she found that she had thrown off her blankets. She could
not dress herself properly without waking Gertrude, but she
wrapped her damp cloak tightly about her shift, lighting a
candle from the coals of the stove, and made her way to the
chapel.

Once at the door, she paused a moment, then blew the
candle out. She would go in quietly and pray; if the priest
were still there, she would make confession of those
things she had done that she knew to be sins - her anger
at Bertram, her doubts of her husband's wisdom in the
organization of Burg Falkenstein, her unkind thoughts
towards the poor drunk priest, and...she was sure...the sin of
pride in her new position as Gräfin - and then she would see
if she could tell him more.

The soft light of two beeswax candles glowed through the chapel, but Margerite could see no sign of a priest. At first she thought she was alone, but as her eyes adjusted to the candlelight, she realized that a cloaked figure was kneeling on the floor, not before the altar and the crucifix behind it, but in front of the statue of Maria in her niche beside her Son. The Virgin's wooden face gazed downward in polished peace, one delicately carved hand stretched out as though to bless the man who knelt before her. Not wishing to disturb the priest at his devotions, Margerite moved forward as silently as she could to stand beside him.

To her shock, Margerite recognised Bertram's black beard bushing out from the folds of his cloak. His eyes were closed, but his face shone like the polished wood of the statue above him, wet with the glistening tracks of tears. Much troubled in her heart, Margerite backed away quietly. Relighting her candle from one of the two that burned there, she left the chapel, shielding the little flame from the rain and wind with her palm until she was back inside the guest-house, where she crept back into her bed without waking Gertrude. Still she could not sleep, for her best efforts could not shut out the thoughts that pressed against her mind like beggars crying for alms.

What wickedness has he done, that he weeps so before the Virgin? Margerite wondered. And the counter-thought, sure as the response of an antiphonal hymn: What wicked man could weep so before the Virgin?

One who has done wrong, and now regrets it, she answered herself. She had hung her garnet rosary over the post of her bed; now she reached for it, running the smooth cold beads through her fingers. Had Bertram committed some crime against this monastery before he came to Burg Falkenstein? Would Ruprecht have taken the man into his service, if he had known about it? Her husband might not be pious, but surely he would not have set a criminal in such a trusted position. And yet, if Bertram's soul were not deeply burdened with guilt, she would not have seen him as she had that night.

And before, she would have sworn on her hope of Heaven that nothing could move the hard-bitten warrior, or touch his coarse heart...I will watch him carefully, Margerite told herself. She shifted under the covers, arranging her limbs more comfortably. Holding onto her rosary, she began to recite an Ave, the familiar words driving the doubts from her mind.

Ave Maria, gratia plena...

A soft hissing sound, followed by an unmistakable pungent scent, broke her concentration. Shocked, she stopped praying, then found that she was laughing.

"Oh, Kobolt!" Margerite said. "The Abbot should not have ordered you locked in here. Gertrude, wake up! Kobolt has made his mark, and you must clean the floor quickly, before the stink sinks into the stone."

Despite Gertrude's best efforts, the musty-sharp smell of Kobolt's spray still hung heavily in the guest chambers when they left at dawn the next morning. Feeling guilty, Margerite dropped another mark and a half into the chapel's offering-box, and only barely managed to look the Abbot in the eye as he bade them farewell and Godspeed.

The weather had cleared a little; though the clouds still moved heavily above, shadowing the black peaks in gray mist, the rain had stopped, and the travellers made good time on the road. By evening, the sky around the lowering sun glowed red, and the walls of Freiburg rose ahead of them. Waving aside her bodyguard, Margerite nudged her horse forward, riding up to join Bertram at the front of the train.

"Do you know where we are going?" she asked. "Is there a place ready for us?"

"I have already sent a man ahead to tell Berthold and Elsbeth that we are on our way. If you can remember," Bertram added scathingly, "they are Ruprecht's associates, with whom the Graf told you we would be staying."

Margerite clenched her teeth tightly, but said nothing, riding alongside him in stiff silence until they had passed through the city gates. Within, she tried not to gawk as though she were…the daughter of a poor knight from the country…but it was difficult. She had never seen houses packed so closely together, many of them with second stories or balconies that jutted out over the street as if their crushing had pushed their upper levels out like teeth growing too close together in a narrow jaw. The streets were thronged with people of all different sorts, as well.

Burghers drew the hems of their rich robes aside from grubby children; women in neat poor clothes carried open baskets full of greens and bread, or closed baskets that bumped against their legs and squawked. Margerite saw a young man in a bright scarlet tunic so short it barely covered his buttocks and a gold-brocaded cape of deep green brushing past a mud-covered beggar woman who turned dribbling eyes after him, extending a three-fingered hand plaintively, while elsewhere a priest turned his head to the side to avoid looking at a blowsy middle-aged woman who stood with her painted breasts halfway out of her bodice.

That must be a whore! Margerite thought. Sermons spoke of them often enough, and back at Hirschenberg everyone knew that Alfrida would go with any man who would give her two chickens or a silver pfennig, but it was very different to see one openly plying her trade on the city streets. On one corner stood a barefoot friar in the brown habit of a Franciscan: his hair straggled long and gray about his tonsure, tangling wildly in his unkempt beard as he waved his hands and shouted, "The last days are upon us! The saints are angry, the wrath of God is coming! You!"

To Margerite's shock, she realized he was pointing to her. "Fine lady, give up your pride, give up your witchcraft, give up your jewels, and go among the poor! The wind of St. Maury is coming; the same great storm that destroyed all of Dublin on St. Maury's Day shall cast down this city, yea, and the proud among it. Humble yourself before the wrath of God! Seek no longer after strange men, nor the whoredoms of the world!"

Margerite stared at him, confounded and frightened, but his pointing finger had already darted away to choose another target among the passers-by, a tall man in dark robes, marked out by his red and yellow hat - the sign of a Jew, required by law to distinguish himself from Christians. "Jew!" the friar shouted. "Give up your wicked ways; convert and know the true faith!" Margerite would have nudged her horse up a little faster, but there were too many people on the street for her to move at more than a slow amble.

The street opened out into a wide square covered with booths and tents, its air raucous with shouting. Many of the merchants had already packed their goods and left, but a few still remained, steadfastly crying their wares. What drew Margerite's eye, however, was the high spire of the cathedral at the end of the square.

Built out of pinkish-red sandstone, the tower rose above the elaborate carving of its arched door to a ravishing tracery of lacelike stone openwork reaching high into the air as if to draw the eyes that beheld it soaring up to Heaven. As she gazed, openmouthed, the deep bells began, singing their evening call out over the city. Although Mathilde was still moving beneath her, Margerite noticed nothing until Bertram's rough voice sounded in her ears.

"Gräfin, you may dismount now."

Caught back to herself with a start, Margerite looked down to see a boy standing beside the head of her horse, his hand lifted towards her. She glanced at Bertram, who was already on the ground, tapping his fingers impatiently against the sheath of his sword.

"Go on, give him the reins," the captain of the guard growled. "I recognise him; he is one of Berthold's servants. Though it is not," he added grudgingly, "a bad thing to be careful in the city, where there are many thieves."

Margerite dismounted, taking care where she stepped to avoid the muck and trash on the street. She waited beside the horse as Bertram directed his men in taking out the iron money-chest and the chests of her personal possessions.

Bertram went before her to the arched door of one of the larger houses, a stone building with a number of deep windows overlooking the square. It was plastered white, gleaming with cleanness above the lowest stones where the feet of passersby had kicked up spatters of mud and dung. Above the door was a coat of arms: a purse, a sword, and a cross, in gold on a red field. Bertram's knock on the door was answered by a thin, nervous, dark-haired girl.

"Tell Herr Berthold that his guests have arrived," Bertram said brusquely.

The girl curtsied. "Herr Berthold says that you shall enter and be welcome. He and the Frowe Elsbeth are awaiting you in their hall."

Hall was, Margerite thought, something of a grand word for the room in which their hosts were waiting: it was only half the size of the hall at Hirschenburg, able to seat perhaps ten or twelve folk at table, and the stone front was clearly only a decorative facade, for all the walls within were of painted wood. Still, as dear as space clearly was in the city, it was no surprise that everything should be smaller. The room was brightly lit, candles glowing about the walls and the fireplace burning high.

Berthold and his wife rose to their feet as Margerite entered. Although Berthold was a merchant, with no trace of noble blood, he and his wife were dressed as though they might be Ruprecht's equals. Berthold, a large man whose head was covered with a generous crop of gray curls, wore a houppeland of dark blue and gold brocade that reached well below his knees, with the side-seams cut to his mid-thigh, trimmed with white ermine; its generous folds emphasized his thick shoulders, billowing over the considerable bulge of his large belly.

Beneath, he wore bright yellow hose with pointed shoes; his wide belt was inlaid with plates of worked silver, the hilt and sheath of his long dagger were elaborately gilded and chased, and his thick fingers were ringed with heavy gold and silver. Elspeth's dress was of bright red velvet, cut a little too tightly for her matronly figure, so that the flesh bulged slightly at her shoulders where the seam pressed against her; the colour was not well-chosen, Margerite thought, for it gave her fair hair an unpleasant orangish cast, as though it had been dyed with saffron, and brightened the natural ruddiness of her plump cheeks until she looked like a cook who had been standing over the fire all day. She wore a good deal of gold jewelry worked in the fragile ItalIan style - too finely made, for the delicate pieces only drew attention to the fleshy hands and throat they adorned.

"Welcome, welcome," Berthold said heartily, blue eyes twinkling with enthusiasm. "Frowe Gräfin, we are honoured to have you guesting with us, and hope you will enjoy your stay in Freiburg. Bertram, so good to see you again!" He stepped forward, lifting Margerite's hand to his lips and kissing it, then turning to clasp Bertram's hand between his own. Margerite frowned slightly, absently wiping the back of her hand against her skirt.

"We are so glad to have you here, Frowe Gräfin," Elsbeth echoed with no less enthusiasm. She cocked her head, looking around sharply. "Where is that girl? Gretel! Hot wine! Come, Frowe Gräfin, be seated, and we shall have refreshments for you shortly."

Margerite let herself be led to a chair, settling gracefully down. Elsbethsat beside her, saying, "Come, Berthold, let us not neglect our noble guest."

Berthold bowed slightly to Margerite. "My apologies, frowe, but there are some matters I must see to with the good captain first."

Margerite realized that they would have to store the moneybox in safekeeping, and see to the quartering of the men who had come with them, and that might well take time. Though Margerite was hungry and wanted to wash, it would have been ill-mannered of her to say so, and the warmth of the little hall was welcome enough.

"Of course," she replied. "I am sure I shall see you at supper, and the conversation of your good wife will be refreshing to me after my journey."

The men withdrew. "I would offer to show you to your chamber now, but we had little time to make it ready," Elsbeth said. "But do not worry, everything will be in order shortly. Gretel!" she shouted again. "You lazy creature, where are you?"

The servant girl appeared, the bronze tray in her hands shaking so that the hot wine slopped over the edge in the pitcher. "Forgive me, frowe," she quavered. "I had to show the Frowe Gräfin's maid to the chamber. She is getting it ready now."

Elsbeth glared at her maid, then turned to Margerite. "Gretel has not been with us long," she apologized. "You must not think that we are always in such a state. Well, Gretel, pour the wine and be about your work."

Margerite sipped slowly at the goblet that was put before her. The wine was not as good as she would have expected from the display Berthold and Elsbeth made of their clothes, with only a trace of honey and a faint dusting of spices to sweeten its sharp taste, but it was hot and welcome after the day's long ride - the more so since, despite the large fire and the sheen of sweat on Elspeth's ruddy face, there seemed to be a chill about the room that she could not explain.

"Have you come often to the city, Frowe Gräfin?" Elsbeth enquired. Margerite was about to say that she had never been into a big city, but something about the woman's manner warned her not to.

"My father's home is some way from Freiburg, nearer to the Rhine," she answered.

Elsbeth nodded. "Ah, you must be more used to Köln or Worms. I have a very good friend, a second cousin of the Archbishop of Köln, and she tells me..."

Margerite let her ramble on as she sipped her wine and tried to relax. Perhaps it was only that the merchant's house, though large for the city, was smaller than anything she was used to, making her feel cramped and nervous. She nodded and smiled, making the appropriate murmurs at the right places in Elspeth's discourse, but otherwise paid little attention until the merchant's wife said, "And I hope you have brought something pretty and fashionable, for Berthold and I have arranged a special dinner for the day after tomorrow. I know you will not have worn your best for travelling, but..."

Margerite had brought the best of Ruprecht's mother's clothes, for she knew that she would have to be able to show the full authority of her position in her dealings with the city suppliers. But Ruprecht had also mentioned something about them being in the fashion of twenty years ago, and that would not stand her in good stead.

Perhaps - she glanced at Elspeth's tight bodice and the rolls of flesh bulging from her sides and belly beneath it - it would be easy and not too expensive for a dressmaker to cut and trim the old gowns, whose beautiful fabric it would be a shame to waste on second-best garments, into a more fashionable shape. And that, too, could be done quickly, without delaying her work here too much.

"I had hoped to see a dressmaker while I was here. Perhaps you can recommend one to me, so that I may make my visit tomorrow morning."

"Of course. There is a very fine woman just across the marketplace, who makes all my clothes. She is a Florentine, who gets a great deal of her materials from Italy, and always knows just what the latest fashions are in the big cities there - I think the Italians have the finest sense of fashion, don't you? There used to be a little Jewish tailor here, who did the most amazing things with sleeves and dagging, but, well..." she shrugged, her golden bracelets jingling... "he was killed when the Death came to Freiburg the first time, so I have made done with Petra ever since."

In due course Gertrude came in to announce that Margerite's room was ready, and there was water warming on the stove, if her frowe would like to wash off the dust of her journey. Grateful for the chance to escape Elspeth's chatter, Margerite pleaded her tiredness. As she rose, Kobolt appeared out of the shadows, following her to the door.

"What is that?" Elsbeth shrieked. "Gretel, did you let an animal in here?"

"It is only my cat," Margerite said. "He follows me everywhere."

"But, Frowe Gräfin, he will soil the rugs and tear up the furniture, and everything we own is of the very best. Can you not put him out?"

Margerite picked up Kobolt, but paused a moment with his warm heavy weight in her arms. She did not know what might become of the cat, roaming free in the city without her: the streets were full of wagons and horses, and his glossy pelt would be tempting to a furrier. But she could not keep him locked in, and, after what had happened at the monastery, she could not deny that Elspeth's fears were well-founded.

"Out, Kobolt," Margerite said kindly. "Do not roam too far, and take good care of yourself. Perhaps we could put a bowl of cream by the door for him, so that he knows to come back here?"

"Oh…we could not do that! The bowl would be stolen as soon as the door closed: these city people are always stealing things."

Margerite hesitated, but at last, though she was little willing to do it, she handed the cat to Gertrude. Kobolt squirmed in the maid's arms as though he understood what was happening, but he did not scratch or bite as Gertrude carried him outside.

As Margerite climbed the narrow staircase behind her maid, the chill in her bones seemed to grow greater, and each breath felt as though she were drawing in a cloud of dust. She could not understand why, for the stairs and walls were very clean, with no dust to be seen on them. But the feeling grew stronger until, by the time she was in her chamber, she was shivering inside her cloak.

"Open the window, Gertrude," she commanded. "The air in here is stuffy, and I can hardly breathe."

"It seems clear enough to me, Frowe," Gertrude answered, but she threw open the shutters nevertheless. Although the evening air that flowed in was damp and cool, it seemed to brace Margerite against whatever was oppressing her so.

As she turned away to let Gertrude undress her so that she could wash and put on one of her more suitable dresses, Margerite heard a heavy thump at the windowsill. Looking around, she saw that Kobolt was sitting on the floor by the window, washing one paw.

"You demon-spawn," she said fondly to him. "You should not have done that. If Elsbeth or any of her servants come in, I shall have to throw you back out the window, you know."

The cat answered her with a brief purring chirp, then began to stalk about the room, sniffing the air. At one inner corner, he stopped, crouching down with his tail twitching. He must smell a mouse, Margerite thought. I would not be surprised if there were mice in this house, with its wooden walls; they are bad enough in stone-built castles. But Kobolt got up quickly enough, completing his circuit of the room.

That done, he sat down for a moment, lifting his leg and washing his substantial testicles. Margerite turned her eyes away from the indecent sight, trying not to giggle, and let Gertrude finish undressing her, dipping cloths into the pot of warm water on the stove to sponge the dirt of travel from her body. The maid was halfway down her back when she stopped with a brief cry of alarm.

"Frowe, he is doing it again!"

Margerite leapt up to catch the cat, but his spray had already hissed onto the corner, and looking around the room, she saw that he had marked the other three corners similarly. She reached for him, but he evaded her with a little leap, scampering frantically around the room once more, then jumping up to sprinkle a few more drops of urine onto the windowsill. "Well, clean it up," she ordered. "Tomorrow you must buy some whitewash, and if we are lucky, we will be able to make it right before anyone sees it."

In any other house, she might not have said that, but she had no mind to admit to Elsbeth that Kobolt had not been in for five minutes before making his mark. And, as she looked about the room, she also had to mark that if its furnishings were what Elsbeth called the best, her taste in furniture was no better than her taste in clothes: the rugs were garish and cheap-looking, and the varnish was worn down in spots on the table, chairs, and bedframe.

Still, the sudden diversion had cleared Margerite's mind, lifting the chill from her bones so that she was able to relax under the gentle touch of the damp cloths, and even - unfashionable as the dress might be - take pleasure in the rich soft feeling of folds of velvet falling about her body as she put on the deep red dress with its white trim. Kobolt leapt onto her lap, and she stroked him, feeling unfathomably grateful to him.

Supper with Berthold and Elsbeth was as tedious as she might have expected. Berthold had nothing to talk about but himself, his family...which he intimated, without quite saying, was a noble one which had come down in the world, but which he was raising to its former glory... and his adventures on the road to Jerusalem - not quite in a declared Crusade, Margerite knew, for there had been no great march on the Holy Land within their lifetimes, but Berthold kept intimating that he had gone to defend the kingdom of Jerusalem.

The coat of arms above the door, Margerite gathered, was not inherited, but his own design: the sword of a warrior, the purse of a financier, and the cross of a Crusader. As always, Bertram sat silently glaring, but Berthold's monologues, interspersed with Elspeth's chatter, hardly left him a chance to speak in any case. After supper, Elsbeth took Margerite by the arm, showing her the entirety of the house. Small though it was in comparison to a castle, even Margerite could tell that it was a fine building for the city, and Elsbeth deserved her pride in it.

The only rooms that she was not shown were Berthold's own bedroom, and the locked room beside Margerite's bedchamber where, Elsbeth said, Berthold kept his finest goods stored for safekeeping. The merchant's wife even led her to a tiny chamber beside her own bedroom, where three candles burned under jewel-toned images painted on a glimmering gilt background: Mary with her Son resting upon her breast, Christ on the Cross, and a saint whom Margerite could not recognise, for the lettering above his head was in Greek.

"This is my little chapel," Elsbeth simpered. "I am Greek by birth - you did not know that? I lost my accent long ago. When I married Berthold and came to live here, he told me that I could continue in whatever faith I pleased, so long as I did it quietly. So I have the Virgin and her Son and St. Spiridion always with me, and whenever I am troubled I come here to pray, for it is the most peaceful spot in the house."

Margerite agreed: the warmth and light of the candles, and the faint sweet whiff of incense in the air, had quite driven out the cold and dankness that lay everywhere else in Berthold's dwelling, creating a little sphere of comfort in the middle of it. Elsbeth turned to leave, but Margerite found herself oddly reluctant to set foot across the threshold, and only managed to make herself step out into the chilly corridor by a stern effort of will.

When Margerite went to bed, she lay drowsy in the darkness for a while. Kobolt purred on the pillow by her head; from the street below, she could hear shouts and drunken singing - not quite loud enough to rouse her to close the window, but loud enough to keep her from dropping straight off to sleep. As she lay there, peacefully listening to the night sounds, she became aware that a conversation was going on in the room next door: Berthold's loud, self-assured voice penetrated the wall easily, answered now and again by Bertram's deep growl. She could not make out all their words, especially Bertram's, but she strained to get some sense out of them.

"...what he sent," Berthold was saying. "How should I question his will?"

"...don't believe..." Bertram answered. "...stated precisely...know the price..."

"And what about my commission?" Berthold's voice was louder now, carrying more clearly through the wall. "I am responsible for our business here in Freiburg…cannot be done cheaply. I always take a commission on handling Order monies."

"…know nothing about that," said Bertram. "Graf Ruprecht…what was promised. Should we…Günther?"

What was promised to Ruprecht? Margerite wondered. By Graf Günther? She pressed her ear hard against the wall, the plaster cool and damp against her cheek.

"That was the amount he sent. But he knows that I always take a commission!"

"Perhaps he forgot," said Bertram, more distinctly. "In any case, you must take it up with him. I am here to carry out my orders, and I will do that, and you will not thwart me, or you will find yourself explaining yourself to Graf Günther."

"But I have been put to some expense!" Berthold exclaimed. "Keeping the Frowe Gräfin and her maid in proper style for these days will not be cheap, and then there is the dinner we have planned for the Gräfin and a certain distinguished gentleman who wishes to meet her: that alone will be barely covered by my commission, and we have already sent out the invitation, so we must carry through. If you do not trust me, I know a man who can be trusted to hold the money until we have gotten word from Graf Günther about its disposal."

What a greasy merchant, Margerite thought, repulsed and amused at once: clearly Berthold's pretensions to some measure of nobility did not last past his purse-strings. But her question was not yet answered, and she kept her ear firmly to the wall.

"Nevertheless," Bertram stated, "you will give me the full amount this night, for I must be about my business tomorrow. This will not wait, for the Order has a strong interest in the matter: Karl must be delayed in his plans, for which war between his vassals is necessary, that he may be forced to turn his eyes from Avignon to his own Empire. And Graf Heinrich has long stood in the Order's way, for he will not treat with the Free Companies - and who knows better than I how much wealth they bring into the Order's coffers, when bandits who want to become great men must find a way to make the profits of plunder respectable? Indeed, he has blocked the Companies' passage through his lands, and sworn to hunt down and hang any of their men whom he may find; and he is strong enough to hold against any gathering of mercenaries with too few men to find a more tempting target elsewhere. You have no choice, Berthold: further the Order's aims as best you may, as you must have sworn to do, or be branded traitor by its brotherhood. I do not know what they would do to you - but I know what we did in the Black Sword Company to those who tried to sell us out."

"Satan's black arse!" Berthold cursed. Margerite could not tell what was happening for a little while then, but at last Berthold said, "Here you are, and much good it may do you."

"You forget yourself," Bertram answered coldly. "Shall I inform the Graf of what you have had to say?"

"You may inform the Graf of whatever you please, for he knows my worth and trusts my word. And save your pennies, for I expect that he will order my commission to come out of your own pocket when he hears how you have treated me - as if you had forgotten my powers to make you regret your actions."

"That is up to the Graf. Good night, Herr Berthold."

Margerite heard a door close, then, unmistakably, the sound of something shattering against the wall. She could not find it in her heart to be sorry for the merchant's discomfiture, for whatever was going on - and she meant to get to the bottom of it, if she had to ask Bertram herself - it sounded as though he had tried to cheat Ruprecht in some way, and gotten the reply he deserved from Bertram. A little warmth of triumph kindled in her on their behalf, but she was still too uneasy to sleep.

The Order, she thought. An alliance in which Ruprecht and Graf Günther - but not Bertram! - were bound, with its own oaths of brotherhood and loyalty...That was not so strange: the hills and woods were filled with knightly Orders, bound together for both war and trade, for in these troubled times, no man could be sure of standing safely alone, not even Kaiser Karl.

It was stranger, that a merchant like Berthold should be allowed into their ranks, when he was no Ritter nor even a nobleman, but clearly the Order had a great many financial dealings with outsiders that called for the skills of a city merchant, and, as she had heard Gertrude say about other servants, when there was no horse to draw a cart, sometimes a flatulent donkey would do. That, too, would explain how Ruprecht had managed to keep Burg Falkenstein stocked and running with such careless accounting: a second income from the Order's business dealings must have covered Burg Falkenstein's own shortfalls.

They would do well indeed, when Margerite was able to get those monies properly recorded and used.But the rest of the conversation, about Kaiser Karl - for that must have been whom they meant by Karl - and Graf Heinrich, and the Free Companies? Even Margerite, a poor Ritter's daughter, had heard of the Companies and the evil they did; she knew that they were excommunicate, sellswords damned as a threat to Christendom.

It was little surprise to her that Bertram had been among their ranks, and it must, she thought, have been dealings with the Companies through his knightly brotherhood that brought Ruprecht to hire the man into his household. *My poor Ruprecht,* Margerite thought. *I think you have been misled - I must watch carefully, to see that this brings you to no ill, for if your brotherhood is so deeply stained with these dealings, it may be a danger to all of us in time.*

At least she would be able to see the mercenaries Bertram was thinking of hiring, and might perhaps be able to have some influence on whether he chose better or worse men. Still, it took her a long time to get to sleep, her mind twisting and turning against its unresolved thoughts like a sleeper trying to rest naked in prickling blankets of heavy wool.

Margerite dreamed, and knew she was dreaming: she could feel the blankets wrapping her limbs as she struggled, but could not open her eyes. Still, the veil of her eyelids was clearing into the darkness, so that she could look into the room. Five golden candles burned there, one at each corner of the chamber and one on the windowsill, their steady light shimmering through the darkness, and a triple line gleamed around the edge of the floor. Kobolt was sitting upon the stove, staring intently at the wall by her bed where she had been listening to the two men.

Suddenly, Margerite realized that something was prowling about outside, and that she was dreadfully afraid of it. Frozen, afraid to move or breathe, she heard it fumbling below the window. *And the window is open,* she realized in horror. But the scratching moved on, around the wall... now, dear God, the thing was scrabbling by the head of her bed, and she could not cry out, only wait as its soft noise moved farther on, to the corner where Kobolt had crouched so intently. The sound of claws was louder there; she could nearly hear the wooden wall splintering beneath them. *If it finds a way in...*

Mother Maria, protect me! She wanted to murmur a prayer, but she was too terrified to open her mouth or reach for her rosary beads. Please God, please Christ, please Maria, holy saints, help me! Margerite squeezed her eyes tightly shut...and opened them on darkness, with the only sound in her ears Gertrude's sleeping breaths. Her limbs were still locked, the fear-sweat beading cold on her brow; and she lay like that for some time, waiting to see if the evil would come back.

What did I dream? Margerite asked herself as her heart slowed and her breath eased. She thought of the tales of the Death she had heard: how it showed itself as an old woman, asking a ferryman for a ride across the river; a knight on a pale horse, passing through a town in darkness; a pair of beggar children, their hands outstretched for alms...Could the Death be walking in Freiburg again? Did I hear it outside my window? Whatever it was had scratched with claws, passed silently through the walls of the house - but not the walls of her room, praise be to Christ and His Mother.

She had heard, too, of how demons would come to the chambers of sinners in their sleep, to terrify them with all the horrors of Hell or ravish them with the temptations of evil. Now, fearful that a cold claw would seize upon her between the moment of thought and that of action, Margerite snatched for her rosary, clasping it so tightly that the edges of the crucifix were a bright pain in her hand. "Ave Maria," she whispered, "gratia plena..."

Margerite was almost to the end of the prayer when the weight landed on her, almost knocking her breath out in a short scream. She writhed in hysterical terror, flinging her limbs about, and the thing leaped off her with a brief indignant meow.

"Kobolt," she sighed, shaking in unutterable relief as she sat up. The moonlight was coming bright through the window; the cat sat in a pool of pale light, looking up at her.

"Frowe?" Gertrude's muffled voice asked from her pallet. "Frowe, are you all right?"

"It was only a dream. Go back to sleep." But it was a long time before Margerite slept, and when she did, it was with the beads of her rosary wrapped around her wrist, its crucifix dangling between her fingers.

Margerite had hoped to break her fast quietly and get early to the dressmaker's, but Berthold was standing in the corridor when she came out of her room.

"Frowe Gräfin," he said, "there is a small matter that needs your attention, which I am sure you will wish to deal with as swiftly as possible, before it is too late." He spoke politely, but there was something Margerite disliked about the way he stood within an armslength of her, looming over her as if to suggest that she was trapped between his bulky body and the wall.

The stove had taken yesterday's cold off her room, but she had noticed it as soon as she had stepped outside her door, and wished for nothing more than to be out in the fresh air, away from the stale chill of this house.

Margerite straightened her back, lifting her chin slightly so that she could look Berthold in the eye. "Yes?"

"The captain of your guard has misunderstood his orders. The money I received from Graf Günther for your husband included a commission for me, as has always been customary in my dealings with the Order, but Bertram has refused to acknowledge this, and has taken the whole sum. Now I beg you, Frowe Gräfin, to restore to me what is right for my troubles."

Margerite looked at him, her heart beating hard. Clearly he thought that she not only knew all about whatever he and Bertram had been discussing last night, but also had the authority to overrule Bertram - and I do, for I am the Gräfin and he, when all is said and done, a hired man! But, unpleasant as Bertram could be to her, it would be petty and stupid for her to interfere out of spite - worse, it would badly serve Ruprecht's interests. And even if the Order is making shadowy deals with the Free Companies, they are on our side, and we may have to trust in them for aid through this war.

Now Margerite was truly glad that she had not been able to keep herself from eavesdropping, so that she had at least some idea of how matters stood.

"If the sum that was sent was the same as the sum that was promised to us, then any cause for complaint you have can only be with the sender. Now, if you will excuse me, your gracious frowe has made an appointment for me with her dressmaker this morning which I should not like to miss." She stared at Berthold until he moved his looming bulk out of her way so that she could pass down the narrow corridor.

The Italian dressmaker fussed and clicked her tongue over the dresses Gertrude carried in for her mistress, thin fingers patting nervously at the wisps of gray hair escaping from her tight bun. "So, so," she said. "Bella, you want me to take in your mother's gowns so that you can appear in the height of fashion? Silly girl, if these bodices are fitted tightly to your maiden's body, you will never get into them again when you have borne a child, and fabric so old will not bear too much reworking.

Keep these as they are for when you have grown heavier and wish to wear something that does not press tightly against your belly, is my advice, and let me make you something new, something that, when you come to court, will have everyone saying, 'Ah, she must have freshly come from Florence!' But I will sew it with broad seams, so that when you have put on weight from childbirth, it can easily be let out by skilled hands, and no one will be the wiser. I have some lovely brocade that will suit your fair beauty; give me a moment and I will fetch it out to show you."

Margerite was tempted, but shook her head, reminding herself sternly that whatever Graf Günther had sent for their succor, before a war was no time to spend too much money on clothes. "I only want these taken in as you can, so that they do not scream to everyone that they are a mother's old dresses. And Elsbeth tells me that she has a dinner with an important guest planned for me tomorrow, so that I must be able to appear well by then."

"Elsbeth!" Petra pressed her thin lips together, snorting elegantly through her narrow beak of a nose. "Elsbeth may also tell me when she will pay me for her last two dresses. She was a good customer when they had more money, but Berthold has nearly lost it all on his business ventures, and yet they still try to live as though they could afford their house on the square. I hope there will be no such trouble with you, Gräfin." The dressmaker's black eyes squinted sternly at Margerite.

"Most certainly not. Gertrude will bring your payment when she comes to collect the work."

"Bellissima! Now, Gräfin, step back here and I shall begin measuring you. A shame to take knife and needle to such beautiful work," she added, glancing at the dresses that Gertrude had spread out over her worktable, "but Christ and all the saints cannot shift the power of fashion."

It was nearly midday by the time the fittings were over. Margerite was glad that she had not ordered new dresses, for the price Petra charged for simply taking in the old ones was more than she could ever have imagined paying for clothes, though mindful of her new dignity, she was careful to keep her shock hidden. She wondered if she should go back to Berthold's house for the midday meal, but she was not eager to face the merchant again - or even, she had to admit, to set foot within the house, with its chill and musty air.

"Come, Gertrude," she said as they left the dressmaker's. "Shall we look for a place to take our meal?"

Gertrude looked around, wide-eyed, at the buildings and throngs of people. "Where shall we go? Frowe, do you mean that we should eat in an inn like..."

"And why not? We cannot be forcing ourselves on our hosts every moment, and I have much to do this afternoon."

They walked past the high sandstone walls and sky-piercing spire of the Münster, following the street southward. They were nearly at one of the gate-towers when Margerite saw the sign of a red bear hanging above the door of an inn. The sweet scent of roasting pork wafted from within, and her mouth began to water.

"We shall eat there," she said firmly.

The Red Bear was quiet and cool within, only a few people sitting at the polished oaken tables beneath the high-beamed roof. Margerite was about to settle herself at one of the places by the wall when she saw, in a shadowy spot well away from the other customers, the unmistakable broad shoulders and tangled black hair of Bertram, sitting with two other men. One of the guard-captain's companions was a short, heavyset man whose reddish-blond hair grew sparse and crisp over his blunt skull, dressed in a mixture of heavy boiled leather and iron plates.

The other was taller, wearing a plain dark tunic and cloak that had clearly seen better days and armed with a battered falchion in a scabbard of cracked and stained leather. His looks marked him as foreign, perhaps Italian or Spanish: heavy featured, black-haired and dark-eyed, with a heavy, close-cropped black beard and the swarthy skin of someone born to southern lands. The remains of a large meal lay on the table before them; the red-haired man was cheerfully gnawing the remnants of meat from a pork rib, and Bertram was slicing the last flesh from a larger bone.

Margerite walked over to them, waiting silently until they realized she was there.

"Frowe Gräfin!" Bertram said. "What are you doing here? Why are you not with Berthold and Elsbeth?"

"That is hardly your business."

"It is my business if you are wandering around the city alone. Two of my men are waiting for you at the merchant's house, ready to accompany and guard you on your afternoon's business, and they can hardly do that if you are not there."

"You may accompany me back when I have eaten, which I shall do after you have introduced me to your companions."

Bertram sighed. "These are mercenaries from the company I have just hired. Frowe Gräfin, this is not really…"

"If they will be fighting for us, I am glad to meet them," Margerite replied sharply. She had been told almost from birth that, if her father or husband was killed in battle, she might very well find herself commanding a castle during a siege, so it was her duty to learn all she could of the mercenaries that would be serving them. More: if these men were as bad as the Free Companies were said to be - but Margerite realized sharply that Bertram had already hired them, and there was nothing to be done. "Gentlemen," she said. Though she was trying to make the best of it, she knew that her voice was cold with anger.

The short man rose, bowing clumsily over her hand. "Frowe Gräfin," he said in a strong Bavarian accent, "I am Paul the Bear, commander of the Bear's Paw Company, and Bertram could not have hired you better. But he knows that. This - " he gestured at the dark man, "is Jochanan, our gunnery officer. We have two cannon and eight handguns, and you won't get better than that in a free company, by God's Blood!"

Margerite raised an eyebrow, not at the oath, but at Paul's declaration. Handguns were not common; she had heard her father speaking of them with other men in tones of mixed admiration and scorn, for devastating as they might be, they were nearly as dangerous to the user as to the enemy.

The dark man also got up. His bow was smoother; his lips did not quite touch the back of her hand. "Most gracious Frowe Gräfin," Jochanan began. Despite his swarthy complexion and ill-kept clothes, his accent was that of a well-educated German from the middle Rheinland. "We of the Bear's Paw Company are pleased and honoured to fight for you, and until our commission is over or we die keeping it, we shall serve you as if we were loyal."

Margerite blinked, wondering if he really could speak German as well as he seemed to; after a moment, Paul burst out in a great laugh. Bertram's face was stern, but she thought she could see his mouth twitching beneath the tangle of his beard - in laughter? Surely not.

Jochanan ducked his head, a look of shame and embarassment coming over his heavy features. "Forgive me, Frowe Gräfin. What I meant was...that is...ah, I am cursed to always say the wrong thing. We shall serve you loyally, in whatever you may require."

"I am glad to hear it," Margerite answered. Her anger at Bertram for hiring the Bear's Paw before she had a chance to say yes or no had already faded. These men were not what she might have expected from the leaders of a mercenary company, and far from what she had feared. She felt more at her ease with Paul and Jochanan than she did with Bertram: the Bear was very much like one of her father's soldiers, and, though she knew the free companies were a Godless scourge upon the land, she could not imagine Jochanan doing her any harm. "Gertrude, see to ordering our dinner. I shall have wine, or beer if the wine is not fit to drink."

"The beer here is very good, Frowe Gräfin," Paul volunteered, draining his stein and holding it up again with a glance towards the woman behind the bar, who hurried to refill it. Margerite nodded, turning her attention to Bertram again.

"You have done well to find a company so quickly," she said, grudging the words, but knowing that they ought to be said.

Bertram shrugged. "I have worked with the Bear's Paw before. They often come through Freiburg, and I knew that if they were in the city, I should find Paul here."

"He's done more than work with us, Frowe Gräfin. Two years ago..."

"I am sure the Gräfin would find that story tiresome," Bertram said, his voice dark and quelling. "She is undoubtedly more interested in your supplies and needs, for Graf Ruprecht has given much of those matters over into her care."

"I can write out a list, if you like, Frowe Gräfin," Jochanan offered, fumbling about in his belt-pouch for a ragged, smudged piece of parchment, an ink-stick, and a pen. Margerite waited patiently as he began to scratch and mumble under his breath.

Suddenly, between one breath and the next, Kobolt was on Paul's shoulder, digging his claws into the mercenary's leather armour. The Bear cried out in surprise, waving his arms, but the cat clung on, sniffing curiously at his face, then licking at the spatters of beer-froth on his short red moustache and beard. When Paul had recovered, he gingerly stroked Kobolt, as though afraid to pull the cat off him.

"Kobolt!" Margerite said. "That is rude of you." She got up to remove the cat from Paul's shoulder, but Kobolt escaped her grasp with an agile twist of his hindquarters, thumping heavily onto the table, where he at once began to scoop froth out of the Bear's stein and lick it off his paw. She was about to apologise, but the two mercenaries were laughing too hard to let her.

"A cat who likes beer!" Paul said. "Frowe Gräfin, if ever you tire of keeping him, he will find a good home in the Bear's Paw Company."

Margerite smiled and shook her head, but Bertram was scowling darkly at her.

"Must that creature follow you everywhere?"

"He comes and goes as he will." Deliberately Margerite drank a good swallow of the cool, tangy white wine in her goblet, holding Bertram's gaze the whole time, daring him to speak again. His nostrils tightened, but he did not press the matter.

Although Jochanan's handwriting was as disreputable as his clothing, his list was clear and exhaustive, detailing precisely what the Bear's Paw Company had and what they would need for each month of active service. They came with their own wagons and were fully equipped as to weapons and war-gear, but they would have to be fed and given... Margerite mentally checked the numbers against her own list...nearly twice the beer and wine of Ruprecht's other soldiers. At the bottom of the list, Jochanan had also added a large quantity of sulphur and saltpetre, with estimated prices for both.

"What are these for?" Margerite enquired. "Do you need to be fumigated against lice and fleas? Surely a tenth of that much sulphur would suffice."

Jochanan shook his head vigorously. "No, Frowe Gräfin. That is for the gunpowder."

"And where in the city shall I go to find it?"

"I know a man, if you will give me the money."

Margerite drew back. The gunnery-officer might seem harmless, even likeable, but she knew better than to give over money to a strange mercenary so quickly - even if Kobolt had heartily approved his commander. But Bertram's lips curved into a small grim smile beneath his beard.

"Have no fear, Gräfin. Whatever else may be said about Jochanan, he is trustworthy."

"As if he were loyal," the Bear added, snorting laughter through the froth of his beer. Gertrude, standing by Margerite's shoulder, giggled, and Margerite could not help smiling with him, while unaccustomed creases even crinkled at the corner of Bertram's eyes.

"I shall see that he has what he requires," Bertram went on. "You need only worry about the supplies of food and materials for which you have come."

When Margerite had finished dining, she, Bertram, and Gertrude parted company with the two mercenary officers. As soon as they were out of the Red Bear, Margerite turned to Bertram, speaking softly so that they should not be overheard. "The budget I have did not plan for feeding an hundred and twenty mercenaries. Graf Günther sent money for their hire; did he send enough for their keep?"

It was too late for her to pretend she knew nothing about the gift - and it rankled too deeply to admit to Bertram that he was privy to secrets which had been kept from her, let alone for her to humiliate herself by admitting that she had been eavesdropping. Better, to suggest that she had known about it all along and was perfectly aware of everything Ruprecht had done and arranged.

Bertram's hazel eyes narrowed, but he inclined his head politely enough. "There is enough. More than enough."

Margerite waited, gazing steadily at him until he gave a low cough. "The Bear's Paw has not found much work in the last months. Paul had little mind to haggle with me, because of that and because...we know each other."

"Yes. How do you know each other?"

Bertram averted his eyes from hers. "I have seen them fight. The Bear is no great strategist, but properly directed, they are among the finest. Like most mercenaries, they will serve for their pay without questioning the cause; but unlike many other companies, we need not fear that they will ravish our own lands on the way to our foe's."

"And this beer allowance? Do they really require twice the drink of a normal fighting man?"

Bertram took the list from her hands, glancing over it as they walked. "Halve that. They will always try those numbers on a new employer, in case they should actually get what they ask for. The other figures look accurate. At least, they are close enough to those for our guardsmen, allowing for the needs of marching on campaign as compared to guarding the walls."

Margerite looked carefully at Bertram. His spine had straightened as he spoke, and his gruff voice had taken on a clearer, almost well-bred tone. For him to hold the post he did, he could not be wholly uneducated - but where had he picked up his learning? She wished again that she could be sure Ruprecht knew what manner of man he was: though he might have fought beside the Bear's Paw as a mercenary once, Margerite was certain that there was a darker shadow over his past than simply being a fighting man who had fallen on hard times, as seemed to be the case with the Bear and his lieutenant.

The negotiations with the merchants for the quantities of food required were exhausting. Flour, oil, salt pork and fish, cheese and spices...Burg Falkenstein had not yet sent the last harvest's wine to market, so they were well-supplied there, and though they would lose the year's income from it, it worked out far cheaper than buying wine in the city. But there was still beer to be purchased, and cheap cloth for bandaging; and plenty of salt as well, for preserving their own meats.

Margerite was glad that Kai had given her a thorough list of expected prices, for the merchants, after one glance at her unfashionable, but fine clothes and youthful face, had without exception decided that she was rich, naïve, and freshly come out of the hinter-woods, and hence the easiest mark in the world for their cunning. She endured the evening meal with Berthold and Elspeth, and slept without dreams that night, untroubled except when Kobolt awoke her by yowling at another tom from the windowsill.

As Petra had promised, the best of Margerite's dresses was ready in good time for her to dress for the midday dinner. Gertrude clicked her tongue as she laced up the tight bodice of pale blue silk, for the Italian woman had cut it low enough to show Margerite's shoulders and the first white swelling of her breasts, and the soft fabric clung tightly to every curve of Margerite's body until its folds belled out beneath the low-slung belt of gilded plates snugged about her hips.

Margerite twirled, letting the skirt flare out.around her legs, then took the mirror from Gertrude's hand to make sure that the gold-brocaded trim at the top of the bodice lay flat and neat against her skin. Dressed thus, with her thick fair hair braided into a gleaming coil about her head, Margerite was sure that she was fit to meet anyone Berthold and Elsbeth could possibly bring before her. Although it is probably no more than another merchant to whom they are in debt, or whom they wish to impress by showing him that the Gräfin von Falkenstein is their guest.

Kobolt miaowed anxiously, stretching up against her leg and pawing at her hip. She disengaged his claws, sweeping his long furry body gently aside. "Not now, cat," Margerite told him. "Stay here if you will, or go out the window and be about a cat's business, but do not try to come with me."

The cat retreated, sitting down by the stove and glaring balefully at the corner that had drawn his attention before. Margerite beckoned to Gertrude, then gathered her skirts in one hand and swept down to the dining hall. Elsbeth was standing before the fire, wearing a gown of tightly cut green damask that was as tight on her ample figure as the red silk had been; she looked like nothing so much as a nursemaid who had borrowed her lady's clothes and jewelry.

She was giving orders to Gretel, who scurried around the table laying out plates and goblets, and her face was already flushed unhealthily with heat and shouting. Margerite could see at once that the work of preparing and serving the dinner would be too much for the single serving maid; Gretel's face was pale and her hands already shook with exhaustion.

"Gertrude, assist," she commanded. Gertrude moved in swiftly, taking the plates from Gretel's hands. A few whispered words passed between them, then Gretel hurried out, leaving Gertrude to finish laying the table.

"That is most kind of you, Frowe Gräfin," Elsbeth said gratefully. "It is so hard to find well-trained servants these days, and unfortunately our cook has gone to visit her family in Regensburg. We should never have let her leave so soon if we had known you would be here, but..." She shrugged her plump shoulders, straining the seams of her dress.

Margerite nodded graciously, pretending to believe her: from what the dressmaker had said, she doubted that Berthold and Elsbeth had more than one servant, and thought it might be surprising if Gretel had seen any wages for a while.

The two women stood talking for a little time, until the door opened and Berthold entered, followed by Bertram and two other men.

"Ha, I see you are here already," Berthold said boisterously. "Frowe Gräfin, good day. Allow me to introduce you to the gentlemen here. This is Damiano, an old friend of mine, who comes of good family in Italy, and this lord is actually a close neighbor of yours: Nikolaus, the younger son of Graf Heinrich von Fürstensee."

Margerite blinked, trying hard to hide her shock. Berthold had handled the money sent for the upcoming war: was it possible that he knew nothing about the purpose behind the gift? But if he did, surely he would never have brought Graf Heinrich's son to meet her...unless there were another plan afoot of which she knew nothing. Resolved to be on her guard, she surveyed the two men cooly as they each bowed over her hand in turn.

The Italian was a man in his middle years, tall and slim, with only a small roll of flesh bulging over his tooled leather belt to show the first signs of age creeping onto his body. His dark hair was slicked back onto his head with scented oils; his clean-shaven face was pleasantly rounded at the edges, and a lively humour animated his blue eyes as he smiled up at her. Damiano's clothes were more exaggerated in cut than Margerite was used to seeing: the sleeves of his patterned golden outer tunic hung down in long fronded streamers, while the pointed tips of its jagged hem barely covered his buttocks, letting his brilliant scarlet hose show off his long legs to advantage.

His shoes were bright blue, their decorative points nearly a foot and a half long. Around his neck he wore a heavy gold chain, and on his left hand was a big gold ring with a smooth-polished black stone, curiously conservative in cut - very similar, indeed, to Ruprecht's amethyst ring, even to bearing an inscription around the stone. In contrast to Damiano, Nikolaus was of medium height and wide-set, nearly verging on fat, though his broad chest and the bulging muscles of his thick arms spoke of considerable strength beneath the padding of indulgence.

His dark brown hair fell casually about his shoulders; his features were oddly balanced, small nose and mouth between wide plump cheeks giving him a rather heavy and sullen look. Nikolaus' clothes were more restrained than Damiano's: his dark green velvet outer tunic reached halfway down his thighs, only shallowly dagged at the edges of the over-sleeves that hung loose over the tightly buttoned blue silk sleeves of his inner tunic; his hose were deep red, almost black, as if to shadow over the thickness of his stumpy legs, and his dark shoes were only modestly pointed. The Graf's son wore several gold rings, including one with a beautiful large square emerald; but on his left forefinger was a simple band of silver with a black inscription graven into it - a love-token? Margerite wondered: it seemed too poor for him.

Or perhaps a piece of special holiness, brought back from Crusade or blessed by the Pope, ringing Nikolaus's finger with the words of a prayer; such tokens were not uncommon. Nikolaus held Margerite's hand for a little too long, his hot mouth lingering unpleasantly on her fingers, so that she had to fight back the urge to wipe her hand on her skirt when he let go of it at last. "Greetings, Gräfin," Nikolaus said. "I am delighted to meet you at last, for I have heard much about you. I have met your noble husband, whom I hold in the greatest esteem, several times, and I believe we have a mutual friend in Graf Günther von Hohenfels."

"Graf Günther has been kind to me, indeed," Margerite said, pretending to a calm she did not feel. Although she did not let her breath quicken, she could hear her heart racing, thrumming an undertone of panic through her veins. Was it possible...surely, from the way he spoke, he could not know anything about the money that the Graf had just sent to support Ruprecht's war against his father? No: his words must have been a formal pleasantry, no more.

"Though my father and your husband have sometimes found themselves at odds," Nikolaus went on smoothly, "be assured that I feel only the best of will towards yourself and Graf Ruprecht, and know that you may think of me as a friend."

Margerite looked at him more closely, trying to guess if there was some double meaning beneath his startling words - the words, perhaps, of a younger son thinking that he could make peace where his father had succeeded only in keeping alive old enmities? Or something darker: according to what Ruprecht had told her, it was Graf Heinrich who had moved to threaten them first, so that Nikolaus could not be unaware of the impending strife, and must have a fair guess as to why she was in Freiburg.

Why, then, should a son seek thus to charm the wife of his father's foe on the eve of battle with assurances of his friendship? Did he mean to win her confidence for the purpose of betraying it - or could it be in his mind to advance himself at the expense of his father and elder brother? Nevertheless, Margerite smiled sweetly at him, just as if his father's men were not at the borders of Ruprecht's land and her mercenary lieutenant not even now mixing gunpowder to hurl cannon-balls and shot against the men of his family. "I am pleased to do so, Herr Nikolaus. It was kind of our gracious hosts to bring us to meet each other."

Once everyone was seated, Gertrude and Gretel poured out wine and brought about the first course, a confection of milk, eggs, and almonds moulded into the shape of fish. The fish had spread out on the plates, the texture being somewhat sloppy, but, Margerite judged, it was a more than creditable effort.

"Tell me, Gräfin," Damiano said, leaning on one elbow and looking at her engagingly across the table, "where are you from, and how did you come to be wedded to Graf Ruprecht so swiftly? I have known him for a little time, and I had heard nothing of his plans for a second marriage."

"My father is the Ritter Martin von Hirschenberg," Margerite answered. She was not sure that she did not catch the flicker of a smile, like a fish's tail flashing through deep water, on Nikolaus' face as she spoke, and she was uncomfortably aware that she had just admitted her birth to be far lower than her position. Nevertheless, she went on boldly. "It was a match of love, such as few are fortunate enough to make." She nibbled a bite of the almond fish from the end of her spoon, dropping her eyes modestly as though embarassed at her declaration, although merely speaking the words had raised her heart again.

"Ritter Martin von Hirschenberg," Nikolaus mused. "I have not heard the name."

"Perhaps you would not have. He dwells far enough from your land. But he is a worthy knight, a trusted companion of Graf Günther."

Nikolaus smiled again, his plump cheeks bulging contentedly, and Damiano nodded. "Ah," the Italian said. "And answer me this, then: did Graf Günther perhaps have a hand in arranging the marriage?"

"It was at his behest that Ruprecht came to my father's castle," replied Margerite. Damiano nodded once more, almost as if he were making a quick note to himself. There was something about the way he and Nikolaus were looking at her that disturbed Margerite deeply: half the cool appraisal she might have expected, half a more searching examination, mingled with... what?

As though she had said something that meant a great deal more to them than her simple words should have allowed, unknowingly speaking in a code that she herself did not understand - like a cook who, ignorant of the degrees of heat and coldness, warmth and moistness, that the learned recognised in different foodstuffs, nevertheless cooked pears in wine and killed lampreys in salt, rendering their danger innocuous by sheer instinct and chance.

"Graf Ruprecht may count himself a fortunate man," Nikolaus said, his gaze lingering on the low-cut neck of Margerite's gown before he met her eyes again. "For you are not only beautiful, but modest, and must be chaste; I see that you wear no rings but your husband's."

Margerite could not keep her eyes from flickering from the single gold band ringing her wedding-finger to the heavily-bedecked hands of the other diners. Perhaps she should have spoken to Ruprecht about jewelry before leaving, but the thought had not even come to her mind, taken up as it was with the needs of preparation for war.

"What fairer jewel can a woman have than a wedding-band?" Margerite answered smoothly. "Even the good sisters who are the brides of Christ have no more noble adornment than the band of their marriage in the Spirit; what else could compare to the sign of the tie between a wife and the husband who leads her and uplifts her soul?"

This remark seemed to abash Nikolaus, who lifted his eyes from their contemplation of the swell of her bosom beneath the tight blue silk bodice. "And does your husband uplift your soul, and bring light out of your darkness, Frowe Gräfin?"

"He does," Margerite answered firmly, anxious to end the questioning. "And now, every game has turn for turn among the players. Damiano, tell me something of yourself. You must be a great traveller."

"Frowe, I am. I trade in…various commodities, and go up and down in the world, seeking those tasks at which I may be best employed."

"And I am sure you have many interesting tales of your journeyings?"

"Perhaps none that would be of much interest to you, Frowe Gräfin."

"Oh, I am sure they would."

Damiano spread his hands out in a shrug. "As you wish, Frowe Gräfin."

As Gretel and Gertrude cleared away the almond fish and brought out dishes of fowl pate, the Italian proceeded to recount the tales of courts he had been at and things done by his high-born friends. Elsbeth was practically shrieking with laughter at each word; Berthold would occasionally break in clumsily with accounts of his own adventures as a merchant, particularly on his journey to the East.

"But the days of crusading glory are over," Berthold said at last, pushing his plate away for Gretel to whisk up. Gertrude began to carry the next course in: each diner got a sizzling golden brace of boneless squabs, their bodies tied up neatly around a buttery stuffing with three little eggs in the middle of each. "Urban may have done his best to proclaim one last year, but what came of that? King Jean of France took the cross, but never stirred a step on the road to Jerusalem, and died in England but two months ago."

"Urban has only been Pope for a year and a half," Nikolaus mused thoughtfully. "And yet he seems to think that he can sway the world with his words alone. Perhaps he has yet to learn the limits of his authority."

"Perhaps he does," Damiano said. "But answer me this, then: how can he be restrained completely when he has the ear of Kaiser Karl so closely, and vice versa? They are friends from their youth, and very much like-minded on certain matters." He glanced sharply at Margerite; then Berthold nodded slightly, and the Italian continued. "This journey of Karl's to Avignon, to try to suppress the Free Companies with an alliance of Papal and Imperial might - an ill-advised venture at best, and one that might have most uncomfortable results if the Kaiser gives all his attention to pursuing it. Is that not so?"

Nikolaus nodded vigorously. "Indeed, this is a matter which goes beyond any brief local inconveniences. And that is something for us to keep firmly in mind, is it not, Margerite?"

"Imperial policy is, certainly," Margerite answered. Another uncomfortable thought had come to her mind: Karl IV had made stringent laws prohibiting local feuds between lords, for the damage they had wrought throughout the Empire, and if Ruprecht's war with Heinrich was not on the wrong side of those laws, it was very near the edge. If his homelands were torn by a series of little wars, the Kaiser would have to turn his attention away from the Free Companies - but what would come of that for those who were testing the borders of his law?

"Of course," Damiano went on, "the Italians are clever people who have little use for Urban the Fifth, as he has little power there: while he dwells in Avignon, he will never be seen as more than a French tool. Do you remember his excommunication of Bernabo Visconti last year, and how he called for a crusade against Visconti himself? Visconti had trampled on Urban's missives, seized ecclesiastical property, and gotten a priest to pronounce anathema against him, and the Pope could not do a thing but curse at him. But that was in Italy; these lands are another matter, as is France."

"I wonder if there will soon be another schism?" said Nikolaus. "Urban was only elected as a compromise, because certain persons could not agree, but he has proven to be troublesome in a number of ways. If there were a Pope in Rome..."

Damiano coughed. "Italians would no doubt prefer it. I have heard rumours that Urban thinks of removing to Rome, but he will have a hard time rooting his cardinals out of the comfortable seat in Avignon: for all the war with the English still sputters and struggles along, there are too many pleasures there in France. I was visiting one of our fellows there only a few months ago, and I have never seen any place to equal the Pope's palace on the Rhone: white horses decked in gold, gold and silver plates, banquets such as you would not believe, and all the pleasures of the city close by. Urban may gripe and complain, but there is more than one cardinal in Avignon who knows what is best for him."

Margerite listened, scandalized but keeping her face from showing it, as the men went on to speak of various cardinals and their personal habits. She had never heard such a conversation, and was only grateful that they did not seem to expect her to take part in it. Even that comfort, however, was taken from her when Damiano asked, "And what do you think of that fine man, Bertrand du Guesclin, whom the new French king seems minded to elevate greatly in the royal service for the works he may perform in the war?"

"I...I do not know," Margerite stammered. "Perhaps, rather, you should tell me your thoughts about him."

Damiano smiled, wiping a shiny smear of grease from his chin with his napkin before he addressed himself to cutting his second pigeon into neat little pieces. "Ah, I think he is one with a great future before him, and well worth marking. At Cocherel, in Normandy - you have not heard of it? Understandable, I suppose, all things considered. He led the French against the forces of Charles of Navarre, and roundly defeated them: the citizens of Paris will sleep the sounder for not having Charles raising his sword on their doorstep. And..." he lowered his voice slightly, "du Guesclin is well-guided, for his wife is a very wise woman, versed in all the arts and sciences of the illuminated. I have seen some of the horoscopes she has cast, and they are truly remarkable. You might very well think on taking Madame du Guesclin for an example, Gräfin. I am sure her powers will have a considerable influence on the progress of the war."

Margerite was saved from having to say anything in reply to Damiano's peculiar advice by Berthold, who coughed loudly, then broke in with, "I understand that King Charles is very sensible in regards to the arts of astrology. Has he a court astrologer?"

"Not that I know of, but I believe the matter is being discussed among the great in France. And King Charles has much need of advice on the stars. For all du Guesclin's latest success, the fate of Brittany is still very much in debate: the English will not give up the support of their candidate, Jean de Montfort, while Charles of Blois still maintains that Brittany is his rightful dukedom and his alone. A few words in the right ears..." Damiano smiled smugly; Nikolaus and Berthold nodded. Only Elsbeth seemed to be paying no attention: she ate steadily, with the beleaguered boredom of a woman who had listened to her husband talk about politics too many times before.

At last the final course, a sweet custard with apples baked into it, had been eaten and cleared away. Nikolaus and Damiano made their goodbyes and departed, but not before Nikolaus had pressed one last, lingering kiss on Margerite's hand and looked deeply into her eyes, saying, "Remember, Frowe Gräfin, that you have a friend in me, and be sure that you can call upon me if aught goes ill." His clammy grip tightened lightly on her fingers, then loosened; he waited a moment, as though he thought she might return the clasp. When she did not, he bowed once more and said, "Farewell for now, then," sauntering out the door with little more than a wave to Berthold and Elspeth.

When she went to her bedchamber that night, Margerite noticed that Gertrude seemed strangely quiet. "What is the matter with you?" she asked finally.

"Frowe, I hope you do not plan to offer my services to that woman often. She did not dare to shout at me as she did at Gretel, but she spoke to me very sharply, as though I were a scullery girl instead of a Gräfin's personal handmaid."

"It was only for the once, since there seemed to be no way her girl could both cook well and serve at table," Margerite reassured her. "I hope she did not offend you too greatly."

"Well." Gertrude giggled, the bright sound of her laughter filling the chamber like a candle suddenly flaring into light. "She would have offended me more, if Gretel had not told me somewhat of her history. Do you know, she is the daughter of a common Greek innkeeper, whose father made his money from fleecing pilgrims on the way to Jerusalem?"

"And Berthold met her…"

"On his way to the Holy Land, when he had lost most of his money in bad business deals and was selling relics and indulgences to make it up. He never made it there: he married Elsbeth for her money and came back here to go into business again."

Margerite thought of the cross on the coat of arms that Berthold had made up for himself, and stifled a laugh. Had she been thinking dark and sinister thoughts about a former pardoner and his cronies? It was no wonder they had little respect for the Church!

And yet, Ruprecht had sent her here and Graf Heinrich's second son was one of those whose conversation had disturbed her so…although, thinking back, she was not sure that some of her unease had not stemmed from the way Nikolaus looked at her, and how he had touched her. Even thinking of his kiss upon her fingers, Margerite found that she was rubbing the back of her hand against Kobolt's sleek fur, as though to wipe away the cold touch of a slug.

"Perhaps when we next come to Freiburg, we shall send ahead to find more suitable people to guest with," Margerite said. "I am sure that Ruprecht would not have sent me to Berthold and Elsbeth if he had had more choice in the matter, or more time to inform his friends here of our arrival."

"I hope so," Gertrude muttered, blowing out the candles.

It was a full three days later when their string of wagons and armed men finally rolled out of Freiburg. Exhausted as she was, Margerite felt very proud, for she had gotten all the supplies necessary, of good quality and at prices low enough that she had not felt extravagant in buying Ruprecht a present: a small gilded hunting horn, finely embossed with scenes of the chase and sounding a sweet, piercing note that made the hairs stand up on the back of her neck.

The journey back was slower than that out, for, with the Bear's Paw Company behind them, they had more than twice the number of men and wagons that they had started with. Nor did they stop at either the monastery or Ritter Wolfhart's castle on the way back: Bertram judged that neither place would be able to put them up, and that they were best in any case to follow the straightest road back to Burg Falkenstein, even if it meant setting up camp along the way.

The mercenaries were already showing their worth in movement, if not yet in fighting: Margerite was amazed by how quickly they made camp in the evening, surrounding their employers as if they expected an attack by bandits or the forces of some Raubritter league, even though it would be a bold group that took on what, by now, nearly amounted to a small army. Once in the night Margerite heard what sounded like the explosion of a cannon, but when she leapt out of the wagon, Paul was already there beside her, his strong arm out to steady her landing.

"Do not be alarmed, Frowe Gräfin," he told her. "It is only Jochanan at work. You may hear these noises now and again, but he hasn't blown himself up yet."

At last they came within sight of Burg Falkenstein again. Margerite felt her heart lifting at the sight of the towers rising above the crenellated walls, and Ruprecht's raptor-head banners spread out proud and crimson against the pale sky. The faint sound of a horn-blast drifted down from the ramparts; they had been seen.

Bertram shouted to one of his men, but by the time the Falkenstein standard had been raised, a column of warriors had already crossed the bridge over the castle's ditch. The defenders stopped; Bertram rode out ahead, taking off his helmet so that they might know him and lifting his signal horn to his lips. Margerite realized she had been holding her breath, and let it out in a deep sigh. If Ruprecht was ready to hold his great castle against the foe so soon, it must be war in earnest now.

Chapter Four

Ruprecht sat mounted and armoured on his horse by the castle's gate as they rode in. Although the great helm with its narrow gilded eyeslits showed nothing of his face, it was figured above with the gold crest of a raptor's head, the golden fabric hanging down behind cut into a deep frond of feathers. A heavy coif of chain-mail spread out over his chest; the vertical ridge of his breastplate pressed hard against his padded red armour-coat with its embroidery of white raptor-heads that matched the device of the shield on his arm.

He held a lance lightly in his other hand, tip pointed skyward, but ready to flick down for the charge at any moment. Looking at her husband, Margerite caught her breath: the full armour and eagle-headed helm, burning golden beneath the sun, had transformed him into something huge and inhuman, like an angel of wrath from the Apocalypse. A tremor ran through her limbs, even as her lips parted to greet him, to reassure herself that this was her own Ruprecht.

"My husband!" she called, her voice clear over the clattering of hooves and rumbling of wagons beside her. "What news? Is the foe upon us?"

Ruprecht lifted the crested helm from his head and handed his lance to his Knappe, riding forward to her. Beneath the great helm, a smooth bascinet guarded his head, his blue eyes shining brilliant out of the openings between nose-piece and the chainmail drape that covered his mouth, chin, and jaw. "Not yet, but our scouts saw you at a distance, and I decided that it would be a good moment to drill the men in springing to defend the castle. Forgive me, my darling, if we frightened you."

"I was not frightened of you, but for you," Margerite replied. She leaned over Mathilde's neck to brush a kiss against the warm metal rings over Ruprecht's lips. Steadying herself with a hand on his shoulder, she could feel the hard plates of his armor beneath the embroidered surcoat. "But you will be pleased by what we have brought back. I have gotten all we needed at a good price, and Bertram has engaged a mercenary company which has two cannon and nine handguns."

Ruprecht leaned back, his brilliant blue eyes blinking in surprise. "Guns! That is good tidings indeed, my darling. And I would know more...but you must be worn out from your travels." He dismounted in a single graceful, powerful motion, the pointed metal tips of his plated shoes clanking lightly against the ground as he landed, then reached up to help Margerite off her horse. "The cooks have promised a fine meal to celebrate your return, but it will be a little while in the making. Go on; I shall come up to your chamber to talk with you presently." He caressed her cheek with the tip of one gauntleted finger, the metal warm and smooth as a kiss against her skin.

Margerite was sitting on her bed in her shift, hair hanging loose and Kobolt on her lap, directing Gertrude in the careful folding and packing of her newly redesigned dresses, when she heard the knock on her door. Ruprecht had taken his armour off, but was still simply dressed in hose and a linen tunic that bore the dark marks of metal, and his golden hair stood up in little disheveled spikes.

"You may leave, Gertrude," he said. "I would speak with my wife alone."

"But my mistress has not yet bathed," Gertrude protested, pointing to the pot of water on the stove, whose gentle steam filled the room with the sweet scent of the rosemary and cicely the maidservant had sprinkled into it. A single glance from Ruprecht quelled her, and she scuttled out.

Ruprecht sat down beside Margerite on the bed. This close, she could smell the musk of his sweaty body: strong, but not unpleasant, a mixture of man and iron and horse. "I am so glad to see you back safely, my beloved," he murmured to her. "I knew that you ought to be safe on the way, or I should not have let you go, but in these times no one's safety is ever certain."

"I was never in danger," Margerite answered, slipping her arm about her husband's slim, muscular waist and moving closer to him. Kobolt raised his black head and miaowed softly, and for a moment, the dreadful dream from her first night in Berthold's house came back to her, sending a sudden shock of chill through her body as though she had inadvertently trodden barefoot on a patch of ice. But Ruprecht would think her silly, or worse, if she spoke of that to him. "It was a very peaceful journey."

Yet Ruprecht's golden brows furrowed as he glanced down at the cat, then looked steadily into her eyes, his shining blue gaze piercing through her. "Was it? Did nothing trouble you?"

Margerite laughed shakily. "Nothing worse than a bad dream after days of travel."

Ruprecht reached down to stroke the cat's soft back, his caress continuing to trail along Margerite's thigh. "Tell me about it."

Margerite told him first about the dream. He nodded slowly. "Such things do happen," Ruprecht said.

He paused, watching her, but the only thing Margerite could say was, "It frightened me."

"Yes. But you were safe, for you have no need to fear such creatures of darkness." Ruprecht stopped. He was looking past Margerite's head, staring out one of the windows that overlooked the ravine, and it seemed to her that a shadow lay over his face, as though his head were covered by a half-seen helm. Margerite did not know whether it disturbed her more to see that he took her tale seriously than it would have if he had passed the dream off as the fancy of a silly girl, but she knew that she felt greatly uneasy.

"Other than that," she said, hoping to get away from the matter, "the worst thing I had to endure was the dinner that Berthold and Elsbeth gave to impress me." She went on to describe the people and the conversation as well as she could. Ruprecht raised a bright brow when Margerite told him what Graf Heinrich's second son had said upon departure.

"So that is the way of it," Ruprecht mused. There was a faraway look in his eyes, as if he were listening to a distant hunting horn that Margerite could not hear, counting the notes that would tell him whether the hart were running or at bay. "You have done better than you know, my love, for you have brought the answer to a question I have been pondering."

"What question is that?"

"The question of what manner of war Graf Heinrich is likely to fight against us."

But Ruprecht would not explain further. Even when she sought to lead the conversation around to Graf Günther, to see if she could get him to mention their knightly brotherhood so that she could voice her misgivings about its dealings with the Free Companies and its apparent involvement with Imperial politics without having to admit that she had learned of the Order and its activities by eavesdropping on Bertram and Berthold, he turned all her questions aside with neat skill, like a master-swordsman gently deflecting the strokes of a novice.

At last Margerite was so frustrated with him that she said, "My husband, perhaps you should call Gertrude back so that she can help me wash."

Ruprecht smiled, and it seemed to Margerite that the shield lying like glimmering fish-scales behind his gaze dropped away, leaving his thoughts clear to her again. He rose, dipping a washing-cloth into the warm rosemary-scented water and lifting the pot to set it by the bed. "I do not think I need to do that," he said, reaching down to tug Margerite's shift gently over her head. Kobolt rose with a protesting miaow, stalking a few feet away to curl up in a shaft of sunlight.

"When I was a young squire riding out on campaign, it was my duty to see to my knight's evening bath," Ruprecht told her. "Come, sit here in front of me and let us see if I have forgotten the skills of washing another." Margerite settled herself between Ruprecht's thighs, and he began to move the damp cloth in slow circles about her shoulderblades, its gentle roughness soothing the strain from her muscles. She sighed gratefully as he rubbed and kneaded at her lower back, easing the tightness of the days of riding.

"Perhaps my memory is failing," Ruprecht said, "but this seems to me a much more pleasant task than I found it as a squire."

Margerite giggled as his hand slipped beneath her to caress her buttocks. "I certainly hope so."

"Of course, it is much nicer to wash a sleek and creamy-skinned back than one that is coarse and hairy," Ruprecht replied, dropping a kiss between her shoulderblades. He bent down to dip the cloth into the pot of hot water and wrung it out again, lifting her hair to wash beneath it and nuzzling the nape of her neck, his breath hot and ticklish against her skin.

Pressing against her from behind, he moved slowly over her collarbones, holding her close as he stroked the cloth downwards to wash her breasts with a slow circling caress, lifting and cupping each in turn. She shuddered as the warm linen passed lightly over her nipples, feeling very wanton with her naked back leaning against Ruprecht's clothed chest. Each soft stroke reached further down Margerite's body, tingling through her belly and feeding the growing warmth between her thighs.

Arching her back, she could feel the hard bulge of Ruprecht's groin hot against her buttocks, and his quickening breaths sighed through her hair. By the time he had rubbed her hips clean, Margerite could scarcely sit still under the sweet exciting torment. The caressing cloth moved down, slow langorous strokes passing over the tops of her thighs to the soft inner flesh, and at last she could bear no more; she turned in Ruprecht's grasp, pressing her naked breasts against him.

"My husband, please take me! I have missed you so much," she gasped. Ruprecht eased her down on her back, unfastening his belt one-handed and pulling his tunic aside to let his swollen spear spring free. Margerite reached for him, grasping the throbbing heat of his prong between her hands and drawing him to her, guiding him in as she opened to his thrust.

"My love, my love," Ruprecht breathed, moving slowly into her. Margerite was almost beyond thought, clasping her legs tightly around his buttocks and arching her own hips up to meet him, flinging herself entirely into the churning maelstrom of pleasure that consumed her flesh as his thrusts grew swifter. A spasm of unbearable delight wracked her limbs, ebbing and surging again beneath the urgings of Ruprecht's body, until at last he too stiffened and cried out, then slowly withdrew from her.

"I shall have to wash again," Margerite said, sitting up and tossing her disheveled hair back with a little shaky laugh. "My husband, what good is washing if it ends with the one washed sweatier than she was before?"

Ruprecht raised himself up on one elbow, his eyes heavy-lidded with pleasure as he looked upon the length of her body. "Perhaps I have lost my touch, after all; I shall have to practice more. I will have a tub brought up here so that you can bathe properly in the evening, anyway."

He sat up, straightening his tunic and rebuckling his belt, and Margerite remembered what she had been meaning to say.

"Sit there a minute, and close your eyes," she told him, leaping up. The hunting horn was at the top of one of her chests, gleaming upon the deep red velvet of a dress. "Now hold out your hands."

Ruprecht did, and she laid the horn carefully upon his palms. "You can open your eyes now."

Ruprecht drew in his breath in a soft sound of delight. "Thank you, my beloved. This is beautiful…you got it in Freiburg?"

"I did. I could not think of anything else that would please you more."

"No." He lifted the horn to his lips. Its soft blast rang high and pure through the room, chill and haunting as the sound of wind whispering through the strings of a harp; the echo of its note died away slowly as Ruprecht lowered the horn, so that it almost seemed to Margerite as if a second horn had answered, clear and far away. "I shall treasure it. Thank you, my bride." Ruprecht slung the horn over his chest.

"Well," he said reluctantly, "I have much that I must see to before supper, and I am sure you would like to rest a little before you join me."

Limbs still weighted by the delicious lassitude of their lovemaking, Margerite did not argue, only kissed Ruprecht and let him leave before she called for Gertrude again.

The men gathered early beneath a gray sky the next morning, a strong cold wind whipping the pennants of the horsemen's lances. Margerite girded Ruprecht's sword onto him with her own hands, fastening the buckle tightly over the thick padded linen of his armour-coat. The mail chin-piece of his bascinet hung loose over his chest; now he kissed her before hooking it up under his steel nasal.

"Wish me luck, my love," Ruprecht said to Margerite, his gauntleted hand heavy on her shoulder. "I leave Burg Falkenstein in your charge. If we are not back and you have not heard from us within a week, close up the gates and prepare to withstand siege - or to discuss terms with Graf Heinrich; but do not surrender unless you have proof of my death."

"I shall do that," Margerite said, biting her lip to keep back tears. "May Christ and all the saints ride beside you and keep you safe."

The chainmail over Ruprecht's mouth muffled his short laugh, and he waved his left hand. "I will sooner trust in your love, my wife."

"That you have, and may it keep you well."

"And you have mine. Hold this keep well - and remember what I told you about trusting Cundrîê and Clingschor. It may be that they will have advice for you while I am gone, and it is important that you should follow their advice."

"I shall do that," said Margerite at once, for she would not have Ruprecht ride off with any doubt in his heart that all was going as he wished at home.

"Until we meet again, beloved." He touched her coiled braid, as she might have brushed her fingers over her rosary for luck, and vaulted up into his saddle. "Knappe!"

Wolfram was at Ruprecht's side at once, handing up the eagle-crested great helm. Ruprecht put it on his head, transforming himself again into the fearful and remote vision of an angel of battle. He touched his golden spurs to his horse's armoured side, moving slowly forward.

Margerite looked up at Wolfram, seeing how the squire's eyes shone beneath the glittering rim of his steel cap. This would be the boy's first battle: she could not let him go without some word to cheer him.

"Farewell, brave Knappe," she said. "Fight well, that I and all of Burg Falkenstein may be proud of your deeds."

"My frowe, I shall!" Wolfram answered boldly. "And though you are far from the field, you may know that I am battling for your sake."

"Knappe!" Ruprecht called. Wolfram bowed to Margerite, then hurried up to attend his lord.

Margerite climbed up to the top of one of the outer towers to watch them go, the train of men and wagons snaking down the hill and along the road. Her hands ached; when she looked down, she saw that she had wrung them together until they were white and bloodless. It would be hard - sweet Maria, it would be hard! - to wait here until Ruprecht's small army came back, with little chance of knowing how matters were going with him. Even if his forces were victorious, a lucky shot in battle could slay the best warrior, and his armour might not be proof against a crossbow-bolt: was that not how the great King Richard of England had died?

She shook herself. Death might be found anywhere in life, but there was still work to be done, and if there were a chance that she might have to hold Burg Falkenstein against siege, Margerite would be ready for it. There were books in Ruprecht's library that spoke of such things: she would seek them out, and learn what she needed to know; and if the men made it back safely this time, she would speak with Ruprecht, and even, if she must, with Bertram, to see what their advice would be when the principles of siege were applied to this castle.

As befitted his place, Ruprecht, in the grand array of his full armour and tournament-helm, rode at the head of his army, in front of his own men; the mercenary company Bertram had hired marched at the rear, guarding the supply wagons. He did not expect any trouble on the way, for, despite what he had told Margerite, there had been no rumours of any preparation for war on Heinrich's part.

The words his wife had brought him from Nikolaus told him that his foe's younger son still held his loyalty to the Order above his loyalty to his father: Günther must have informed the young man how matters stood, and Nikolaus, in turn, would do his best to see that the war was carried out as the Order intended, with a great deal of noise and raids back and forth across the border, but with neither party making a full-fledged effort to either conquer the other or offer reasonable terms of peace, and thus bring the trouble to an end.

The risk, of course, was that Heinrich would take the opportunity given by Ruprecht's declaration of war to march directly against Burg Falkenstein with his full force, in which case Ruprecht would find himself hard-pressed indeed; but that was a chance that must be hazarded, and if it came to pass, Ruprecht knew that his castle could hold out for a long time until Günther's aid came, and thus still fulfill the will of the Order. Ruprecht's force was still nearly an hour's ride from Ritter Sigmund's castle when they saw the small band ahead of them on the road. Sigmund's banner, a golden lion on a black field, waved above the riders, and the dull gleam of armour and helms told Ruprecht that his knight had come out to meet him in person.

"Hail, Ritter Sigmund!" Ruprecht called out as soon as they were close enough.

"Hail, my Graf!" Sigmund replied, his hoarse voice muffled by his helm. "What tidings bring you here in such force?"

"Grim tidings, my friend, for we have a war to fight!" Ruprecht replied.

Ritter Sigmund drew his sword, holding it high above his head. "By God and the oaths I have sworn you before Him, I am yours to command."

Ruprecht nodded, the raptor crest of his tourney-helm lowering and lifting weightily. "And therefore you have the trust of my border, a trust that you shall soon need to defend for my sake as staunchly as you did for my father's. Let us ride on to your castle, and there I shall tell you more."

Inside Sigmund's great hall, Ruprecht, Sigmund, Bertram, Paul, and their chief lieutenants gathered about the table. Ruprecht waited until Sigmund's servants had filled their cups with wine, then called Wolfram to fetch his maps.

"Graf, forgive me," Ritter Sigmund said, leaning his meaty elbows on the table and looking Ruprecht in the eye, "but what is the cause of this war?"

"I go to war to reclaim Burg Düsterstein, which Graf Heinrich disputed with my father and which he has unlawfully given to his knight Friedrich, unrightfully called von Düsterstein, for these many years. I have borne Heinrich's insults for too long; the time has come for me to strike back, and reclaim what is mine - for my father's honour, my own, and that of the son I hope shall soon kick in my new bride's womb!"

Sigmund stroked his thick blond beard, nodding. "And so, do you mean to lay siege directly to the castle? That would seem risky to me, since, even if you call in all your knights from your border keeps, Graf Heinrich's army could easily take us from the rear if we were to encamp about Burg Düsterstein."

"I know that, as well…ah, none too soon, Wolfram." Ruprecht took the maps from his Knappe's hand, spreading them out across the table. "We will ride first to Burg Düsterstein, to strew ashes and read out our cause for war, as Kaiser Karl has decreed must be done; then we shall withdraw for three days as the law prescribes, to give Heinrich a fair chance to reply. I do not think, however, that he will yield the castle to us without a blow struck. When we have heard his answer, then we shall begin our attack - not upon Burg Düsterstein, but on Heinrich's villages, that he may know how fully our words are meant. Now, Sigmund, I know that you would gladly ride out with me, but you are the closest to Heinrich's lands, and thus in the most danger: if Burg Eichenwald falls, that is our first shield broken. You must hasten to ready yourself for defense, for if you are besieged with enough force, it may be some time before we can come to your aid."

"It shall be as you command, my Graf. I never failed your father, and I shall not fail you while I live."

Ruprecht looked at Sigmund's earnest face, heavy weathered cheeks red above his full fair beard and his blue eyes gazing sternly from their nests of deep creases. He felt a sudden surge of affection for the older knight, to whom matters of right and wrong were so simple. Another man might have asked more questions: what real cause had Ruprecht had for war, why did he need to strike now, why did he think he could defeat Heinrich, carrying battle to the other Graf's lands while he was still outnumbered?

But obedience to his lord and to God, and the joy of taking part in a good fight, were the only justifications Sigmund seemed to have ever required in his life; and for that, Ruprecht both loved and, somewhere in his heart, might have envied him. But it was also the way of life that men such as Sigmund were born to be tools of those with greater wisdom and power, and Sigmund was, indeed, his tool - not to be ill-treated or broken carelessly, but to be used, and used up, at need.

Ruprecht knew he himself was just such a tool to Günther, and Günther to the Imperator of the Order: but through will and wisdom and strength, and with the help of Margerite's vision and understanding, Ruprecht knew that he might yet rise to command those under whom he now served.

It was no more than half a day's march between Burg Eichenwald and Burg Düsterstein. Ruprecht commanded the mercenaries and the bulk of his force to stay behind at Ritter Sigmund's castle. This foray was simply to make the announcement of war required by Kaiser Karl's recent laws, and to draw Heinrich's attention: Ruprecht would strike elsewhere when the three days prescribed by law were up.

Accompanied only by a small band - three Gleven of three horsemen and a spearman apiece, including his own, his twenty best foot-fighters, and the mercenary Jochanan with two of his handgunners - Ruprecht rode quickly through the wooded valley where Sigmund's burg stood, coming out soon into pleasant meadows and fields. He was skirting the border between his own lands and Heinrich's now.

Once he saw a small group of three mounted men, undoubtedly outriders of Heinrich's, silhouetted against the top of a low green hill but he paid no attention to them: they would not attack his company, and if they bore word back to Heinrich of what they had seen, so much the better. As they rode northeast, the land grew higher again, rising into dark pine-covered hills.

Although a light veil of cloud grayed the sky, the sun managed to burn pale through its misty shroud now and again, and Ruprecht could tell that it had not yet reached the midday height by the time he saw Burg Düsterstein looming before him.

The small castle lived up to its name: built of roughly-hewn lumps of gray stone, it squatted low and square upon an outcropping of rock among thick pine-woods. Ruprecht had never been inside Burg Düsterstein, for Graf Heinrich had taken it before he was born, but even if it had had more windows than the narrow arrow-slits that showed dark above the walls, it could not have ever gotten direct sunlight within: the wooded hills shadowed it in every direction.

Yet it was a site of no little importance, for it was the sole guard of the northeastern quarter of Heinrich's lands where they curled about Ruprecht's: while Ruprecht's father had held it, it had served as a constant threat to the Graf von Fürstensee; while Heinrich held it, it offered him a clear march through the richest parts of Ruprecht's territories. It was a sufficient cause to justify war - if Ruprecht had thought that he could either harass Heinrich into negotiating for it or successfully besiege and hold it against Heinrich's forces.

As they came within sight of the castle, a horn sounded from within the walls, and Ruprecht saw the iron-bound gates swinging closed. He smiled: they would be ready to hear his words.Ruprecht took his crested tourney-helm from Wolfram, lowering it over his bascinet. He signalled his other men to halt; the Knappe raised his banner, and Ruprecht rode forward with his squire behind him and Jochanan's two gunners flanking them, stopping just outside arrow-range and waiting.

"Ho!" he shouted. "Ritter Friedrich! Are you within?"

At last Ruprecht saw the dull gleam of daylight on a helmed head above Burg Düsterstein's low battlements, and a man's tenor voice sounded sharp through the distortions of the helmet.

"Hail to you, Graf Ruprecht von Falkenstein! Say to me, what brings you across your border to the territories of Graf Heinrich von Fürstensee? Do you come in friendship, or with your sword drawn for war?"

Ruprecht drew his sword, holding it aloft. With the other hand, he reached for the scroll that Wolfram passed up to him.

"Hereby, as is set out by the Kaiser's law, with yourself as witness, I do read the cause of war. Because this castle, Burg Düsterstein, was held by my father and his father and his father before him, having been built to guard the north of our family's lands, and because it was taken by Graf Heinrich von Fürstensee neither by sale nor agreement nor by fair and knightly force of arms, but by recourse, upon dispute, to a Kaiser who did not possess it to give, I, Graf Ruprecht von Falkenstein, do hereby declare and affirm my ancient right to Burg Düsterstein by blood and law, and say to Graf Heinrich that if it is not returned to me, it shall be war between us until I have won Burg Düsterstein back." He handed the scroll back to Wolfram, taking a small bag from the Knappe's hand. "These ashes I strew upon Graf Heinrich's soil, in token of the scorn in which I hold his unrightful ways and the devastation I shall wreak upon himself and his lands until such time as Burg Düsterstein is in my hand again." Ruprecht upended the bag, scattering the ash. The fine dust floated on the breeze a moment, then was lost. "So I, Graf Ruprecht von Falkenstein, have sworn it."

Ruprecht slashed his sword sharply downward. A huge crash of sound dazed his ears; the air was suddenly full of swirling smoke, sharp with the stink of gunpowder. His horse reared, and he heard Wolfram cry out softly as the squire struggled to restrain his own steed. Gaining control again, Ruprecht cast the scroll onto the ground and wheeled his horse without waiting for Ritter Friedrich's reply; Wolfram and the gunners followed him briskly back to his band, and they turned to ride away.

When they were out of sight of the castle, Ruprecht realized that Jochanan was jogging breathlessly by the side of his horse, the loose sole of one shoe flapping loudly against the ground as he ran and the battered sheath of his falchion swinging perilously on its frayed belt-loop. "Herr Graf," the mercenary panted, "Stop. Stop!"

"Who are you to tell me to stop?" Ruprecht asked, urging his horse a little faster.

"Herr Graf! I am sorry," Jochanan gasped. "I did not mean to offend you...Forgive me, I am sorry...One of the guns...did not fire, Graf, and...gunner says he thinks...it is still sputtering...I must have a moment...make sure it is not going ...to blow up....I beg of you! Please let us stop."

"See to your weapon, then," Ruprecht said, reining his horse in. The mercenary stopped gratefully, shoulders slumped and head drooping towards his chest as he struggled to get his breath back. Then, "That was only the blast of a single gun?"

"Herr Graf, it was," Jochanan answered, his head coming up proudly. "It would have been much louder if they had both gone off."

"Well. I have no doubt that Heinrich will get the message in any case, and the news that we have guns will help to make him less willing to assault us straight-on. But...how often do your guns miss fire?"

"Every so often," Jochanan admitted. "I am always working on the formula, trying to make it more reliable. But it is in the very nature of gunpowder that sometimes it will not explode if you throw it into the heart of the fire, and sometimes it will burst almost before a spark touches it." He held up his hands. The left was missing two finger-joints, and the right one, and when Ruprecht looked closely at the gunner's craggy face, he could see that Jochanan's close-cropped black beard hid a flower of pink scar-tissue on the left side of his jaw.

"Working on the formula?" Ruprecht enquired. "That sounds almost like the words of an alchemist...but if you think there is danger from your other gun, you had best go see to it now."

"Thank you, Herr Graf!" The mercenary hurried off, taking the offending weapon from the man who was holding its long wooden stock gingerly at arm's length and walking off into the woods with it.

Ruprecht watched him go, musing. He was nearly certain that Jochanan was a Jew, although what he might be doing with mercenaries, when Jews were forbidden to bear weapons throughout Christendom...well, each man had his tale, and hard-pressed as the Jews had been since the first coming of the Death, the only surprise was that a mercenary company would accept a man who had undoubtedly never touched sword or spear until he was an adult; but of course Jochanan's skill with gunpowder made up for that.

More disturbing was the hint that the man was an alchemist as well as a gunner, for a Jewish alchemist was likely to be versed in more things than gunpowder and distillation. The Order dealt with Jews of wealth and power now and again, just as it dealt with Saracens, but no Jews had ever sought admittance to it, and there were some few of them who were counted among the bitterest foes of the Order.

It was not inconceivable that Jochanan had been planted in a mercenary company as a spy: but Ruprecht would question Bertram on his history later, for it was also possible that a Jew who would take employment as a mercenary among Christians was a renegade, and hence well-suited to the Order's uses. A dull boom sounded from the woods; a flock of birds arose in twittering alarm, and a few green leaves drifted free on the wave of concussion. Ruprecht jumped; Wolfram whirled about wild-eyed, his hand on his sword.

"Soft, Wolfram," Ruprecht said to his squire. "Let us see if we still have a gunnery officer."

He started to turn his horse towards the place the noise had come from, but Jochanan came walking out of the woods, a few more black smudges staining the gray wool of his disreputable tunic. The metal tube at the end of the wooden pole in his hands seemed whole, and he looked cheerful enough, so Ruprecht kneed his horse into a walk, waving the band on again.

Ruprecht's forces stayed at Ritter Sigmund's castle that night, then bore south again. There was a stretch on the southern portion of their mutual border which was held, on Heinrich's side, between two castles nearly a day's ride apart. Striking at one of the villages there would not be too risky: they could be in and out before either castle could muster to defend its people, and they had enough strength to defeat any one of Heinrich's knights' bands easily if it came to a battle.

The only question was whether Heinrich, when he heard the news, would ride directly to Burg Düsterstein in the expectation of engaging Ruprecht there, or whether he would hover farther down the border, awaiting just such a raid as Ruprecht meant to make. On the third night after Ruprecht's declaration of war, his force made camp in the woods near the middle of the border, only a few miles away from Heinrich's Burg Mittelfeld.

Ruprecht had ordered Wolfram to set up his tent a little way from the others, on the opposite side of the camp from the mercenaries, for he would need quiet and safety from intrusions - particularly if there were any truth to his suspicions about Jochanan, who had already shown a curious talent for stumbling into the wrong place at the wrong time. Ruprecht ate at the same campfire as Bertram and Paul, the three of them wiping the grease of the sausages from their fingers with hard pieces of bread and washing their meal down with leather tankards of thin wine as they discussed their plans for the raid.

Paul seemed to be concerned chiefly with the deployment and arrangement of his men beside Ruprecht's troops, and asked no further questions; but Bertram kept pressing for more information about their route in, and that, Ruprecht could not yet give him.

"You must trust my judgement," Ruprecht said at last, sipping lightly from his tankard. The flickering firelight played over Bertram's cheekbones and forehead, deepening the hollows of his eyes beneath his black brows and losing his mouth in the shadow of his beard; now, as the captain of the guard scowled, he looked very much like a gargoyle snarling from a candlelit wall. His expression might have daunted another man, but Ruprecht knew that Bertram would never dare raise hand to him. "I shall tell you our goal and direction of march at dawn tomorrow, and you and I shall have enough time to make our last decisions of strategy then."

Bertram grunted, tearing a bite from the end of his sausage; Paul drained his leather mug, refilling it from the wineskin at his side. "More wine, Graf?"

Ruprecht declined with a smile and a wave of his hand. In truth, he thought, looking up at the stars glimmering faint and clear between the woven blackness of the pine-branches overhead, save for the matter they were discussing, this was not so unlike some of the longer hunts he had been on: the warmth of the flames holding the night's coolness at bay, the sausages popping and sizzling on their stick over the fire, their golden fat dripping down to flare up on the coals; the wine slightly sharp in his mouth, but welcome after the day's riding - perhaps too welcome, for it was tempting to let Paul refill his tankard, but Ruprecht knew that he would have to have his head clear that evening. So thinking, with only a slight pang of wistfulness at having to leave the other men's company, he rose gracefully to his feet.

"Bertram, you will take charge of the second watch," he ordered. "Set Michael to oversee the first, and Gottfried the third. I am going to my tent now, for I have much to think on."

The days after Ruprecht had marched out ground wearingly and swiftly on Margerite. She had little time to rest, for she must see to the disposal of all the supplies she had brought back from Freiburg, while giving directions to the castle folk, not only for their daily business, but for the things they must do to prepare in case of siege. Despite the whirl of work, however, she could not keep her thoughts from turning to her husband, soon, perhaps, to be facing the storm of arrows and the keen edge of the sword.

Nor could she block from her mind the dreadful visions that tormented her: Ruprecht's helm split down the middle, bright blood and the gray of brains staining his fair hair; the firm muscles of his white chest carved open by the stroke that had shattered his heart; the slippery coils of his guts spilling out amid grass and mud...But men must go to war, she told herself firmly as she walked up and down the spiraling oaken staircases, or sat in the great hall waiting for Kai to bring her yet another of his lists. And women must wait for them, and trust in Christ to bring them home safely.

Still, if it had not been for Kobolt following her about, chasing after her skirts and purring softly in her lap and dropping his dead mice before her feet, Margerite wondered if she might break under the strain: it was only to the cat that she could whisper her fears, for she must show herself strong even to Gertrude, and Kobolt's golden eyes looked back knowingly into hers as he put a paw on her hand, as if to reassure her.

Margerite would not have slept at all at nights, she thought, if it had not been for the hot possets Cundrîê brought her: strong red French wine, spiced and sweetened with honey, with the musky aftertaste of herbs. Kobolt had sneezed and spat at his first sniff of the drinks, and Gertrude had muttered darkly, but Margerite drank her draught every evening as if she could bring her husband safely home by following his wishes.

The first three nights, worn out and lulled by Cundrîê's potion, Margerite slept deeply and without dreams, barely able to open her eyes and drag herself from bed when Gertrude awoke her in the mornings. But the fourth night, nearly as soon as she had closed her eyes, it seemed to her that she could feel herself flying again, circling high beneath the starry darkness and looking down at the shadowed mountains and valleys below.

Where am I? she wondered, tilting her wings against the wind. But as she flew, it seemed she heard a voice speaking through the air that rushed about her.

O thou bright spirit, my bride, Margerite, Gräfin von Falkenstein! Falcon-queen, princess of the air, by the vows of love that bind us, arise and come to me.

Though the words clanged strangely in her ears, ringing backwards and forwards as though they echoed within a sounding-bowl of metal, it seemed to her that she knew the voice: it was the voice of her falconer, who had brought her to him, whispered to her and stroked her and fed her on good meat, that she might fly for him. Now she narrowed her long wings, arrowing swiftly over woods and fields and the shimmering snakes of brooks, until she saw the little campfires burning low in the woods, and the wagons and tents ringed about them.

One of the tents glowed with a dark light that hurt her eyes and made her want to look away, the colour of an amethyst afire; and yet the call was drawing her closer to it, so that she must soar low above the banner that draped limply around the pole at its peak. Fly forth, her falconer's voice urged her. Fly forth, and tell me what you see.

She soared upwards again, glad of the clean night air that flowed through her feathers like the tingling cold water of a brook. Below she saw a small river winding through the broad valley; the gray stone of the keep at the river's banks seemed to stand out pale beneath the starlight.

Fly on, the voice pressed. Fly higher, see farther: look to north and east.

She followed the line of the river, slowly circling more and more widely around it. A second keep, greater than the first, stood silhouetted behind the pines on the first high line of hills to the east; below, she could see the small square houses of a village, and farther to the north, more westerly, the low-burning flames of more campfires, the light of their coals gleaming on the armour of those few men who sat on guard.

What do you see? How many?

She struggled for words, for numbers, but her keen bright falcon-sight had stripped all such thoughts from her mind. Not more than had been at the first camp, but not fewer by many; all the tents were dark, save for a faint unnerving shimmer about the peak of one.

Where will they go? What is their path?

As the question shaped in her mind, it seemed to her that she could see the dust of the men's passing still on the eastward road behind them, churning up like a river frothing into a dry bed; it pooled at the camp, then surged on towards the forested hills to the west.

Well-done, my falcon, my bright spirit! the falconer cheered her. Fly home, now; hasten back, for you have gone far tonight and done well. Fly home, my heart-bought bird, and sleep in peace, knowing that all is well…

The moon was down, and the second watch had begun. Bertram sat beside the outermost fire with young Eckhardt beside him, listening to the soft rustling of the wind through the pines. The padding inside his iron-plated leather jerkin kept him warm enough, but the links of his chain-mail coif were chill about his face, and when he touched the helmet on the ground beside him, he could feel its icy metal even through his gloves.

"Do you think there will be much plunder?" Eckhardt asked eagerly.

"We are only going to burn a village, not take a castle," Bertram replied. "If we find anything to plunder, it will be such things as are valued by those who do not have much."

Eckhardt rubbed his knuckles over his narrow jaw, scratching absent-minded at the scant growth of yellow hairs there. "There is a girl I should like to take something home to," he said after a little while. "If, maybe, I should find a necklace for her, or even a little silver ring…"

"A girl, is it?" Bertram said. "And does she have a name?"

Eckhardt turned his face away, dropping his eyes. "She does. It is…mayhap presumptuous of me, but I helped the Gräfin's maidservant Gertrude when she needed a man to lift and carry, and she seemed pleased to stand and talk to me afterward."

Bertram's gloved hands tightened into hard fists against his sides; the grimness grated like sand in his throat as he said, "You are a good young man, Eckhardt. Such women are not for you: I would advise you to bring your trinkets to another."

Eckhardt stared up at him, pale eyes shining wide from his long face in the firelight. "Why? She is the Gräfin's serving maid; I am a man-at-arms to the Graf. There is not such a gap between us that it cannot easily be bridged, should it please us."

"Not if you take my advice." Bertram closed his mouth firmly, knowing that he should say no more. Eckhardt, too, subsided into silence, but after a little while, he spoke again, his voice softer and less brash. "This will be my first battle."

"I know."

"Is there…much I should have to fear?"

Eckhardt looked up at Bertram again, and in his plaintive words, it seemed to Bertram that he heard his own voice in youth, the same words that had whispered themselves over and over in his head as he sat in the tent sharpening weapons and polishing armour by candlelight, his hands shaking so that he had to grip whetstone and cloth until his knuckles were white. He had not been able to speak so to any other, for it would have been a shame and a reproach ever after; but he had wished that he could.

"You are strong and trained as well as you could be in the time you have been with me," Bertram said gently. "From the folk of the village, you have little to fear. If Graf Ruprecht chooses one of the larger villages, there may be some men with real weapons, but the mounted fighters will be dealing with the chief threats. Unless it be sheer bad luck that a pitchfork or scythe do you some harm, or you are careless enough to try and loot a body that you have not made sure is dead, you should do well enough. If we are seen riding in - if our path is badly chosen or unlucky - we may have to contend with the forces from one of Graf Heinrich's keeps, though they probably will not attack a group our size by choice. But should that happen, and if they close with us, keep your wits about you. It is no shame to you to run from an armoured horseman. But you may well come to blows with another man-at-arms, and there is your weakness: you are not as good with a sword as I should like you to be. Use your spear to keep your enemy at a distance - use it as a quarterstaff if you must - and you will have a better chance of survival: and if you cannot kill him before he closes with you, then hold him off until another can finish him, for once a foe has gotten past a spearman's guard, it is time to say a funeral Mass. As for fear..." Bertram paused, thinking back on other battles he had been in, on men slain and death risked for the sake of mere plunder, or worse. "This is no Crusade, and the keeping of every man's soul is his own. Since we have no priest with us, and if you have not been shriven - then pray, as best you can, for the mercy of the Virgin, who can intercede with Her Son for even the wickedest of men."

Eckhardt nodded soberly, then turned his gaze away, sinking into his own thoughts again. Bertram watched him for a moment: an ungainly lad, perhaps, with his long limbs sticking out like a stork's from his jerkin of boiled leather whose iron breastplate had been made for a larger man and his long nose pricking from under the flared rim of his old pot-helm, but a good one. It would be a cruel tragedy if he were to be drawn in by the Gräfin's maid, his decent soul unwittingly falling to the evil that had consumed Burg Falkenstein even as it had rotted the root of Bertram's own home...

And my own soul, Bertram reminded himself. He looked at the fire, the gray ash shells of half-charred pieces of wood crumbling over the glowing coals that still gnawed at their hearts, little flames leaping up here and there as gusts of wind stirred them to burn out the little that was left within. Wearily, he reached over to toss a few more sticks in, watching as the droplets of resin beneath their bark caught and flared, the fire creeping up around them.

It was on such nights, watching alone by the fire with his weapon-fellows sleeping around him, that Bertram's heart felt its own weight most painfully. Dark memories, rising like ill mists seeping up from beneath the cover of a poisoned well...he did not dare think too closely upon them. If he did, he knew the barrier in his heart would give way like stone crumbling from a rotten wall at the edge of a precipice, toppling him into the dark abyss below.

Of the scars on his sword-arm, one had not come in battle, but from the edge of his own knife: a thin white thread along the muscle of his forearm, long-healed, but still, sometimes, aching with the echo of that keen cut, as though it called for a second blade to fulfill its promise. Bertram shook his head violently. Self-murder was the last despair, the final turning-away from God: though he had not deserved it, either then or by his deeds afterwards, Mother Maria's mercy had saved him from that sin and the surety of Hell.

As his blood had poured out, the blackness rising about his brain, he had felt a woman's soft touch on his wrist, had heard - he thought - a woman's voice murmuring words that he could not afterwards remember. But he had woken with a strip cut from his tunic and wrapped tightly about his arm as a bandage, though whether he had done it himself in his delirium or whether it had been done by another, he would never know. Still, his life was not over, and there was time for redress: for the wrongs he had done, even more than those he had suffered.

And yet, it seemed to Bertram as he sat staring at the little flames creeping up around the blackening bark, that all he did only sank him deeper towards Hell, as if he were struggling in quicksand that softened with every flailing of his arms. For Graf Heinrich, by all accounts, was a good man and a good ruler, who upheld the Emperor and his laws with the strength of his right arm.

It was hard enough to fight for Ruprecht: but worse now that the Graf was married to that witch-wife, who played so mockingly at innocence and even dared to take the Sacrament in her mouth, all the while flaunting her great black tomcat with its unnatural cleverness and malice. It was worst of all, Bertram thought, to look at Margerite's fairness of face and body, remembering how he had been betrayed by just such a female.

He had not rested his head upon a woman's warm bosom since fleeing his home; for all the sins he had committed, he had not even quenched his lust with a whore once, let alone ravished an unwilling woman, and the memories of desire that Margerite's tight-laced bodices and softly rustling skirts raised in him were worse than the pain of festering wounds.

At least - Mother Maria's mercy - she seemed to care no more for him than he did for her, and did not seek to use her body to taunt or influence him. Still, he wished that she had never come to Burg Falkenstein. The fire was dying down. Bertram heaved another log onto it, shattering the half-burned pieces beneath so that their charred shards fell asunder in the glowing bed of coals.

Eckhardt's eyelids were drooping beneath the shadow of his helm-rim; Bertram rose and kicked him lightly in the ribs. "If you're sleepy on watch, boy, stand up and walk, or you'll be hanged some day for nodding off on duty."

Ruprecht was at the door of Bertram's tent at dawn's first gray light, fully armoured but bare-headed, with his plain fighting bascinet beneath his arm. The Graf's blue eyes glowed with a hectic brilliance, his golden hair floating in a soft halo about his clean features; another looking upon him might have thought that his look of spiritual exaltation was the light left by a holy vision. Bertram resigned himself to listen to whatever plan Ruprecht had conceived in the darkness - to listen to it, and to carry it out as best as he could.

"I think we can safely march straight in," Ruprecht said. "Heinrich should have long since received my declaration, and he will have gone to Burg Düsterstein; if he did not delay too long, he may even be there today."

Bertram only grunted. He had no doubt that Ruprecht had used some magical means to find out where Heinrich was: why else should he know this morning what he had not last night? But his part was that of a hard-bitten warrior who believed in nothing but what he could see, so he made the token protest, "If he has not done as you expect, are we ready to meet him?"

"If Heinrich is waiting for us near the border, he has not had enough time to muster his full forces," Ruprecht replied smoothly. "It would be no bad chance, for your Free Company brings our army up to a size fit to take his on directly, especially with Jochanan's guns on our side. It is almost a pity that we did not bring the cannon, but they are heavy to move and expensive to fire, and I do not think we shall need them after all. Now, rouse the men and get them into marching array, for I wish to be back on our side of the border by sunset."

Although the early morning was overcast, a faint mist wisping through the trees, the clouds burned off swiftly, the sun beating down hot upon the helms and armour of Ruprecht's men. Soon the iron plates that covered Bertram's body and limbs were warm, his sweat dampening the padding of his jerkin, but, trained to ride and fight in heavier armour through any weather, he paid it no heed.

The first hazard they had to pass was the river that flowed through both lands, running along the border for a short way. The only way to cross it was by fording it; and the ford, a few miles north of Heinrich's southernmost keep, would certainly be guarded. As they reached the flatlands sloping down towards the river-bed, Bertram commanded the archers and gunners to the front, flanking the four swiftest Gleven: Graf Ruprecht's, his own, and those of the Ritters Dietrich and Wilfrid, a pair of sons of minor nobles with no inheritance who had chosen to take service and hold land under Ruprecht in hopes of someday gaining castles of their own.

If any of the guards escaped the arrows and tried to run, the mounted units would chase them down and finish them. The moment Bertram spied the men arrayed on Heinrich's side of the ford, his heart sank. There were a full eight mounted Gleven, three of them led by men whose fine armour proclaimed them to be knights, as well as thirty or forty infantry men and twenty archers.

It might have been enough to discourage Ruprecht, had he relied only on the soldiers of his own who had come with him, but with the mercenaries on their side, it would be a slaughter, and a sore blow of itself to Graf Heinrich. Yet it was Ruprecht's men who would have to cross the ford to do battle, and there would be losses on their side that they could badly afford.

"Foot-soldiers, cross behind us and spread out to come in from the flanks," Bertram directed. "Gunners, aim at the knights...Now!"

The two mercenaries braced the ends of their long gun-sticks against the ground, drawing their hot wires from the small brazier Jochanan carried, stretching them out to touch off the powder through the holes in the ends. Bertram had seen guns fired before; he closed his eyes against the first brilliant flash, but he could do nothing to block his ears against the deafening boom.

Around him, the horses were rearing and plunging, terrified by the explosion; but even as he struggled to regain control of his own mount, he saw one of the knights on the other side, his chest a red ruin of tattered flesh and iron-shards, toppling to the ground, while the man behind him had been pitched headfirst from the screaming horse that lay shatter-legged on the ground. But Graf Heinrich's men had not been thrown into disarray; Bertram saw the horsemen spreading out, the archers bending their bows.

"Archers!" Bertram shouted. "Fire!" The low song of the bowstrings thrummed through the air even as the first enemy arrows rattled off Bertram's shield. Though the bows were little danger to the knights, they were doing their work against the more lightly armoured infantry. Across the river, several more men had gone down, and someone on Ruprecht's bank was screaming, a thin high sound that spoke of an arrow in the guts.

Ruprecht spurred his horse into a gallop, calling, "Forward!" Even as Bertram urged his own steed on and lowered his lance, he had to spare a heartbeat of grudging admiration for the Graf: first up out of the river, he would be the most vulnerable to the charging horsemen ahead. Their charge slowed as they rode into the water that churned almost up to the horses' bellies, froth drenching the riders' legs. Bertram leaned forward in the saddle, urging his mount as the horse gathered its strength beneath him for the plunge upward.

The guns spoke again; a wide spray of blood fanning out from a shattered helmet as another man fell backwards from his steed. Ahead, a bright lancetip tearing a streak of splintered wood from Ruprecht's shield as the Graf's own lance swung harmlessly past his man. He braced his own weapon against the rider coming down the bank at him.

The shock of their meeting nearly knocked him from the saddle; his own blow landed squarely on his foe's chest, but there was not enough momentum behind it to either pierce or unhorse. About him, the riders were dropping their lances and drawing swords. Bertram kicked his horse hard sideways to dodge a last lance-thrust from one of his foe's Gleven-flankers and pulled his blade free, wheeling to chop down at his enemy.

The man parried hard; steel clanged and sparked on steel as they traded blows, Bertram trying to bear the other man down with his strength and weight. His foe was good, swinging the heavy blade with the easy speed of a lifetime's training: one of his blows glanced ringingly off Bertram's helm, knocking it sideways to half-block his vision.

But Bertram had fought in worse gear: the askew helmet did not stop him from hooking the other man's shield with the outside corner of his own, forcing the opening that let him bring his sword down with his full strength upon the joint of arm and shoulder, shearing through the mail rings and cutting deep into the bone.

The blood spurted hot into Bertram's face as his foe reeled back, his momentum helping Bertram to wrench his sword free and strike again, his tip sinking in deeply over the rim of the other's breastplate.

Bertram disengaged, his eyes flickering about for his next target. The surviving horsemen were all engaged; he turned to the aid of his Gleven-fellows, striking from the flank at the broad-shouldered man who was systematically hammering Wilhelm's shield into pieces, then wheeling just in time to block the blow that would have taken Hans' arm.

From the corner of his eye, he saw Ruprecht's sword stabbing in beneath the helm of the knight he battled; then Bertram was busy defending himself again, hacking and cutting in a flurry of blows. Heinrich's foot-soldiers had closed in before Ruprecht's could cross the river; one struck hard from behind at Bertram's leg, and he only managed to deflect it with his shield-rim by sheer luck before bringing his blade down to cave in the man's iron-bound cap of hard leather.

But the mercenaries were running up the bank now; through the noise of battle and the ringing the gun-blasts had left in his ears, Bertram could distantly hear the battle-cry of the Bear's Paw Company, "Glück!"

The battle went swiftly after that: it was not long before Heinrich's men had all been brought down, leaving Ruprecht's troops tired and bloodied, but victorious. After a brief conference with Paul on the subject of plunder, agreeing that the Bear's Paw should have half of whatever was worth taking away from the battlefield, Bertram deputized three of his men to search the bodies together with three of Paul's soldiers; then turned to seeing to the wounded. Despite their disadvantage of position, Ruprecht's forces had fared better than he had expected.

There were only twelve of their own men dead, plus five mercenaries; no more than thirty-five with wounds that would keep them from marching on and fighting. Of those who had been killed or seriously wounded, only eight had been among the mounted warriors who had borne the brunt of the fighting; but it was always thus, for even the light horsemen had better armour than most of those who fought on foot. Unfortunately, Ritter Dietrich was among the dead, and the loss of a knight was a great one, but Heinrich had lost three to their one.

When Bertram and Paul had done their best to stanch and bandage the bleeding of the wounded, Ruprecht directed that those who could not go on should be taken back across the river to the wagons with the dead, together with the fifteen horses they had captured alive, and there withdraw well out of sight to wait for their return. That done, the Graf signalled that the rest should gird themselves again and march forward.

The sun was just past midday when they came upon the village. It was a large settlement, with perhaps as many as two hundred houses and three or four times that number of adult inhabitants. Ruprecht detailed six Gleven to ride about the edges and kill anyone who tried to get away with a call for help. He did not bother with any of the folk working in the fields, simply rode straight for the great oak tree in the center of the village square and grabbed the nearest peasant-man by his collar.

"Bring to me whoever is in charge here," the Graf said in a pleasant tone. "If he is not here in the time it takes to say two Paternosters, we shall begin to burn the village and slaughter every soul in it."

The peasant ran as though the hosts of Hell were at his heels - truly so, Bertram thought, his lips twisting bitterly at the irony - and within moments a better-dressed man was striding out of the door of the best house on the square. The village headman's ruddy face paled at the sight of the army ranked before him beneath the raptor-banner of Falkenstein, and he hastened to fling himself to his knees before Ruprecht's horse.

"What do you want of us, noble Graf Ruprecht?" he asked pleadingly. Drops of sweat trickled down his pale cheeks; his dark eyes were wide with a hopelessness that Bertram had seen many times before - often on the faces of men who wept and begged him not to strike. If Bertram had been closer, he knew that he would have smelled the familiar stink of fear rising sharply from the man's plump body: he judged it even odds that the peasant would loose bladder or bowels.

"Call out all your able-bodied men, with no weapons or knives on their persons. I will have your stores of food, animals, and such other things as we choose, and then I will burn this village as a message to your overlord Graf Heinrich. However, if you and your folk obey, you will be allowed to live; if you try to fight, every living creature in this village will die. The same thing will happen if you try to get a message out, for my men have you surrounded outside the village and they will signal me if they see anyone running. Do you understand me?"

The headman nodded, biting his lip as the tears flooded to his eyes. His life, hereafter, would depend solely on the lords' mercy: the best he and his folk could hope for hereafter was to be enserfed, bound for the rest of their lives to work the fields of others. Yet that choice, at least to a peasant, was better than trying to fight and being cut down, and after a moment he turned and began to shout orders in a cracked voice. Ruprecht spoke briefly to Paul; the mercenary commander, in turn, directed a number of his men to check the villagers for weapons and line them up in rough cordons in the square.

"Is this everybody?" the Graf asked the headman.

"Yes, noble Graf...except for Peter, he is lying in bed with a fever, and Josef, he broke his leg two days ago when he fell off a ladder..."

Ruprecht cut him off with a curt gesture. "Good. Men of mine will accompany a few of them to collect your wagons and round up your animals; the rest will bring out your food and goods for loading. Bertram and Paul, choose twenty men each and sweep the houses. Tell those within them to take what they will of what is left and come to the square if they value their lives."

Bertram selected his twenty from his Gleve and the footsoldiers, including young Eckhardt after a little thought. Curtly he directed them: two men to a house, watch each other's backs and shout for help if there was any trouble, and try not to kill if they could avoid it. The villagers were docile enough now, but they could turn in a moment if any serious fighting broke out: Bertram had seen it happen before, any number of times.

Methodically the pairs of soldiers worked from house to house to clear out food and valuables: one man would stand with sword drawn, glowering menacingly at the women and old men or children inside to make sure none of them tried to hit his companion from behind as he rifled their belongings, then delivering Ruprecht's message.

There was enough to steal, for this had been a prosperous village: silver and bronze ornaments, a few worthwhile weapons and mismatched pieces of armour; even bolts of good linen and wool. Bertram smiled grimly as he passed over an iron cauldron: it was too bulky to be worth hauling back, but once the Company had been in such straits that one of his comrades had tried to knife him for the right to loot a pot not half the size. Thus I have come up in the world, he thought in disgust.

"Hai!" Wilhelm said, breaking Bertram out of the dangerous reverie he had very nearly fallen into. Something clanged on the floor. "None of that, girl."

Bertram looked around to see his Gleve-companion holding a pale-haired maiden with her arm twisted up high behind her, her back bent so that her small breasts arched out. She could not be more than thirteen or fourteen, he judged. An iron skillet on the floor by her feet showed what had happened: she had undoubtedly tried to brain Wilhelm, and - Bertram realized with sickening resignation as his second unsheathed his dagger with his free hand and cut down the front of her shift - was about to get raped for her pains.

"No noise, and stop struggling, or I'll kill you," Wilhelm grunted. The girl's feeble wrigglings ceased at once: she stood stock-still in his arms, trembling like a doe in the grasp of the hounds.

"Good work, this searching houses," Bertram said, reaching out to pluck the dagger from Wilhelm's hand before the soldier could protest. "But I like the look of those tits, and I don't want your seconds. Out: I'll catch up with you in a few minutes, and if that silver cross from three houses back never gets counted in the plunder, no one will know but us."

Wilhelm looked at him a moment, then shrugged phlegmatically and shoved the girl across to Bertram, departing as Bertram pushed her towards the bed. Her shoulders felt unbearably soft and delicate beneath his hands, as though he could tear her apart by tightening his grip carelessly; the tears were spilling from her blue eyes now like streams tumbling over the rim of a snow-edged mountain pool.

As soon as the door closed behind his Gleve-man, Bertram let go of the girl. "Don't say anything," he said harshly. She shook her head, staring wild-eyed and backing away from him. "Take whatever you have left that you want to keep and get to the square: Graf Ruprecht will fire the houses soon." Bertram stepped up on the bed, shifting his weight until the timbers creaked rhythmically for the length of an Ave.

"How...how can I thank you?" she quavered tearfully when he stepped down again. "Why...?"

"Light a candle to Maria for me," Bertram grated, "and pray for the soul of an evil man." For there had been enough women like her that he could do nothing for, and most of them were dead. He whirled and stamped out, not forgetting to fumble at his breech-tie as he stepped through the door.

"That was fast enough," Wilhelm said.

"You learn to be fast, if you want to spew your load, grab your loot, and get out with a whole arse too," Bertram replied. "Come on, there's more work in front of us."

When the whole village had been ransacked and everything worth taking piled on the villagers' own wagons, Ruprecht tersely gave the order to fire the buildings. The flames leapt greedily from thatch to thatch, sparks leaping up brilliant against the black streams of smoke that billowed into the air.

As soon as the last one had caught, Ruprecht nudged his horse forward, and his army followed him, the wagons rumbling behind with their plundered oxen and horses. As swift a march as they could manage back across the border; then, when they had gone far enough, they would rest in safety, and be at Burg Falkenstein the following day. Bertram had seldom seen a campaign run so smoothly, but he knew that the beginning of a war would not necessarily promise how it would end.

Chapter Five

Margerite was sitting in Kai's chamber with the seneschal and Ruprecht's bailiffs, discussing the taxes levied by the Graf on the various villages in his lands and how they should be adjusted for the war, when she heard the signal horn blowing distantly outside. Without waiting for either of the men to respond, she leapt to her feet, running down the spiral staircase and out into the courtyard, across to the round guard tower at the gateway to the outer bailey. The soldier who stood at the foot there was fully armoured, but his helmet was resting by his feet, and he showed no sign of alarm.

"I heard the horn," Margerite panted. "What does it signal? Are foes approaching?"

The guard tipped his head back, looking down at her from his lanky height and giving her a gap-toothed grin. "Not unless you have some complaint of your husband...forgive me, Frowe Gräfin. I did not mean to be impudent."

The sudden wash of relief that flowed over Margerite at his news left her light-headed, too joyful for anger at the casual taunt the soldier might have given any village girl, but she could not let it pass. "Remember," Margerite said coldly, "that I am mistress of this castle, and until the Graf has come back, I am your highest commander. Let us begin again. Tell me what the horn-call means." She stared up into the soldier's pale eyes until his gaze dropped, and he hung his head a moment before straightening as he would have before a male superior.

"Frowe Gräfin, the signal-call says that one of Graf Ruprecht's men has reached the outer guard, and reports that all is well."

"Fetch him to me. I shall await him in the Great Hall."

When the messenger entered, helm dangling loosely from his hand by its strap, Margerite was glad to see that Ruprecht had sent his squire on before: he must expect a free road back to Burg Falkenstein. Wolfram bowed low before her. The Knappe's face was streaked with dust and sweat, his square jaw black with several days' growth of beard and his thick dark hair disheveled, but he was grinning, his blue eyes alight as he spoke.

"Most noble Frowe Gräfin, I bring you good news," he said. "We met the first forces of our foe as we crossed the river, and Graf Ruprecht led us on to victory over them. He rode at the head of the van in the charge across the ford, and he brought down the first among Heinrich's knights with mighty blows; though he was in the thick of the fight, no sword could pierce his bright armour, nor any craft break through his guard. I myself rode beside him, and slew my man, my first kill in battle; after that there were others, for we utterly destroyed all those who stood against us, and that will be a great blow to Graf Heinrich. And our arms were strengthened by the thought of the fair frowe who waited for us, for with the memory of your bright eyes and white hands serving as our battle-banner, we could not be defeated."

Margerite stroked Kobolt, who lay purring in her lap, and smiled graciously at the young man. "Your news brings me all the joy I could hope for. You are a brave Knappe, and I am sure Graf Ruprecht is as proud of you as I am. But tell me more, Wolfram, for I am sure more than that happened in the days you were gone."

"First the Graf rode to Burg Düsterstein to deliver the news of war, with the strewing of ashes and the sounding of thunder. After that, we crossed into Graf Heinrich's land again, and that was where we won the first victory of the war. And then we rode on to one of his villages, stripping it of food and goods and burning it behind us - but that is a lesser matter, for they were peasants, who gave up without a fight." The disappointment was clear on Wolfram' grimy face as he spoke the last words. Margerite kept herself from laughing at him only with an effort.

"A lesser matter in terms of knightly glory, perhaps, but no little one in terms of conducting a war, as you will soon learn, my young courtier," Margerite said gently. "Can you tell me how much plunder you took, and of what sort?"

Wolfram' brow creased, and he squinted off into the shadows behind her as if he were trying to make the answer pass before his eyes. "There were...a number of wagons, several more than we had brought with us...twelve, perhaps? Please, Frowe Gräfin, do not cast the lightning of your angry gaze upon me if I cannot remember, for the Graf did not ask me to take account of what we got, and I was riding in front beside him the whole while."

"As is your duty," Margerite assured him. "Well, I shall know soon enough. How long will it be before the train arrives back?"

"I would say that they are but three or four hours behind me, radiant Frowe Gräfin. Graf Ruprecht sent me on ahead, that you might make ready to receive the men home."

Margerite nodded, well-pleased. The news of the plunder that Ruprecht had taken was especially welcome, for that would nicely fill out Burg Falkenstein's storehouses and make it easier to keep their mercenaries in good humour. And if the war dragged on through harvest-time, in spite of all the supplies she had fetched back from Freiburg, Ruprecht's folk would need every crust of bread and dreg of wine they could get in order to make it through to the next harvest. But most of all, she was glad at the news that Ruprecht would be home soon, alive and unharmed.

"And so I shall. Run to the kitchens and call Berthe to me - no, wait. Gertrude!"

Gertrude stepped into the hall at once. "Your wish, frowe?"

"Bring two large cups of the best wine, for Wolfram has ridden hard and brought joyful tidings today. Ruprecht is coming home!"

Gertrude was back in moments, pouring out the wine for her mistress and the Knappe. Margerite lifted her goblet. "Wolfram, I drink in thanks for Graf Ruprecht's success, and in thanks and blessing to the good squire who has brought this news to lift my heart."

"And I, in turn, drink to the beauty of the Frowe Gräfin, to whom all our battles and our bravery are dedicated," Wolfram replied. They touched rims and drank. Wolfram drained his goblet's bowl empty, for which Margerite did not reproach him, for he had clearly ridden hard to get her husband's message to her as soon as he might.

But she only sipped, for there would be much to be done if a feast were to be arranged so quickly - and it must, for economy with their food would do no good if the soldiers were not encouraged and kept in good heart by being allowed to celebrate their victories - and provision made for listing and storing Ruprecht's plunder as well.

The feast went by in a blur for Margerite. She paid little attention to the succulent flesh of the roasted capon before her, or the sweet hot bread; she was too caught up in the sight of her husband alive and beside her, his golden hair flying as he laughed and shouted toasts to his victorious men. Ruprecht was so strong, so vital, and he could easily have been lost to her: with all her heart, she thanked Mother Maria that he had come back safe.

It was late when they at last arose from the table, leaving the courtyard to the ribald singing and raucous noisemaking of the soldiers. Margerite expected Ruprecht to come to her room with her - they had been so long apart! - but when they reached her door, her husband only kissed her once, and said, "Sleep well, my love. We are both tired, and there is much to do tomorrow."

Margerite was disappointed, but there was little she could say. A wife had the right to demand the marriage-duties from her husband, even as a husband did from his wife, but if Ruprecht were exhausted after his campaign, it would be unjust of her to press him. "Good night, my beloved," Margerite answered, watching him go, then turning to open her door. Gertrude had put everything in good order, and Cundrîê had already come and gone, leaving her night-draught steaming on the table.

She drank it down gratefully, barely wrinkling her nose at the musty aftertaste, and let her maid undress her for bed. Again she was flying, circling high above the castle. Beneath the strange shimmering that seemed to half-hide it from her sight, she could see the leaping fires in the courtyard, the little dark shadows of men stumbling about in their ruddy light; and a small candle seemed to burn pure and clear at the top of one of the round towers overlooking the ravine.

Fly onwards, my falcon-queen, the familiar voice whispered to her. Fly east; fly with all haste, the wind in your wings - hurry, lest you come too late!

She narrowed her wings, plunging through the cold night-air like an arrow - not thinking of the target, yet sure of her flight. The hills fell away beneath her; she swept across the river-valley, the moonlit water rippling silver beneath her, and up again, over dark woods and gray crags, to the great square castle that sat high upon the rocky mountainside. Beneath her, the helms of the sentries on the walls gleamed like silver-sheened pearls in the moonlight.

Most of the windows were dark, black arrow-slits dull as scars against the gray stone walls, but light shone through one, and it was to that one she flew, swooping through the insubstantial veil of glass to come to a perch upon the back of a huge oaken chair. Three men sat within, talking wearily in the light of the low-burning candles. All three were brown-haired and broad-built, dressed in fine silks and velvets, but one was older, his hair and thick beard grizzled and eyes scored by the deep-graving claws of age, and even sitting, he was taller than the other two by a good half a handspan.

The others were young men, alike enough to be brothers, with the same rounded faces and small features; but where one's face was lively, with an uptilted nose and firm-set mouth, the other's seemed sullen and misbalanced. A pang of unease went through her as she looked at the young men, for it seemed to her that she had seen the second before, but she could not recall where or when...could not recall who...

The older man spoke, and it seemed to the falcon that his voice echoed within her head, as though she were whispering along with him.

"Nikolaus, why do you think that simply fortifying the border will have more effect upon Ruprecht than raiding across into his lands? Explain this to me again."

The sullen one raised his left forefinger, the candlelight glinting painfully from the graven silver that ringed it. "What does he want? He wants Burg Düsterstein, but he is not strong enough to take it; he knows if he besieges, we will come upon him from behind and hammer him against the castle walls like a clay pot on an anvil."

"Not so very like," the older man said dryly. "Not if he has more guns than those he showed at Burg Düsterstein, and a larger force in reserve than the army that slew my good knights Helmbrecht and Wolfgang and Albrecht at the ford north of Burg Mittlefeld, together with all their men." He shook his head. "Who would have thought Ruprecht would bring so many men for a simple raid on a village? But if he has such an army, we are not the stronger by much: I would not wish to engage him in battle unless we could make sure that the ground was on our side. And if that is so, he will know that, and be bold. Christopher?"

"Father!" said the other young man enthusiastically. "Ruprecht cannot be allowed to get away with what he has done unscathed. I say that we should ride out against him tomorrow. Only by hurting him can we make him draw back, and spend his men and strength in protecting his own."

"But he will not strike too soon again," Nikolaus said. "I think that he will be guarding his own lands already, for he must expect us to return blow for blow. Let us threaten, but not act yet: let Ruprecht wear his men down with marching, and sap their courage with waiting, while we hoard our strength and watch until we can catch him unawares."

"And how much should we bear before we act?" Christopher asked. "This is no council of priests, to suggest that we suffer Ruprecht's depredations in Christian humility. Let us go against him now, for that will save us much in men and substance which otherwise Ruprecht will destroy, if we give him the chance."

The older man leaned his chin thoughtfully on his hand, looking at the two before him. "The counsel of the elder son is rash, and that of the younger son is cautious. We have spoken thus all evening without a decision, and the candles are burning down." He picked up the quill pen before him, dipping its point slowly into the ink and looking at the blank parchment lying pale upon the table.

"We shall garrison our border-castles with our full strength," he decided. "Tomorrow I shall call up the musters from Burgs Hellental and Waldenstein. Let those poor men whose homes Ruprecht burned be given such weapons as they can wield as well, and pressed into strengthening the border-guard: since we must do our best to give them the means of survival, they may as well do something to earn it, and they can hardly till the ground in peace with Ruprecht threatening at our borders. But to Ruprecht, I shall send the message that Burg Düsterstein is ours, lawfully given us by the Kaiser some thirty years ago and lawfully held. We shall not surrender it to him, and if he will not withdraw and pay reparation for what he has done, it will be feud unto the death."

"Father," said Christopher, "a thought has come to me. If we are to wait and send messages and refuse to act, might we delay Ruprecht for a time by offering him a price for Burg Düsterstein - a price that we know he cannot meet? For we all know that the Kaiser has done his best to put an end to private wars within the Empire: if we do not finish this swiftly, as I think we should, we may find that greater lords than ourselves are displeased, but if we show that we have made an effort to resolve the matter, then we will not be in the wrong if a judgement should be made between us. And I think that Ruprecht must have something other than Burg Düsterstein in mind, for I see no reason why he should have chosen to pick a quarrel over it now. If we write to him, he may return some negotiation, and we may have a better chance of finding out what he really wants."

"I agree with that," Nikolaus said swiftly. "And even if Ruprecht rejects the offer at once, as he will, it may lead him into thinking that we have grown weaker, and thus into acting rashly."

"That is a strange ploy," the old man mused, looking at his two sons. "But I will agree that there may be more behind Ruprecht's declaration than the desire to gain back Burg Düsterstein, and that it may be worthwhile to wait to act until we have found out why. So be it: I shall write the letter, offering him the castle - at a price Kaiser Karl would not like to meet."

"Well-done, Father!" Nikolaus enthused.

Christopher smiled ruefully, one corner of his mouth twisting downward. "I would still prefer to act now, but I am glad my plan has found favour with you. Goodnight, Father."

The two brothers left the room. Their father stared at the pale parchment for a moment, then sighed, dipping his pen into the ink once more and beginning to write.

Take wing again, fair falcon, the voice said in her mind. She beat her wings hard, rising from the back of the chair; though the wind of her leap into flight did not so much as bend a candleflame, she was aloft, diving through the window again and out into the cool night. Fly home, fly swiftly, come back to me...

216

Margerite awoke slowly, blinking her eyes against the shaft of sunlight slanting in through one of her windows across the bed. Gertrude was leaning over her, gently shaking her shoulders.

"Frowe, forgive me," Gertrude said, "but I could let you sleep no longer. The Graf wishes to see you as soon as you are ready."

Margerite yawned, stretching out her arms and arching her back. She had dreamed...it was fading from her mind already, but she had dreamed of flying. And a castle room... had she really dreamed Graf Heinrich's second son, arguing with his father and brother about something? She could not remember: her head was still muzzy with sleep, and standing up made it no better.

"Brew me some mint tea, and see that it is strong," she told Gertrude as the maid began to dress her. "You should have awakened me earlier, for it is unhealthy to sleep too long."

"You would not waken, frowe. Perhaps you drank too deeply at the feast last night?"

"But I did not. I watered my wine and sipped carefully, as my husband did, for we both knew that there was much work ahead of us. He did not even come to my chamber..."

Gertrude patted her shoulder. "I know. Well, I shall fetch your mint tea, frowe, and tell the Graf that you will be a little while." Then the maid glanced up, her brown eyes glittering like clear glass. "If you want only to sleep in the morning for no clear cause, and are beginning to feel tired all the time... frowe, could it be that you are carrying a child already? You and the Graf have done more than enough to make one."

Margerite laid her hand upon her flat belly, a little leap of excitement fluttering in her heart. "Now pray to Maria that it is so! Oh, nothing could make me more joyful than to bear my husband's child so soon."

Gertrude sniffed. "If it is so, we shall see if you are still saying that when you are waddling like a cow and squatting to piss five times an hour. And I would wager a silver mark that you will regret those words when you are screaming in childbed and cursing every man that ever set his seed in a woman."

"I have seen as many babies birthed as you have," Margerite replied calmly. "And I have never known a woman who did not say that all the pain and travail of Eve's curse was worth it, when a healthy child was lifted to suckle at her breast."

"That is so, frowe, but it is a long road from here to there. Still...do you think you are bearing? It may be so, for you have not had your courses since you came to this castle. Will you tell the Graf yet?"

"You know that they do not come upon me as regularly as they do with some women," Margerite admitted. "But still, if they do not come soon...No, I shall leave it until I am certain. Ruprecht should not be bothered by raising a hope that may come to nothing, least of all with his war to lead. Bring my tea to me in the great hall."

Ruprecht looked fresh and rested, his blue eyes clear and a small smile on his face as he petted the gray head of one of his mastiffs. "Are you well, my wife?" he asked as Margerite sat down beside him. "Your maid said that she had trouble rousing you."

The surging excitement of the thought that she might even now be carrying Ruprecht's child still echoing in her body, Margerite touched her belly gently. "I am very well, my husband. Gertrude told me that you wanted to see me."

"Always," Ruprecht said, stroking a finger down her cheek. "But there is a matter I should particularly like you to see to. Although our battle at the ford was a great success, I did lose a few men there. I want you to speak with Bertram, to find out how matters stand with their families and be sure that they are well provided for."

"That is a noble thought." Margerite did not wish to speak the words that came to her mind next, but she knew that she had to. "But...are such things provided for in our accounting? Even with what you brought back, we will have little enough left over from the expenses of the war to maintain Burg Falkenstein and its lands in the next year."

"One way or another, the wives and children of the dead will be in our care. And my men will fight better if they know that, should they fall in battle for me, their families will not suffer for it."

"Then I will find the money for it," Margerite replied, smiling back up at him.

"And there is one in particular I should like you to see to yourself. Ritter Dietrich was among those killed; if you will, go to his wife and see what her plans are - whether she wishes to remarry and stay on the land he held from me, to return to her family, or to come here to Burg Falkenstein for a time. In any case, I will see to it that she is able to do as she desires, for Dietrich was a good man and a good comrade, and he died as befitted a knight. Bertram will escort you, for he knows the way well."

"That is a sad duty, but I shall undertake it, and have Father Hans say a Mass for his soul." Margerite's voice trailed off: though she knew it was a grievous lapse in faith, she could not help wondering if Christ could truly hear the wine-slurred prayers of Burg Falkenstein's priest.

Ruprecht sighed. "You are a good woman," he said quietly. "I owe Günther much for bringing us together. Now, you shall probably find Bertram either out in the yard with the men, or in the chamber where he looks after the affairs of the soldiers - you know where that is?"

Margerite shook her head.

"It is in the guard-tower above the chapel, on the top floor. Margerite, are you sure you are well? You should eat something, for you are very pale. Did your dreams disturb you last night?"

"I dreamed…I do not remember what." Margerite's stomach was beginning to turn slightly, but when the servant laid bread and cheese before her, she found that she had eaten more than half of it almost without realizing as they spoke. "But there is truly nothing for you to worry about. If my dreams have been unquiet, it is only to be expected in times of war."

"Well, you may sleep in peace for a little. I think Graf Heinrich will be some time in gathering himself from the blow I have dealt him; I should not be surprised if he tries to negotiate now, though I do not expect much to come of it, since he is a stubborn man and his eldest son Christopher is much the same."

Margerite frowned, a faint sense of unease quivering within her like a little fish in deep water. The name seemed to echo up from the lost depths of her dream…Christopher and Nikolaus, Christopher and…

"I wish I could remember my dream better," she said wistfully. "Before, they were always so clear in my mind upon waking, but since you left on campaign, they have come back to me only in wisps and shards."

Ruprecht looked down at the mastiff to his left, absent-mindedly taking a crust from the table and feeding it to the great dog. "You have nothing to fear, beloved. Be easy and joyful in your mind, for I am sure that your dreams bode nothing but well for us."

As Margerite went up the stairs of the guard tower, Kobolt bounding behind her, she began to feel her heart sinking within her. She would not have confronted Bertram in his stronghold for anything other than Ruprecht's request, for while he might be their servant, this was truly his realm as much as the kitchens were Berthe's or the mews Johann's, where she and Ruprecht might command, but not rule.

But she gathered her courage about her as she would have pulled her cloak tight against snow-spattering winter winds, and opened the door without knocking. Bertram started up from behind his table, thrusting something into the pouch at his belt. His hazel eyes were wide and angry, and Margerite could see his white teeth snarling like a boar's tusks inside the black thicket of his beard.

"What do you want, Frowe Gräfin?" he asked roughly. "This is no place for you."

Kobolt leapt onto the table, pouncing upon the parchments there as if he had heard a mouse rustling inside them and knocking them askew. Bertram pushed his chair back, the heavy muscles of his shoulders and arms bunching beneath his plain gray tunic as his hand flickered towards the hilt of his sword. A spark of fear shot along Margerite's nerves: if she tried to stop him from striking, he could brush her hand away like a butterfly, and her rank would do her no good if he did not choose to acknowledge her. But he dropped his hand abruptly, glaring with the fury of one who had been thwarted.

"Kobolt!" Margerite said sharply, though she could not help feeling a guilty gleam of pleasure at Bertram's discomfiture. "Bad cat."

Kobolt looked up at Bertram with an insolent purring chirp, then jumped down with a hard kick of his back legs that sent the uppermost page flying, scampering over to twine about Margerite's ankles and gaze up at her adoringly.

"Frowe Gräfin," Bertram said icily, "you should put that animal outside." He held up one of the parchments so that Margerite could see how the ink had been smeared about on it.

Unwilling to give him the satisfaction of overcoming her, Margerite drew herself up and said, "I need the names of those men killed in the battle, and an account of their families."

She did not expect the frown that darkened Bertram's brow further, nor the sharp edge to his voice as he said, "Why?"

"Because the Graf requires it! Do you pay so little attention to those who fight beside you that you cannot tell me these things?"

Bertram sat down again, back straight and forearms crossed on the table, his eyes staring at a point above Margerite's head as he spoke, his voice flat and precise. "In order of rank, the dead are Ritter Dietrich, Karl son of Wolfhelm..." As he listed the names, Margerite felt a brief pang of guilt. If nothing else, the deaths of those under his command had clearly not passed without touching the grim man. But she pressed on, nevertheless.

"And their families?"

"Ritter Dietrich was two years married, and had no children. His wife Alfrida is the third daughter of Ritter Walther von Marienfoss, a vassal of Count-Palatine Robert the Tenacious. Karl had three children by his first wife, all of whom are grown, none by his second, and four young ones by his third, as well as his mother, to see to. Richard had..."

Margerite had a good memory, and had no doubt that she would not forget any on Bertram's list, but he was looking at her as though he had won a victory of some sort.

"They shall be seen to," she said crisply. "Now, the Graf has charged me to see to Ritter Dietrich's wife, and he tells me that you will be able to escort me there. I shall be ready to ride shortly: see to it that our horses are ready, along with whatever guard you think we may need."

She withdrew without further words, following Kobolt down the stairs and out. She would lurk inside the ruins of the pleasure garden for the count of twenty Paternosters and twenty Aves, so that Bertram might not think her too eager for his convenience; but she could not bring herself to delay longer, for Ritter Dietrich's poor wife must be suffering doubly in the knowledge of her husband's death and the fear for her own future.

Margerite and Bertram rode down towards the castle gates in silence. As they neared the main guardtowers, a sharp stink reached Margerite's nostrils, the smell of sulphur and scorched brass. "Faugh! What is that?" she asked. "It smells as though the Devil himself has passed by."

Bertram pointed to the round tower overlooking the ravine. "Jochanan has set his gunpowder works in the top chamber there. If he blows himself up, he will not take much else with him."

"How dangerous is his work?"

"Although Jochanan seldom has to fight hand-to-hand when battle is joined, he risks his life more often than any member of the Company. Have you not noticed his missing fingers? Either of those explosions, or a few dozen others, could as easily have taken his head off. He lives a charmed life, perhaps because..."

Bertram chopped his words off abruptly, turning his face away from Margerite as though to hide an expression that might have betrayed something to her. Though that mess of beard hides his face well enough, Margerite thought.

Ritter Dietrich's house was a fair distance from Ruprecht's castle. It was past time for the midday meal by the time Margerite and Bertram came within sight of the small stone manor nestled in its green valley between the low forested hills. The man who came out to take their horses was wizened and badly stooped by age, but he moved spryly enough as he led the mounts to the stable. A young girl opened the door for them, showing them along the narrow stone corridor to the manor's hall.

Frowe Alfrida was, Margerite judged, in her late twenties, but a dusting of gray already dimmed her light brown hair, and she rose with care to greet them. Her thin face was very white, the hollows beneath her red-rimmed eyes shockingly dark, and the black linen of her dress hung from her sharp collarbones as though it had been made for a larger woman.

"Greetings, and welcome, Frowe Gräfin, Hauptmann Bertram," she said. Her voice was low and clear, and would have been beautiful, if it had not been torn by the ragged edges of grief. Margerite felt her own heart wrenching within her with a sharp twinge of sympathy and fear, for she knew that it could have been herself standing there in a mourning dress, waiting to see what tidings would follow her husband's death - could yet be. Sword-edge, lance-tip, crossbow-bolt...any of them could leave her as bereft as the widowed Alfrida.

"Greetings to you, Frowe Alfrida," Margerite replied. "Sit you down, for I would speak with you - Bertram, you may leave us."

Bertram stood there a moment, looking at the two women. Abruptly he bowed to Alfrida. "I grieve the loss of your husband," he said. "I was proud to ride with Ritter Dietrich, and he died bravely."

Alfrida nodded, and Bertram departed the room, leaving Margerite alone with the new widow.

"Can I offer you food or drink, Frowe Gräfin?" Alfrida asked dully when they had seated themselves. "I know that you must have a long ride from Burg Falkenstein."

"Both would be welcome."

The fare Alfrida's servants brought in was simple, but good: white bread, pork sausages heavily spiced with pepper and sage, fresh summer cheese with a sprinkling of caraway seeds through it and a rich, honeyed brown beer.

"Frowe Alfrida," Margerite said as she began to cut her sausages, "the Graf has sent me to tell you that we at Burg Falkenstein share your grief at the loss of your husband, of whom Graf Ruprecht thought most highly."

"Dietrich was ever loyal to Graf Ruprecht," Alfrida said. "I do not doubt that he died willingly for his lord. It was a better death than that of my first husband, who fell to the plague two years ago."

"Even so. Now, the Graf would know what your wishes are, if you have thought on them..." Margerite fell silent. It seemed harsh to make a newly-widowed woman choose her future so soon, but that was the way of things.

"My dowry was not great," Alfrida said slowly. "And though it will be hard to live here without Dietrich, it would go harder with me if I were to leave."

"Graf Ruprecht wondered if you might mean to remarry and stay on these lands."

Alfrida rested her chin on the tip of her narrow forefinger, her blue eyes darkening in thought. "Has he a husband in mind for me? When I have finished my time of mourning for Dietrich, I will be willing to marry again."

"I do not know if there is anyone in his mind. He has not spoken to me of it, if that is so."

It occured to Margerite that Alfrida might be a good match for Wolfram: the Knappe might well win his spurs in Ruprecht's war. Young and impractical as he seemed to be, it would be to his gain to wed a woman of some knowledge and experience, and perhaps his light heart would serve to lift Alfrida's spirits.

"Tell the Graf, then, that I shall stay here, and keep the holding in order, trusting in his protection until a fitting husband can be found for me. Assure him, also, that he need not fear loss of war-trained men or revenues from here: I know well how to hold these lands."

"I shall tell him that," Margerite promised.

The meeting with Alfrida had left her feeling saddened and thoughtful: lost in her own concerns, she barely noticed the grim figure of Bertram shadowing her like a stormcloud across the sun. What would she do if Ruprecht were killed in one of his battles? She - and her child, if she bore one - would be the inheritors of his lands: Burg Falkenstein, and all the lesser castles and villages that went with it, would be hers to hold. But could she hold them alone, without a man to protect her? Some women did just that: even with a living husband, Margerite knew that she might have to command Burg Falkenstein's defense if the castle were attacked while Ruprecht was away.

However, as a widowed Gräfin, she would be a most
desirable prize: she could hardly expect not to remarry,
and she might have to do that swiftly, lest a worse husband
be found for her than she could find for herself. Or...she
glanced across at Bertram, hulking on his horse beside her,
and shuddered. If Ruprecht were killed, would he try to
force her into marriage, raping his way into title and power?
Such things had happened before: a marriage could be
forced and consummated before Margerite could send for
help. If the thought had come to Bertram's mind already -
accidents happened in battle all the time, and in the thick of
the fight, who could really say which weapon had struck a
man down?

Again she remembered the dark foreboding that had
come over her as she saw Bertram holding Ruprecht's
horse at Burg Hirschenburg, and shuddered. The days after
Ruprecht's return passed quickly: the plunder had to be
divided and stored, the quartering of the mercenaries seen
to - for nearly an hundred and fifty men beyond Ruprecht's
usual band were something of a strain on even Burg
Falkenstein's space - and past that, the cows, fed fat on the
burgeoning green summer grass, were coming into their full
flush of milk, which had to be made into butter and cheese
daily and stored up against the coming privations of winter
and war.

Four days had gone by when the messenger came riding
up in full armour beneath Graf Heinrich's gold and black
banner, halting his roan stallion just outside the gates of
Burg Falkenstein and waiting to be hailed in.

Ruprecht and Margerite received the messenger in the
great hall. He had few words for them, simply stating,
"Graf Heinrich sends you this," and handing over the rolled
parchment that had been tucked into his belt.

Ruprecht glanced at the seal, then drew his dagger to
break it. He read over the letter, and smiled. "You will
guest with us tonight," he said to Heinrich's messenger.
"Tomorrow I shall have a reply for you to take back.
Gertrude, see this man to guesting quarters."

When her maid had led the messenger out, Margerite reached over for the parchment. Ruprecht let her have it, watching with a faint amused curl of his lips as she read.

"This is ridiculous," Margerite said, slapping the letter down on the table. "The price Graf Heinrich names for Burg Düsterstein would buy this castle and three more like it, if one were minded to sell for a good offer. What can he mean by sending us this? Is it only an insult?"

"I think not," Ruprecht answered. "I think he wishes to delay, and perhaps find out more of my plans if he can. Well, I shall write back to him, and let him think that negotiations are continuing and that his lands will be safe for a little while. And two days hence, even as he is receiving my reply, we shall be riding towards his borders again."

This time, though the whole of the Bear's Paw Company would go with him again, including the six of Jochanan's nine handguns that would shoot, Ruprecht decided to take only half of his own men, leaving the other half at Burg Falkenstein under Bertram's command.

"Now that war has truly begun," he explained to Margerite, "I cannot risk leaving this castle too lightly defended. You have enough men to hold out if it should chance that Heinrich gets word that I am away and decides to make a direct attack on us; and since I do not mean to engage his full force if there is any way to avoid it, I will not need them."

"That sounds sensible enough," Margerite agreed. "But must it be Bertram that you leave behind?"

"Who better to guard you, and Burg Falkenstein, while I am gone? You do not have to have him eat at table beside you; you have only to trust his skills as a warrior and commander."

For a moment, Margerite felt impelled to speak of her misgivings about the dark Hauptmann. But she pressed her lips tight shut before she could begin. If Bertram were at Burg Falkenstein, there would be no risk of him arranging an accident for Ruprecht in battle; and she would be alert to make sure that he did not betray the castle from within.

"If that is your wish, I am well-content, my husband," she said, leaning against the solid warmth of Ruprecht's shoulder and looking lovingly up at him.

Though she was still anxious, Margerite was not as terrified for her husband this time as she had been before. To her disappointment, her courses had come upon her, and though the loss of blood left her tired, as always, some of her seething nervousness seemed to have drained away. She knew that this was natural, for when a woman did not conceive, her unhealthy humours were likely to gather in the womb until her courses purged her of them, for which reason a woman's menstrual blood was likely to corrupt whatever it touched.

And every night she dreamed. She still could not remember her dreams clearly, but she knew that she was flying in them, and that somehow they brought her comfort. Ruprecht had said that he thought they boded well, and Margerite was beginning to feel it so - to feel that, as long as she dreamed of flight and soft whispering in her ears, Ruprecht would be safe and well.

And thus it was: her husband was back after ten days, and again he came riding with wagons of plunder behind him. Ruprecht had not brought back nearly as much this time, for Heinrich's defenses were up along the border and he had been forced to travel fast and light, but Margerite cared only that he was home and victorious. And this time, he came at once to her bed as soon as he had washed, making glorious love to her before they went down to celebrate his success with his men.

When she had eaten her fill, Margerite went to walk among the soldiers, speaking warm words of praise to them, especially those who had been wounded. As she worked her way slowly around the courtyard, Paul lumbered up to her. The Bear had clearly drunk well, for the firelight showed a deep flush on his blunt face, and the tankard in his hand kept sloshing over as he waved it about. Kobolt leapt up on his chest, clinging to his leather jerkin and sniffing enthusiastically at the beer on his breath; he laughed, holding his mug up for the cat to scoop the froth from.

"Another victory for us, Frowe Gräfin!" Paul declared. "By God's Blood and all the saints, I think your husband is the best commander I have ever served under. He seems to guess every one of the enemy's moves as though Christ were sending him personal letters about it, and he had us in and out of there with no trouble, slick as a stallion's prick into a mare - beg pardon, Frowe Gräfin. This is good beer, too: I think I've drunk near half a barrelful tonight. You wouldn't guess it, would you?"

"A soldier is worthy of his hire," Margerite responded. "Graf Ruprecht is very pleased with you and your men."

"Is he? That's good, that is. Hey, cat, leave some of that beer for me - " for Kobolt, tired of playing with the froth, had stuck his muzzle into Paul's tankard and was lapping thirstily. "Do you give him beer often? He seems to like it. Will he drink wine, too?"

"He drinks from my goblet, when he can get onto the table without being noticed."

"Fine cat." The Bear scratched behind Kobolt's ears, then pushed the cat's head out of the mug and took a deep swig for himself. "A question for you, Frowe Gräfin. Are there any stocks of healing herbs you can spare for us? My own are going low, they get used up fast in the field. I have no woundwort left, and only a few handfuls of knitbone. I need more St. Johannes' Wort and sanicle, as well."

Margerite frowned. The medicinal herbs and ointments were kept in the kitchens with the culinary herbs, and she had only glanced at them briefly in her explorations of the castle, but she seemed to remember that the stocks were far lower and poorer than she had expected from the size and careful tending of the garden in the herber.

Well, it was time to start harvesting and drying this year's supply, in any case. She would see to it that it was properly done, and perhaps send down to the midwife at Tiefensee with orders that she go out and gather a larger supply, since they would need a full load of medicinals for the war.

"Come to me tomorrow, and I shall see what I can do for you."

"My thanks, Frowe Gräfin. My men will thank you too."

Margerite was in the herber the next morning, puzzling over some of the plants she did not recognise, when Gertrude came running up to her breathlessly.

"Frowe, you must come quickly. There is a woman in Tiefensee dying in labour, and no one can rouse Father Hans to give her the last rites. They say the child's arm is halfway out, but its head is still in."

"Can the midwife not turn it?"

"It is the midwife who is giving birth, frowe."

Margerite hastened out of the garden, her eyes darting about the courtyard. "You!" she shouted to the young guardsman who stood near the chapel door - was it Gertrude's Eckhardt? She thought so. "Throw a bucket of water on Father Hans and haul him out of there. Tie him on a horse if you have to, but get him down to the village. Gertrude, fetch...no, I'll do that myself. Tell someone to get Mathilde ready for me."

She hurried to the kitchen, opening the chest where the herbs were kept. If it had not been so unbefitting to her sex and station, Margerite would have cursed loudly as she squatted down and rummaged among them. There was less there than she had thought, and none of the herbs that were best for helping women to give birth.

"Frowe Gräfin?" said Wolfram' voice from behind her. Margerite rocked back on her heels, glaring up at him. "Frowe Gräfin, can I help? You seemed to be in a hurry..."

"Not unless you know where there is some wild thyme oil to be had," she snapped. "Or motherwort, or raspberry leaf, or Lady's mantle, or any of the herbs that are best for easing pain - an ointment would be best."

"Oh, but I do, Frowe Gräfin. A moment: I shall be back."

"Bring them to me in the courtyard!" Margerite shouted to him as he ran from the kitchen.

By the time she had reached the stables, Eckhardt had propped Father Hans up on a horse and was leading him along. The priest swayed dangerously in the saddle, but at least his eyes were open. Margerite mounted up, telling Gertrude to hasten down to the village as quickly as she could.

Wolfram was out of breath when he reached her, panting as if he had run up and down all the stairs in the castle without pausing for a heartbeat, but the bag in his hands bulged satisfyingly full.

"Here are all the herbs you wanted, Frowe Gräfin. There was no ointment for pain, but I have put in mandrake and hemlock, so you can make your own draught."

Margerite blinked. Those were powerful herbs, more likely to kill than to soothe - she might have chosen to bring them to a bad birthing in case there was nothing she could give but the easing of pain, but Christ and all His saints preserve her from having to use them! But there was no time to wonder about the Knappe and his herblore, if a woman was dying in the village below. She nudged Mathilde into a trot, then into a canter, overtaking Father Hans and Eckhardt within a few moments.

Once in the village square, Margerite reined in her horse, looking frantically about her. She had seen the doors closing as she rode through, and now the square was deserted save for a couple of children playing games in the dust. There was no time to waste: she dismounted and hastily tethered her horse, striding to the nearest door and banging on it.

"Frowe Gräfin!" exclaimed the plump woman who opened the door, sinking to her knees before Margerite. Margerite did not wait for her to say anything more.

"Where is the house of the midwife?" she demanded. "I have come to help with her birthing, and the priest is on his way behind me."

The peasant woman's eyes opened very wide, and her hand twitched up as if to cross herself against evil. "Frowe Gräfin, I...Frowe Gräfin, she is well attended. You do not need to trouble yourself, for I promise she is being looked after."

"Where is she?" Margerite said, only keeping her voice from rising to a shout with great effort. She did not know what was wrong with the people of Tiefensee, but whatever it was, she was in no mood to humour it. "Tell me now!"

The woman pointed, her plump finger trembling. "Down there, near the end of the street."

Margerite glanced quickly, and now she saw the roughly carved wooden plaque showing a woman nursing a baby. She did not waste any more time, but hastened quickly towards the midwife's house. She could already hear the birthing mother's moans as she neared the door; without bothering to knock, she shoved it open and entered.

The midwife's house was bigger than most of those in the village, with several rooms. The birth was not taking place in the bedroom, but on a bed of old blankets laid over straw in the Stube, the oven-warmed parlour. A dreadful stench already hung in the air: the birthing mother had loosed her bowels and bladder, their stinks sharp above the iron odour of her blood. Three women were crouching about the bed, one grasping the midwife's hand as she strained and screamed again.

Her knees were drawn up; she was half-leaning back against the wall, staring white-faced and wild-eyed between her legs. Margerite saw at once what Gertrude had told her: the child was coming neither headfirst nor breech, but had gotten stuck sideways in the birth canal, with one tiny hand protruding from its mother's bloody dilation. Clearly the women attending either did not know how to turn a child that had gotten so far down the canal, or were afraid to try; but Margerite knew that if something was not done, mother and baby would both die.

"Frowe Gräfin!" said the oldest of the women. "Frowe, you do not need to be here. We are seeing to the matter."

"Not very well! Move aside, for I believe I know what to do."

"This is no affair of yours, Frowe Gräfin," the old woman insisted stubbornly. "Please, you should not trouble yourself."

Margerite ignored her, rummaging through the bag Wolfram had given her. Among the smaller bags of dried herbs was a clay bottle, which Margerite uncorked and sniffed: Maria be thanked, it was wild thyme oil, with no hint of any stranger herbs in it. She tied up the long folds of her sleeves over her shoulders - praise Christ, she had worn one of the untailored dresses today, instead of the recut ones with their tight sleeves to the wrist - and poured the oil over her hands, crouching down between the midwife's legs as the women reluctantly made room for her. If only she could give the woman some herbs to ease her muscles, to make it easier to turn the child...but the sedatives Wolfram had brought would almost certainly kill baby, or mother, or both in their condition.

Behind her, Margerite heard a soft crooning yowl, and glanced back without thinking. Although she had not seen Kobolt come in, he was sitting against the wall by the stove, swishing his tail and staring wide-eyed at her. She would have tossed him out, but there was no time to waste on such things; she would just have to trust in the attendants to keep the cat from getting too close to the birthing.

Gently Margerite worked her hand in towards the other woman's womb, feeling up along the child's arm to its shoulder. The midwife heaved and moaned, her muscles contracting hard along her swollen belly.

"Shhh, shhh," Margerite murmured. "Be easy, for your child will be out safely soon." The baby squirmed, slippery beneath her fingers as she pushed slowly and steadily, trying to urge it up a little higher so that it could turn. She had never done this before, but at the age of twelve she had seen her mother turn a baby that was trying to come out shoulder-first.

Now it seemed to her that she could almost hear her mother's voice, a gentle murmuring within her head. Be sure that no part of the child is stuck in the birth canal, or it will not turn. Rub the mother's belly gently with the other hand, to ease the muscles as much as you can, for her body will be fighting against you...

Margerite reached up with her free hand, pressing down rhythmically as another contraction rippled over the midwife's stomach. "Stop pushing," she said breathlessly. "Let me get it back up...do you understand?"

The midwife nodded painfully, drops of sweat dripping from her darkly matted hair onto her bare breasts. "Turn..." she gasped.

"I am turning it. Be easy, let your child move."

One more gentle push, and Margerite suddenly felt the baby sliding back, the opening of the womb tightening around her hand - and, thank all the saints, the arm slipping back inside: she had been afraid that she would have to break it to get it into position. She withdrew, moving up to press against the slick mound of the midwife's belly. There was the baby's head, there its rump...

Margerite put one hand on each, trying to rotate it about. The midwife tossed her head back and screamed, her muscles all hardening as though her body were trying to armour the child within. Margerite waited until the spasm had passed, then pushed gently again, slowly kneading the baby's rump backward and its head forward.

Her shoulders and back ached from the strain already, and she could feel the sweat running down her face and between her shoulderblades - what fool had stoked the stoves so high for heating a birthing-room? But now the head was down, ready to come out. If the child's ordeal had not killed it already...but no, its heartbeat was still strong, a fluttering pulse beneath its mother's taut-stretched skin.

Or weakened it until it could not live, for children often died when their membrane ruptured too early in the birthing, as this one's had done… where was that wretched drunk of a priest? At least a layperson who knew the rite could baptize a child in cases of last resort, and there was a pot of warm water by the birthing-bed.

"Now push," Margerite told the midwife. "The child is in place; push with all your strength."

The birthing mother bore down, grasping the hand of the woman who held her so tightly that the other woman cried out, her moan a soft echo of the shriek that ripped its way through the midwife's throat. A tiny spurt of urine jetted out above the bloody lips of her vagina, but Margerite could feel the baby moving within her, and urged her on. "Again! Again, it is coming."

The midwife heaved and shuddered, panting like a hound in full chase. She was beginning to open, and Margerite caught the first glimpse of the baby's slick head. "Push down," she ordered. "Your child is beginning to crown."

A brief grimace that might have been a smile flickered across the midwife's face. She tightened her hand on her comforter once more, straining every muscle. "Maria!" she cried out. "Mother Maria, help me! Aaaah!" But the baby's head was coming out, and Margerite could feel the smile pulling hard against her own face.

"You are doing well. Keep pushing, for the head is nearly through."

The midwife's contractions were coming hard and regularly; Margerite kept talking to her, guiding her through the rushes of straining as the child's head slid free and the knob of the foremost shoulder squeezed into view. "You are almost there, be brave. The shoulder is through, it is nearly out." She held the baby's head carefully, pulling it slightly upwards to ease its body's way out. Suddenly the second shoulder popped through, and the baby slid out in a rush of slippery fluid.

Margerite nestled it against its mother's trembling thigh, patting it on its back until it gulped air and let out a high wail. But her own breath was still bated back, for she knew that the turning might have ruptured the mother's womb: she was waiting to see if a gush of blood would follow. But none did, and when the slick dark cord that still bound the child to its mother had slowed its hard pulsing, she dared to look up.

The three peasant women were still sitting about her, and she could not read the thoughts behind their furrowed brown faces, but they were gazing at her as though they expected something. But, Maria be thanked, Gertrude was standing by the door, and she at least could be relied on.

"Get me a clean string to tie off the cord with," Margerite ordered, "and see to it that there is water boiling." Gertrude had the string in her hand within moments, and Margerite tied the cord an inch from the child's navel, then sliced it through with her dagger. She watched carefully to be sure that the baby would not bleed through the cord, but her knot was holding firm. Lifting the child up - it was a boy, she saw - she handed it to Gertrude to be washed.

The midwife moaned again, more softly, and her belly gave another heave. Dark blood dribbled out of her; a tingle of warning ran through Margerite's body, but there was not much. The afterbirth was coming, and Margerite slicked her hands freshly with the wild thyme oil to help ease it out gently in a single piece - if any is left within, her mother's voice said firmly inside her head, it will fester and then the mother is sure to die in childbed fever.

But all looked well: the slick bluish-red mass was firm, the membranes separating from the womb as neatly as a deer's hide peeling away from the flesh beneath the edge of a hunter's knife, and no rush of blood followed.

"There, it is all out," Margerite said soothingly. The midwife was leaning back against the wall, breathing hard with her eyes closed. Margerite washed her hands in the pot of warm water by the birthing-bed and stood, stretching and twisting to ease the aching muscles of her back. "You may clean her up now," she said to the three attendants. One of the younger ones ducked her head, dipping a cloth into the pot and beginning to sponge away the blood and mess about the new mother's thighs and buttocks, while Margerite went to the stove to brew up some of the herbs she had brought.

They were neatly labelled in their little cloth bags: raspberry leaf, motherwort, and Lady's Mantle, just as she had asked of Wolfram. Gertrude had already gotten a second pot of water heating, and Margerite dropped the dried leaves in, watching them swirl on the surface.

"Frowe Gräfin," the older attendant said. She was standing as well now: tall and straight-backed for an old woman, her blue eyes glaring severely beneath the tangles of iron-gray hair that had escaped from her braid. "We thank you for your help, but mother and child are both well now. I would not have you trouble yourself further, for you must have much to do in these days, and need not bother yourself with the matters of lowly folk."

"But I choose to!" Margerite snapped. "You would have lost both of them if I had not come, and what would Tiefensee have done for a midwife then? Before God, I have never met anyone who would not be grateful for such help as I have given, rather than trying to chase me away. Now, whether you wish it or not, I shall stay a little while and be sure that she does not begin to bleed, and also that she drinks a good cup of the tea I am brewing for her, which will help her womb to settle itself and strengthen her in recovering from the birth."

"Frowe Gräfin, it is kind of you, but there is no need. Gerhild has plenty of brews of her own that she makes for mothers who have given birth."

"And she is hardly in a condition to make them, is she?" Margerite asked, looking back at the midwife. Gerhild, now clean and decently covered from the waist down, was gazing fondly down at the child that her younger friend was holding to her breast, but she was still deathly-white from the exhaustion of labour, and clearly too weakened even to hold up her own son.

Kobolt miaowed as if to second her words, and the old woman started, drawing her skirts back and staring down at the cat as if a fiend from Hell had come up through the floor. Angrily Margerite reached down, picking Kobolt up and cradling him in her arms - daring the peasant woman to say something about it. "And if I had not heard of this," she added sharply, "Father Hans would still be up at Burg Falkenstein, instead of...where is he, Gertrude?"

"Waiting outside until he is needed, frowe," Gertrude replied. "Eckhardt is looking after him."

"Your presence does us too much honour, Frowe Gräfin," the old woman muttered, but she retreated.

Margerite stayed until she was able to get a cup of the strong herb tea down Gerhild, who sniffed at it and smiled wanly up at her. "You are kind, Frowe Gräfin," the midwife said in a hoarse whisper, her voice broken by the hours of screaming. "I could not have turned the child any better myself, and when they told me the arm was showing, I resigned my soul to Christ."

"We were fortunate, and your womb is strong," Margerite replied. "Since you are a midwife, I do not need to tell you how to look after yourself in the next days - but do you think these women will be capable of taking care of you?" She would not bully a woman who had just given birth, but she could hear the doubt in her own voice, keen as an edge of glass sliding along glass.

"They are good women, Frowe Gräfin. They are only overwhelmed by your presence."

Margerite bit back her retort, patting the new baby instead. He blinked up at her, blue eyes pale in his crumpled red face, then gave voice to a loud wail. She smiled, unconsciously touching her own stomach. If she had conceived on the night of Ruprecht's return, then the child would be born in mid-March, just a little before Easter…

"Shall I call Father Hans in to baptize your son now?" Margerite asked.

Gerhild looked down at the child in her arms. "His colour and heartbeat are good, and he is suckling strongly." She frowned, and Margerite knew what she was thinking: either she or the child could still die suddenly, for a long labour might do harms that could not be seen at first. "Yes, Frowe Gräfin, please call him."

"As you wish," Margerite said. "May Christ and Maria bless and keep you both. I shall come down here tomorrow to be sure that you are still doing well."

"And Christ and Maria bless you, Frowe Gräfin, for the great work of charity you have done this day."

"Come, Gertrude; come, Kobolt," said Margerite. Gerhild would need her rest, and she had no mind to stand longer in the hot birthing-room with the three peasant women staring so uncomfortably at her.

Father Hans was standing outside with Eckhardt beside him. The priest still listed unsteadily, but he was able to ask, "Frowe Gräfin, are my services needed?"

"You have a child to baptize," Margerite answered crisply. "God willing, there will be no more for you to do - but you shall stay in the village chapel for the next two days, lest you be needed again. Eckhardt, you may go back to the castle."

The priest bowed clumsily to her and stumbled in. Looking at the closed door, the resentment begain to boil up hot in Margerite again.

"What do you suppose is wrong with the people of this village?" she said to Gertrude. "I would have expected those women to at least offer me a piece of bread and a cup of small beer, if they had nothing better - and I know they did, for that was not a poor house and the cheesemaking has been going on for weeks."

"If you are hungry, I am sure Berthe can cook you something far nicer than anything to be found in this village," Gertrude said timidly.

"No, it is not the food itself, but…They do not know me, but why should they speak so coldly to me when I was doing my best to help them?"

"I do not know, frowe. Perhaps you can ask Gerhild tomorrow."

Margerite untied her horse's reins and mounted up, starting back to the castle at a slow walk so that Gertrude could keep up to her. Suddenly the maid giggled, a plump hand covering her mouth. "I know something that may interest you, frowe. You know the mercenary gunmaster, Jochanan?"

"Yes," Margerite said cautiously.

"Well, Eckhardt thinks he is a Jew. Can you imagine that?"

"And how does Eckhardt know this? I have never seen Jochanan wearing a Jewish hat, as the law prescribes."

"When they were marching on the first raid, Eckhardt saw Jochanan pissing, and he swears there was no hood on his pizzle! And later Eckhardt saw him turning down a perfectly good pork sausage. He knows the sausage was good because he ate it himself."

"You," Margerite said severely, "have no business talking to Eckhardt about anyone's pizzle, and he should not have mentioned it to you. As for Jochanan himself…" She paused. If Jochanan were really Jewish, he was breaking nearly every law she had ever heard of concerning the Jews.

But then, the Free Companies were always halfway on the wrong side of the law at best, and she was uncomfortably aware that employing them was very close to being unChristian, illegal, or both. Yet, if Ruprecht were to win the war, there was really no choice, and she could find little evil in either Paul or his lieutenant.

"I do not see that it matters," Margerite said at last. "But you should keep your mouth shut about it, and so should Eckhardt. Jochanan is one of the most valuable men in our army, and we do not need anyone asking questions about him."

"O, very well, frowe." Gertrude giggled again. "What do you think a pizzle looks like without a hood?"

Margerite smiled to herself. "When you are married, you may uncover your husband's, and then you will know. But if I catch you trying to find out before then, I will have the skin whipped from your back."

Margerite knew Gertrude did not believe her threat, for she had never whipped the girl, but at least she subsided into a respectful silence.

When they had gotten back to the castle, Margerite went up to the library with the remainder of the herbs. To no surprise of hers, Wolfram was leaning back in a chair with his long legs crossed at the ankles, softly reading the passage from Tristan in which Brangaene discovered that Tristan and Îsôt had drunk the love-potion meant for Îsôt and Mark.

" 'O woe!' she said, 'for that same flask,

And the drink within its glass,

Of both of you will be the death.' "

Margerite coughed quietly. Wolfram leapt to his feet, setting the book carefully aside, and swept her a deep bow. "Most gracious and noble Frowe Gräfin! Did all go well? Is there anything more I can do to bring joy to your goddess' heart?"

Margerite sighed. "Wolfram, where did you get these herbs?"

"I..." The Knappe's heavy-boned cheeks flushed red, and he looked away, avoiding her eyes. "I got them from Cundrîê," he mumbled.

"And where does Cundrîê keep our herbs?"

"She tends the garden, Frowe Gräfin."

That was one mystery explained; but Wolfram had not answered her question. "That was not what I asked. I need to know where our stores of medicinals are, since clearly most of them are not in the kitchen. Do you know where Cundrîê keeps the herbs she has harvested?"

Wolfram shuffled his feet, looking down at the toes of his boots. "You will need to ask her, Frowe Gräfin."

Margerite stared at him for a little while. She could see the Knappe growing more and more nervous under her gaze, and she was quite sure that he was only telling her a few grains of the truth. Still, there was a more important matter she had to bring up with him. "Do you know anything about herblore, Wolfram?"

The squire's head came up, and his blue eyes brightened. "Only a little, radiant Frowe. I have learned…" He swallowed hard, as though to keep something solid from escaping his throat, then went on… "what many men who go to battle do, about the herbs which are best to stanch bleeding and keep wounds from festering and dull pain."

"Dulling pain…yes. Wolfram, you brought me mandrake and henbane. Do you know how dangerous they are? Do you know how likely they would be to kill a badly wounded man if you gave them to him on the field?" Margerite's hands were shaking on the bag of herbs, and she could hear her voice growing shrill: for she could not rid herself of the thought of Ruprecht's squire, in his ignorance, giving his lord a deadly poison in the effort to heal him or ease his pain.

"Frowe Gräfin? If you wish to teach me more of the lore of herbs, you shall find me the most willing of students, both for the sake of knowledge, which is the queen of the world's endeavors, and for the sake of the noble teacher." Wolfram looked down at her, his square-jawed face completely open and sincere. With an effort Margerite restrained herself from shouting at him any longer. He was a very young man, after all, and he could not do better than seeking to learn after he had found his knowledge lacking.

"Then I shall teach you at least enough so that you are not a danger to those around you. Come: we may as well begin by harvesting some of the fresh herbs in the garden, since the time has come for that - " and since, if Margerite admitted the truth to herself, she would rather gather and label and dry every herb she needed with her own hands than have to ask questions and perhaps even beg advice of Cundrîê.

The next morning, Margerite rode down to the village again to visit Gerhild, bringing with her a basket of cheese and honey and good white bread. The midwife's husband, a burly, grayhaired man who might have been twenty years older than his wife, answered the door, showing her in at once with all courtesy and paying no attention to Kobolt, who pounced in behind her. Gerhild was better today, sitting up in her bed with her long brownish-blond hair tumbling loose about her wiry shoulders as she nursed her child.

"Welcome, Frowe Gräfin," Gerhild said. Her voice was still hoarse from the screams of her painful labour, but she sounded stronger. "As you see, I am doing well, thanks to you."

"I am glad to see it," Margerite replied. "After all - " she smiled - "there may come a day when I need your help as badly."

"Are you bearing, Frowe Gräfin?"

"I do not know, but if not, I hope that I soon will be."

"Ah." Gerhild stroked her son's head. "For all the pains and dangers of Eve's curse, there is nothing better than bringing a child into the world - otherwise I would never have dared it, after all I have seen happen to women in labour. I hope for your sake that you may soon bear one of your own, and that your bearing is easy."

The two of them talked for a while longer, and finally Margerite steeled herself to ask, "Gerhild, is there something wrong with the women of this village? You were in no state to notice yesterday, but the women who were with you kept trying to send me away, even after I had delivered your child. Why should they behave so?"

The midwife bit her lip, large gray eyes thoughtful in her triangular face. "The folk of Tiefensee are not much used to visits from Burg Falkenstein," Gerhild said slowly. "Things were different when the Gräfin Radegund - the Graf's first wife - was alive. He and she would ride down here together, and we were always glad to see them. But after the Death came back and she died...she was the last person in these lands to die of the plague...Graf Ruprecht has not been the same since."

"What do you mean?" Margerite asked, the hairs prickling up on the back of her neck. She did not want to hear this, and yet she could not tear herself away, nor change the subject. But she bent down to pick Kobolt up, holding the big cat's solid warmth tightly to her body against the cold that seemed to shiver in the depths of her bones. "Tell me."

"He...I hardly know how to explain it, Frowe Gräfin. He would go into rages, and do things that...set everyone in the village in fear of him. Most especially, if he thought that someone might have done harm to the animals he hunts or the woods he hunts in. There was one lad who had barked a young oak tree to make a whistle - killing the tree, yes, but there were plenty more growing beside it. Graf Ruprecht put him to death in a frightening manner. Since then, most folk here think it best to be out of sight when the Lord of the Wood rides by, or they hear the sound of his hunting horn."

The midwife's high cheekbones had gone very white, and her child had stopped suckling and was beginning to cry softly, as though he could taste the sharpness of his mother's distress in her milk.

"No one was bettered by the Death," Margerite said, "and Ruprecht's woods are his to protect…Was that all?"

"Yes, Frowe Gräfin," Gerhild said. Margerite thought that she spoke too quickly, but she could see no gain in pressing the matter.

"Well, I shall be coming down here more often, so perhaps you can tell the folk of Tiefensee that I mean only good towards them and they may as well greet me kindly."

"I shall do that, Frowe Gräfin. There are already many who know how you came to save my life yesterday, and believe me, they are grateful to you."

Margerite and Gerhild talked for a while, but Margerite knew that she could not linger too long away from the castle, with all that had to be done. She made her farewells to the midwife and her husband, and rode back up towards Burg Falkenstein, her heart heavy and thoughtful.

Although she had never seen Ruprecht in one of the rages Gerhild had mentioned, she could imagine it easily enough: those men who seemed to hold their tempers the most tightly leashed were the worst when they exploded. And she had seen him terrifying in full armour, and drawing his sword to lash out when startled; Margerite had no doubt that, when provoked, Ruprecht could be a very dangerous man.

And yet he had never so much as raised his voice to Margerite, nor given her reason to think that he would ever do her harm. It was that thought that strengthened her homeward way, taking the harshest chill from her realization of the fear in which the Tiefensee village held her husband.

The eagle might be a terror to his prey, a mortal danger to his foes: but to his mate he was companion and guardian and love. When Margerite awoke the next day, Kobolt's plumed tail draped across her face and head still dazed from her dreams of flight, she found that she was blinking against the sun. She had slept well into the morning, later than she had ever slept in good health before.

"What is wrong with you, Gertrude?" she asked irritably. Her head was aching, as though she had drunk too deeply the night before, and the lassitude of sleep weighted her limbs. "Why did you let me sleep so long?"

"I could not rouse you, frowe," Gertrude said, her voice unusually meek. "Frowe, I think you should stop drinking those draughts Cundrîê brings you at night. You mutter strangely in your sleep, and you have not been yourself in the mornings."

Margerite frowned, throwing off her bedclothes as Kobolt leapt to the floor. After seeing the herbs Cundrîê had given the Knappe, she was less sure that the old woman's draughts were truly harmless - but she had been drinking them every night for a month now, and never seemed to take ill from them. Even now, the sleepiness was falling from her and the pulsing headache was fading. "We shall see. Hasten to dress me, for I should not have slept so late."

When Margerite reached the great hall, she saw to her annoyance that it was empty except for Bertram, who bowed briefly to her.

"Frowe Gräfin," he said. "You are awake. The Graf bids me tell you that he had to ride out early today, in hopes of forestalling Graf Heinrich's first attack across our border. All being well, he should be back before St. Johannes' Eve."

I should have been awake to wish him farewell, Margerite thought sadly. Though she did not know why, she felt guilty, as though her conversation with the Tiefensee midwife had somehow been responsible for the deep sleep that had kept her from seeing Ruprecht off.

As Ruprecht had promised, he was back two days before St. Johannes' Eve, swinging into the hall in a high good humour. "We did not even have to join battle," he said. "Just as I had guessed, Graf Heinrich is not ready to meet our full forces. He sent small bands that could move quickly to plunder our villages, thinking to slip them past our guard - but we were ready for him, and his men turned back well before we could close with them. Now we shall have a little respite, and I think that we shall celebrate Midsummer's with a stag hunt, and before this sun-wending we shall see here the men to whom I wish to show honour. What do you say to that, beloved?"

"I think it a fine plan," Margerite answered, tilting her face up for a kiss. Ruprecht's chin was scratchy with golden stubble and grimed from the chainmail of his bascinet, but she did not care: he was there for her, and his war was going better than she had dared hope. "Shall I ride in the chase with you?"

Ruprecht grinned down at her, his blue eyes warm as the summer sky with admiration. "If you will, I shall be delighted. You have had little enough time for rest and pleasure since our marriage; leaving all the cares of Burg Falkenstein behind for a day to ride in the woods will be good for cheering your heart."

Ruprecht was out in the woods all the next day with his Knappe, the Ritters Wilfrid, Götz, and Dancwart - Ritter Sigmund had not been called, because Ruprecht would not take him from the border, though he had sent a letter assuring the knight that his exclusion was not from lack of favour and promising him a fine hunt when the danger was over - and a few of his other favoured men, letting the jowly leithunds sniff out the trails of stags as the men examined the tracks and droppings to judge the sizes of the beasts.

A large breakfast was served in the great hall the following morning, and there among the breakfast dishes, the hunters spread out the fumes they had brought back in their grass-stoppered horns. Margerite watched with keen interest as each of the men in turn showed off his stag's droppings, describing the tracks of the animal that had produced them and giving his thoughts on size and condition. Wolfram proudly prodded at the thick oblongs before him: he had not seen the beast, but its fumes showed it to be at least a hart of ten.

"But what of the tracks?" Ruprecht asked. Wolfram held his index fingers apart to show the length, adding that their edges were crisp, as if freshly made.

"Did the tracks of the hind feet fall before or after the marks of the forefeet?"

"Ah...before, I think."

Ruprecht shook his head firmly. "It may be a finely horned stag, but it is not well-fleshed, to have made such tracks, for only a thin-flanked hart can place his feet so. We shall not hunt him if we can get a better, though..." he waved his goblet at Ritter Wilfrid's fumes, which were sheened with a trace of slime... "he may be a finer chase than Ritter Wilfrid's stag, which seems to have suffered some ordeal of late."

"But what of your stag, Graf Ruprecht?" Ritter Wilfrid asked when the others had all spoken of their beasts. "You have not put out any fumes; did you find nothing?"

Ruprecht grinned, pulling out the plug of damp grass at the end of his hunting horn and shaking out three long, thick masses. Although Margerite knew only the basic elements by which a stag might be judged, she drew in her breath: these fumes had obviously been dropped by a hart far better than any of those represented at the table.

Wilfrid shook his curly blond head, staring ruefully down at Ruprecht's fumes. "You tricked us all, Herr Graf," he said without rancour. "Why did you not show these at the beginning?"

Ruprecht's merry laugh rang out over the table. "I have been watching this stag for three years now, and every year he has grown better antlers. This year he has reached his head of thirty-two at full, which no stag can outstrip; next year his pride will begin to lessen again, and I would take him while he is in his greatest strength. But there was always the chance that a strange beast of the same quality might have wandered into the woods while I was unawares, and that one of you might come upon him: stranger things have happened upon a hunt."

"That is not likely, when you are so often hunting through the forests," Ritter Wilfrid said. "But you have defeated us fairly, Graf; now tell us where we shall seek this stag."

The men went out in the afternoon with Joachim and Ruprecht's best leithund to harbour the hart, making sure that the stag was still in the area where Ruprecht had found him the day before. They were merry when they came back, for they had followed his tracks close on to a thick covert where they thought he was bedding, and his fresh fumes were as promising as those he had dropped the day before.

"We shall rise at dawn, and take to our horses when we have broken our fast," Ruprecht said to Margerite, and she agreed eagerly, caught up in the men's excitement.

Joachim went into the woods with the leithund and two of his kennel-boys before the hunters had risen, to make sure that the stag was still within the covert they had marked. The rest of the hunters ate a good breakfast, fine red jellies of wine and meat set out among large plates of finely sliced smoked trout, cheese, and wheaten bread, washed down with white wine from Ruprecht's land and red Ahr-wine. The sun was well-up when one of the kennel boys came running back in.

"The stag is still in his covert, Herr Graf, noble lords," the youth announced breathlessly. "The Master of Hounds awaits your word to seek him out." Ruprecht arose from his seat, taking Margerite by the hand.

"The hunt is begun," he said.

The hunters mounted in the courtyard, leading the coupled ruorhunds, who would chase the deer down when the leithund had found its trail, along the path they had followed the day before. The day was very bright, the light breeze mild and warm on Margerite's face as she rode along beside Ruprecht.

The hunters were all dressed in green: Margerite wore a dress of dark green patterned with gold brocade, and Ruprecht shone resplendently in a close-cut tunic of pale green velvet trimmed with ruddy fox fur over deeper green hose, with a dagged gold ruff lying over his broad shoulders like a second short cape beneath his hip-length cloak of green linen, his sword dangling from a leather belt trimmed with gilded plates, and the hunting horn Margerite had given him slung glittering across his chest.

The woods rustled softly about them as they rode along the trail that had been marked with peeled sticks yesterday; the air was sweet with the scent of the little violets and wild strawberries growing at the shadowed roots of the trees, and the sunlight through the leaves cast a dappled veil of green and gold over the path. They were in sight of one of the trails through the holly thickets where the stag had been bedding when Ruprecht unslung his horn, blowing a single lingering note to let Joachim know that he might start the search.

Farther along, Margerite heard the sound of the Hound-Master and his leithund crackling through the twigs, the soft murmurs of "Hoy, hoy! Good Hänsel, so, so...nose to the ground, good boy. My sweet darling, my fine hound, wise little Hänsel."

The huntsmen moved slowly after Joachim, a little way to the rear, following him by sound and the fray-barked branches he left to mark the trail. Margerite sat straight on her horse, nearly quivering in excitement. Her sight had brightened as if she were looking through a clear crystal, each green leaf or green-black needle on the trees standing out as if carved with a sharp-edged chisel.

The glossy leaves of the low holly bushes gleamed like dark polished metal; the white strips of peeled wood upon the branches that marked their way shone like banners against the dull gray bark. The high twittering of the birds above them sang sweet in her skull, keen as the prickling of little needles, and she could feel the blood rushing and thrumming through her body.

Suddenly, Margerite heard the sharp crashing ahead, the sound of something large fleeing through the thicket. A high, clear horn-call split the air: three long notes, to tell the hunters that the stag was moved. Ruprecht spurred his horse on with his coupled hounds beside him, Margerite following closely and the other men bringing up the rear. Joachim stood upon the trail, his brown leithund straining at the lead. "Herr Graf, the great stag is running: the chase is begun."

"Uncouple the hounds, then, and let us after him!" Ruprecht cried joyously. Joachim at once unloosed Hänsel, then the ruorhunds that had come up with the horsemen, and urged them on.

A thrill went up Margerite's spine as the running-dogs leapt forward behind the leithund, their deep voices baying musically, and Ruprecht urged his gray-black steed into a full canter behind them. She kneed Mathilde up, the mare surging forward between her legs to follow Ruprecht's horse in its headlong careering after the fleeing stag. Thin twigs grazed her cheeks stingingly, bringing the blood to rush hot through her head; she swayed in the saddle as Mathilde turned hard behind the hounds.

"There!" Ruprecht shouted from ahead. Margerite looked up, and saw the stag in full leap over a dark low wall of holly-bushes - his huge crown of antlers trailing back from his head like dagged red banners, the great muscles of his shoulders and hindquarters rippling beneath his polished bronze hide.

The dogs bayed louder as he landed and was gone through the underbrush again, tearing forward with flecks of foam flying from their mouths. Ruprecht did not slow for the bushes, but in a moment was aloft behind the hart, his great dark steed flying easily over the thorny thicket. Caught up in the fury of the hunt, Margerite did not slow to ride around, but dug her knees in, leaning back as Mathilde's muscles bunched beneath her, leaping into the air as if weightless.

Margerite did not even feel the bump of landing: her horse surged ahead at once to follow the hounds, and it was as if she were still flying through the air, the wind howling about her as she pounded through the woods in Ruprecht's train. Ahead ran their quarry, and Ruprecht was sounding his horn in the music of the chase, its high silver note shivering maddenly through the drumbeat of her heart in her ears.

Faster, faster: the trees blurred into shimmering streaks of green and brown tearing past her as flashes of sun through the branches burst into her eyes, the barking of the hounds rising into a wild cry like the howling of wolves. The twigs pelted across her face like hailstones in the stormwind; and then, as Ruprecht's horn rang out again, it seemed to Margerite that the golden and green world burned suddenly colourless, silver and black, as though Midsummer's day had become Midwinter's night.

The brilliant sunlight flashed silver and cold as the light of the moon, glinting off white snow beneath the black shadows of bare branches, and its brilliance sparkled in her eyes like a torrent of glittering white snowflakes whirling through the night. The ruorhunds ahead, baying and slavering for the blood of the hart, had all gone wolf-gray, and a white mist curled up from the flying hooves of Ruprecht's gray-black steed. Ruprecht's green cloak fluttered black as a raven's wing behind him, rimmed with silver like a sheen of ice; his hair gleamed sheer silver in the unearthly light, and when he glanced back at her, his face shone white as a bone beneath the moon.

Margerite cried out in terror, jerking at her reins. Mathilde swung aside, and in that moment all was as it should be again, the gold and green of summer shining warm about her. She urged her mare on behind Ruprecht's mount again, but the knight's mighty horse was already far ahead, following hard on the hounds and their quarry. Ride as she might, Margerite could just barely keep in sight of Ruprecht.

Distantly, from behind, she heard the other horns blowing now and again to answer her husband's, and knew that the rest of the hunters were still following on, but not too close. Suddenly the belling of the hounds changed, their barks growing fiercer and more frantic with joy. Ahead of her, Ruprecht had slowed his furious pace, and Margerite was able to catch up with him easily, leaning forward to look ahead.

The huge stag, his muscular sides dark and dripping with sweat and the breath foaming hard from his mouth, was at bay beneath a great oak. His dark eyes rolled desperately, and his breath came in harsh snorts, his limbs trembling with exhaustion and despair. Yet, though brought to bay, the hart had not given way to defeat: he lowered his high-crowned head and pawed at the grass with a forehoof as the hounds leapt and barked about him, swinging his antlers threateningly to keep them from his flanks.

"Halloo, halloo!" Ruprecht called out, pitching his voice high to carry through the woods, and Margerite joined in above him. "Halloo, halloo!" He put his horn to his lips, blowing a long single that rose and swelled to shiver through the warm summer air, then a flurry of shorter notes, ending with another long call. As the sound died away, Ritter Wilfrid rode out from the green shadows of the wood, followed shortly by Wolfram and the rest of the hunters.

Ruprecht did not delay too long, for the great stag's antlers had already grazed one dog's flank, leaving a long red streak along its golden hide, and the others were dancing and giving voice about him so wildly that they were in danger of falling to the hart's prongs with every swing of his head. He dismounted lightly and drew his sword, the sunlight flashing gold along the keen edge of polished steel as though the blade were afire. Alert to the single moment of his opening, Ruprecht leapt in between the dogs, dodging the sweep of the stag's awesome antlers, and thrust his sword in behind one shoulder.

The hart stiffened, the gleam of life already dulling in his dark eyes. For a moment he stood, a bright streak of blood bubbling out in the white foam dripping about his wet mouth, then slowly went down to his knees, toppling to his side on the ground. The hounds, well-trained as they were, stood back panting. Ruprecht lifted his horn to his mouth again to blow the long echoing notes of the death, and the other hunters took up the call, the notes of their horns rising in a high clean chord through the trembling leaves.

As the sound of the mort died away and the hunters dismounted, turning the stag over onto its back, Ruprecht unfastened his cloak and laid it over a nearby stump. He pushed his sleeves back, his solidly muscled forearms bare and pale below the fur-trimmed edges, and sleeked his disheveled golden hair back behind his ears. This stag was his: no one would deny him the unmaking. Margerite, still breathless and shaky from the ride, leaned up against her mare's warm saddle to watch as Ruprecht drew his golden-hilted dagger and crouched down at the hart's head to begin the Entbästung, the skinning and removal of the chief cuts of meat.

"Wolfram, cut the Furke," he commanded as he skillfully made his slits in the warm body, slipping his blade beneath the hide to part the delicate transparent membranes holding skin to flesh. The Knappe went to the oak tree, gazing up into its leaves thoughtfully for a little time before he finally reached up to break off a long forked branch, snapping away the twigs and pushing the butt-end into the earth by the body of the stag.

Ruprecht cut apart the stag's deep red flesh with the ease of many years' practice: breast from back, ribs from spine, quartering the legs and shoulders away neatly from the body, then turning it over to slice away the long thick muscles overlying the back above the hindquarters. Breast, shoulders, flanks, legs: he laid them all neatly together, and the Entbästung was done. Next came the Furkîe, where the hunter carefully opened the stag's belly, laying open the ruddy layers of muscle to show the innards.

Ruprecht's golden hair fell about his face in a shimmering veil as he slipped his hands into the bloody cavity, delicately feeling about to cut out the liver and flick away the dark gall-bladder with a neat twist of his knife, then to separate the kidneys from their membranes. He sat up on his heels, shaking his head back before he reached down to cut the stag's testicles free from the scrotum. These pieces, the special delicacies, he tied onto the Furke with a net bag that dangled heavily at the branch's fork.

The hounds rustled, sniffing closer with ears pricked up and eyes alert. Veteran hunters all, they knew that after the choicest meat and organs had been cut from the stag's body, they would receive their Curîe, their reward for a good hunt. Ruprecht took out heart and lungs, slicing the heart crosswise into four equal pieces, and laid them upon the four corners of the bloody hide, then cut quickly through the points above the stomach and at the end of the bowels to free the digestive track, heaving the gray slithery mass of intestines over to the hide as well.

There, Wolfram and Joachim, who had at last managed to find his way to the scene of the death, helped to slice the stag's guts up for the hounds; Ruprecht's dagger grated between the bones of the spine as he cut the stag's mighty head free, turning it upright.

"Za, za, za!" he called. The hounds came running on, feeding greedily on the pieces that had been laid out on the hide for them; but Hänsel the leithund was allowed to gnaw his fill from the stag's neck, for of all of them, he had served best and it was his mind that must be kept most firmly on great stags as his quarry.

Delighted by the enthusiasm of the hounds receiving their reward, Margerite almost did not notice the black streak slinking stealthily through the grass towards the Furke with its heavy burden of meat. It was only the soft purring chirp that alerted her in time to leap over to the forked stick and grab Kobolt as he pounced upward, clawed paw extended to snag one of the stag's testicles where it bulged through the net.

"Bad cat!" Margerite scolded. "How did you get here?"

Ruprecht glanced over at them. There was a smear of drying blood on his forehead where he had absently pushed his tangled hair back, and the wild brightness of the hunt still played in his eyes like blue foxfire; for a moment, Margerite was almost afraid to look at him. Then he laughed, and she realized that he was happier than she had ever seen him before, even at their wedding or while making love - as though the hunt had driven out every shadow of sadness that dimmed his heart.

"If he dares to brave the hounds," Ruprecht said, still laughing, "he may have a share of the Curîe, for he must have run long and well to catch up with us."

Margerite looked up through the branches, their green interlace brocaded against the blue sky. The hunt had begun in mid-morning; now the sun was lowering into afternoon. They had run most of the day, on the year's longest day - no wonder her legs were shaking and her feet unsteady under her, after such a chase! Seeing how late it was, she felt suddenly weak with hunger as well, her mouth dusty as a long-dried streambed, but although Wilfrid and Götz were unhooking their wine-flasks, and another hung from Ruprecht's saddle, Margerite did not want to interrupt her husband in his hunter's ritual by asking for it.

Kobolt sprang out of her arms, as if he had understood Ruprecht's words, and made his way in among the hounds. Margerite watched anxiously, but they left the cat alone: it was not unlikely, she thought, that they had already learned what his powerful claws could do to a tender nose.

"Beloved wife," Ruprecht said, "will you weave a garland and crown of flowers, so that we may bear the forest-king's head back to Burg Falkenstein in proper state?"

As the huntsmen set to cutting branches and binding the pieces of meat onto their carrying-sticks, Margerite bent gladly to the task Ruprecht had set her, braiding slender green-leafed twigs into two rings and plucking flowers to weave into them. Dark violets and the star-leaved twigs of sweet woodruff with their tiny puffs of white blossom; ruddy anemones and blue columbines; the white flowers of wild garlic and the golden rosettes of dandelions: they made a noble crown and garland for her to set upon the antlers and about the neck of the stag's head, now enthroned upon the solid shaft of a spear.

That done, Ruprecht took up the head and mounted again, holding it before him in triumph as he rode. The other hunters followed, each carrying a piece of the stag's body in the place which, relative to the rest, it had held in life, with Wolfram in the middle, bearing the laden Furke. Joachim had taken charge of the hounds again; but Kobolt scampered along in the woods beside the hunters, a flash of golden eyes or black tail showing now and again out of the undergrowth. The courtyard had been set up for the Midsummer's feast by the time the hunters got back, long tables arranged in a ring about the heaped wood that would be set alight at sunset and great oaken barrels of wine and ale standing beside them.

Ruprecht rode straight to the high table where he and Margerite would sit with his knights, driving the butt of the spear he carried deeply into the hard-packed earth so that the stag's antler-crowned head would look upon the feasting from aloft. The sun was already well on her way towards the horizon, but there would be good light for a few hours yet. Before the hunters dismounted, several servants came to them with goblets of wine.

Margerite lifted hers high to salute the stag's head, letting the sweet golden drink flow cool down her throat with reckless abandon. Strong on her empty stomach, the wine mounted in her almost at once, warming her cheeks and humming softly in her ears. Tossing his goblet back to the manservant's waiting hands, Ruprecht leapt from his horse and reached up to help Margerite down, his strong arms catching and steadying her so that she hardly felt her feet touch the earth. He brushed his lips lightly across hers, and Margerite thought she could taste the stag's blood in his mouth, a whisper of salt beneath the sweetness of the wine.

"Let us go and make ourselves ready, my beloved," Ruprecht said to her. "The day is wearing on swiftly, and soon we shall be leading the sun-wending dance."

When Margerite came back down to the courtyard, face and hands washed and hair neatly combed, but still dressed in her gold-brocaded dress of hunting green, the first tinges of pink were just beginning to glow pale in the western sky. The courtyard was full now, the men and women of the castle lined along the long wooden tables or standing in small groups, talking and laughing. Ruprecht's musicians were seated to the side of the high table, beneath the stag's head, and as Margerite walked down to take her place, they began to play, the singer's clear tenor voice ringing brightly over the sounds of merriment.

"Summer's green on field and wood,
The meadow's blossoms shine,
My frowe walks o'er them, fair and good,
And sips the sun-bright wine.
O, let the stag before her bend
His mighty-antlered crown,
As earth and sky and rustling wind,
At her feet lay them down."

Margerite seated herself, and Gertrude poured out wine for her. Ruprecht was only a few minutes behind: like her, he had washed and tidied himself, but was still wearing his hunter's green and gold array. It was not long before the servants began to carry food out from the kitchens. Berthe, undoubtedly frustrated at the daily economies of wartime, had seized on the opportunity to outdo herself. Perhaps at Ruprecht's order, the feast at the high table was all in green and gold to match the colours of the hunt.

They began with the stag's liver chopped and cooked in wine, mixed with breadcrumbs and tangy verjuice and gilded with egg yolks and saffron. After that followed little pastries enclosing a savoury mixture of veal and cheese, their upper crusts glazed in swirls of saffron-yellow and parsley-green; then an assortment of small birds, partridges and thrushes and larks, whose skins had been coated with egg-whites and dusted lightly with a sprinkling of gold-leaf flakes so that they glittered in the reddening light of the sunset.

Next, a small roast pig was brought out, dressed in its own green coat; when the coat was unfastened, the diners saw that the swine's body was stuffed with capons and doves. There were also pancakes filled with fine-chopped veal and cream and covered with a rich green sauce of parsley and sage, and rabbits stuffed with sausage, the golden egg-yolk glaze a gleaming polish along their pale bodies and well-cooked haunches.

Lastly, as the main meal was being cleared away, the servants carried about high-heaped platters of lightly fried cakes dripping with honey and fruit preserves. The sun had sunk to the horizon now, glowing red above the dark sweep of rolling woodlands below; the peak of the mountain beyond the castle's ravine glimmered golden in its last light against the darkening blue of the eastern sky. Ruprecht arose, giving Margerite his arm and leading her to stand before the heaped wood for the bonfire.

"A torch!" he called. "Let Burg Falkenstein's frowe kindle the sun-wending fire!"

Wolfram bore up a torch, the flames curling high into the cooling air, and gave it into Margerite's hands. For a moment she held it, staring at the hot yellow fire leaping and spitting from the resin-soaked pine: it almost seemed that she could see strange burning shapes coiling within the flame, eyes looking out at her...

With a shudder she thrust the torch into the piled wood. It caught at once, flames running along the tinder and small twigs like burning oil, catching hold on the bark of the dry branches and flaring up quickly. Blinking the brightness away, Margerite stepped backward quickly; she might have stumbled, but Ruprecht was there to steady her.

The minstrels struck up their music again, and Margerite heard the opening notes of a galliard plinking from the strings of the lute, the beating of the little drum a gay call to dancing. Ruprecht lifted her hand in his, and she saw that the other folk had moved away to leave them a clearing by the fire, standing about to watch.

Uncertainly at first, her feet finding the steps only slowly, Margerite let Ruprecht move her into the dance: it had been some time since she had last danced. But soon the steps were beginning to feel more familiar, her body moving more easily to the lively whirl of the music. When Margerite was dancing steadily and confidently, Ruprecht began to dance more daringly: swooping in and out, twirling and leaping to the notes that rippled about them, but always coming back in to meet her, so that she never feared that she would misstep or miss his rhythm.

Though he was by far the better dancer, his skill seemed to sweep Margerite up so that her simple steps felt like the inevitable counterpoint to his more complex ones, the two of them touching and parting, blending and moving together as perfectly as falconer and falcon, hunter and quarry, lover and beloved…

Her gaze fixed on Ruprecht as they danced, Margerite found herself rapt in the vision of him: strong and graceful as a leaping stallion in midair, golden hair flying loose about his shoulders and muscular legs rippling beneath his tight hose, moving in the dance with the delicate and powerful precision of a skilled knight in battle.

The music rose in a loud tinkling of cymbals: Ruprecht leapt into the air once more, landing lightly on the balls of his feet with one arm behind Margerite's shoulders and the other hand holding hers just above her breasts. He bent his head, kissing her as he drew her closer to him, and a storm of shouts and applause drowned out the minstrels.

"The first dance for me," Ruprecht said breathlessly in her ear. Margerite, too, was breathing hard, overwhelmed by the warmth of his body pressing against hers. She would have clung to him forever, but presently he disengaged her, though he still held her hand. "Others would dance too: shall we lead them in a ring?"

As if they sensed the Graf's thoughts, the minstrels began to play again, a lively dancing-tune. Ruprecht reached out to take the plump hand of Ritter Götz's wife, and Margerite let the knight close his hard hand carefully about hers, moving into the first steps of the ring-dance about the rising bonfire. Now and again, flowers and green wreaths sailed over the heads of the dancers, tossed into the fire for luck by those who watched and waited their turn.

Only... Margerite saw him from the corner of her eye, now and again, as the steps of the dance turned her about... only Bertram neither danced nor clapped and stamped: he stood in the darkness by the wall, and his face, shadowed into hiding by black beard and hair, was turned away from the merriment, as though he could not bear to see the joy of others. But it was no night for thinking about Bertram, and the whirl of dancing and music soon drove him from Margerite's mind.

She danced in the courtyard until late in the evening, revelling thoroughly in the chance to delight and enjoy the company of the folk of Burg Falkenstein. Even the Bear's Paw company had been invited to celebrate the sun-wending: Margerite danced a few times with Paul, though he could hardly do more than lumber unsteadily from foot to foot, and also with Jochanan, who was agile enough most of the time, but apt to sometimes lose the rhythm, as though he had been dancing to a tune that was similar to, but not quite the same as, the one she heard.

Eventually, however, she grew tired, and settled down in her seat again, sipping her wine and watching the festivities. Gertrude was still up, dancing rather more closely than she ought to have been to her young Eckhardt, and Margerite smiled to herself, watching the two of them. There would be a betrothal soon: she would speak to Ruprecht about it when the right moment came. It would work out well, since Eckhardt, as a guard, was already to be counted among the castle's folk; it would mean no great change in life for either of them, and would reinforce the good stations their services had gained them.

Suddenly someone cried, "The wheel! They are lighting the wheel!" The dancing stopped, and Margerite saw everyone's head turning to gaze up to the top of the mountain where a great flare suddenly leapt into the night sky. In its brightness, she could see the spokes of a wheel half again the height of a man, and the black silhouettes of the folk about it, reaching out to guide and steady the burning wheel with their sticks as it began to roll in a torrent of sparks. Margerite watched its flaming path down the dark mountainside with delight, for several of the villages near Burg Hirschenberg had done something similar at Midsummer's.

Although the burning wheel could not be seen for long from the castle courtyard, she knew that the Tiefensee folk were rolling it down to the lake: if it was still burning when it plunged into the water, it would promise a good yield of wine that year. For a moment Margerite thought regretfully of what Gerhild had told her, wondering if Ruprecht's first wife had once been the one to light the Midsummer wheel above Tiefensee, as well as the castle's bonfire.

But the dancing was beginning again, and though she was still too tired to join in again, she was well-content to sit with her goblet of wine in her hand and Kobolt in her lap, watching the dancers and listening to the lively tinkling of the music. When she began to yawn, Margerite arose from the table. The outer edges of the bonfire had burned low now, and here and there some of the younger folk were leaping across the coals for a year's luck. Margerite felt herself ready to go to bed, and looked about for Gertrude, but the girl was nowhere to be seen. Perhaps she has gone ahead of me, Margerite thought.

She glanced around herself to see if Ruprecht was anywhere near, but she could not see him either. By herself, she walked into the inner courtyard, making her way across it in the bright light of the moon. She had thought to go straight up to bed, but as she passed the herber, the glimmer of the white roses tumbling about its walls and the pale blossom-platters of the linden tree above the love-seat caught her eye. She walked in to stand there for a moment, gazing about herself in contentment. By night and moonlight, the neglected garden did not seem like an overgrown mess, but rather like an enchanted woodland grotto, and the words from Tristan came to her mind.

"The sweet linden sweetened for them
With her leaves the shadows and air,
And through her shadows the winds were
Sweet and soft and cool...
There they sat, all in each other,
The true lovers..."

Margerite did not notice Ruprecht stepping out from beneath the linden's shadow, but suddenly he was there before her, his fair face pale and hair bleached by the moonlight to a shimmering fall of flax. Without speaking, he drew her to him, kissing her deeply. His mouth tasted of meat and blood, strong with raw wildness, and his breath was hot upon her face. Margerite felt overwhelmed, almost frightened, but she could not break away from his firm hold, and as he kissed her again she found herself embracing him as well, clinging so tightly about the hard muscles of his back that her arms trembled.

Gently Ruprecht moved her backwards, into the shadow of the wall where no one passing by the gateway could see them. Margerite realized that she was terribly aroused, the thin linen shift beneath her dress caressing her swollen nipples almost painfully as she shifted position, to feed the urgent, needing pleasure throbbing between her thighs.

"Ruprecht," she murmured softly, almost pleadingly to him. "Oh, my love..."

Ruprecht put his finger to her lips to silence her. We should not be doing this here, Margerite thought dizzily. We should go up to my chamber. But she could not bear to wait, not with him here, so close, his hands caressing her body so lightly, so skillfully through her hunting dress, the hard muscles of his thighs pressing against hers as if to urge her to open to him. She sighed soundlessly, her head going back as his hot greedy kisses devoured the sensitive skin of her throat. She could feel Ruprecht's hand moving up her thigh, lifting her skirt as he freed himself with the other hand.

He crouched slightly, embracing Margerite more closely, and then she felt him rising up into her, felt her knees weakening in the overwhelming rush of pleasure as she sank down fully upon his spear. Ruprecht was holding her tightly, supporting her against the wall even as she rocked upon him and he thrust upward again and again. Against her will, Margerite felt her mouth opening to cry out the ecstasy pounding through her body, but Ruprecht bent over her, fastening his lips on her own so that she could make only a tiny muffled mewing into his mouth as her body shuddered and spasmed with delight beneath his relentless assault.

When at last he withdrew and let go of Margerite, she staggered and almost fell, her trembling legs too weak to hold her up. Ruprecht caught her at once, slipping his hand about her waist, then crouching to lift her in his arms as if she were a child. He carried her easily up the four flights of castle stairs to her bedroom, where Gertrude was waiting.

"A joyous Midsummer's, my love," Ruprecht said to Margerite when he had set her down upon her bed.

"Joyous indeed, my dear husband," Margerite replied, smiling sleepily up at him. "A fine hunt, a fine feast...and finest of all, our dancing together."

Ruprecht smiled, and kissed her softly on the lips. "Finest of all, indeed. Sleep in peace, my beloved bride." He left quietly, his shoes soundless on the stone floor.

Gertrude looked at her mistress, tapping her fingers lightly against her leather belt. "Was it the dancing, or the wine, that made you too weak to walk to bed by yourself?"

Margerite stretched pleasantly, yawning in a delightfully sensual lassitude - which could not be sin, for God made man and wife to rejoice in one another, she reminded herself hastily.

"The dancing," she replied. She would have said no more, but when Gertrude undressed her, the maid saw the traces that could not be hidden, and snorted.

"Dancing, indeed, frowe! If Eckhardt and I had done such dancing, we would be looking for Father Hans to marry us even now."

Margerite was too tired and happy to answer Gertrude. She only waved her hand limply through the air, as if to brush away a fly, and let the maid sponge her thighs clean, though when she crawled into bed, she was careful to keep her legs together, hoping that no more of Ruprecht's precious seed would drip out before it could kindle a child in her womb. It seemed to Margerite that she stood in a strange room, hung about with green silks. Seven green candles burned there, one upon the black marble top of the altar in the middle and six ringed around it in a circle on the floor.

On the altar lay the body of a white dove, her head neatly severed; a bowl of golden liquid with heavy trails of ruby fluid stirred through it; a mummified adder coiled about itself; a forked and armed mandrake root; a stag's fresh testicles, hairy and bloodied, in their net bag as she had seen them dangling from the Furke that afternoon; a swallow-feather pen, its tip stained red; and a parchment with seven strange signs inscribed on it. She heard a man's voice chanting, as if from far away, but she could make out none of the words, nor could she see him.

Then a dark shadow dimmed the light of the room, and a great heaviness seemed to weigh upon her. The shape of a man in black robes took form from the air: he was tall and gaunt, black-haired and black-eyed with a long, severe, sorrowful face. Upon his hand was a seal ring of lead, and he was crowned with a diadem of the same dull gray metal. When he spoke, his voice was deep almost beyond her hearing.

"I, Aratron, ruler of the sphere of Saturn, have come to answer your conjuration. My powers of stone and earth, of alchemy, magic, and medicine, are at your hand, by the sigil of mine which you bear. Take this might, to use as you will." He pressed his leaden seal to the corner of the parchment, and the sign he had touched gleamed briefly black. The man's voice chanted in answer; Margerite still could not understand it, but the Saturnine spirit bowed his head and was gone.

The second being to appear was a powerfully built man robed in blue, crowned in glittering tin and sapphires. His long hair was brown and curly, his face open and friendly, yet noble beyond compare, as Margerite had sometimes imagined that Kaiser Karl must be. He spoke with the strong surety of a great ruler, leavened with a note of good humour: "I, Bethor, ruler of the sphere of Jupiter, have come to answer your conjuration. My powers of wind and air, of rulership and wisdom, are at your hand, by the sigil of mine which you bear. Take this might, to use as you will." As the ruler of Saturn had, he touched his ring of bright tin to one of the signs on the parchment, which flashed blue for a second. He listened to the chanting a moment more, bowed his head, and was gone.

Margerite stared in awe, knowing - though she did not know how she knew - what she saw. These were neither angels nor devils, but those powerful spirits whom God had set to rule the spheres of the planets and all in nature that proceeded from their essence. It seemed to her that she could feel the power in the room growing, like the heaviness in the air before a thunderstorm, as each of the spirits appeared.

Phaleg, red-haired, armoured, and crowned in iron for Mars; the golden-haired, gold-clad, radiant youth Och for the Sun; Hagith of Venus, with her long copper hair flowing down about her full breasts, whose sinuous movements of hips and shoulders beneath her green silk gown made Margerite almost ashamed to look at her; agile, quick-moving Ophiel of Mercury, whose body seemed to shift and flow beneath his purple gown; and lastly, the Moon's ruler Phul, shimmering in white and silver.

As Phul pressed his silver seal-ring to the parchment, it seemed to Margerite that she heard a note of music like the ringing of silver upon crystal, swelling outward into a great sevenfold chord that sang in her bones and seemed to shake through the very realm of the stars.

Then an eighth deep note joined the chorus, quivering through the earth, and Margerite began to shiver from the beauty of it, her thighs aching with an echo of the desire that had come upon her in the garden with Ruprecht.

The parchment upon the altar drew her eye again: now she could see that thebody of the snake lay upon it, the mandrake root within its coils.Before her eyes, the stag's testicles seemed to glow with an aura of coruscating sparks glittering out towards the parchment, drawing in its weight of power, and she felt something pressing warmly against her womb from within.

Suddenly, then, Margerite felt a mighty stormwind blowing about her, rain and hail lashing at her and half-blinding her eyes, so that she saw the candle and the things set before it only through a hazy veil.

The note of a hunting horn rose clean and wild through the sounds of the storm, sweeping away the last echoes of the great chord, and the warmth pressing at her womb was suddenly gone. She thought that she cried out then, but could not hear her own voice until she awoke in bed, sitting upright and gasping for breath, with gray light seeping through the shutters and Gertrude shaking her shoulders.

"Frowe! Frowe, what is wrong?" the maid was calling anxiously.

"It was only a dream," Margerite said, trying to calm her shaking voice. "Perhaps I was dancing and drinking wine too long last night; that is a great cause of dreams." Already the details were fading swiftly from her mind: she tried to call them back to her, but could draw up only a blurry memory of awe and beauty, and the faint echo of a hunting horn.

A knock sounded on the door. Gertrude glanced over suspiciously. "It is that woman, I am sure. Shall I tell her to go away?"

"Let us see what she wants," Margerite sighed. "There may be some matter that I will have to deal with."

Gertrude snorted, but held her tongue, opening the door. Cundrîê stepped in, carrying a tray with several covered dishes arranged upon it.

"I have brought something for you to break your fast with," she said. "The Graf thought you looked a little pale at the feast after the day's long hunt. You should rest in bed this day, and eat well."

"I am well enough," Margerite started to protest, but Cundrîê waved her hand imperiously.

"It is the Graf's wish," she said. She set the tray down on the table and left. Kobolt leapt up on the table at once, nosing at the largest of the dishes, then reaching out with his paw to knock the cover off.

"Away with you," Gertrude scolded, tossing the black tomcat onto the floor. He jumped up onto the bed, curling himself into Margerite's lap and purring as he looked wide-eyed into her face.

The dish that had tempted Kobolt was small strips of roast dove breast in a sauce seeded with pepper - strong and fine food for breakfast, but when Margerite had taken her first bite of the rich dark meat, she found that she was quite hungry, and could only bring herself to give the smallest bits to Kobolt when he stretched out a hopeful black paw towards her plate.

Cundrîê had also brought a goblet of unwatered wine sweetened with honey and cinnamon, a bowl of cabbage leaves stewed with pickled cucumbers and flavoured with rosemary and anise, and, oddly enough, a piece of dark soft rye bread. Margerite was not used to eating so much early in the day, and when she was done, she found herself feeling a little drowsy again.

"Go about your business," she ordered Gertrude. "I think I shall take my husband's advice and rest. He cannot chide me for being lazy when he was the one who suggested that I should do little this day."

When Cundrîê came back for the tray, she bore a large book in her hand. "You may find this to be of interest to you," the ugly old woman said. "It will tell you of the science of the stars, and of reading their configurations to understand how they shape matters on the earth below. Wars have been won and lost before through knowing the influence of the planets."

There was something in Cundrîê's words that seemed familiar - yes: in Freiburg, Damiano had spoken of Madame du Guesclin's knowledge of astrology as a factor in the warring in France, and suggested that Margerite might do as the Frenchwoman did. Margerite was loath to take the book from Cundrîê - but, she assured herself, the Church had never named astrology as a forbidden art, and there could be little harm in learning the patterns of the spheres as God had set them.

And she was already regretting her declaration to Gertrude that she would stay in bed that day: it would be wearisome without something to occupy her mind.

"I thank you for your tender concern," Margerite said, taking the book. "I shall see if I find it interesting."

Ruprecht and his army rode out again a few days later, going to make their warning procession along the border and perhaps, if they got the chance, to strike quickly across it. Although his earlier successes had heartened Margerite, she found after a couple of days that she was growing uneasy.

Perhaps it was because none of the dreams of flight that she had come to think of as signs of Ruprecht's safety had come to her; perhaps it was because she was sleeping lightly and uneasily, for though Cundrîê still came to her with a cup of hot wine every night, the old woman's draughts seemed to have lost their power to ease her.

She seemed to have lost some of her taste for food, as well; she found herself able to do no more than pick at the midday dinners Berthe cooked up for her, and often supper seemed to turn her stomach. Though Ruprecht's minstrels played while she dined, she took little pleasure even in them, for the notes of the lute seemed jangling and off-key, and the singer's tenor voice sounded in her ears with the sharp edge of wine about to turn to vinegar.

And, as if Margerite did not have enough to concern her, it seemed as though she could go nowhere without seeing either Cundrîê or Clingschor ghosting along the passage ahead of her, or suddenly rounding a corner where they had not been before.

She was almost beginning to feel hunted, or constrained, as though the old couple were not servants, but guards. Finally, one morning after a particularly uneasy night, Margerite decided that her ailment of thought must be due to the endless waiting inside the walls of Burg Falkenstein: surely she had never stayed cooped up so long in her father's keep?

I shall go down to Tiefensee, Margerite said to herself. It would be good for her to speak to Gerhild again, to see that the midwife and her babe were keeping well, as she would have done at her father's keep. With that in her mind, she felt more cheerful: she told the cook to make up a basket of nourishing foods, cheese and white bread and a brace of jugged partridges, and put a bottle of strong red French wine in as well.

Margerite was just passing out of the castle's inner gates when she heard Clingschor's deep bass behind her, "Frowe Gräfin, where are you going?"

"What is that to you?" Margerite replied. "Is there some matter that I must see to now? If so, tell me at once."

"Are you going down to Tiefensee?"

"As it happens, I am. Have I not the right to see to my own villagers?"

Clingschor's black eyes glinted down the long thin beak of his nose at her, and the deep creases bracketing his mouth darkened as he frowned. "It is not fit for the noble Frowe Gräfin to go among peasants. That is below your station, and unpleasing to the Herr Graf. You should have learned from your readings by now that it is the nature of strength to rule weakness, not to cosset it, and that gold loses its worth when it mingles with base elements, but becomes more worthy when it is purified and refined by the proper processes. Frowe Gräfin, you are a highborn woman of wisdom and power, and it is your nature and place to rule from this castle, not to sit in the village inn with those who tend your fields and flocks. If you wish a report on the coming harvest, or have an order to give to the Tiefenseers, you have only to tell Kai, and he will see to it."

"That is not the teaching of our Lord Jesu Christ," Margerite answered, suddenly angry. "Did he not go among the lowest folk even as the highest, and did he not teach that the poor were blessed in God's sight? I will go myself to see how matters are there, and if the Graf has a complaint of that, he may tell me himself." Defiantly, she reached down to pick up Kobolt, who was rubbing about her ankles, and held him one-handed to her breast. The big cat draped himself over her shoulder, purring happily and swishing his plumed black tail.

Astonishingly, Clingschor smiled, showing his long yellowed teeth as his face wrinkled into a goblin-mask. "It is well that you have learned to let nothing thwart your will. Remember that, when you have forgotten the foolish notions that guide it now." He turned, his shapeless robe of black silk swishing against his bony ankles as he walked away.

But the sense of triumph that had been swelling in Margerite's bosom drained away like wine spilling from an unstoppered skin as she made her way through the outer courtyard. She did not know, in truth, whether her anger at Clingschor had sprung up from revulsion at his unChristian advice, or simply because he had sought to stand in the way of her right as Gräfin to do what she chose.

Margerite wished, with all her heart, that she could talk with Father Hans, and ask his judgement as to whether she had spoken from charity or pride. But she might as well ask one of the wine barrels in the castle's storage room as its priest: she would get the same counsel from either of them.

Kobolt put a paw up to Margerite's face, his velvety pads stroking her cheek gently as if to comfort her. "You are a good tom," she said to him. "And at least you seem eager to go to the village - is there a she-cat there whom you wish to visit?" Kobolt purred, ducking beneath her chin and rubbing his head hard along her jaw. As she walked, her doubts and troubles began to fade from her mind: the sun was shining warmly through the leaves, and the air was sweet with the scents of grass and meadow-blossoms.

She was glad to be out of the castle for a little while; she had not realized how troubled she was, with nothing to do save work and worry. By the time she came to the midwife's house, Margerite's heart was almost light. She knocked once on the door; Gerhild's low voice called, "Come in."

The midwife was sitting at her table with her long honey-brown hair down about her shoulders, suckling her child at one bare breast. Her cheeks were pink with health, her breasts well-swollen with milk. She started to rise to greet Margerite, but the Gräfin waved her to sit.

"What brings you here this day, Frowe Gräfin?" Gerhild asked. "Is all well with you?"

"All is well," Margerite answered. She knew it was not true; and yet she could not put words to the things that had been troubling her. Perhaps later, she told herself. She set her basket on the table and let Kobolt leap to the floor. "I have brought you a few things to eat, for I know that nursing can take much strength from a woman's body."

"It can do that," Gerhild agreed. "Your care is most gracious, Frowe Gräfin, and I thank you."

"And how is your son?"

"Little Dietrich is growing strong and well now - you see how eagerly he suckles? He will be a big man, like his father."

Margerite cooed over the baby, helping Gerhild to rewrap the swaddling cloths about his limbs so that they would grow straight and strong. When Dietrich had fallen asleep at last, Gerhild said, "And how are things with you at the castle? You seem more troubled than before."

Margerite was ready to deny it, but the midwife's luminous gray eyes were gazing straight into her own, and Margerite knew that though she might lie, she would never be believed.

"It is hard for me with Ruprecht away at war," she hedged. "Fearing for him, I cannot rest easily. And...I wish that he had not left Bertram in charge of the guard, for he is not a pleasant man."

Gerhild raised a slanted brown eyebrow. "Really? I have heard from the lads who serve there that, though he may be stern, he is a good man. If he trains them harshly, it is only to keep them alive when they must defend themselves on the field, and he has made life easier for more than one young man from Tiefensee."

"That is not the man that I have seen," Margerite declared strongly. "He scowls at me, and it is plain that he hates me. And...I know now that he is a mercenary from the Free Companies. He is hardly fit to fight with Ruprecht's men, let alone to command under my husband."

Gerhild looked at her gravely. "I think that you judge the Hauptmann too harshly. For all the ugly brush on his face, I have heard that he well knows the manners that are fit for a castle: it is he who teaches the lads how to carry themselves as members of the Graf's guard, or when they are called upon to serve in the Graf's hall, so that they do not stumble around like dung-footed peasants in the sight of those better-born than themselves. And he can read and write, and he fights on horseback, I am told, as well as any knight. Bertram may have been a mercenary once, but he is no man of low stock."

"I had thought as much," Margerite admitted reluctantly. "But whatever his birth, if he were a man of honour…" He would not be here, she thought, but would not say. It sounded too much as though she were speaking against her husband, though the idea had never crossed her mind: it was only that the post of Ruprecht's Hauptmann was too good for a former mercenary, or a disgraced knight.

"No one has ever thought that he might be otherwise. It is true," Gerhild added, "that he has little to do with women: he has never even visited Ada's house late at night. But he has never said aught improper to any of the lads, either, so I do not think that he harbours unnatural vices. Perhaps he was unhappy in love once. It takes some men so."

"I cannot imagine a woman ever turning to him."

"Well, each has her own thoughts on what she wants a man to be," Gerhild replied. "There are many women in this village who think that you must be brave beyond the ordinary to have wedded Graf Ruprecht, and to dwell content in Burg Falkenstein."

"What do you mean by that?" Margerite asked tautly.

The midwife's triangular face paled beneath her light summer tan, but her gray eyes were steady on Margerite's. "I spoke to you before of Graf Ruprecht's rages, which have the folk here in fear of him. As may be: there are worse overlords, to whom cruelty is not a means of revenging a broken law, but simply a sport. But I think you will be little surprised if I say that none of the lads who serves up at the castle would like to come upon those two old servants of the Graf's in the darkness."

"I am not fond of them myself," Margerite admitted. "But as for fearing them - why should a strapping young man fear such withered old creatures? I think even Gertrude's young Eckhardt could break either of them in half without shedding a drop of sweat." Yet, even as she spoke, she could not keep from shivering, and she was sure Gerhild knew, as she did herself, that her words were empty bravado.

"You see," Gerhild said softly. "But I should not fear Bertram, if I were you. Whether he cares for you or not, I think he will do you no harm."

They spoke of smaller things a while longer, then Margerite made her excuses and left. She was halfway back to Burg Falkenstein, Kobolt scampering through the grass ahead of her, when she remembered that she had wanted to tell the midwife about her disturbing dreams. Another time, Margerite told herself. And if it displeases Cundrîê and Clingschor for me to visit in Tiefensee, so much the better.

Still, Margerite's unease did not lift in the days that followed. She was beginning to feel like a hawk kept in condition, but not flown for too long, so that she must bate and scream to relieve the endless strain of boredom interwoven with the tension of waiting for a flight that never came. Thinking on that, it came to Margerite that perhaps she would go hawking, since she had not gone out with a bird in some time.

Enid, Gawan, and Ruprecht's goshawk were still deep in moult, and the eagles were too heavy for her to fly, but she remembered that there was a sparrowhawk in the mews as well, and, though too small to take prey larger than partridge or wood-pigeon, the little birds made up for their size by being the only hawks that could be flown between St. Margaret's Day and Lammas.

Margerite ordered Gertrude to fetch her a light cloak, for the day was cool and damp, and then commanded her horse to be readied and supplied for a day out before she walked down to the mews. Johann was sitting quietly among the birds, his close-cropped red head bent low over the delicate stitching of a small leather hood. When Margerite entered, the little falconer laid his work aside and rose smoothly to bow to her.

"What is your desire, Frowe Gräfin?"

"I would go hawking today. Yes," she said, raising a hand to forestall his protests, "I know that the sparrowhawk is the only one fit for flying now, but it will please me greatly to set her at a brace of partridges or thrushes, or whatever she may find."

"Hmm." Johann bit his lip, looking down at the rushes lying over the floor. "Well, Frowe Gräfin, the bird is yours to command, but I must warn you about her. Even for a sparrowhawk, she is high-tempered, prone to carry her prey, and often slow in coming back to the fist. You might find better sport if I went with you to bear the burden of one of the Graf's eagles."

Margerite thought about it for a moment - but Ruprecht had spoken with such pride of his eagle-hunts for roedeer, and with the rigors of the war, he had never had the chance to show her what his great birds could do. It seemed to her that letting the falconer take her out with the eagle would be almost like being unfaithful to Ruprecht, by depriving him of a delight that was rightfully his. And besides, she felt little inclined towards company: a long ride by herself was what she desired, with only the bright uncaring gaze of the sparrowhawk on her.

"No. I will take the sparrowhawk. Be sure, I have flown such birds before, and know well enough how to handle them."

"As you will, Frowe Gräfin." The falconer looked up into her face pleadingly. "But take the greatest care with her, I beg you. Although the Graf seldom flies her himself, he would be heartbroken if she were lost. He won her in a tournament in Triers four years ago, and she was the favourite bird of the Gräfin Radegund."

"I shall fly her carefully, and treat her tenderly," Margerite promised. "What is her name?"

"Frowe Gräfin, she answers to Cundwîr, and this is the whistle to which she is trained." Johann pursed his lips, letting out a sharp three-note burst.

Ruprecht's beasts have more wholesome names than his servants, Margerite thought briefly as she repeated the whistle for the falconer: Cundwîr, Parzival's Grail-maiden, was certainly a better companion than Clingschor, or even Cundrîê. But, of course, Ruprecht could not have been responsible for the naming of the old couple, and it was unworthy of her to blame them for what they could not help.

When she walked out of the mews with the sparrowhawk on her gloved hand, Mathilde was saddled and waiting, but to her great annoyance, Margerite saw that Bertram was standing beside the horse.

"Where are you going?" he asked harshly.

"I am going to ride out for a day's hawking," she answered. "Have you news of something important, that it should keep me from the field?"

"You should not ride anywhere alone," Bertram declared. "A single man could take you captive, and then what would befall? You should stay here in safety; but if you must ride out, then you will ride with a guard of men about you."

"You credit Graf Heinrich with...I do not know what, but I doubt very much that he has sent one man, or even a small band, to lurk in our woods in hopes that I might come riding by someday. I do not need a guard, as if I were a prisoner, and I wish to be alone."

"You shall not be," Bertram stated flatly. The two of them glared at each other for a moment; Cundwîr, as if sensing the rancour between them, bated and shrieked, her voice shrill and painful in Margerite's ears. Margerite found herself briefly tempted to take the sparrowhawk back to the mews and go up to her chamber to sulk over her embroidery, but she knew that would do her little good.

"If I must have a guard, then I suppose that one man may come with me. But let him ride well behind me, and make no sound, for I do not wish to be disturbed or chattered at."

Bertram frowned, his broad forehead creasing alarmingly. Beneath his black beard, Margerite could see his lips twisting, as though he had bitten into a fruit and found it foul. "If you will have only one guardsman," he said slowly, "then it must be myself, for with the Graf gone, I am the best fitted to defend you at need."

Margerite almost relented then, for if she did not wish to have castle guardsmen about her, far less did she wish to spend the day under Bertram's baleful stare. But she recognised the truth of his words; and if he stayed well behind her and left her alone, he would be easy enough to ignore.

"So be it, then," she said. "Ready your horse and mount quickly, for Cundwîr is ready to fly, and I do not wish to wait long."

The dampness of the day had turned to a light drizzle as they rode out, a gray veil hanging over the dark peak of the mountain behind the ravine and dulling the green of the fields below. Cundwîr fluffed her feathers against the dewy mist and glared about herself, but, in spite of the chill, Margerite found that she was already feeling better as Mathilde's walk quickened to take her ahead of Bertram, following the path along the river to Tiefensee. The lake's surface was gray as burnished pewter, the occasional gust of scattering raindrops rippling across it like a cast of delicate hammer-marks on metal.

Several ducks dabbled among the reeds at the edge, and Margerite thought regretfully of her peregrines moulting in their mews, for duck was a fine quarry for falcons. But each thing in God's time, she reminded herself: for the health of the birds, it was best not to disturb them now, and she would have good enough sport with the little sparrowhawk.

For some time, Margerite skirted the fields, hoping that a partridge or quail would start up. But she saw nothing fit to fly Cundwîr at: though a lark twittered ahead in the gray sky, it had already flown too high and far for a sure kill, and, mindful of Johann's warnings, she did not want to loose the sparrowhawk at a quarry she did not have a good chance of taking down.

At last she decided that there was little hunting for her in the open today, and turned towards the treeline: sparrowhawks were at their best over fields, but in the woods there would be a fair likelihood of starting out pigeons or thrushes. The woods seemed very still beneath the gray sky, with only the occasional rustling as a gust of wind whispered through the branches.

The dark needles of the pines dripped lightly, but steadily, as the mist beaded on them, the little drops rolling down to fall from the sharp tips onto the carpet of dead needles and damp earth beneath. Even the roe-deer who roamed freely in the wood seemed to have hidden themselves: though now and again a line of delicate hoof-prints in the forest mould crossed the trail, Margerite did not see so much as a flash of ruddy hide through the trees, nor hear any light crackling of branches, save for the twigs that snapped beneath her own horse's hoofs as she rode.

She was almost ready to turn back when the pigeon flew up ahead of her in a low clapping of gray wings. At once she tossed Cundwîr into the air. The sparrowhawk arrowed straight for her quarry, but though the slip was close, Cundwîr had not gained the height for a strike, and the pigeon was staying low, keeping beneath the protection of the trees' branches in its flight.

Undaunted, the sparrowhawk swerved above her prey; Margerite spurred her horse on to keep sight of them, her hands clenched white on the reins in nervous excitement. Cundwîr dropped again, and for a moment Margerite could not see either hawk or pigeon.

"O, strike well!" she murmured as if the sparrowhawk could hear her, cantering down the trail. "Have you got it?"

But as she rounded the bend before her, she heard the tinkling of Cundwîr's bells above her, and looked up. The small hawk was sitting sulkily at the top of a pine, with no sign of the pigeon anywhere. Margerite sighed. Perhaps she ought to have known better than to loose Cundwîr at a pigeon in the woods, after all. But at least she had not taken flight for the wild, and now, Mother Maria willing, Margerite could lure her down and ride in search of some better prey for her.

Margerite held up her gloved fist hopefully, calling, "Cundwîr! Cundwîr," then whistling the three sharp notes Johann had taught her. The sparrowhawk glared down at her, ruffling her brown feathers up and shifting uneasily from foot to foot with a tiny jingling of bells. "Cundwîr!" She whistled again.

After a few minutes of this, Margerite gave up, reaching into her bag for the lure instead. It was a well-made one, a pair of dried lark-wings bound back to back, with a small chunk of meat tied onto it. She tossed it into the air, swinging it temptingly on its string. Margerite knew that she was good at handling a lure so that its movements looked like those of a bird in flight, but Cundwîr only looked down at it in contempt, then tucked her head down to smooth her feathers with her beak.

Margerite resigned herself to a long coaxing, alternately swinging the lure and lifting her fist, punctuating her sweet calls with keen whistles to the bird. She had not been at it long, however, when she heard the sound of hooves behind her. Turning her head, she saw that Bertram was riding up; when she looked back at the soft noise of ringing above, Cundwîr was already in flight, circling high above the woods, then sweeping suddenly westwards and out of sight.

"Why did you disturb me?" Margerite asked furiously. "You frightened the hawk, and now we shall be all day getting her back."

"If there is anyone of ill intention in these woods, they must have heard you and will know where you are. We should ride back to Burg Falkenstein and send Johann out: let him search for the bird, for she knows him well and will likelier come to his fist than to yours."

"I lost her, and I should find her," Margerite insisted stubbornly. "Perhaps you know little of the honour of falconers, but I will not come back to Johann without the hawk unless there is no other choice. She went that way, and I shall follow her, whether you wish to come with me or not."

Bertram sighed, but turned his horse to follow Margerite's through the underbrush, making their way in the direction of Cundwîr's flight. Twice more they caught sight of the small brown shape circling through the air, but the sparrowhawk seemed to be wilfully fleeing from them.

Margerite watched her flight with as much wistfulness as despair: the sharp curve of the little raptor's wings through the air reminded her keenly of the dreams that had not come to her since before St. Johannes' day, the rushing wind bearing her up and the sweeping exaltation of flight, half-remembered upon awakening, but all the dearer for the mist that lay between waking thought and the realized desire of the dream.

The rain was growing heavier, thickly veiling the mountains' ridges and dulling the sky. Margerite pulled her cloak tight about her neck to keep the heavy drops that fell from the branches from rolling down her back.

"Are you ready to return now?" Bertram finally enquired. "She will not fly in this weather; she must be waiting in a tree somewhere."

"And if she is, she will be the easier to find," Margerite replied. "We shall go on...shhh!"

For it seemed to her that, through the soft pattering of the rain on the damp forest floor, she had heard the faint tinkle of bells again.

They waited in silence for a time. Margerite was about to command that they ride forward once more when she heard the soft jingling more clearly, off to the left. "This way."

The two of them rode slowly, for the bushes were thick and the horses were not finding their way easily. But suddenly they were in a little clearing at the side of a hill; and above, Cundwîr perched on the scraggly branches near the top of a pine whose jagged crown had once been blasted by lightning.

Margerite lifted her fist, calling, "Cundwîr!" and whistling yet again. This time, to her surprise, the sparrowhawk lifted into the air, flying straight down to settle on her glove. "Fair bird, good bird," Margerite soothed, her body feeling shaken and limp in the great wave of relief that washed over her. She reached down into her saddlebag for the tidbits that she had brought with her to reward the sparrowhawk, letting Cundwîr snap greedily at the little dark pieces of meat.

"Well, you have found her," Bertram said, his voice almost disappointed. "I trust you do not want to fly her again today."

"No," Margerite admitted. "But I am tired and hungry. Since the rain seems to be stopping again, we shall pause here to eat before we go back. There is bread and cheese and wine in my saddlebag, and a cloth to spread upon the ground: fetch them out."

Glowering, Bertram did as she had commanded. It seemed to Margerite that she could almost hear him thinking that the Hauptmann of the Graf's guard had no business acting as servant, even to the Gräfin, but he said nothing. The rebellious hawk still on her fist, Margerite eased herself down from Mathilde's back and settled herself upon the thick piece of gray wool.

Now that she had the leisure to look around herself, Margerite saw that, beneath the overgrowth of brambles, there was a small grotto carved into the hill, lined with rough-cut stones. At its foot was a stone basin. Though it was filled with dirt and rocks and overgrown with moss, Margerite could still see that there was a word cut into its rim. Curious, she rose and looked more closely. It read MARIENBRUNNEN: Maria's Spring.

As Margerite stepped back in surprise, she caught her heel on something, stumbling and nearly falling. Cundwîr bated and screeched in protest, but Margerite regained her balance, squatting down to see what had tripped her. Beneath the thickly piled mess of rotting needles and earth, she could make out a gray edge of carven stone: the fold of a garment, the curve of an arm. At once she realized what she must have found, and a shudder of awe and sadness went through her.

"Bertram!" she said sharply. "Bertram, this was once a shrine to Mother Maria. But it has been..." Her voice trailed off, for she did not know the right words. Cast down? Defiled? Years of weather might have choked the basin and the stream that must once have led into it, but it would have taken a strong man to cast the statue so far from her pedestal.

Bertram came over slowly, as though he feared to come too close. As he looked at the half-obscured word, then down at the statue, he drew in his breath. "Yes. It must have been."

"Well, it is not past mid-afternoon. There is plenty of time for us to clean it as best we can, in honour of the Virgin who must once have blessed this place."

Bertram stepped back, hazel eyes widening as he stared at her in surprise. "You cannot mean...is that what you want?"

"Of course it is!" Margerite snapped. "I do not know what happened here, but it will do Mother Maria honour for us to restore it, and good to our souls." She went over to a tree at the edge of the clearing, tethering Cundwîr to a low branch by her jesses, then came back to the basin, to begin scooping rocks and mouldy dirt away with her bare hands.

After a moment, Bertram silently joined her. Now and again she caught him looking at her - wonderingly? - out of the corner of his eye, but he said nothing, working with precise, ferocious speed. It was not long before the basin was cleared, and Bertram was scraping away the thick layers of moss to expose the leaden rim of a pipe leading into the hill.

"The water must have flowed out here," he said. "But the pipe is clogged. If you will, you may be able to clean it out with a long stick, and I will see to Her statue."

Margerite found a stick on the ground, prodding it in and dragging the muck out of the pipe bit by bit as Bertram dug. At last her work was rewarded by a trickle of water, thin and brown at first, but gradually growing stronger and clearer as the spring's own flow cleared away the last of the blockage.

Margerite could smell the water, a sharp metallic scent with a strong hint of sulfur, and she knew what manner of place this was. There were many such shrines where Maria or a saint had blessed a stream, that the afflicted might come to and drink of it or bathe in it and find healing, and often pipe and bowl were set to guide the waters and make it easier for sufferers to partake of their blessing.

Reverently Margerite bowed her head, dipping her two cupped hands into the cool water and lifting them to her lips. "Mother Maria, bless me," she murmured. The spring's taste was strong and medicinal, heavy with the acrid scents of its healing power, but Margerite drank it gladly.

As she straightened up and looked behind her to see how Bertram was getting on, she saw that he had paused in his labours to stare at her again. "What is the matter?" she asked. "Have you never seen anyone ask the Virgin for blessing before?"

Bertram flushed, glancing away from her. "It is not…" he mumbled. Then his back straightened, and he looked her in the eyes, his gaze suddenly so keen and bright that Margerite found her neck stiffening in the effort not to turn away. When he spoke again, his voice was very clear, almost cultivated in its deep intonation. "I may have misjudged you, Frowe Gräfin. I beg your forgiveness."

"Misjudged me in what?" Margerite asked. But Bertram did not answer, only bent to his digging once more. She could see the red flush spreading up from his beard across his cheekbones, and wondered what thoughts he had harboured about her.

Nothing good, surely, Margerite said to herself, but she found that she could not rouse the anger that Bertram's coldness usually kindled in her. As he knelt clearing the earth away from the statue of Maria, heedless of the wetness soaking in through the knees of his trousers and the drops of rain gathering in the black tangles of his hair to run in sodden trails down the back of his gray tunic, Margerite could not help remembering how she had seen him in the monastery, weeping before the Virgin.

He seeks redemption, she thought. And no man is so evil that Mother Maria may not be moved to beg mercy for him, if he calls to her. She remembered, as well, how Gerhild had spoken of Bertram's kindness to the young men he trained in arms: was he yet atoning for his sin, whatever it was?

"You have my forgiveness," she said softly to Bertram. She was not sure whether he heard her or not, for he made no reply, only heaved at the statue, the muscles of his broad shoulders writhing and his face contorting with the effort until she came free from the mould, tilting slowly upright.

The statue of the Virgin was nearly four feet tall, the gray stone deeply stained by her years of lying in earth and moss and mould. Her hands were clasped beneath her cloak, and her head was inclined downward: from her pedestal, she would have seemed to be looking down in pity and love.

Maria's face was not skillfully carved: the jaw was too angled, the bones of the cheeks too prominent, so that she had the look of one ravaged by sickness and hunger, but nevertheless, there was something in the cast of the Virgin's dark-socketed stone eyes that struck to Margerite's heart: wide with a serenity that belied her gaunt face, they seemed to speak of profound understanding and pity, of a wisdom that saw and a heart that was moved by all things in the world.

Looking at the statue, Margerite felt at once abashed and exalted, and she knew that, whatever the craftsman's defects of skill, he had prayed to Mother Maria with a true heart as he worked for her glory, and she had answered him. Bertram looked up to see that the stone platform beside the stream-pipe was clear, then crouched down, wrapping his arms about the statue just below the hips.

His legs straightened; the muscles of his back and shoulders bulged, straining hard at the seams of his tunic, and his face looked as though the blood darkening it would burst through the skin. He took a first step, then a second, and Margerite saw that his feet were sinking nearly ankle-deep into the wet mould. She stared, breathless, as he trod heavily to the platform and paused a moment. The seam down his back split with a sharp rending sound; Bertram grunted deeply, and, in a single desperate burst of strength, heaved the statue back up into her place.

He staggered back, breathing hard. The blood drained slowly from his face as its contortions smoothed, leaving him pale and - for the first time that Margerite had ever seen - almost peaceful in appearance, though he was trembling with the aftermath of his struggle. Margerite did not want to speak, lest she break that peace: she only waited, silent, as Bertram sank to his knees before the Virgin, his lips moving slowly.

After a time, Bertram rose again, going towards the horses. "We should begin to ride back," he said. "I believe I know roughly where we are, but it may take a little time to find the proper road."

"Will you not drink of Maria's waters?" Margerite asked.

Bertram looked down at her. His disheveled black tangle of hair and beard, wilder than ever and standing out in wet spikes over his face and head, hid most of his expression, but in his hazel eyes, Margerite felt that she could see something of the harsh thoughts in his soul, flailing him and driving him on like the knotted hempen lash of a flagellant.

"She has given more," Margerite said gently, "to many who have done less for her. Does not the workman deserve a drink to refresh him?"

As if in a trance, Bertram turned, walking back to the fountain. The water was spilling over the rim of the basin now, dripping down the wet gray stone in little clear rivulets. He knelt beneath it, opening his mouth as the healing drops ran down his face like rain. As Margerite watched, she felt herself overwhelmed by...she knew not what, but she found that she was weeping silently, and yet there was no sadness in her heart.

As they rode back to the castle, Margerite, thinking aloud, said. "We ought to bring a few of the castle-folk down to clean up the shrine properly. Cut the path back again, clear up the brambles..."

"No!" Bertram said, shaking his head violently. She looked at him in startlement. "Forgive me, Frowe Gräfin, but..." His dark brows furrowed, his gaze turning inward; his fists clenched and the muscles of his arms tightened, as though he were wrestling with something within. "I do not think that such a mission would find much favour in Burg Falkenstein, and...what would the Graf say to it?"

"He would say..." Margerite checked herself. She had been about to say, He would say that I might command our servants as I will, but, to her sadness, she realized that she was not sure. Ruprecht tolerated her keeping of Sundays, even made no complaint at the lack of meat and cheese on Fridays, but how would he react if she took some of his men from their work for the sake of restoring a shrine he cared nothing about, especially in the middle of a war?

"It would be best not to speak of it to any other," Bertram said, his voice flat, almost hollow with resignation. "When I can, I will come down here to tend to it - and, if you wish to pray at the shrine, I will accompany you."

"So be it, then."

"And, Frowe Gräfin - I bid you to be careful. I thought that you knew all the ways of Burg Falkenstein, but I see now that you cannot."

"What are you speaking of?" Margerite asked him sharply.

Bertram looked up at the dripping leaves above them. With his hair and beard slicked down by the rain, Margerite noticed suddenly that his brow was wide and well-shaped, the line of his jaw sharp and clean: shaven and trimmed, he might be a handsome man.

"Best not to ask me any further, Frowe Gräfin. Your innocence may be your strongest shield, if it has protected you this far - Perhaps what I mean is only that Burg Falkenstein is not a place where the care of one's soul is easy, as you must have seen for yourself by now. I myself was once..." He stopped, looking away, and she knew that he would say no more.

Margerite rode on, her heart downcast. It was coming to her painfully, sharp and uneasy as the first pangs of tainted food in her belly, that the life of the spirit was one thing she would never be able to share with Ruprecht, any more than she could share it with Cundwîr or Gawan or Kobolt. Like them, he was a magnificent creature of the earth; and like them, so far as she could tell, his fierce heart could be moved by neither sacraments nor Passion nor the love of the Virgin.

Yet, unlike the beautiful hunting beasts, Ruprecht was a man, baptized at birth and with every capability for understanding the needs of the soul - and doomed, at death, to the long torments of Purgatory, if his eyes would not open in life. Margerite knew that she herself was no nun exalted beyond the world by her vocation: she loved the pleasures of the earth too well, and the lawful delights of her marriage and position, and she would not even have chosen to forego the trials that being Ruprecht's Gräfin had brought upon her.

Yet she also knew that without the comfort of her trust in Mother Maria and Christ, she would not be able to bear the greater sorrows that her life had brought and would bring her again; her joys would not be as keen, nor her heart capable of the same exaltation. It saddened her beyond measure that this aspect of her being, and of the greater world beyond, was something to which Ruprecht was and would remain blind.

Blind - or worse, choosing to deny. Uncomfortably, Margerite thought of the books that Cundrîê had brought her, books that were not kept in the library, but hidden somewhere else in the castle. There was no harm in natural philosophy of itself, but of late, she had begun to wonder if some of what she was reading went beyond philosophy and into heresy: Clingschor's disturbing exhortations to her were certainly against the teachings of the Church. Although the wild accusations of sodomy and unholy rites made against the Templars by the French had been disproven in Germany, that had been over thirty years ago, and many strange cults had since sprung up in the wake of the Death.

It would not have surprised her in the least to learn that Cundrîê and Clingschor were farther down the road to Hell than most, and their influence could be doing Ruprecht no good: if she were in danger, as Bertram had hinted, was he not in danger threefold? And yet Margerite did not know how she could speak of the matter to her husband, for preaching at him would only set him more firmly against doing what he ought to for his soul's sake - or even, if she bothered him too greatly with it, rouse his wrath against her.

So thinking, Margerite was able only to exchange a few polite words with Johann when she brought the sparrowhawk back to the mews, then left swiftly. The four flights of spiralling staircase seemed longer and steeper to her than usual, her legs leaden as though all the life-blood had drained from them. It was only that she reached the top that the unease in her belly clenched, and she felt the first stickiness of blood between her thighs.

She had forgotten that her courses were due upon her - perhaps in hope that they would not come - but they were, and the tightening cramp of her womb warned her that it would be one of those rare times when the pains of Eve were hard upon her. Kobolt was waiting in her room, curled upon her bed with his plumed tail wrapped over his nose and his yellow eyes gleaming above its black veil. As soon as she entered, he leapt up, rubbing about her legs and miaowing anxiously.

Margerite bent to pet him, grimacing as another pang twinged through her belly. Other women had warned her that the ache of a bleeding womb, keen as the pains might sometimes be, was only a slight foretaste of the pains of childbirth; but Margerite would willingly have traded her lighter cramps for all Gerhild's agony, for the latter was redeemed and made blessed and joyful by the birth of a child, while the monthly bleeding betided only the disappointment of her hopes.

"Gertrude!" she called. "Gertrude, come swiftly! I need you."

But instead of Gertrude's light tread, Margerite heard the rustling whisper of Cundrîê's silken robe, and the grayness filtering through the windows cast the old woman's ugly face into a stony gargoyle-relief. "What do you wish, Frowe Gräfin?"

"Only that you fetch Gertrude for me," said Margerite. Then, unwillingly. "No: my courses have come painfully upon me. I would have you make a tisane to ease them."

The hooded dark eyes glared unnervingly; Cundrîê pressed her sunken lips together, looking Margerite up and down. "So you are not with child."

"Pregnant women seldom get their courses!" Margerite flared. "No, I am not."

Cundrîê's gray head drew back slowly, like the head of a snake recoiling before a strike. "I see. I shall fetch your tisane, and mayhap it will bring you easing. Would you like a book to occupy your mind, as well?"

"I know where the library is," Margerite said. Although Cundrîê's tomes of astrology and alchemy were strangely fascinating - as far as she could understand them - Bertram's strange warning was still ringing in her mind. *I thought that you knew all the ways of Burg Falkenstein...Burg Falkenstein is not a place where the care of one's soul is easy.*

She wished, suddenly, that she had thought to look for a Book of Hours in Freiburg, one of those beautifully illuminated texts with prayers and passages from the Bible, on which she might meditate.

Mother Maria, Margerite thought, *guide me through this darkness. Help me to know how to warn Ruprecht against whatever corruption is in the mind of his servants, and to save him - and myself - from that peril of which Bertram would not tell me. I fear we are all in danger from Ruprecht's companions: from Cundrîê and Clingschor within, and from the dealings of his knightly brotherhood without, as they seek to sway the mind of Kaiser Karl from the counsels of the Pope.*

Margerite shivered, feeling suddenly very cold and vulnerable. She wished now that she had spoken about the Order with Ruprecht when she came back from Freiburg. Even if that had meant admitting that she had listened at the wall like a gossipy maid spying on her betters, she might have been able to get some answers out of him, and might know more of how matters really stood now, with the war the Order seemed to have fomented and with Ruprecht himself, in his dealings with Graf Günther and the other members of his knightly brotherhood.

When Ruprecht came back, perhaps...after he had lain with her, when his heart was warm and mild towards her, then she would confess her small crime to him, and offer her wholehearted help. And then, perhaps, once he had learned to fully trust her...perhaps she could open his eyes to the inner perils of his castle. If he does not know already, Margerite thought. She shivered again.

She knew that a woman's mind was weakest during her courses, as Eve had proven weak; she prayed to Mother Maria, who was free of Eve's curse, that her thoughts were no more than the fears of a brain disordered by the humours of which her womb was now purging itself. If her dreams were the work of the Devil, if Ruprecht had already been lured into mortal sin by his strange servants, then she did not know what, except the grace of the Virgin, might save the two of them.

Margerite dreamed again that night, winging dizzyingly high above Burg Falkenstein. But this time she heard no voice guiding her, no calling and no patient questions. Instead, she was flying north, the black sky smoothing almost unnoticed into the pale blue of daylight. Below her lay a castle greater than Burg Falkenstein, high-built and walled. Fountains sparkled in its courtyard like sprays of diamond among the close-mown green lawns and paved pathways; well-tended oaks and lindens shaded benches of marble and well-wrought wood.

Below, a young man stood with his hand on a woman's white arm, both of them dressed in fine clothes of bright silk and rich velvet. Though distant, their faces were clear to the falcon's long sight: her delicate features and sharply arched eyebrows beneath a coronet of thick coppery braids, his strong, clean-shaven face framed by the simple and elegant cut of his brown curls. It seemed to her that there was something familiar about the young man, as though she had once seen his face through a veil of dark fog.

He said something to the woman, who laughed and waved her left hand, the large cabochon stone of the ring on her forefinger gleaming with a deep ruby glow in the sunlight. The black words engraved in the gold about the stone were clear, to the falcon's eye, as the tail of a mouse whisking through the grass far below: EX TENEBRAE LUX.

Even as she read the ring's message, the scene below her shifted like mist in the wind. It seemed to her that the stones of the castle grew glass-clear to her gaze, that she was looking at the same young man, but haggard and unshaven, his brown hair standing on end in wild points. He was locked into a chamber with great iron bolts across the door and guards standing before it; now he staggered forward, shouting through the thick oak planks.

"I am innocent!" she heard him call. "Jürgen, Erich, how long have you known me? Can you, at least, not believe me?"

The guards turned their backs and put their hands to their ears, their young faces twisting as if it hurt them to hear his cries. With the lines of pain graven into his face beneath the dark scurf of fresh beard, he looked more familiar yet to her. She struggled to remember, to call a human name into her wild falcon thoughts...

"Bertram," Margerite whispered. She was awake at once, her eyes open to the darkness. Gertrude was sleeping still, a deep-breathing heap on her bed. Maria be thanked, she had not heard her frowe speak the Hauptmann's name.

Margerite tried to calm herself, thinking of what the dream could have meant. For her to see Bertram as a young nobleman, clean-shaven and well-favoured...though his hair had been brown instead of stark black...

My mind is growing disturbed, Margerite said to herself. And it is shameful for a woman to dream about a man who is not her husband. Yet she was not long from Maria's shrine: could the dream have been sent to her by the Virgin? She cast her mind back, trying to remember the details more clearly.

"I am innocent!" he had said. Innocent of what? Something dreadful, to have brought such a high-born man to the state in which she had seen him. But a strong enough accusation, whether true or false, could destroy as surely as undeniable proof: every woman who must look to her name for chastity knew that.

There had been something else, as well, something nagging at Margerite's mind like a uncut toenail snagging in the soft leather of a shoe. She twisted her hands together, the smooth gold of her wedding ring turning under her fingers. Yes: the woman's ring, which looked so like Ruprecht's, save for the ruby stone where Ruprecht wore an amethyst. The motto, which she had never bothered to read on Ruprecht's ring: EX TENEBRAE LUX - From Darkness, Light.

Now that she thought on it, she remembered that Damiano had worn a similar ring, except that it had been set with an onyx - and Wolfram wore one also. An emblem of the Order? It must be, but why would a woman wear the sign of a knightly brotherhood?

A dreadful suspicion was beginning to grow in Margerite's heart. Resolutely, she pushed the blankets aside, grasping for her shift and pulling it over her head. She kindled a taper from the ash-blanketed coals in the stove and walked out, down the corridor that led towards Ruprecht's room.

As she had thought he would be, Clingschor was standing in front of her before she was halfway down the hall. "Where are you going so late, Frowe Gräfin?" he asked, his deep bass voice echoing unnervingly from the stone walls.

Margerite did not answer. She was looking at the old man's hands, white and thin as jointed bones against the black silk of his sleeves. Then she had to struggle not to let her knees sag beneath the relief that rushed over her like the current of a strong river, for Clingschor - as she had desperately hoped, as she had feared would not be the case - wore no rings, not even a plain band.

"What can I do for you?" Clingschor said. "Do you wish Cundrîê to make you some hot wine?"

"No." Margerite straightened her back, bold in the knowledge that matters were not as bad as her imagination had made them for a moment. Spurred on by the heady mixture of relief and nervousness burning through her veins, she told him bluntly, "My chamber-pot was full, and I did not wish to wait for Gertrude to clean it. Out of my way, for I must do that which no one can do for me." She would not have spoken so to any other man for shame, but Clingschor neither blushed nor flinched as he ought to have done, only stepped aside with a small ironic bow.

"You should flog your maidservant for her carelessness, Frowe Gräfin," he said. Margerite did not reply, but swept past him and down the stairs with all her dignity, hoping that he would not notice the flame of her taper trembling in her hand.

When she was back in bed, it took a very long time for Margerite to stop shivering. But at last the warmth of her blankets and her own tiredness began to overcome her. I will dream no further this night, she told herself firmly. I have seen all I can bear for now: be still, my soul.

As she began to drift towards sleep, she felt the soft brush of a long-furred tail across her face, and heard the deep rumble of Kobolt's purr. Margerite smiled drowsily at the thought that the black tomcat was standing guard against her night-troubles. Thus comforted, it was easy for her to let the last of the tension seep from her muscles and the thoughts from her mind, and soon she slept without dreams.

Chapter Six

Ruprecht and his men came home sooner than Margerite had expected, several of them with limbs swathed in makeshift bandages or riding in the supply wagons. They had run into one of Heinrich's raiding bands, who had had their backs to the river and been unable to flee: Ruprecht's soldiers and the Bear's Paw Company had wiped them out, but not without suffering some losses.

When Ruprecht came to Margerite's room that night, though he had bathed and dressed in clean clothes, the flickering candlelight showed her the shadows beneath his eyes and the little lines of tiredness gathering at their corners. For a time he sat upon her bed, stroking her hair with one hand and Kobolt's head with the other, and did not speak.

"My wife, are you well?" Ruprecht said finally, his brilliant blue eyes meeting Margerite's searchingly. "Cundrîê told me that you had suffered a…a women's difficulty."

"It was no more than all women who are not with child suffer every month," Margerite replied, baffled. She could not understand why Cundrîê had spoken to Ruprecht of such a thing, nor why it should seem to so worry her husband, save for the disappointment of both their hopes of a child.

"You must take better care of yourself," Ruprecht went on, and Margerite could hear the strain of worry behind his voice, as though his words bore a great weight she did not comprehend. "Perhaps it would be better if you did not go out on horseback so often, and climbed the stairs no more than you must. I know that you have taken great burdens upon yourself in the course of this war, more than you ought: you should rest, and let Kai and Bertram deal with matters of supplies and accounting."

Margerite put her hand upon his arm. "Ruprecht, my love, no woman needs such care until her child is already showing in her belly. It was only…" she flushed at shame for having to speak to her husband of that matter, but he seemed so worried and sad that she had to console him, no matter the cost. "It was only my monthly courses, coming when they were due, according to the curse that God laid on Eve. If we got no child last time, mayhap we shall have better fortune now." She leaned her head upon Ruprecht's broad shoulder, looking up at him.

But, though he sat with Margerite for some time, his speech with her punctuated with kisses and light caresses, Ruprecht did not seek to make love to his wife tonight, only, after a while, rose and bade her goodnight. When he had gone, Margerite did not call Gertrude back in straight away. Instead, she sat by herself, feeling more than a little lonely. Why had he not lain with her, when she would so gladly have welcomed him back after his battle? And she, too, had thoughts of which she would like to unburden her heart: why did Ruprecht forsake her, when now, of all times, she needed to speak freely to him?

It is late, and he is tired: he has ridden and fought, and seen some of his men die. Give him time: he will be more himself tomorrow, Margerite counselled herself. And telling him your fears about his servants and your doubts about his knightly brothers is hardly the way to greet a husband just come in from war. She called in Gertrude, eager to lose her forsaken thoughts in the serving maid's chatter, and Gertrude did not disappoint her: she had managed to find some time to speak to Eckhardt when the men had returned, and gleefully recounted all his deeds to her mistress as she helped her undress.

Margerite listened with half an ear, glad of the soothing noise of Gertrude's light voice, but her full attention snapped back to the maid when the girl turned her head and the glitter of something bright at her throat caught Margerite's eye. Margerite looked more closely: the servant was wearing a little silver crucifix - a piece not too fine for her position as the Gräfin's maid, but one Margerite had never seen on her before.

"Where did that come from?" Margerite asked.

Gertrude giggled, her hand going to her neck as if to cover the pendant. "Eckhardt gave it to me at the Midsummer dancing. He got it on the Graf's first raid, when they looted the village - he said Hauptmann Bertram had given it him as his share of the spoils, and warned him to keep it by him to protect him against evil. I would not have thought the Hauptmann to be a good Christian, would you?"

"The state of Bertram's soul is not a matter for you to judge," Margerite said, rather more sharply than she had meant to.

She could not rid herself of the image of Bertram kneeling beneath the stone bowl of the holy spring, the water running over his upturned face as he gazed at the Virgin. The thought was comforting and troubling at once, and she could not say why: it was easier for her to turn from that to the problem of Gertrude and Eckhardt.

"But if Eckhardt is giving you pieces of silver jewelry, and you are wearing them so blithely, we shall have to arrange a betrothal soon, lest your chastity be doubted. I think that Ruprecht believes that I ought to have a better-born maidservant, and I do not wish him to have any reason to send you away and leave me in Cundrîê's care, even for a little time." Again Margerite wondered uneasily what the old woman had told Ruprecht about her courses, and why? The thought writhed about the bottom of her mind like a snake in the darkness, a snake she could not see, though she could hear the dry rustling of scales on stone.

"Well, Eckhardt's father is dead, but his mother and sister live in Tiefensee together with his old grandfather. It is the old man you will have to deal with, and I think…" Gertrude giggled again… "you will find that an interesting task. Eckhardt says he is the only man in the village who is not terrified of the Graf. He will even risk taking a bow out to the vineyard when the deer are eating the grapes, and no one else would think of doing that, for they fear Graf Ruprecht's wrath too greatly."

"As well they ought, when it comes to a question of shooting his deer," Margerite said severely. Yet this too was discomforting: she remembered, all too clearly, Gerhild's voice saying, He would go into rages, and do things that… set everyone in the village in fear of him. There was one lad who had barked a young oak tree to make a whistle…Graf Ruprecht put him to death in a frightening manner. "Still, old terror or not, I think I can deal with the man. If," she added belatedly, "you want to marry Eckhardt. If you do not, you ought to return that crucifix to him and stop talking to him."

Gertrude clasped her hand protectively about the silver pendant. "O, frowe, of course I want to marry Eckhardt! He is sweet and brave and handsome, and we will be ever so happy together."

Handsome was not the word that sprang to Margerite's mind when she thought of young Eckhardt's gangly body and horselike face, but she said nothing about that: it was unkind to mock the blindness of love. "And he is willing to marry you?"

"I am sure he is. He has already spoken of what life is like for the castle's guardsmen who must leave their families in Tiefensee, and mentioned several times that those couples who both work inside Burg Falkenstein seem to be the happiest."

"That seems clear enough," said Margerite, smiling. "Very well: I shall start making plans for your betrothal, though we must send word to your family at Hirschenberg, and it may be a little while before that can be done."

"I am content enough to wait, frowe, so long as I do not have to wait too long."

Margerite scrutinized her maid carefully. "Are you likely to start putting on flesh around the middle too quickly if your marriage is delayed?"

Gertrude's round cheeks flushed, her brown eyes gleaming as though she were torn between embarassment and pride. "Frowe, I am still a virgin...but I am more than ready to make Eckhardt my husband. He has kissed my lips," she admitted in a lower voice, turning her gaze away, "and once he laid a hand upon my breast."

"Well, see to it that he does no more until your wedding night. But you should be married by Christmas, if all goes well." If Eckhardt lives through the war, she did not say. Even a woman knew that most of the casualties in any battle were among unseasoned foot fighters like Eckhardt, rather than the well-trained, mounted, and armoured knights; and no one would bother with capturing Eckhardt alive to hold for ransom. Gertrude was in far more danger of losing her beloved than was Margerite, and, thus thinking, Margerite added, "Even by Michaelmas, if I can arrange it."

"Thank you, frowe!" Gertrude dropped to her knees, pressing Margerite's hand to her lips. "I will be good until then; I promise I will not give anyone cause to doubt my chastity."

"Be sure you do not. But I shall be glad to see you wedded, and hope that your marriage is as happy as mine has been."

Ruprecht made one more long foray that month, leading his men out on a hot bright day with the sun beating down on their helmets. Margerite's dreams of flight were coming to her almost nightly again, and, though she could still remember little of them, she welcomed them with all her heart. She hoped that the war would be over soon, for the haymaking had lagged somewhat behind. Soon it would be time for harvesting the grain that rippled golden over the fields around Tiefensee and all the other villages in Ruprecht's lands, and then for picking the grapes swelling and ripening on their neatly terraced rows of vines.

They would need every man at home for that work, if much of the harvest was not to be lost; and the strain of supplying the soldiers on their way and feeding the Bear's Paw men was beginning to show in Burg Falkenstein's stores. But Ruprecht had been as successful as if God himself were guiding him, and Margerite knew that Graf Heinrich must thus be in worse straits than they were.

He cannot hold out too much longer, she comforted herself now and again. Even if Ruprecht is not able to capture him or take Burg Fürstensee, the toll we have taken on his villages and troops must force him to seek a resolution soon. Still, the worry was beginning to grind on Margerite's nerves.

Ruprecht had not made love to her before he left, and sometimes when she saw Cundrîê ghosting through the castle or bent over her herbs, she had to struggle not to take the old woman by the shoulders and shout at her, "What did you say to him? Why have you done this to me?" For she was sure that Cundrîê must have told Ruprecht something that made him fear that he would harm her: there was no other reason for him to have gone out again without lying with her.

The only times when she felt truly at ease in her mind were those warm afternoons when she rode out with Bertram guarding her, following the twisting pathway through the woods to the Mariabrunnen shrine. She and Bertram - though he had done most of the work, in truth - had tidied the place, trimming back the overgrowth in the clearing and washing the stones of the grotto clean of dirt and moss.

Although the stains of her burial were too deeply ingrained in Maria's stone to clean away, the dark cast seemed somehow to suit her: Mother Maria, shadowed by her agony at her Son's death and by the sins of the world - a shadow that could not be lightened, as the shadow of the grotto was, by the candles that Margerite and Bertram brought to burn before her, kindled by the tiny fires Bertram struck from a piece of flint with the back of his knife.

Whenever she came to the shrine and looked upon the statue of the Virgin, or sipped of the spring's mineraled waters, Margerite felt herself comforted and at peace, in a way that she could not be in Burg Falkenstein's neglected chapel.

It was one such afternoon, as they sat together in the shade of the pines, that Bertram shyly said, "Frowe Gräfin, I would speak to you about young Eckhardt."

"Is all well with him?" Margerite asked. Then she realized that it was a foolish question, for Eckhardt had marched out with Ruprecht: Bertram could know no more about him than she did herself.

"Mother Maria willing, I hope so. But he has told me that Gertrude spoke to you about their plans for wedding."

"Indeed she did. I think it a fine match - do you know a reason why it should not take place?"

"No." Although Bertram did not smile, his harsh-lined face seemed less grim and severe as he said, "Rather, I would speak on his behalf. Although I have trained him as well as I could in the time I have had him, and he has been eager and willing to learn, he is not the best fighter in Ruprecht's army..."

"And foot fighters are always the first to die in war."

Bertram raised his eyebrows, hazel eyes wide with surprise. Margerite smiled at him. "You forget, I grew up in an outlying keep. Though my father's castle was never attacked, Christ be praised, I heard the speech of soldiers from the time I was a small child, and helped to tend their wounds and pray for the dead when they came back from battles."

For a fleeting instant, Margerite almost thought that she saw Bertram's lips curve beneath the black tangle of his beard, and she was sure that a look of relief smoothed the deep lines of his forehead. Again she thought fleetingly, I wish he would trim that beard and cut his hair.

Only because he is the Hauptmann of a Graf's guard now,she hastily added to herself, and ought to look more the part. Still, Margerite could not help thinking on how he had appeared in her dream, nor could she keep herself from looking for the strong lines of his remembered features beneath the thick hair that hid them.

"Then you will be able to judge for yourself the matter I had thought, from courtesy, to put before you," Bertram said. "Because he is young and soon to be wedded, and because he is a good youth who promises well, if he lives, I should like to pull him from the ranks of marching soldiers and keep him on castle guard-duty for the rest of this war, replacing him in the army with Ludwig, who is older and has seen more fighting. This will weaken our home defenses by the weight of a man, which I would not ordinarily counsel; however, I will pledge to work more closely with Eckhardt, and be sure that he can fulfill his part should Burg Falkenstein be suddenly attacked."

Margerite sat still for a moment, taken aback by the request. It was not a very great thing that Bertram asked - save to Eckhardt and Gertrude; and for her maid's sake, she should have thought of it herself. But she would scarcely have thought that such matters would move Bertram's heart. And he would know, far better than she, that he would bear the brunt of any danger that sprang from his decision, since it would be he who fought alongside Eckhardt if the castle were attacked, and would suffer whatever risks came from having the weaker warrior by him.

"I do not think there is much to fear from exchanging the two men," Bertram went on, as though Margerite were a fellow commander, hesitating as she weighed the tactical situation. She felt oddly warmed by the compliment his advice implied - if only Ruprecht would trust in her so! "If we are attacked, the advantage lies with those within the walls; and if their force is great enough to get through..." He shrugged. "Ludwig is no Sigfrit, to hold off an army single-handed."

"I do not doubt that you are right. Very well, it shall be as you say. And..." Margerite lifted her hand, thinking to lay it upon his arm, then dropped it again lest he take her touch amiss. "I thank you for thinking of it. My father often said that a good commander must sometimes be mindful of his men's hearts, as well as their worth on the field; this is very like something he would have done."

"You do me too much honour, Frowe Gräfin," Bertram said, a bleak note in his voice. Inwardly, Margerite cursed her hasty speech: if Bertram had lost high rank, as she was sure in her heart he had, it was ill-done of her to remind him of it.

But, as if Bertram could feel her inner twinge of distress at his tone, Margerite saw his shoulders settle as if he were shrugging off whatever memory had pained him through her words. He pointed to a pair of turtledoves, sitting gray and quiet in the scraggly top of a pine above them, and said, "Those pigeons would make good quarry for your little sparrowhawk, if she were better mannered - though it will not be too much longer until you can take your falcons out for finer sport again."

Ruprecht and his troops came back on the thirtieth of July, tired but triumphant. Ruprecht had taken some of his men deep into Graf Heinrich's territory to destroy yet another of his villages: though they had needed to retreat too quickly to bring back much plunder, they had dealt one more sore blow to the rival Graf's chances of keeping up his side of the war for much longer.

Meanwhile, the rest of Ruprecht's men, under the command of Ritter Wilfrid, and the Bear's Paw company had marched north from Burg Eichenwald towards Burg Düsterstein, where they had found a smaller host marching from that castle to Ruprecht's northernmost village. The lesser army had attempted to avoid them, then to flee, but Ruprecht's men had pursued and dealt them heavy casualties before they managed to reach the safety of Burg Düsterstein.

"We could have besieged them there at our leisure," Ruprecht said, telling Margerite about it over his welcome-cup of wine in the great hall. "But a siege will do us no good, only tie up our troops and leave our lands defenceless. Unless we were to besiege Graf Heinrich within Burg Fürstensee itself…and that would still be too risky, for I do not think that we can trap him within its walls: his army is still at least the equal of ours, even with Jochanan's guns to even the score."

"But there should be no need for that," Margerite said, sipping at her own wine. "If it is only his concession of Burg Düsterstein and its lands we want, he should soon see that he cannot hold out much longer against the war we are fighting. My husband, I am so proud of you!"

Ruprecht smiled, putting his arm about her. "My dear wife, I could not have done half of what I have done without you. At the risk of sounding like my Knappe, I will say that you have been my guiding spirit in this war."

Margerite could only lean her head against his shoulder, cherishing the warmth his words awoke in her heart.

"Tomorrow," Ruprecht said suddenly, "we shall go out after roedeer with one of my eagles. You have never seen them fly, and you well deserve a day of enjoyment."

Although Ruprecht did not come to her chamber that night, Margerite was well content when she fell asleep, and glad when she awoke with the dream-memory of the wind through her pinions. Ruprecht, too, was in good spirits when she met him to break their fast in the great hall.

"It is a fine day for hunting with an eagle," he declared. "Bright, but cool enough, and with a little wind to bear the eagle up. For this hunt, we must ride up the mountain: an eagle does not do well when flown off the fist on open ground, because they are too heavy to quickly reach their height."

Margerite nodded agreement happily enough: she knew nothing of flying an eagle, and she was too caught up with the sight of her husband radiant in his hunting green and gold, his fair hair wafting about his face like a saint's halo, to think of much else.

The two hawkers rode down from the castle along the edge of the gorge, until they could cross over the river easily and take the path up the mountain. Margerite glanced back at the harsh crags dropping sharply down behind Burg Falkenstein, and a thought came to her mind.

"Is there no way down to the river from our castle?" she asked. "It seems a worrisome thing to me, to have no escape in case of siege."

Ruprecht's golden brows drew together, and Margerite could see the tightening of his shoulders beneath the green velvet of his tunic. There is a way, she thought, or else he would not be disturbed!

"There is a path," he said slowly. "But it is difficult to reach and hard to follow. One man, if he were very strong and agile, might be able to make his way down the back of Burg Falkenstein if it were needed…Yes, if we were besieged and needed to send a messenger out, we could. Out on a rope through the rear window of the main hall and down to the ravine path: from there a single man would have a good chance of passing unseen behind any besiegers."

Margerite nodded. "That is well to know."

Ruprecht looked at her a moment, then turned his gaze away, looking up into the shifting patterns of the green alder-leaves above them. Suddenly he laughed.

"Thus is the price of being Graf and Gräfin: we cannot go hunting alone," he declared. "Even when we command no one else to go with us, we are accompanied…look!"

Margerite looked where his free hand was pointing, to see Kobolt halfway up a tree, clinging to its rough bark with all his claws as he glanced about wide-eyed.

"Perhaps he has learned that when we hunt, there is fresh meat for him. He is a very clever cat, and has a keen sense of where food can be found…as Berthe has complained to me often enough."

"He will have to discuss the matter with Ginovêr, here," Ruprecht answered, stroking a finger gently along the eagle's breast. "I believe that he will not find an eagle as easily awed by a claw across the nose as my poor hounds."

The two of them rode until they came to the top of the mountain, where the pines grew more thinly. "Now we shall let him fly, that he may wait on his quarry," Ruprecht declared. He raised his heavy-gloved left arm sharply, and with a beating of wings that swept Ruprecht's hair back as if he faced the stormwind, Ginovêr was in the air, swooping low among the trees until the updraft from the gorge caught him, lifting him to circle slowly above the two hawkers on their horses.

"We shall ride down this way, for there are many roedeer and the sound of our passing is like enough to flush them out," Ruprecht told Margerite. "Ginovêr only needs to see one running and gain a moment's clear way through the trees, and then she will have it, for there is no bird I have ever flown to match herself and her mate Artûs in cleverness and speed, not even your beautiful peregrines. And for all their majesty, there are few who have ever been able to train eagles to take worthwhile game, and few who can fly them well. Indeed..." Ruprecht looked seriously at his bride, all the merriment gone from his face in a moment. "Should I die before you, and before them - if some ill chance finds me in battle, say - I would like you to bring Ginovêr and Artûs up here and set them free, to fly and mate at their own will."

"If it should ever come to pass so, I shall do it," Margerite promised. "But God grant I never have to!"

Ruprecht and Margerite rode down beneath the dappled shadows of the pines, the mountain air soft and cool on their faces. Both of them had slacked their reins, letting their horses find the path as they gazed upwards, watching the eagle soaring above them.

"There is always a little risk in this hunting," Ruprecht said softly, "for Ginovêr can cross the distance between two peaks in a few minutes, where we will need several hours to ride. More than once, I have reached herself or Artûs too late to lure them from their prey, and an eagle is a proud bird, who does not give up what she has slain easily. But it is well worth it to see her stoop."

They were near the foot of the mountain's far side when a sharp rustle sounded in the undergrowth and the roe-deer shot across their path. Margerite had only time to see the ruddy flash of its coat; she thought she had marked the short prick of horns as well, but could not be sure.

Ruprecht's breath hissed out through his teeth as he reined his horse in, staring up through a break in the pine-branches. "Now watch!" he said. "Ginovêr will stoop soon, the moment it passes through any clearing."

As Margerite stared up at the eagle, it seemed to her that a wind lifted her from herself, so that she looked down upon the world from high above the mountainside. The deep green glow of the sunlit pines, their needled branches interlacing in a sharp canopy above the forest's floor; the jagged crags of rocks jutting out through the trees; the sweep and lift of the wooded land...and, between the trees, the ruddy back of the fleeing roedeer darting beneath the branches like the back of a trout flashing beneath the dark waters of a river.

She could feel the huge power of her wings, the strength gathering in her great talons as her keen eyes judged the path of her prey, her heart sharpening towards the single point where she plummeted upon the roebuck like a thunderbolt from the bright sky.

The shock of the eagle's strike jolted through Margerite's body, flinging her back to herself. She stared about, blinking in stunned shock; but Ruprecht had already spurred his horse on, shouting, "Ride! We must catch her as quickly as we may!"

Margerite dug her knees into her own steed's side, urging the mare forwards behind the flying black hooves and tail of Ruprecht's mount. Her ears still sang with the sound of the air of the heights, and the wind of her riding streamed about her as though it blew through feathered wings; when her horse leapt over the rippling waters of a narrow creek, she felt herself soaring again, with no shock of landing.

She did not know how long she rode behind Ruprecht, but when her husband at last pulled up his horse, both steeds were blowing hard, their glossy sides wet and matted. Ginovêr mantled over the body of the roebuck in the middle of a small clearing, her great wings spread low to hide her prey; but her beak was bloodied, and Margerite could see that she had already broken into her kill. Kobolt crouched near her, the black plume of his tail lashing as he stared wide-eyed at the two humans, his eyes glowing like molten gold.

As Ruprecht drew nearer, Ginovêr's feathers puffed up and she opened her beak in a loud screech of warning, then drew her head back as though she meant to strike at him like a snake before lowering her beak to her prey again. Ruprecht prudently stepped back, turning his head to look at Margerite.

When she met his gaze, she drew in her breath: his blue eyes seemed to glow brilliant from within, like silver mirrors turned to the sun, but their wide black pupils seemed hollow, as if no living man looked out of them. Yet she was not afraid, for the wildness of her flight still beat in her soul. Dazed and breathless, Margerite reached out, taking her husband by the hand.

"My bride," Ruprecht said, his voice low and hoarse. "My huntress, my fair falcon...come to me." He drew Margerite in, embracing her fiercely. Ruprecht's mouth was hot on hers; she could feel the hammering of his heart beneath the hard muscles of his chest, beating in furious time with her own. It seemed to her as though his touch was setting her aflame, the desperate need-fire burning between her legs so that she could not bear to stand there any longer, but pulled him down to lie over her, her hips already thrusting against him.

Dimly, she felt Ruprecht's hand lifting her skirts, grass and moss cool against her backside; she heard Kobolt's wild yowling and the noises of the eagle tearing at her roedeer as if from far away, but they were nothing against the roaring wind in her ears, nothing against the feeling of Ruprecht at last plunging into her, his heat filling her own and kindling it up again and again as she stared into the blinding light of his eyes, her body clasping him with wings and talons like a falcon clinging to her prey.

When at last Margerite convulsed and cried out, the sensations enflaming her body were so strong that she thought she had fainted for a moment. She came back to herself only slowly, lying panting on the earth by her husband.

Her skirts were up about her waist, but she had not the strength to lift her hand and push them down; the droplets of sweat were chilling slowly on her face, and her limbs were trembling as though she had run beyond her strength.

Kobolt had crept up beside her, and was lying nestled by her right thigh, his purr vibrating softly through her flesh. Ruprecht raised himself shakily on one elbow, leaning over Margerite to drop a gentle kiss on her bruised lips.

Ruprecht's bright hair was disheveled, the flush fading only slowly from his fair cheeks, but the strange light had gone from his blue eyes: they were brightened by no more than the kindness and love that Margerite always saw in them when he looked upon her. He blinked, as though he had been wakened suddenly from a dream into the full light of day.

"I did not mean to do that," he said wonderingly. "I…"

Margerite laid a finger upon his mouth. "I could have asked for nothing more, my dear husband, my love." They lay together for a little while longer, until Ruprecht at last pushed himself up, tying his hose again and pulling down his tunic, and walked unsteadily over to Ginovêr. The eagle had fed full, and made no protest when Ruprecht approached and lifted her up, though Kobolt darted in at once and began tearing ravenously at the edge of the great breach Ginovêr's beak and talons had left in the roedeer's ribcage.

Still exhausted by the violent passion that had overcome them, Margerite and Ruprecht rode slowly back to Burg Falkenstein, saying little. But Margerite's heart was content, for she was sure that whatever fear or worry had kept her husband from her bed must be broken now: she could take it only as God's gift to restore the lawful ways of their marriage.

By the time Ruprecht had reached his chamber at the top of Burg Falkenstein, he was shaking so hard that he could barely stand. Since learning that Margerite's body had passed out his first effort to kindle a child of Power, he had striven with all his will to keep himself from going to her at night.

Even before going out to battle, when the dark fear singing at the roots of the hearts of all men had told him that he must try to plant his seed before he left, for he might never ride back to Burg Falkenstein; even when coming back from battle, lightheaded with the relief of life won and renewed and with the delight filling his heart as he looked upon Margerite's sweet face - even then, though Ruprecht knew their separation saddened her as much as it did himself, his Will had remained master of his heart and body, and he had managed to hold himself back.

But today...he did not know what had come upon him, save that it had seemed akin to that strange rush of wild might that had nearly overwhelmed him as he performed his rite on Midsummer's Eve.

He was not even sure he remembered all of it: the eagle mantling bloody-beaked over her prey, yes, and Kobolt staring at him, those wide golden cat-eyes seeming to swell to take in the whole of his mind, as though the cat were his own familiar...then clinging to Margerite desperately, driving into her with all his strength as she lay on the earth with her skirts up; but he did not remember climaxing, only coming slowly to himself beside her and realizing what he had done.

For if it had set a child in Margerite's womb already, his plans would be as naught, for the son he desired must be a firstborn, by a woman who had borne no other. But if that were so...then Ruprecht would be spared the ritual he had readied himself to do that night, the full rite at which his first plans had balked. So thinking, Ruprecht slowly raised his head. For a long time he stared at the heavy tapestry hanging over the doorway to the hidden staircase.

His mother had woven the hunting scene many years ago: the green of the trees and the hunters' garb was beginning to fade to a drabber colour, the ruddy coats of the mastiffs and mastiffs graying, while the bright scarlet of the blood spurting where the spear-heads were sunk into the boar's side had dulled to the colour of blood long shed and dried.

The Death took her, he thought, and God did nothing, nor did his priest stay to give comfort to her as she died. And when it came back...

Radegund had been the first in Burg Falkenstein to sicken: though there was plague in Freiburg once more, and rumours of outbreaks in the monasteries and towns between Burg Falkenstein and the city, she could not be stopped from going down among the Tiefensee villagers, to see that all was well with them and bring food to those who were sick and old.

She had gone to bed early, saying that she had ridden too long and was tired; and before dawn, Ruprecht had heard her maidservant's scream through the single wall between their chambers, and run in to see, in the dim glow of a single candle, the flush of fever burning hectic on Radegund's cheeks and the dark swellings rising on either side of her neck.

She had cried out softly in pain, tossing from side to side; her gray eyes had been open and staring, but though she had looked upon Ruprecht, she had not seemed to see him, nor hear him when he knelt beside her bed and clasped her burning hand in both of his. Ruprecht had worn the onyx ring of the Order of Light-Bearers then: he had been...much like Wolfram, young and enthusiastic, his mind aflame with the desire to learn the secrets hidden within the shadowed parts of the universe.

Since his mother's death fourteen years before, he had put no trust in Christ; when, as a young squire at Graf Günther's court, his knight had dropped certain hints of forbidden learning and power beyond the human world, he had eagerly seized upon them, taking to heart the Order's motto EX TENEBRAE LUX: From Darkness, Light.

He had risen swiftly, from silver ring to gold to onyx-set before he became a knight, but had not been able to set his hand to the next trial: the deliberate sacrifice of a human life, which would begin his Ordeal - an Ordeal that would end with either the amethyst ring upon his hand, or his eternal death. To this day, Ruprecht did not know for certain what had finally shored up his resolution. Perhaps it was his own fear of the Death, for by the second day of Radegund's agony, his head had been light and swimming and he had begun to walk unsteadily, whether from terror or the first grip of fever he was not sure.

Or perhaps it was that he could no longer bear to look upon what his beloved wife had become, screaming and twisting upon her bed in excruciating pain as the black lumps swelled upon her flesh and her skin began to mottle as though she were rotting alive, as her waist-length chestnut hair matted into thick ropes that chafed on her skin, while the handfuls of incense burning in her chamber only overlaid a sickly sweetness on the dreadful stench rising from her: her sweat, her breath, the thick and turbid black urine that dribbled from her now and again, all stank so vilely of corruption that only the Order's training of will and control of the bodily urges kept Ruprecht from trying to vomit with every breath he took in her room.

And thus, before her third day of dying had dawned, he had lifted his wife's foul and wasted body and carried her down the staircase to the chamber of his magic. There he had made a bed for Radegund and wrapped her warmly, though she was so far gone in the pain and madness of her disease that there was no saying whether she knew what he was doing or not. There, at last, he had called upon Lucifer, Star of the Morning, to receive his offering and his dedication in return for ending the Death within his lands; and there he had lifted Radegund's blanket aside and plunged the knife in beneath his dear wife's plague-blotched breast, to end her pain and...damn his soul irretrievably?

Ruprecht did not fear damnation: he had gladly taken it on himself with his first oath to the Order. Nor would he choose to give up the amethyst ring that had been bestowed on him when his Ordeal was done, and the powers and rank that came with it. And yet, he knew that if it had not been for the Death, he might never have been able to steel himself to the deed, even if it had only been a peasant child bound within the circle and not his heart's greatest love.

But that was over and done: and if Ruprecht woke sometimes in the night weeping, with the dream of Radegund's wide green eyes and long red-glinting hair still before his eyes, there was no one but himself to know it, for even his Knappe was not permitted to share his bedchamber.

Now there was Margerite, whose winged soul had ravished his heart into love before he knew it, and who was already his partner in magic, though it might still be hidden from her waking mind. And for the sake of their child, his will must be strong and steady where before it had wavered: he must ready himself to do what he needed to do, without fear or hesitation.

Yet Ruprecht stared at his mother's hunting tapestry for a moment longer before he opened his mouth and softly spoke the name, "Cundrîê."

Although he did not hear the door to his left open or close, the old woman was at his elbow nearly at once.

"As you will, master," she said, her voice ringing softly clear and inhumanly beautiful through his room.

"It may be that I set a child in Margerite's womb this afternoon," Ruprecht said. He hated to admit his failure, lest it be reported to Graf Günther, but without that, he could not correct what he had done. "Brew a draught that will take it from her now and painlessly, without doing her any harm. For this night I shall carry out the ritual of which I have spoken to you before, that I may get a son of power. And…be sure that she sleeps so soundly this night that nothing will wake her before dawn, for she must suffer neither fear nor pain."

"Master, it shall be done," Cundrîê answered. And though Ruprecht did not see her go, she was there no longer.

Margerite was in her chamber before the evening meal, sitting in her chair while Gertrude combed and arranged her hair.

"You are very disheveled for one who has only ridden out to watch an eagle's hunt, frowe," the serving girl said. "If it were not your husband with whom you had gone, I should be most worried. Did you have more sport than the hawking, perhaps?"

"Have I told you that you are most impudent, Gertrude? It is not for you to ask about the Graf and I?"

"O, very well, mistress. Only I know that he has not come here in some time, and I know what a stallion is like when kept too long from mares."

"Gertrude!" Margerite said. Then she relented, for she was too content to hide her happiness. "It may have happened as you think, yes."

"That is good news, frowe, for I know you were pining without him."

Margerite was about to reply when the door opened, and Cundrîê wafted in, carrying a large silver goblet of steaming wine.

"What are you doing here at this hour, Cundrîê?" she asked. "It is too early for my eventide cup, and I do not need a soothing brew tonight."

"You shall drink this anyway," the old woman replied. "It will only bring you rest, and strength, and health to your womb."

"My womb does not need your help!" Margerite flared, for she still blamed Cundrîê for Ruprecht's long absence from her chamber. Kobolt, lying on the bed, lifted his head and miaowed as if in agreement. "Take your draught away: I do not want it."

Cundrîê stared at her, and though her ugly face was calm, her black eyes glittered like chips of polished onyx. "It is the will of the Graf your husband that you drink it," Cundrîê said, lifting the cup to her. "Take it. If not for your own sake, for the sake of setting his mind at ease."

"What have you told him?" Margerite asked. "Why should his mind not be at ease?"

"Take it. The Graf wishes you to."

Reluctantly, Margerite accepted the goblet, for she could see that Cundrîê would not leave until she did. The smooth stem was warm in her hand, and in the steam that rose from the bowl, she could smell the musky tang of the herbs that had been brewed into the rich red wine, underlying the sweetness of honey as though the bees who had made it had fed on strange plants.

She lifted it to her lips for a cautious sip, careful not to scald her mouth on the hot metal rim. Cundrîê nodded in satisfaction and left. Margerite looked down at the dark drink steaming in its figured silver bowl. For a moment, she thought of casting it into the chamber pot, but the taste still lingered on her tongue, haunting and seductive, and the scent rose to curl sweetly through her nostrils. Almost without knowing what she was doing, Margerite raised the goblet to drink again.

A soft, powerful blow struck her hand, knocking the goblet away to scatter its contents in a dark fan of droplets over the fresh rushes and strewing-herbs on the floor. Kobolt had leapt into her lap; he stood there now with the points of his claws in her thighs, lashing his black tail and staring wildly about himself.

"Whatever is the matter with you, cat?" Margerite asked. She tried to stroke Kobolt's soft head, but he had caught sight of the goblet, still rolling gently from side to side on the floor. He jumped down, striking at it with his paws as he would strike to toss a mouse in the air, then arched his back and hissed, bristling out his magnificent black tail, and ran away to leap onto the bed, clawing at the pillows and growling.

"There must have been a strong dose of valerian in the draught, to drive the cat thus mad," Margerite said, to herself as much as to Gertrude. Then a yawn caught her by surprise, stretching and cracking her jaws. "But perhaps Cundrîê was right in saying that I needed rest, for I am very tired. Gertrude, I shall lie down now. Wake me in a little while so that I may join Ruprecht at supper."

In her dream, Margerite was flying again; but now she soared low, circling over Burg Falkenstein. Where before she had never been able to see the castle clearly, now it was as sharp as a daylit crag in her sight, the crenellations of the walls standing out like torches against the darkness. It seemed to her that she could see through the stone, looking within to where the scullery maids slumbered by the coals of the kitchen fires, to where Kai's long body tossed restlessly on the bed in his seneschal's chamber and Berthe rumbled and snored in a heavy mound beneath her blankets.

Burg Falkenstein slept; but on the top floor, a single small taper glowed, moving from Margerite's room down the winding spiral of the staircase. She looked closer, and a single thought came to her mind: What is Gertrude doing, creeping about so late at night? But she could not hold it: she was flying, circling, though her wings seemed strangely weighted, so that she could not gain height.

The serving maid made her way down the stairs to the side door into the courtyard, walking out beneath the stars. In the herber...although the moon was down, the falcon could see him clearly...waited young Eckhardt, shifting from foot to foot as he looked up through the rustling dark branches of the linden tree whose broad trunk and shadows hid him from anyone who might glance through the gate.

But Gertrude was not halfway across the courtyard before a black-cloaked figure stepped out of the shade, seizing her by the wrist and dashing the taper from her hand. The candle's flame glowed down like a spark falling from a bonfire, guttering to darkness on the earth; Gertrude tried to whirl back, but could not break away.

"Come," a voice murmured. Gertrude stared upward, her eyes wide.

"Graf Ruprecht?" she whispered. "What do you want?"

"Come with me," he repeated. Ruprecht was all in shadow: from where she flew, the falcon could not see his face. Unable to free herself, Gertrude followed him with dragging steps, back into the castle and up the dark staircase to his chamber.

"What do you want?" the serving maid asked again. "Are you going to...Graf, you must not! I am about to be betrothed, and think of Margerite: how could you betray her?"

"I do not mean to betray Margerite," Ruprecht said, his voice strangely cold and hollow. He raised his hand to beckon, and Clingschor and Cundrîê were suddenly there, their twinned faces gleaming white against their dark hoods like maggots writhing on black earth. One of them moved to either side of Gertrude, pale hands closing upon her arms.

"No!" Gertrude shrieked, her plump face twisting in terror. She backed up, flinging herself about desperately and opening her mouth to scream. Ruprecht clamped a hand upon her face to stifle the sound, but she ducked away from him, turning to drive her knee up between Clingschor's legs.

The old man grunted at the blow, but showed no other sign of pain; Ruprecht grabbed Gertrude about the shoulders, and she struck out at him desperately, raking her nails down the side of his face. Then the chain at her neck snapped: the silver crucifix Eckhardt had given her glinted, flying off to clink against the stone wall and drop, and suddenly the strength of fear seemed to be gone from the maid's limbs. She stood panting in their grasp, glaring at Ruprecht.

"I should have known," she gasped. "You may rape me, Graf, but you shall not have me willing, and you shall not stop me from telling my frowe either. What do you think she will say to you, when she learns that you had to use her serving maid to sate your lusts?"

Ruprecht only shook his head, a dribble of blood running down his cheek where Gertrude had clawed him. "Be comforted, if it is any comfort to you, that Margerite shall not know what has happened to you this night. Clingschor, Cundrîê, downstairs."

He drew aside the large tapestry that hung upon his wall to show an oaken door, opening the iron lock. Beyond was a staircase - a staircase hidden in the castle's thick stone walls, with no exits or entrances save at top and bottom. Ruprecht walked down it; his servants lifted Gertrude between them and followed.

The way down seemed to glow with flickering foxfire: down behind the slumbering glow of the smithy, through the two round rooms at the foot of the guard-tower by the herber, and down again to two chambers below the smithy. Now the falcon's sight was blurred again by the shifting veil of light that hung over these rooms; but dimly, as she watched, she could see the four shapes arranging themselves...see the pale flash of white skin as Gertrude was stripped and bound, the deep violet glow of the silken robes in which Ruprecht arrayed himself and the light that shone ever more brightly from the amethyst on his left forefinger.

It seemed to her that she could see the faint-sparkling tides of power already swirling in about the castle, converging and gathering on the room in which Gertrude lay naked before the Graf and his two servants, their shapes like black holes in the shimmering whirls of energy. A rod of fire burned in Ruprecht's right hand, a star-white sword in his left: he uplifted the wand, and the falcon heard his voice shivering through the deep stone foundations of the castle.

"LUCIFER, SATHANAS, STAR OF THE MORNING!" Ruprecht called, and with each word his face seemed to grow brighter, as though he were drawing all the shifting banners of light that played about the room into himself.

"Lucifer, everlasting Power, Lord of the World and Prince of the Air! Light in the Darkness, Lord of Knowledge, Master of Hell and Sovereign of the Damned; fairest and mightiest of angels, cast flaming from Heaven! Thou flame made brighter by the Lake of Unquenchable Fire, burning more beautiful against Hell's horrors; thou Star of the Morning illuminating Night's blackness! I call thee from the keep of Unconquerable Will: the walls of my pride are black steel, the walls of my mind are glittering adamant. Thou, whom no downfall could defeat; eternal foe of God, Serpent of Wisdom and god of this world! As the walls of Eden were breached, that thy Light might enter into the minds of men, I breach now the gates of Earth, to bring thy Light and Power forth into the darkness veiled by human flesh!"

Ruprecht spread his arms wide, as though he were casting heavy velvet curtains aside; and in the gap between wand and sword, a red spark seemed to kindle and grow. The falcon could not look straight at it, but it seemed to her that she could see the fires leaping and the dark shadows darting between the flames, and her wings trembled beneath the blast of the heat that rose from it, so that she must sink from the air and perch upon a stone crenellation.

"LUCIFER, SATHANAS, STAR OF THE MORNING! The Way is open; rise now from the Adamant Throne, let thy wings of flame bear thee through the depths of the Abyss, and come thou forth, as Lord of Earth! The Way is open; thus do I unbar the gate for thee, with the blood of a stainless maiden."

The white glow of Ruprecht's sword and the deep red flame of his wand moved downward; the deep violet light of his robes shadowed Gertrude's pale flesh. It seemed to the falcon that the air rent with a sound like a great piece of silk ripping; and only faintly beneath that sound could she hear Gertrude's last despairing gasp, "Maria!" Then the light within the room burned too brightly for her to see, and the hot sulfurous wind rose up to beat against her, tearing her from her perch and flinging her away.

Then Margerite's eyes were open: she lay naked on her bed, staring at the brightness that filled her chamber. Though the windows were black and no candles burned, every corner of the room shone more clearly than in the full light of day. She tried to move, to lift her hand and call for Gertrude to comfort her against the dreadful dream, but her lips and throat seemed frozen, and her limbs lay limp, not so much as twitching to her command.

The door opened; Ruprecht walked in. Margerite could do nothing but stare helplessly at him. His naked body seemed to glow from within, his golden hair a fiery halo about his transfigured face and the sharp-drawn musculature of his white body almost translucent, as though his flesh had become the rippling glass walls of a burning lantern. He was terrifyingly beautiful as she had never seen him before, like a bright star in human shape, and the blue brilliance of his eyes seared her gaze like lightning.

Unable to move, Margerite could only tremble helplessly as Ruprecht lifted the black silk cords dangling from his hand like a whip, binding her hands and feet to the bedposts with knots soft as ropes of air. He stroked a fingertip lightly over her mouth, and it seemed to her that his touch set her lips aflame with a dreadful pleasure, so that her body shook with longing for his kisses. He knelt between her legs, bending over her body: his tongue slipped into her mouth, sliding hotly between her lips, and she would have cried out beneath that ravishment if she could have.

Ruprecht's tongue traced a trail of fire down Margerite's throat, keen as a knife; each beat of her pulse beneath his mouth seemed to spurt an ecstasy of heartblood. Her nipples flared like the hot sparks of stars as his fingers tightened upon them; her back tightened, trying futilely to arch and toss under the hot flood of sensation flowing through her, but the bonds on her wrists and ankles held her tight, so that the ecstatic agony of her ravished senses could not break through the paralysis that gripped her.

She could feel the heat beating off Ruprecht's body between her legs, as though his flesh were gold still glowing from the casting, but for all her desire, she could not tighten her limbs to grasp him, only suffer the exquisite torment of his skin brushing tingling against hers now and again as he shifted position, soft as the caress of amber-sparking fur against the delicate skin of her inner thighs.

His fingers trailed lightly over Margerite's body with cruel gentleness; the pounding of her heart hammered resoundingly in her ears, so that if he spoke words, she could not hear them. She ached to thrust her hips upwards, to pull him to her and into her, yet she was still bound and helpless, unable even to cry out to release a little of the unbearable sensations mounting within her.

Then his mouth was upon her again, the fiery trace of his tongue moving down over the sensitive skin of her belly to lick along the edge of the golden curls at her groin. Margerite did not know whether she wanted to cry to him to stop, that it was shameful, that she could bear no more, or to urge him on. But she had no power to do either; she could only lie splayed before him as his hot tongue flickered down like the tip of a whip, caressing the soft damp petals between her legs as he had kissed her mouth.

She could feel her womb clenching and releasing, pulsing rhythmically beneath the mastery of his tongue's thrilling strokes circling her most private parts. Each time his tongue grazed the little bud at the top of her vulva, a shock of pleasure twinged through her body, making her jerk involuntarily against her bonds, but he would not linger there. In that corner of her mind left to her, Margerite thought that she would go mad with the tormenting pleasure of his touch, but there was nothing she could do to either stop him or make him finish.

Margerite was nearly beyond thought by the time Ruprecht reared up again, the clear light of his face shining over her body like a lantern of dazzling adamant. Then, at last, she felt the touch of his spear between her legs, her body opening to him in helpless pleasure as he pressed deeply into her. His cock felt burningly cold within her, as though the icy silver light of a star pierced her body, but she could do nothing but take it in, welcoming the touch finally penetrating her to her depths.

Slowly he pulled out, filling her shuddering flesh again and again until there was nothing left in the world for her but the sensation of his measured thrusts forcing her to answer to his rhythm, to take him into her again and again until his last blow burst through her with an ecstatic force that convulsed her body and rent her awareness into flying shards of light spinning down into the darkness. Margerite awoke to the sound of her own scream in her ears, thrashing desperately against the bedclothes.

The dim gray light of early morning was filtering through the windows; she sat bolt upright, looking frantically about the room. Kobolt was playing with the rushes on the floor, pouncing and tossing, but she could see nothing of Gertrude.

"Gertrude!" she shouted, hoping that her maidservant had only gone out to fetch water for her morning wash. "Gertrude!"

But no answer came. The stove was cold, its coals burned down to a thick layer of gray ashes, and no fresh fuel had been laid beside it.

"That girl is lazy," Margerite said to herself, clutching desperately at the comfort of the ordinary words. "She slept too late, and now she is hurrying down to the kitchen, hoping that she can fill the stove and light its fire before I awaken."

But the memory of her dream was dreadfully clear in Margerite's mind: she had seen Gertrude struggling with Clingschor and Cundrîê and Ruprecht, had seen...whatever happened deep beneath the castle, to the ringing of Ruprecht's blasphemous words.

Terrified, Margerite touched her wrists, then her ankles, where she had been bound with the silken cords. There was no sign of chafing, no sign that she had been tied - but she had not been able to struggle. Her fingers trembled as she reached between her legs. She was a little sore there, yes... but had she not been so after making love to Ruprecht the afternoon before? She was shivering deeply now, bone-cold and praying in the depths of her heart that the door would open soon and Gertrude would walk in, contrite at having overslept and perhaps complaining that her mistress had cried out in her dreams and kept her from a good night's rest.

"Gertrude!" Margerite called again, and again she received no answer: there was only the sound of Kobolt's paws rustling through the rushes on the floor, and the slight tinkling of metal.

"Kobolt, what have you got there?" Margerite said breathlessly. "Let me see it."

She got up, crouching down beside the cat. Something glinted silver beneath his paw: suddenly Margerite was scrabbling desperately through the rushes, seizing upon Kobolt's plaything. When she held it in her hand, she stopped, staring in horror. It was the silver crucifix Eckhardt had given Gertrude, and the chain was snapped through, just as it had been in her dream. But...how had it come here?

"Kobolt, where did you find this?" Margerite asked, her voice thin and taut with fear. The cat looked up at her wide-eyed, then scampered across the room again.

"Gertrude!"

Margerite waited for the space of ten Aves, her panic mounting, before she called again. At last the door swung open, and she drew in a furious breath, ready to berate her serving girl for all the fear she had suffered. But it was not Gertrude who stepped inside, but Cundrîê, carrying a bucket of water in one hand and a basket of wood in the other.

"Where is Gertrude?" Margerite asked. Though she tried to keep the terror from her voice, she could feel it shaking in her throat: she had seen Cundrîê...

"I do not know, Frowe Gräfin," Cundrîê replied, her beautiful low voice smooth. "I can only tell that she has not tended to your needs this morning, so that must be my task now. If you will wait a few minutes, I shall have the water hot for your washing. Which dress do you desire to wear today?"

"It does not matter," Margerite said. "I want only to know where Gertrude is, for..." She stopped. For my dreams were evil, and I fear that some ill has befallen her, she had been about to say: but if there were truth in what she had seen...

She shuddered, her hand going to cover her womb. Even now, it seemed to her that she could still feel the shameful twinges within her of that burning cold she had welcomed so desperately, the last echo of - Ruprecht's? - touch not faded completely from her flesh.

"It would not surprise me if she has run off to be with the young man she visits at night," Cundrîê said calmly. "She took advantage of your trust and sound sleep, Frowe Gräfin. You should not concern yourself too much with her. Now, it promises to be a fair and warm day outside, so I think that the dark velvet may be too heavy for you. Perhaps the pale blue silk which you had recut in Freiburg: I know that it pleases the Graf when you wear that. Do you wish to?"

"I...yes, I will wear that," Margerite said. Her hand clenched about the silver crucifix, until the ends of its arms pressed painfully into her skin. Suddenly unwilling for Cundrîê to see she had it, she waited until the old woman's back was turned and head bent over her chest of garments, then dropped it behind her bed, praying that Kobolt would not drag it out again.

Margerite suffered Cundrîê's touch in her dressing, though her flesh crept beneath the old woman's cold and bony fingers as Cundrîê combed and arranged her hair. Her legs shook as she descended the spiral staircase; she could not keep from glancing anxiously before and behind, desperate to see some glimpse of Gertrude's brown braid or tidy woolen skirts.

She stopped before the door of the great hall, reluctant to go in. Ruprecht would be there, breaking his fast at the head of the long oaken table: how could she bear to look into his eyes again, or feel the touch of his hand on hers, after she had dreamed that...what? That he had killed her maidservant? That he, or...Someone else in his shape, had come to her, bound her and ravished her in a manner that she could not think about?

But she was the Gräfin of Burg Falkenstein, and sooner or later, she must look upon her husband and speak with him again; even let him lie with her at his will, though before she would have sworn an oath upon the bones of St. Peter in Rome that Ruprecht would never come to her without her consent.

Margerite opened the door and stepped into the hall. To her relief, Ruprecht was not there: there was only a servant boy, scurrying to bring her morning meal of bread and watered wine.

"The Graf rose early to go hunting," said Cundrîê from behind her. Margerite started, whirling to face the old woman. "He is likely to be out all day, so you must amuse yourself as you will."

After she had eaten, Margerite called for her horse to be saddled. If Gertrude had simply slipped out on Eckhardt's account...perhaps more had happened than she had bargained for; perhaps she was only waiting at his family's house in the village until she could gather her courage to tell her mistress, and would be there even now, ashamed and missing her maidenhead, but alive and well.

The weather was as bright as it had been the day before, the sunlight glinting off the ripples of the river and the reflection of the sky shining blue from the surface of Tiefensee. The day's warmth and the steady rhythm of her horse beneath her were beginning to calm Margerite, letting her tell herself that she had suffered no more than a bad dream - that, with her husband away doing battle two weeks out of every three, it was a wonder that horrors did not dog her dreams every night.

The streets of the Tiefensee village were deserted; only a few chickens pecked their way along the streets, a mongrel hound dozing beneath the baker's window in the sweet scent of fresh bread. When Margerite reached the village square, however, she saw that it was thronged with people - that every peasant in Tiefensee seemed to be standing there, staring up at the gibbet that had been raised before the broad green branches of the linden and the two nooses dangling empty from it. Beside the gibbet, Ruprecht sat mounted on his gray-black steed: the body of a stag was thrown across its neck before him, and Margerite could see the arrow-shaft sticking out of its paunch.

She knew enough of hunting to be sure that a beast shot so
would have died badly, and her heart caught in her throat,
for she also knew that Ruprecht would never have taken
such careless aim. Beneath the gibbet stood four prisoners:
an old man, his face half-hidden by a great curly mass of
gray-white hair and beard; a woman of middle years and
a maiden of about Margerite's own age, their eyes swollen
red with weeping and hair disheveled; and young Eckhardt,
his glance darting frantically over the crowd as if he were
searching for someone.

The women looked very much like Eckhardt, with the
same straight brown hair and horsy faces: Margerite
remembered that Gertrude had said the boy had a mother
and sister. Did he do Gertrude some harm? Did Ruprecht
find out about it? She spurred Mathilde up, and the peasants
drew back from her path as though she were flailing about
herself with a whip.

Ruprecht turned his head, looking at her in startlement.
His blue eyes were wide and dazed, the sunlight burning
a golden halo about his hair, and to her horror, Margerite
could not help thinking that she saw the last afterglow of her
dream bright in his flesh, shining out of the grim mask into
which his fine features had set themselves.

...now she brought her hand to her mouth to keep herself
from crying out...down the side of his cheek was a long
scabbed scratch, just like the mark she had seen Gertrude
leave upon his flesh in their struggle.

"What are you doing here, my beloved?" Ruprecht asked.
"This is none of your affair: I have a simple matter of justice
to administer, that is all. You may stay if you wish, of course,
but there is no need for you to watch if you would rather
not."

"I...what has happened?"

Ruprecht laid his hand upon the corpse of the stag before him. "The old man shot this stag at dawn in the vineyard. For killing my beasts, the punishment is death; and so it would have been for him alone, if he had simply slain it cleanly. But he was drunk and clumsy: he shot it in the guts, and followed it at once, so that it had to run for a mile or more with the arrow chewing at its bowels. Then he lost the trail, and it was only by chance that I found it on my way, and was able to track my stag to where he had fallen, and put him out of his last pain. I followed the trail back, and came upon the guilty one."

Margerite nodded dumbly, her eyes still searching the crowd in hopes that she would see Gertrude standing there - terrified for her love, perhaps, but still alive.

"Do you wish to leave, or will you stay?"

Margerite wanted to go, but she could not make herself rein her horse about, could not surrender her hope.

"So be it," Ruprecht said. He raised his voice, lifting his hand above the heads of the prisoners. "I, Graf Ruprecht von Falkenstein, do hereby pronounce the sentence of death upon the unlawful murderer of my stag, and all his living kin here. Let the womenfolk be brought to the gibbet." He gestured; two of his guardsmen grasped Eckhardt's mother and sister by their bound hands, pushing them forward. Father Hans stumbled up to meet them; the women knelt before him. "You, Eckhardt..." Ruprecht looked down at the young guardsman, and for a moment Margerite seemed to see the dreadful set of the Graf's features softening, as though he truly regretted the words he must speak. "Because you have served me well, and fought bravely among my troops, you shall not suffer the shame of hanging, but be beheaded with honour. Let a block be brought forth; Bertram, draw your sword."

Eckhardt looked up, his eyes squinting against the sun's brightness in his face as he stared pleadingly at Margerite. She had no words of comfort to give him; she wished with all her heart that Gertrude could be there to bid him farewell... that she knew where Gertrude was, or could be sure in her heart that the maidservant had not died before her beloved.

But that thought strengthened her, so that despite the dark undercurrent of terror dragging at her limbs, she was able to cry out, "Ruprecht, no! Punish the one who is guilty if you must, for that is your right when your deer have been poached, but not the others. Let them live: is not the loss of a kinsman enough?"

The light of the sun caught Ruprecht's blue eyes as he looked at her, and Margerite froze. His gaze was not that of a human being: it was harsh and pitiless, knowing no more of mercy or compassion than the fierce stare of an eagle. She wanted to collapse weeping beneath it; only her years of learning to comport herself as the mistress of her father's castle held her upright, staring back at him.

"Leave, Margerite," he said. "Leave, or be silent."

With all her heart, Margerite wanted to flee, but she could not turn away: the sick feeling was in her soul, that she could have done something to prevent what was happening now. Had she seen to the betrothal earlier, she might have pleaded for Eckhardt's life, at least; she might have spoken to his grandfather, and learned what was in his mind...been able to dissuade or warn. Mutely she shook her head: she must stay, and pray that her presence at least brought a little comfort to Eckhardt in his last minutes of life.

Father Hans had finished with the women before two of the Tiefensee men had carried a butcher's block into the middle of the square. Eckhardt knelt before it, closing his eyes against the sight of the scarred wood, stained with old blood and splintered from years of axe-blows. His lips moved as he softly murmured something; Father Hans put a shaky hand on his head, giving him the final blessing.

As if determined to die like a soldier, Eckhardt shuffled forward on his knees, laying his head on the block. Bertram stepped up beside him, the Hauptmann's sword flashing in the sunlight. Bertram's face was deathly white beneath his black beard as he lifted the blade in both hands, his hazel eyes fixed on the man who knelt before him.

"Now, Bertram," Ruprecht said. The bright blade slashed down, biting deep into Eckhardt's naked neck and the wood beneath with a solid thunk. The bound body jerked back, the blood fountaining brilliant red into the sunlit air; Eckhardt's head rolled free on the other side of the block, coming to rest face-down a little before the hooves of Ruprecht's horse.

Margerite had seen hangings before: she did not watch as Eckhardt's mother and sister were hauled into the air, but she could not help hearing the strangled noises of their dying, nor seeing, from the corner of her eye, how their arms jerked and legs kicked against the air where they dangled. Ruprecht sat perfectly still on his horse, his face fair and remote as that of a saint carved in stone.

"As for you," he said to the old man who stood glaring up at him, bright blue eyes venomous beneath the thicket of his gray-white eyebrows, "you shall have the punishment that is most fit for you." Ruprecht unslung his bow, nocking an arrow. "Cut the bonds on his hands and feet," the Graf commanded, "and let him run. If he can get free...he shall be free."

One of Ruprecht's men drew his knife, slicing through the rough hempen ropes tying the last prisoner's ankles and wrists. "Go!" he said roughly, with a hard push between the old man's shoulderblades. The old man stumbled, then began to run, dodging and weaving; the folk around him melted away from his path as if he bore the plague. Ruprecht waited, his arrowhead tracking the old man's movements; then Margerite saw the slight smile curling his lips as he released the bowstring.

The arrow sang through the air, sinking deeply into the old man's lower back. He staggered and twisted against it, though he did not go down; but as soon as his body turned, Ruprecht loosed a second arrow, and this one went through his side into his guts.

Ruprecht rode slowly over to where the old man lay moaning softly in agony. "Up!" he said. "My stag gave you a good run with an arrow in his bowels; now you will give me one. Up, and flee for what is left of your life!"

The old man pushed himself up. Spittle was dribbling into his beard, and his eyes rolled wildly in pain and terror. Margerite bit her lips until she could taste the blood; she would have sworn that Ruprecht's victim would never stand again, but from somewhere, as if a greater terror than the arrow in his guts were driving him, he found the strength to rise, tottering along a few steps before he actually broke into a stumbling run again.

Riding in slow chase, Ruprecht unslung the hunting horn from his neck and blew upon it: the three long notes of the mote, blown to show that the stag was moving. The high sound shivered through Margerite's body, and she found that she could not stop shivering when its echo had died away, even when she could no longer see Ruprecht or his human quarry.

The stink of fresh blood and open bowels was beginning to fill the warm air; Margerite could hear the buzzing of flies like the low hum of fever in her ears as they gathered over the pool of blood drooling from Eckhardt's head and the long darkening stain on the earth by his headless body. Suddenly Margerite knew that she could bear no more.

She clamped her knees tightly to Mathilde's sides, urging the horse on. The villagers got out of her way as they had fled from Ruprecht; she kneed Mathilde into a full gallop, tearing down a side street and back along the edge of the lake, back to the woods.

Faintly, she heard the call of Ruprecht's hunting horn once more: the mote again - how could the old man still be running? Margerite did not know and could not bear to think on it. She fled wildly down the path that she and Bertram had broken towards the shrine of Maria, for she could think of no other place that might still the dreadful horror that shook her body until she could barely hold to Mathilde's reins and keep her seat steady on the horse's back.

Mathilde had slowed to a walk by the time Margerite reached the shrine, for even in her distress, Margerite could tell that she had run her steed too hard. "I am sorry, Mathilde," she whispered, dismounting and stroking the horse's wet cheek. Mathilde nickered agreeably, butting her head lightly against Margerite's hand.

Margerite crossed the clearing, going to her knees before the fountain's overflowing bowl. "Mother Maria, help me," she prayed. "I am so frightened...I do not know what..." Then she was weeping, the great sobs racking her body so hard that she could neither see nor speak. She wept for Eckhardt and his family, their lives wasted for an old man's drunken guilt; for Bertram, who had been forced to wield the sword that took his comrade's head; for Gertrude, whatever fate had befallen her; and she wept for herself and Ruprecht, for the love that had seemed so fair to her and whose memory now seemed a burden past bearing.

It was not so much Ruprecht's cruelty to the poacher and his family that had undone her, for he was well within the bounds of law in dealing his justice. Her own father had hanged his fair share of criminals, including a young boy of ten years caught in the act of stealing one of his horses: a lord must carry out his laws, even the harshest, when necessary. Rather, it had been the inhuman look transfiguring Ruprecht's face, so closely kin to the shining power that had possessed him in the night, that had terrified Margerite.

Now she could not deny that all her fears were true, that her suspicions of black magic and heresy were not fevered imaginations born of a womb too long empty, but sober truth: Burg Falkenstein's lord - her husband - had given himself over to the Devil.

Even when her tears had run out, Margerite could not stay her sobbing, rocking back and forth on her knees in front of the dripping basin. The breaths rasped harshly out of her torn throat; her whole body shook as though she lay deep in the fever of the Death.

"Frowe, be easy," a deep voice said beside her, and Margerite felt a warm hand upon her shoulder. She looked up to see Bertram there, offering her a damp kerchief. Gratefully she took it, wiping her face and blowing her nose. The Hauptmann's eyes were very red in his pale face: she wondered if he, too, had been weeping.

"I cannot," Margerite said. "I cannot, for..." She rose to her feet, trying to hold herself straight and gather some tatters of dignity about herself, but the effort was too much for her. Before she knew what she was doing, she was clinging to Bertram, shaking against his solid warmth. He held her quietly, waiting for the fit to pass, until at last she stood still, her head resting against his broad chest.

This is not proper! Margerite thought, suddenly realizing that she was in the embrace of a man who was not her husband. She moved to step away from Bertram, and he let his arms drop.

"Now you have seen why the folk of Tiefensee fear Graf Ruprecht," Bertram said. "This is not the first time he has taken harsh vengeance on poor folk who trespassed upon his woods."

"I knew that," said Margerite shakily. "It was bad...bad enough...poor Eckhardt, who wanted to marry Gertrude and stay at Burg Falkenstein! But that is not all. I dreamed...I dreamed..." Like a stream breaking through the rocks and earth that dammed it, the words suddenly began to pour out of her mouth. She told Bertram of her dream that Ruprecht had taken Gertrude beneath the castle and done something unspeakable with her, and of waking in the morning to find the maidservant gone, her broken crucifix on the floor and the scratch-mark left on Ruprecht's cheek.

The only part she could not speak of was how he had come to her after, for the shame of that was too strong within her: she could not have told another woman, let alone a man. Bertram's face grew grimmer as he listened, until Margerite almost feared to look him in the eye: again he seemed like the dark soldier she had first seen at Burg Hirschenburg, a man of blood without pity or mercy. Yet she could no longer keep her thoughts secret, and now she blurted out the questions that had been seething in her mind, for she was sure that Bertram knew the answers.

"You warned me before, but would not tell me of what I should beware. Now I know more of the evil within Burg Falkenstein - and within Ruprecht," she added miserably. "Who are Cundrîê and Clingschor, and has this anything to do with the Order that is supporting our war?"

Bertram's voice was gentle as he said, "Frowe Gräfin, forgive me. I would not choose to tell you of this if I could keep you from it, for the answer to your questions will be a heavy burden; but it seems that you have already learned most of it by yourself. What has Graf Ruprecht already told you of the Order?"

"Ruprecht has told me nothing. But when we were in the merchant's house, I overheard you speaking of the Order late at night. I did not mean to eavesdrop, but you were in the chamber next to mine, and the wall beside my bed was thin. From that, I know that it is a band of knights and merchants, which deals with the Free Companies and sought to sway Kaiser Karl from his crusade against them."

"Other than that?"

Margerite shook her head. "Nothing."

"Then may Maria give you the strength to bear this. The Order of Light-Bearers is not a chivalric brotherhood, as you thought, but a band of men and women who worship the Devil and practice black magic. Your husband Graf Ruprecht is a member, and has been for years. He is not yet a ruler among them, but he is of some importance in their counsels and workings, as may be shown by the ring of amethyst he wears - lesser members have plain rings graven with their motto, or rings set with onyx, while ruby is for the rank of Princeps. The Order is spread throughout Europe, its members being for the most part in places of power, for they seek to gain control of whatever affairs of men they may to increase their own power and do the work of their Master. As for Cundrîê and Clingschor - I know not what they are, only that they came from Graf Günther. Servants of the Order, at any rate, and no doubt spies, watching Graf Rüprecht for Graf Günther, and the rest of us for Graf Ruprecht. I would not stake my soul that they are human," he added reluctantly.

To her horror, Margerite found that she was not surprised by Bertram's words. She could not disbelieve nor doubt: she could only whisper, "My dream?"

"I do not doubt that, however it may have been, you saw the truth of Gertrude's fate. Was she still a maiden?"

"Yes."

"The Order..." Bertram's voice broke. He coughed, swallowed hard, and spoke again. "The Order has been known to use the blood of maidens in their sacrifices, most often young children, although they prize more highly a woman who has come to full-grown years and held to her chastity."

"Bertram - how do you know this? How do you know all of these things?"

"I am not a member of the Order, nor have I ever been," the Hauptmann said roughly, and she could hear the harsh pain in his throat. "I...was greatly harmed by them once, and have sought to learn more of them, that I may strike a blow in return. Thus I came to Burg Falkenstein. This war," he went on grimly, "is not the least of the ills to which I have lent my hand, fighting against a good man at their direction, for the sake of winning their trust and gaining my revenge. For that reason, and of your kindness, ask me no more about myself."

"I shall not," Margerite said. But she remembered the dream in which she had seen him, remembered him crying his innocence - and the woman with the ruby-set ring. What he would not tell her, she could guess, and feel its truth as surely as she knew the truth of her dreaming.

A young man's heart and trust won by the woman whose betrayal had tainted all of Eve's daughters in his mind; a crime committed, frightful enough to doom the youthful nobleman on sparsely planted evidence; an escape from the bolted chamber where he waited trial; and then wandering, with no skill but his sword to keep him alive...where should such a man go but the Free Companies?

A man of Bertram's prowess and intelligence could not long be overlooked: he must have quickly risen to command, and then discovered the hand of his foes there. "But Bertram, why did you not warn me before? Why did you say nothing of this, when Gertrude's life could have been saved?"

"I did not speak to you at first because I believed you to be already an initiate of the Order. You were Ruprecht's wife, given to him by his superior in the Order, Graf Günther; you even seemed to be followed by a familiar spirit, as many of the Order's magicians are."

"A familiar spirit?" Then Margerite realized what he must mean. "Kobolt is only a tomcat, who fights and hunts mice and sprays in the corners like any other cat. You can ask..."

She bit her tongue. She had been about to say, You can ask Gertrude, when the sickening shock of realization had hit the pit of her stomach. Bertram could ask Gertrude nothing, nor could Margerite ever call her maid to speak for her again. Though her tears were all cried out, her throat choked her words off.

"I realized that," Bertram said, "when you gave me orders to clean this shrine, and I saw you praying. I did not tell you then, because..." He crossed himself. "It seemed to me then that you were wholly innocent, clean of any taint of your husband's magics. And if Ruprecht had shielded you so long, then I thought, I hoped...I knew not what, but perhaps that instead of the worse corrupting the better, the better might be acting to cleanse the worse. So I held my tongue, and waited - and chose wrongly, for you are right: Gertrude's death is another upon my head. Gertrude, and poor Eckhardt, and..." He stopped, looking down at the ground. "But would you have believed me, if I had told you what I knew?"

"No," Margerite admitted, the words tearing through her throat like shards of broken glass. "I would not have - not even then. I suspected Cundrîê and Clingschor, but I would have gone at once to Ruprecht and told him of your accusations." But if you had told me the morning after I saw you in my dream, when I guessed at what meaning the Order rings might have...If I had thought to ask you then... Poor Bertram, Gertrude's death is on my head as surely as it is on yours.

"So."

They stood there, neither of them speaking until Margerite put her hand on Bertram's arm. "And so you must not blame yourself, Bertram. I am as much at fault as you, for I fought so hard against believing any ill of Ruprecht, and did not dare speak to him for fear of losing his love. And now - Maria help me, for I am defiled, and shall never be clean again!" She whirled away from him to sink down sobbing again, for it seemed to her that she could still feel the touch of Ruprecht's magic through her body, even in her deepest and most secret places.

But Bertram did not turn from her: instead he knelt down beside Margerite, gently laying a heavy arm about her shoulders. "You are not defiled," he insisted, "for you have done nothing, nor taken any hand in Ruprecht's evil."

"But I must go back to him, and be as his wife and lie with him...and oh, I cannot bear it!"

She held tightly to Bertram, clinging to his strong body like a drowning swimmer clinging to a rock against the force of a raging torrent. He embraced her carefully, his touch comfortingly warm and human upon her. As the spasms of sobbing ebbed, she looked up into his face. The water in his eyes glistened in the sunlight, the streaks and speckles of green through his brown irises shining like shafts of sun through a clear pool.

Hardly knowing what she was doing, Margerite found that her lips were meeting Bertram's, the taste of tears salty between them. She felt the tremor running through him, and knew that she should pull away now, but she could not: the only thing she could think of was that she needed to have him with her, needed the comfort of his human touch to drive away the horrors she had undergone.

"My frowe," Bertram said breathlessly. "You cannot..."

Margerite kissed him desperately again, stilling his words with her mouth. Incredulous and shaken, Bertram reached slowly to pull the pins from her hair, letting it spill down over her shoulders and touching the shining fall with the tips of his calloused fingers as though he feared to shatter her.

The hazel eyes of the young nobleman from her vision stared down at her; the look on Bertram's shadowed face was that of a dreamer about to pass through a door, not knowing whether horror or beauty waited on the other side, and as if in a dream, he helped her to unlace her bodice and draw off the pale blue silken gown and the shift beneath it.

"You are so beautiful," Bertram murmured, his voice broken and hoarse. "I do not deserve...my frowe, why?"

"Please come to me," Margerite whispered. She did not have the strength to try to explain to him: she could only summon up the simplest and most honest words. "I am frightened, and alone, and you are my only trust. I need you by me."

Bertram unlaced his breeches and pulled his tunic off. Beneath the light pelt of pale hair on his chest, his heavily muscled body bore a number of scars, from withered white tracks to seams still a shiny red. It was further proof of his humanity, set against the memory of Ruprecht's perfection, and Margerite welcomed the sight in the depths of her soul.

He sank down beside her in the grass, kissing her and stroking her shivering body as he might have touched a frightened horse. Bertram's caresses were not as skilled as Ruprecht's, but clumsy and almost shy, as though he had not touched a woman for years.

For her part, Margerite could hardly do more than cling shaking to him, letting his warmth and strength seep into her chilled flesh; but gradually his soothing movements began to ease her. Bertram was ready for her, his thick shaft standing up hard between their bodies, yet he made no move to enter her. Margerite realized suddenly, too, that she was glad of that, for after what had happened to her, she did not think she could bear being pinned down beneath a man's weight.

Yet she wanted him inside her, his touch within scouring away the memory of the burning cold that had pierced her. She lifted her leg over his hip, sliding her body up a little and reaching down to guide him into her. Bertram gasped as the head of his shaft entered Margerite's body, his arms tightening upon her and hips moving with hers as she began to rock slowly back and forth upon him, letting the sweet relief build within her.

Bertram held Margerite for a little while when they were done, but then he suddenly let go, turning his head to the side as if he could not bear to look at her.

"What is wrong?" Margerite asked. Though her heart was still uneasy within her, her body was much eased, the shaking of chill gone from her limbs and the last dreadful tinglings washed from her womb.

"Frowe Gräfin, forgive me," Bertram said, his voice muffled. "I should not have done this to you."

"What do you mean?" Margerite said, bewildered. "You did not…"

"I assoiled your chastity - and here, of all places, beneath the gaze of the Virgin!" Bertram ground his face into the earth, as though to drive the sight from his eyes.

"Bertram!" Margerite protested, reaching out to him; but he flinched back as though the touch of her hand were a hot iron.

"Do not touch me! It is my fault, for the corruption of the Order upon my soul. I curse them!" He sat up, staring wild-eyed with bits of grass and earth matted in his beard. "Dear God, I curse them, for having brought you into their foul snares. And I - I should have held strong, but I could not, for your beauty and the love I bear you. O, had I refused to slay poor Eckhardt, and died for it, it would have been the better for both of us than to have committed this sin, and defiled Maria's holy shrine with it."

"Bertram! If there is fault, it is mine more than yours, for I wished you to come to me. And I am little regretful of it, for how can Ruprecht be my husband, after what he has done to me? Yet," Margerite added more softly, "it is I who should ask forgiveness of you, for you gave me only easing from horror, where I can see that I have brought you pain."

Bertram shook his head wearily. "If you knew how long it has been since I last lay with a woman in love, and what has befallen me in the years between, perhaps it would seem no wonder to you that I was willing to seize upon your weakness. Yet knowing why a thing is so does not amend it, nor does it lessen my sin against you and against the Virgin. No, Frowe Gräfin, I can only beg your forgiveness, and promise that I shall not deal with you thus badly again, however the desires of my heart may urge me."

"Bertram, you have my forgiveness, though I do not think you need it. As for what may be between us..." Margerite paused. She had not thought past the turmoil of her soul in that moment, neither taking into account what might befall the two of them or what they should do afterwards. "I do not know what may come to pass. But this I know: that when we are by ourselves, I should like you to call me by my baptized name, for..." she shuddered... "I am the Frowe Gräfin only by virtue of being married to Ruprecht, but Margerite is the name by which Christ will receive me on the day of my death, and, though you may not think so, I swear by the Cross that I think you have saved my soul this day. Will you do that?"

Bertram looked into her eyes for a long time, his green-brown gaze darkly shadowed beneath his black brows. He is in pain, Margerite thought: if only I could bring comfort to his soul, as he has brought it to mine! But at last he nodded, and took her hand in a firm grasp, as if sealing a compact between soldiers.

"I will - Margerite."

"Thank you, Bertram." Margerite leaned forward to brush her lips against his. He did not flinch back again, but neither did he make any move to answer her kiss, only rose to his feet, lifting her shift and gown from where they lay carefully draped upon the grass and helping her to put them on before he dressed himself.

"We should depart separately," Bertram said. "I will delay in the woods some time; you follow the straightest path back, and I shall circle about and return from another direction. If you are asked, say only that something frightened your horse, and you became lost. Perhaps you slipped from her back: that will answer any questions that might be asked."

Margerite put her hands to her head, pushing back her loose hair. She could find no fault with Bertram's plan, and said so.

"That is well. Ride carefully, Margerite."

"And you, Bertram."

Margerite gave her horse over to the stableboy and made it up to her room without anyone but a few of the servants seeing her. Alone save for Kobolt sitting regal in one of the wide windows, she was about to call for Gertrude again when she caught herself, remembering once more that her maidservant would never answer her again.

She did not weep, for she had no tears left, but she sat for a time before propping her mirror up on the table and beginning to comb her own hair and, clumsily, to put it up again. After a while, she realized that she was ravenous, for it was well past time for the midday meal. And sooner or later, despite all she knew now, she would have to gather her courage to face Ruprecht and take up her duties as Gräfin again.

And yet I could leave. I could give over the life of the world, and become a nun…

But what convent would take her? A Gräfin with no dowry - for Ruprecht would never give her one to become a Bride of Christ, of that she was sure. Perhaps she could humble herself, risking rape and murder on a long journey to a cloister that had never heard of Burg Falkenstein and going to them poor and barefoot, but she had no doubt that sooner or later Ruprecht, or other members of his Order, would find her: she did not think he would let her escape him. And what if I am with child already? The thought struck Margerite with a dreadful weight, ringing in her heart with a truth that, for all her hopes, she had never felt before.

She touched her belly, wondering. Once with Ruprecht in the woods; once with Bertram, and once with… her mind shied away from the thought. And if a child were growing in her womb, would it be born fair, or dark-haired? She and Ruprecht were both fair: a dark changeling would tell him, without a doubt, that she had betrayed him. And yet the thought of bearing Ruprecht's child, which a day before had been her dearest hope, now filled her with dread.

"I do not know," Margerite said aloud. "I cannot even know that I am with child, not until..." Her courses would be due in a little less than half a month, and even if they did not come down then, she had often gone late: the midwife at Burg Hirschenberg had told her that this was not too unusual, especially for a young woman who had never borne a child.

But good sense was no match for the awful certainty that filled her; it seemed almost as if she could feel the tiny thing squirming within her already, innocent - pray Christ it was innocent! - of any knowledge or sin beyond the first sin of Father Adam that all humans bore. And...I could rid myself of it now. Margerite knew that a child was no more than the potential of life until it had been six weeks in the womb.

She had known women who rid themselves of five-weeks' children and received only light penance, for abortion was not murder until after six weeks, and in any case there was no blame given to a woman who took herbs to bring down her courses when they were a little late. Such herbs were easy to find, for they grew thickly in the Burg Falkenstein herber.

Pennyroyal and tansy, thyme and wormwood, celandine and rue, and a host of others: brewed into a strong decoction, they would put an end to any fears she might have about bearing a child - whoever its father was. Margerite pressed her hand against her stomach, as if she thought that a babe might already be bulging against its flatness. There was no way to tell so early: she could not really be sure for another month or two, and a simple draught would bring down her courses and end her doubt.

"But...could I?" she whispered. If a child grew in Margerite's womb, it was her child, shaped from her own flesh and blood; unless she wanted a wet nurse, it would suckle at her own breasts. Again it seemed to her that she could feel the slight movement within her, as if her thoughts had disturbed the tiny creature, as if it were pleading with her to be born.

"I cannot," Margerite said to herself. "Rest easy, little one. Whoever your father is, you are mine, and I shall take care of you."

At her words, Kobolt leapt into her lap, purring and rubbing his head against her stomach. She scratched behind his ears, letting him lick her fingers. "Did you think I was talking to you, cat? No doubt you did, vain creature. Well, Kobolt, some of us cannot catch mice and rats for our dinners, and I have had nothing since breaking my fast, so I am going down to the great hall. Would you like to come with me, Herr Tomcat?" The cat answered with one of his purring chirps, winding about her ankles as she opened the door, then pouncing ahead to lead the way down the staircase.

Ruprecht was in the great hall with Bertram and Wolfram and Paul, going over their campaign maps again. Margerite seated herself quietly beside Ruprecht, grateful that she would not have to speak. The Graf seemed himself again, staring at the point Paul was indicating with his stubby finger. His face was quiet, all the madness washed from it; handsome, a little pale with tiredness, but his blue eyes still bright and alert, he looked like the man Margerite had married.

Ruprecht leaned his chin on his hand, the muscles of his forearm cording beneath the blue sleeve of his tunic, and for a moment Margerite felt that she wanted to touch him, to reassure herself that all she had seen was only a phantom dream and that everything between them was as it had been yesterday. Instead she signalled to a servant for food and wine, sipping at the cool sweetness and listening quietly as the men discussed their next move.

"Ruprecht!" a voice called from the door. They all looked up, to see Father Hans lurching unsteadily into the room. The priest's graying hair was disheveled, his cassock stained with spilt wine, and Margerite could smell the fumes from his unshaven mouth long before he reached them; but when he spoke, his voice was clear enough.

"Ruprecht, that was your fault this morning."

Ruprecht was on his feet at once, facing down the priest. "What do you mean by that, Hans? That man shot my deer; should I let criminals go unpunished?"

Father Hans did not back up or quail before his lord's wrath. Perhaps it was the wine giving him courage, perhaps it was only because he had known Ruprecht since the Graf's boyhood. "He shot the deer because the deer are devouring the Tiefensee vineyards. I have heard the village folk complaining often enough in these last weeks. And do you know why those animals are ravaging your lands?"

"Why is that, Hans?" Ruprecht asked. His voice was quiet: before, Margerite might have taken it for the mildness he always showed the old priest, but now she shivered in fear, for it seemed to her that she could hear the dangerous edge in it, cold as the depths of lake-water beneath the sunlit shallows.

"Because you have not been doing your duty! Has there ever been a year before when the fat deer flocked out of the wood like cattle? No, because you were hunting every day, and you knew when your herds had to be culled to keep them from overunning field and vineyard. But this year you have spent all your time in war, and given no thought to your duties at home - you, whom your men used to name Lord of the Woods. Graf, I beg you: go to the forests and hunt for yourself, or give the men of Tiefensee leave to protect what they have planted, else you will lose harvest and harvesters alike."

Margerite held her breath. She was sure that Ruprecht would kill the priest there in the hall for his words, for she had never known anyone to speak to him so. Christ, forgive Father Hans his sins, she prayed urgently. He is a drunk who should never have been anointed, but if he dies for the sake of his flock, he will have died as a priest.

Even as she thought that, she found that she, too, had risen to her feet: she had not been able to protect Gertrude, nor sway Ruprecht's wrath that morning, but if he drew his sword to strike at the priest, she would try to hold his arm, and trust in whatever love had been between them to keep him from cutting her down as well.

But, to her surprise, Ruprecht sat down, a look of thoughtful contemplation on his face. "I will not give peasants leave to hunt my deer," he said. "But we can hold and gather our strength for a week or two, and the meat will be useful both on the march and through the winter, if we have enough salt to preserve it. Margerite?"

Shocked by his words, it took Margerite a few moments to gather her thoughts. "I...yes, that is. We have plenty of salt, for I bought as much as I could in Freiburg, thinking that we would have to keep a great store of meat through the winter."

"So it shall be," Ruprecht said. "You have what you want now, Hans. Go back to your chapel, and drink your wine to celebrate if you wish."

The priest bowed, stumbling out. Margerite sat down as quietly as she could, praying that Ruprecht had not noticed her getting up. But he turned to her, inclining his head in his courtly fashion. "My darling, a hunt such as this will have to be bow and stable, for we have not the time to pursue lone deer by force. Will you ride with us to shoot, or to watch the shooting?"

"No." Realizing how blunt her refusal sounded, Margerite hastened to soften it. "I would gladly ride to the chase, but I am no great shot with a bow, and find little sport in watching the driving of deer. I shall stay here, and be sure that all is ready for smoking and salting the venison you bring back."

"You are a fine and noble wife," Ruprecht said, and she could see nothing in his eyes except the glow of pleasure and admiration. "Later we shall have time to ride to the chase together again, as you wish it." Before Margerite could move her hand, he had caught hold of it, raising it to his lips and kissing her fingers lightly.

The touch of his mouth sent a queasy shiver through her, remembering, but she did not dare let it show, thinking only, O, Mother Maria, please do not let him come to my bed tonight! But when the evening meal had been cleared and it was time for her to go to bed, Margerite found herself lingering in the hall with Ruprecht.

At first she did not know why she was so reluctant to rise and go to her chamber alone, but then she remembered: Cundrîê would be there in Gertrude's place, and it would be the old woman who undressed her and saw her to bed. That fear gave her the courage to speak to her husband, saying, "Ruprecht, my maidservant Gertrude is gone."

"Is she?" Ruprecht asked, looking at her mildly. His face seemed clear and innocent, with only a little surprise to be read upon it. He twirled the stem of his goblet idly in his fingers, looking at the reflection of the candlelight swirling on the surface of the pale wine. "Did she tell you she was leaving, or did she simply run away?"

Margerite longed to fly at him, to scream that he knew better than she where Gertrude was, but Bertram's words of warning were still with her. She knew that her only protection was her seeming of innocence, and so she said, "I awoke this morning, and she was gone. I thought she might have gone down to the village, and when I saw...what happened to Eckhardt, to whom she was to be betrothed, I wondered if she had fled from here in terror, lest the same punishment befall her." Margerite could not keep the accusation from her voice, but it did not matter: she would have spoken the same in any case.

"It would have gone better if you had left before the judgement," Ruprecht said. His voice was calm, but it seemed to Margerite that a shadow came over his face...one of sorrow? Regret? Margerite could not tell. "If that is so, we will find her tracks when we are beating the woods, but I can hardly waste men in a search for a missing servant-maid now."

"And if she is not found," Margerite said, tightening her hand on the stem of her own goblet to keep the tremor of her fingers from showing, "I shall need another maidservant."

"Why? Have you found fault with Cundrîê's help?"

"She has served well enough to assist Gertrude, but she is an old woman, who seems to have many other duties. I want a maid who is nearer to my age, and," she added in hopes that Ruprecht would think her desire frivolous rather than reading the fear in it, "more familiar with the fashions of today, for Cundrîê hardly knows how to dress me in those clothes I had remade in Freiburg. I could train one of the Tiefensee girls quickly enough, I think."

Ruprecht shook his head. "No, I had been thinking that it would be better for you to have a handmaiden who had something of a proper education and manners fit for a Gräfin's servant. I will send away for one; surely one of my friends' wives can find a girl who will suit."

The goblet shook in Margerite's hand so that the wine nearly slopped out of it. When Ruprecht spoke of his friends, he might very well mean the Order of Light-Bearers; had she only exchanged one spy for another? But she forced herself to give a little laugh, and to smile at him sweetly, as she said, "That would be most kind. I will be happier if we can find Gertrude, for I am very worried for her, but even if she should come back, I will be glad to have a second maidservant."

To Margerite's relief, Ruprecht did not follow her up to her chamber; nor did he come to her in the nights following. He was courteous and kind to her, as always, but very much preoccupied with his riding into the forests, first to count the deer, then to begin their cull. Margerite was glad to lose herself in the work that brought: the fires burned high in the Tiefensee courtyards, smoking and drying the haunches of red deer and roedeer that hung above them; the salt baths had to be prepared for curing some of the flesh, oak bark collected for tanning the hides, and all done at once, before the summer warmth could spoil the meat...it was as if the November slaughtering had come three months early.

Margerite had no time to ride to the shrine with Bertram, nor even to speak to him; but sometimes she glanced at him to find him hastily dropping his eyes, his lids lowering too late to hide a glimmer of wordless pain and longing, and often she wished to take his hand, to feel the gentle reassurance of his strength and remind herself that she was not alone in the burden of knowledge she bore.

Margerite was, however, alone with her second burden: for her courses did not come down when they were due, and, as certain proof, she had begun to empty her stomach into her chamberpot every morning. Now, no matter what she told herself, she knew that she was with child: it almost seemed to her as though she could feel the weight in her womb. When she was not thinking, she found herself moving more slowly and carefully, as if to protect the babe beneath her heart; her small white breasts had not yet begun to swell or grow tender, but sometimes her nipples tingled oddly, as if her child already longed to suckle at them.

She wished that she could speak of these things with Gerhild, to see if other women underwent them, but she did not yet want to give voice to her knowledge, for the sake of the worries that flung themselves endlessly to tear at her joy like a pack of mastiffs about a boar. What colour would the child's hair be when it came from her womb? And even if its looks did not betray her, what would Ruprecht do with it?

She, or Gerhild, could baptize it at need, but neither baptism nor attendance at Mass had saved Gertrude from her fate. Would he kill a daughter in unholy sacrifice, or raise a son to follow after him in the black arts he practiced? And...though she seldom gave voice to this thought, even in her mind, it was always smouldering like a coal eating away at the roots of her thoughts: what would look out of her child's eyes when it was born?

For she no longer dreamed of flying, but when she was on the verge of wakening, it sometimes seemed to her that, through her closed lids, she could see a seed of light kindling within the darkness of her womb, and she could not drive away the memory of the brightness glowing from Ruprecht's transfigured face, etched upon her sight like a lightning bolt against black night, nor forget altogether the star-cold burst of brilliance that had spewed into her body.

As always, the Order answered Ruprecht's request quickly. There was a convent in Passau, the abbess of which held the rank of Archbishop in the Order - equal to Ruprecht himself. That convent could sometimes supply young girls to Order members, for the sacrifice of either maidenheads or lives, or for use as servants and magical assistants, as the need might be. Now they had a fourteen year-old, a maiden of noble birth who had been orphaned in the return of the Death and sent to a convent by the cousin who had taken over her lands.

She would suit well enough for both of Ruprecht's purposes: she would do as Margerite's maidservant, and, since he no longer dared to risk the health of his wife and the child Cundrîê had promised she was carrying by sending Margerite out to spy upon Heinrich's movements, he would be able to use the girl in certain rituals of the body by which greater power could be raised to the magician's will.

The convent girl was delivered a week after Ruprecht's summons. It was his good luck that he was in the castle when the two riders were seen coming up the path, rather than out at his hunting, for he was able to meet them at the gate. He knew the man who accompanied the maiden well enough: Damiano, a Monsignor in the Order, who often ran errands for his superiors - the same man whom Margerite had met in Passau. Ruprecht greeted him warmly, inviting him to stay for a few days and take part in the hunting, but Damiano shook his head.

"I will leave the hunting to you," he said. "I must be gone tomorrow, for there are many things happening, and I have words to bear to others. It was only good chance that I happened to be passing in the right direction when your girl needed someone to accompany her."

Ruprecht looked at the girl, who hung back fearfully from his gaze. If he had not known her age, he would have guessed her to be no more than eleven: hunched in her novice habit, she looked very small and frail, blond hair hanging lankly about her pinched face. Her breasts had not yet begun to blossom, and her shape beneath the black robe was that of a boy, her hips still narrower than her shoulders.

Ruprecht sighed to himself. He would not be able to use her as he had planned: the rites of binding and scourging were meant to cause pain and fear in the victim, yes, but she must be able to feel pleasure as well, even against her will. Besides...he had to admit it to himself, for a lie to oneself was a weakness that, sooner or later, a demon would be able to pry its way through...he knew that, faced with the half-grown body of a frightened child, he would not be able to summon up his own desire to complete a sexual ritual. Still, she would grow, and as a virgin, she would still be of some use in his magic.

"What is your name, child?" Ruprecht said to her.

"My name is Eva, Herr Graf," she responded timidly.

"Damiano, forgive me for leaving you so quickly, but I wish to speak to Eva about her duties in private before I introduce her to my wife." Ruprecht clapped his hands sharply, and the servant boy who had stabled the horses came running back. "Take Herr Damiano to the great hall; see that he is fed, and given wine, and a guest-chamber readied for him. And see to it that Eva's possessions are taken up to the Gräfin's room."

"Herr Graf?" Eva said. "Forgive me, but I have nothing but the clothes I am wearing."

"That shall be seen to. Now, however, you shall come to me. I will see you at suppertime, if not before, Damiano."

"Of course," Damiano replied glumly. Ruprecht remembered that the Italian was quick to sulk if matters had not gone as well as he hoped, or if he thought that his meager importance had been underestimated, which was undoubtedly the case now. Damiano was useful and widely travelled, so Ruprecht would have to spend some time soothing his bruised temper that evening, but for now, it was more important to sort things out with Eva before she had a chance to speak with Margerite.

Ruprecht led the girl up to his chamber. When the door closed behind them, he grasped her by the shoulders, looking down into her green eyes with his most penetrating gaze. "Do you know who sent you here, or why?"

Eva tried to look away, but the force of Ruprecht's will held her paralyzed. She was barely able to gasp out, "Herr Graf, the Abbess told me a great lord's wife needed a maidservant. That is all I know."

"Did the Abbess..." Ruprecht paused. If he were to use her in his workings, however, he would have to tell her something of the Order, if she did not know about them already. Better that she be sure there was nowhere she could flee, no safe place to go if she failed him or tried to escape him. "Did she ever have you assist her in her secret mysteries - in any works of magic?"

"She swore me never to speak of such things, Herr Graf!" Eva blurted, and Ruprecht saw that she was staring at the amethyst ring on his left forefinger: the Abbess, he knew, would wear its mate. "She said that demons of fire would rip the skin from my flesh and the flesh from my bones if I ever told anyone what she did. I cannot tell you, Herr Graf!"

"But you have answered my question well enough without telling me," Ruprecht said sardonically. The child was either clever enough to need close watching, or the Abbess had already given her some instruction in the ways of demons and their subtle speech, or both. "You cannot tell me what she did, but you can tell me what you did, can you not?"

Eva's face twisted in thought. "Yes, Herr Graf. I dressed in white silk and carried a bowl of water, and I held a censer and swung it about the room. And sometimes I bled a few drops of blood, and sometimes I gave up a hair, and sometimes I made water into a phial. And I did personal service to the Abbess."

"Did you ever see a demon?"

"No, but I saw a nun possessed by one."

"What you shall do here," Ruprecht told her slowly, "is not that different from what you did in the convent, save that you shall have your duties as maidservant to the Gräfin as well. Do you know of the nature of the Order of Lightbearers?"

Eva nodded, a quick birdlike jerk of her head.

"Then you should know that the Gräfin is set higher in the Order than I, though that is known by only the fewest, and she wears no ring for the sake of secrecy. She is cold-hearted and cruel, and would have no qualms about having you slowly torn to pieces with red-hot irons if she so chose. Her magic does not need your help, and you are not to bother her with as much as a single word about what you and I do together - if you do, it will be your death. Do you understand?"

"Yes, Herr Graf," Eva answered, her voice almost inaudible. The girl was trembling as though she herself were possessed, her thin face gray with terror, but Ruprecht pressed on. "And her cat will know, for it is a demon and her familiar. The same is true if you say a single word to anyone else of what I do, of what you do, of what my servants Cundrîê and Clingschor do, or about anything connected with magic or the Order. Your answers to me were clever enough, but if that cleverness ever turns against me..." He reached out, touching the tip of his ringed forefinger to her breastbone. "I have servants of a kind that can creep within your ribs like rats and gnaw your heart with tiny bites of fire until it is all consumed, and keep you alive while they feast on your bowels and your brain. Do you understand?"

"Yes, Herr Graf," Eva whimpered.

Ruprecht lowered his threatening finger. "But so long as you understand and obey and serve well, you shall be treated well, and no harm shall come to you. Cundrîê!"

"Yes, Herr Graf?" At the low voice beside her, Eva looked up. Her face went whiter still; she jammed a fist into her mouth to muffle her small shriek, and Ruprecht smelled the sudden acrid stink of piss.

"Cundrîê, you have frightened her," he said reproachfully.

Cundrîê laughed, the soft clear laugh of a young maiden ringing strangely from her ugly face. "I thought you wished her to be frightened, Herr Graf. But no matter. Say to me, what is your command?"

"Take this poor girl and get her cleaned up, and then find clothes for her suitable to her station as Margerite's maidservant."

"As you will, Herr Graf. Come, Eva."

The girl would not suffer Cundrîê to touch her, but followed docilely enough. Ruprecht breathed deeply, sitting down to compose himself. This was neither what he had expected nor wished for, but a magician who let surprise or compassion shake his will would be subjected to those beings he commanded soon enough.

He had achieved the first part of his goal in regards to the maidservant, anyway: she would do her duties for both Margerite and himself, and never breathe a word to his wife about his doings. Now that Eva was well and truly broken to his will by the terror he had set upon her, she could easily be tamed and calmed by a time of decent treatment and a few good meals, and would soon be a worthwhile and valuable instrumnt of his magics.

Margerite was sitting in her room, picking at a piece of embroidery and staring out one of the wide windows overlooking the ravine. The weather had turned cool again; she had been overseeing the preparation of another few tubs of salt brine when she began to feel chilled and faint, and had come up to sit by her stove and warm herself in quiet. When the door opened, she jumped and turned around, expecting Cundrîê. Instead, a young girl in a damp novice's cassock stood there, cringing beneath her glance.

"May it please you, Frowe Gräfin," the girl said quickly, "I am Eva, sent to be your maidservant by Graf Ruprecht."

Margerite blinked in surprise. Eva's low voice was cultivated enough to show some education, but she was thin and frightened as a street waif, and surely far too young to do a chief servant's duties.

"How old are you, Eva?" she asked.

The girl's chin trembled as though she were about to break into tears, but she answered clearly. "Fourteen, Frowe Gräfin."

"Well. And where did you come from?"

"From the Convent of the Holy Cross in Passau, Frowe Gräfin."

"Where are your clothes? Have they been brought up?"

"Cundrîê said that I might cut whatever Gertrude had left behind for myself, Frowe Gräfin - if it pleases you," Eva added quickly. Margerite was already beginning to grow irritated with the girl's frightened servility, and her words made it worse.

Gertrude's small wooden chest sat untouched in the corner, as it had since her disappearance; somehow, though she did not know why, Margerite felt that to give her maid's clothes away would be like sealing her death, and the loathing of that deed sat heavily in her chest. Yet she knew that Eva would have to wear something beside her cassock - which was not only unsuitable, but wet through from her journey, and beginning to smell in the warmth of the room as though someone had pissed on it along the way.

Gertrude, Christ and all the saints help her soul...if she were to come back, if she were not really dead, Margerite would gladly give her as many of her own fine dresses as the maid could fit into.

"Let us see how we manage. Are you good with a needle? You are smaller and thinner than Gertrude, I believe."

As if to drown the thoughts that yammered in her heart with direct action, Margerite marched over to Gertrude's clothes-chest, flinging it open and reaching in for a pair of garments - the embroidered dress of blue linen and its undershift that she had worn at her wedding, she remembered, let out at the seams and taken up in hem and sleeves when she had given it to Gertrude as being too poor for the Gräfin. A sudden pang of pain went through her, so that she stayed doubled over a moment longer than she needed to, until she could compose her face again.

"Take that cassock off. You will not wear it again; give it to someone who needs it more than you do." Although, looking closer, Margerite could see that the black wool was thin and worn; the garment would have to be cut into pieces for any further good to be gotten out of it.

Eva stood shivering, her arms crossed above the pale buds of her little nipples. Her ribs stood out sharply under her skin, her hipbones keen as axe-blades edging her sunken belly. "Did they never feed you at the convent? Never mind, you shall have good food here. Put this on."

When Eva had pulled the shift on, Margerite saw with some surprise that it fit her well enough - was even a little short in the hem and tight at the cuffs of the sleeves. Gertrude had been plump and round-breasted, but when Margerite really looked at Eva, she saw that the girl was actually quite broad through the shoulders, and big-boned as well. It was no wonder that she looked starved, if she had been fed on rations designed to quell the fleshly desires of contemplatives, like a mastiff puppy given the meals of a greyhound.

Eva was taller than she looked, too, an inch or so taller than Gertrude and only a little shorter than Margerite. Unkindly, Margerite thought that in her mistress' dress, when she straightened her back and squared her shoulders, Eva looked like nothing so much as a young squire guising as a woman for Fastnacht. Then the girl ducked her head, her eyes slipping away when Margerite tried to meet her gaze, and again she had the look of a small and frail child.

This girl has been ill-treated by someone, Margerite thought. I wonder where she came from before the convent? But she only said, "Gertrude's clothes seem to fit you well enough, although they may not when you have gotten a few meals into you. Now take this out and get rid of it: I can smell it from here." She prodded the habit with her toe, and got a reproachful miaow out of it, for Kobolt had crept beneath the folds when she was not looking, and lay there sniffing in its stink, purring blissfully and kneading with his paws.

"Your cat, Frowe Gräfin?" Eva asked nervously, keeping her distance from the pile of black cloth.

"Yes. His name is Kobolt. You must give him a bowl of milk every morning, and watch to see that he does not leave dead mice and rats on my bed or in the rushes where I will step on them. You have no reason to be afraid of him," she added more sharply when the girl kept staring at the cat as if she did not dare to dislodge him from his resting place. "Toss him off of there and get about your work. If you have any questions, ask me, and I will tell you what I want."

Eva paled as though Margerite had threatened her with a whipping. "Frowe Gräfin, I would never disturb you. Never!"

"And how, silly child," Margerite asked, exasperated beyond endurance by her new maid's nervousness and still aching with the pain of knowing that Eva had taken Gertrude's place for good, "do you expect to serve me if you do not know what my wishes are?"

"I had thought Cundrîê would tell me," Eva whimpered. "Is she not chief of the castle's servants, Frowe Gräfin?"

At the thought of this frightened child left to Cundrîê's unholy mercies, Margerite's irritation cooled swiftly. "I suppose she is." How could she warn Eva without telling her anything? She would have to be so careful, and keep such a close watch on the girl! "But she is an old woman and seems set in her ways, and what she wants is very seldom precisely what I want. You are to come to me for instructions, not to her - you are to seek her out as little as possible. Do you understand?"

At Margerite's last words, Eva shied involuntarily with fright, and Margerite wondered for a moment if she would faint.

"I understand, Frowe Gräfin," she said, barely moving her lips.

"That is well. Eva, you look as though you have not eaten for weeks. After you have disposed of this rubbish, you are to go to the kitchen and tell Berthe that I want you fed as much as you wish to eat. I think that you were not cared for properly in the convent, and I want no servant of mine looking as though Burg Falkenstein can afford no better than crusts of bread and water for its own. You will feel better with some food and a cup or two of wine in you, though do not drink too deeply, because I am sure you were not used to wine at the convent and it will easily go to your head."

"Thank you, Frowe Gräfin!" Eva gathered her courage, prodding at Kobolt until at last he rose, stretching majestically, and strolled off the habit. The maidservant snatched it up and fled from the room.

Margerite was able to hold her tears back until the door had closed, but when she went to shut Gertrude's chest again, they burst forth in a storm, the hot drops running down her face and spattering her hands. Gertrude was gone, truly gone. Margerite had seen it often enough, how the dead only seemed absent until the time came to parcel out their clothes to the living.

She knew how absurd it was to be crying over a few pieces of linen, but she could not stop herself. Unless something happened that she could not guess at, Gertrude would never have a decent burial, nor could Margerite openly mourn her: this giving might be as much of a funeral as she would ever get, and it was the sadder because only Margerite knew about it.

"For your sake," she said, as if Gertrude could hear, "I will be kind to the girl, although she is already driving me mad. Pray to Mother Maria for me, that I may be patient with her, and teach her how to act like a Gräfin's maidservant instead of a whipped cur."

The weather turned sharply at the end of August: suddenly yellow tinged the edges of the leaves in the orchard, and the mornings were cold and damp with fog. It was on just such a morning that Margerite, walking through the inner courtyard, heard the pounding hoofbeats on the hard earth of the outer bailey, and a man's strained voice shouting, "Graf Ruprecht! I must see Graf Ruprecht!"

She hurried towards the inner gate, her skirts swishing about her ankles. Bertram, running from his guard tower, overtook her halfway, his sword already drawn.

"Hold!" he bellowed, his powerful voice carrying easily through the mist to the guards at the gate. "Who is this, and what does he want?"

Margerite caught up to him at the narrow entrance flanked by round tower and castle wall. Two guards stood with their spears pointed at the rider without. He must have ridden a long way without rest, for his dun horse was close to foundering, standing splay-legged with its head down and foam dripping from nostrils and mouth. He was helmed and armoured in leather with iron plates sewn onto it, and a dark stain of blood had spread outward from a rent in the leather over his left shoulder.

"I come from Ritter Sigmund von Eichenwald," he gasped. "The Ritter Sigmund sent me to tell Graf Ruprecht…that Graf Heinrich's men have surrounded his castle, and he is besieged within. He cannot hold out more than two weeks at best: for the love and faithfulness he ever bore to Ruprecht, and his father before him, he begs your aid." Beneath the nasal of his helmet, Margerite saw his mouth twist in pain, his face whitening. He slipped from his horse in a half-faint; his feet struck the earth hard, jolting a soft moan from him. Bertram was there to catch and steady him at once, helping him in towards the castle.

"Run!" Bertram snapped to one of the guards. "Find Graf Ruprecht…I know he has not ridden out yet today. You, sound the alarm, then fetch Paul the Bear and Jochanan to the great hall. Come, friend," he said, more gently, to the wounded messenger. "You are safe now; you have only to give your message to Graf Ruprecht yourself. How badly are you hurt?"

The messenger lifted his arm, biting his lip. "Crossbow bolt. I was nearly out of sight of Heinrich's men when it struck me. They came on us late yester-evening, and there were too many to do battle with, so we had to flee back to the castle; but on the way, Ritter Sigmund gave me his orders, and I broke away from the main host."

"I shall see that your wound is tended to," Margerite said. "Bertram, take him in; I will join you there as soon as I have what I need to clean and bandage his hurt."

Bertram glanced down at her. For a moment, he almost smiled, and her heart warmed within her at his look. "That is well-done, Frowe Gräfin."

Margerite walked to the herber as fast as she could, seeking among Cundrîê's strange plants for the ones she recognised. Most of the herbs had already been harvested and dried, either by herself and Wolfram or by the weird woman, but some of them were springing up freshly around their cut stalks.

She gathered a frondy handful of yarrow and the ruffled, spear-head-shaped leaves of betony: she would make them into a poultice with some of the freshly dug comfrey root drying above the kitchen fires. If the messenger's wound had fevered in the course of his ride, he would need something to draw out the poison: Adder's Tongue did not grow in the herber, but she had seen to it that there was a stock of it in the castle.

Weakened as he must be, she would not dare to give him any of the stronger herbs against pain, but a decoction of willow bark might serve to bring him some easing. Margerite paused a moment, looking down at the remains of the pennyroyal, its new shoots already bursting out with shiny little green leaves. She was not even a month late for her courses: if she picked a handful, mixing it with some of the dried rue and wormwood in the kitchen...Her hand moved towards the herb, dropped again: for all her thoughts and fears, she still could not do it.

By the time Margerite had finished grinding and mixing her herbs, and steeping the willow bark into a strong brown tea, the messenger was propped up in a chair in the great hall, weakly watching Ruprecht and his commanders as they debated. He had taken off his armour, and Margerite could see now that his face was flushed, eyes bright with fever. When she drew his torn sleeve aside, the edges of the wound beneath were puffed out, red and shiny.

"I will pour wine into this to clean it, and it will hurt," she said softly to him. He closed his eyes and his breath hissed out through his teeth as the pale stream splashed over his injury, but he did not cry out. "Brave man," she said approvingly. "Here, drink this." She gave him the cup of willow-bark tea, and he sipped at it while she smeared the poultice over the ugly gash in his shoulder and wrapped clean bandages about his arm. "Christ willing, this will draw the fever out and you will begin healing cleanly."

"Thank you, Frowe Gräfin," he said, his voice hoarse and exhausted. "You are most gracious, to tend me with your own hands."

"You have more than earned it," Margerite assured him, wiping the traces of the gritty mess from her fingers with her last cloth and going to sit beside the men.

"Aye, he must want something," Paul was saying. "But if his army is encamped around Burg Eichenwald, will it not be easy for us to come upon them and take them? If we hit them all at once, and the shock of Jochanan's guns is on them..." He looked to Jochanan, and his lieutenant nodded.

"But he must be expecting us to ride to Sigmund's rescue!" Ruprecht said, striking the table with his fist. "What else could we do? And why else would he have besieged a castle that is little closer to Burg Falkenstein than is his own Burg Mittellfeld? He does not need it as a base to strike against us: he has at least two fortresses of his own on the border that would do just as well. No, he has some trap planned: I am sure of it."

"What can he do?" Paul argued. "He can hold, or march. No one can do both at once, unless he splits his forces, and then we can take both parts easily, one after the other."

"There are villages within easy march of Burg Eichenwald," Bertram said thoughtfully. "It will be little trouble for him to send smaller bands away to devastate them, without risking his main force. In fact, they will have to do that for supplies for their army, for Graf Heinrich cannot have much left, after the destruction we have wreaked on his lands. Harvest is nearly over: he must somehow regain much of what he has deprived us of, or he will have lost the war without ever once engaging us in full battle. We should take steps to prevent it."

Ruprecht's gaze was strangely searching as he looked over at Margerite. He had grown thinner in the last weeks between the rigors of his hunting and of alternately ordering out the patrols and riding with the troops himself. The bones of his face stood out more sharply than they had, and it seemed to Margerite that there was almost a pleading look in his bright eyes, though she could not imagine what he thought she could tell him.

"It is true," he said at last. "But Heinrich is fighting us now as we fought him, I think; and if we send our troops out in smaller numbers to scout and protect our villages against lesser bands, I suspect that we shall find that there are greater forces waiting to chew us up piecemeal, as we have been chewing on him."

"So what are we going to do?" asked Paul, almost plaintively. "Herr Graf, no war was ever won by sitting down and waiting. I say we should charge in and take Heinrich where he sits."

"I am with that!" said Jochanan enthusiastically. "We have the two big guns ready to go, seven of the little ones in operation, plenty of powder, and the makings for more. I think we can take them...you may call me bloodthirsty, but I'm bloodthirsty."

They all looked at him incredulously, Ruprecht raising one fair eyebrow and Paul muffling a snicker. The gunner hunched his shoulders, his dark eyes dropping. "Uh. Sorry."

Ruprecht sighed. "Nevertheless, holding back for a little time is exactly what I mean to do. For Sigmund's sake, we cannot simply let Burg Eichenwald fall to the foe, or how should any of my other knights ever put trust in their Graf? But I do not mean to walk straight into whatever trap Heinrich has laid, either. He must know, as well, that when he has taken the offensive so closely that I do not dare to leave Burg Falkenstein without a good part of my troops left behind, lest he steal a march on us and we come back to find ourselves trying to besiege him within my own castle, or, at the least, seeking to come to terms with him on ransom for the Gräfin Margerite."

The Bear frowned, his small eyes squinting: the thought had clearly not crossed his mind. But Bertram nodded soberly. "That is true enough, Herr Graf. Yet, if we must ride to Sigmund's aid sometime, would it not be better to do it before Graf Heinrich has had the chance to reprovision himself from our villages?"

"We shall wait a little time, to see what Heinrich is doing, and to be sure we are ready to meet him" Ruprecht said. "Jochanan, mix up as much powder as you can, for I think we shall need it."

"As you will, Herr Graf," the gunner said, his heavy features brightening at the thought.

"Bertram, Paul, make sure that every man's weapons and armour are ready for battle - that no shaft is cracked and no strap broken. I want Burg Falkenstein to be prepared for siege as well, ready to slam the gates shut and take what action we can against an outside army, for I have grave misgivings about this."

Margerite found that, as she was listening, she had put both hands over her belly, and was rocking slightly, as if to protect and comfort the child growing within her. Yet, although the men's speech disturbed her greatly - the way in which Ruprecht spoke about attacks on Burg Falkenstein, about siege and even her own capture, was too grimly matter of fact for her to set it aside as simply another possibility in the practicality of war - in a way it was almost a relief, to be worried about weapons and provisions and the movements of troops, rather than the dark thoughts that had haunted her, waking and sleeping, all month.

"Margerite, what is the state of our supplies like? If we were to be trapped here, how long could we hold out?"

"If we hasten to claim our portion of the harvest from all our villages and see to the slaughtering of all extra cattle and swine at once, then well into the winter, at least," Margerite answered confidently. "Through the winter, if everyone went on half-rations from the beginning, though I would not like to starve our fighting men so soon. But it is well," she added, "that your hunts brought in so much meat."

"See to the preparations. If we are able to engage and defeat Heinrich, well enough: there will be little lost by doing so, save that the peasants will grumble. But if we are defeated, or beaten back into Burg Falkenstein, we will need whatever we can get, for help may be some time in coming." Again, Ruprecht looked very pensive, and Margerite wondered if he knew something more than she did.

She remembered how the Bear, half-drunk, had spoken of his uncanny ability to guess where Heinrich's troops were, and she wondered now if that had something to do with the black arts he practised, and if whatever magic he used or demons he served had brought him news of ill to come: the thought sent a cold shiver down her spine. At least, Maria be thanked, Ruprecht had not sought to come to her bed that month, and that was not the least of mercies.

Margerite rose. "Eva!" she called. The servant girl appeared at once. A month of feeding had put better flesh on her bones, so that already the seams of Gertrude's clothes strained across her shoulders when she bore a basket of fuel in for Margerite's stove or helped to carry the wooden tub in for her frowe's bath, but all the gentleness Margerite had shown her had done nothing to lessen her cringing, or the stark look of terror on her face whenever her mistress rebuked her, however softly.

"Frowe Gräfin, I am here," she whispered. "What do you wish?"

"See to that man there." Margerite pointed at the messenger. "He needs rest and careful tending if he is to recover: make sure that he has a warm bed. I shall be speaking with Kai in his chamber, so come there when you have taken care of him."

"Yes, Frowe Gräfin," Eva said, bobbing a nervous curtsey and hurrying to the side of the wounded man.

The next week was filled with frantic activity: the sounds of hammering on wood and beating on metal filled the Burg Falkenstein courtyards from dawn onwards every day, and Margerite often found herself taking her meals on her feet, a goblet of wine in one hand and a piece of bread in the other as she directed the slaughtering and the disposition of the wagonloads of flour and dried beans and peas that rolled in through the main gates every morning.

At times it seemed to her as though she was living in the middle of a great beehive, the air buzzing about her with the rising excitement of the preparations for what would likely be the final turning point of the war. Worn out as she was when she went to bed every night, she found herself lying awake, and it seemed to her that, beneath Eva's soft snuffling breaths, she could hear the stones of the castle thrumming deeply like a great lutestring, as though something were stirring at its foundations. When at last she fell into exhausted sleep, she tossed and turned uneasily, as if her soul were fighting against her body's weariness for wakefulness.

The preparations had gone on for a little more than a week when, on one of her troubled nights, Margerite awoke in the darkness to the rough licking of Kobolt's tongue on her ear and the sound of his loud purr.

"Get off me, cat," she mumbled, turning over, but sleep would not come back to her. Something was wrong, and after a few moments, she knew what it was. She could not hear Eva breathing: she knew, as surely as if the full brightness of day were streaming in through her windows, that she was alone in the room.

"Eva?" Margerite said, hoping that the maid would answer, and prove her feeling wrong. But no reply, not so much as a muffled grunt, came from the pallet in the corner.

Cautiously Margerite got up, feeling her way over to Eva's bed. The blankets were thrown back and disheveled; the bed was empty.

"Eva!" she called, more loudly, but no answer came. A terrible panic came over Margerite then. She seized the half-burned candle from her table, opening the stove and blowing upon the ashes until she saw the glow of the last coals flaring red beneath her breath. Another few breaths, and the candlewick kindled to flame, its brightness casting huge leaping shadows upon the stone walls.

The poor, frightened child...what had Ruprecht done with her? Was she even now beneath the castle, suffering the same horrible fate as that which Gertrude had borne? And... the horror took Margerite so that the candle nearly fell from her shaking fingers...would the same thing come to pass again as had happened before? Her womb twinged at the thought: would he come to her again?

She crept out of the room, walking down the corridor to the western staircase. She was about to step into the stairwell when she heard the door opening behind her - the door to the corridor leading northward, towards Ruprecht's chamber. Like a frightened animal, she dodged behind the edge of the wall, shielding her candle's flame with her hand. But she did not flee: if she saw what she feared, she would still be able to run; and if he were not waiting there for her, it might be that she would have a chance to save Eva from whatever had befallen her.

The candle-flame wavered before Margerite's door, gleaming off white linen and pale hair. It was Eva who stood there, and she was alone. Margerite leaned against the stairwell a moment in relief, collecting herself before she hurried back down the hall. Eva shrank back against the stone wall, holding her candle before herself as if its light could shield her from Margerite.

The girl's eyes were almost black in the darkness, twin golden flames reflecting tiny from her swollen pupils. As Margerite breathed in deeply, she could smell the faint scent rising from Eva's skin: hyssop, mugwort, and vervain, underlaid with the sweetness of frankincense, as if the maid had been lingering in a well-censed chapel.

"Where have you been?" Margerite demanded.

"I..." Eva's gaze darted about nervously, like a cornered doe desperately seeking out a gap where she could slip between the trees and run. Suddenly she dropped to her knees before Margerite, still holding her candle up as if it were an offering to the Virgin. "Please, Frowe Gräfin! I have done nothing wrong, I swear it! I have obeyed you and the Graf - I am sorry I was gone when you wanted me. It will not happen again, Frowe Gräfin!" She was weeping in terror, the tracks of tears shiny on her pale cheeks.

"You are not to go wandering about at night!" Margerite whispered to her sharply. Overcome by relief, her own heart was pounding so loudly in her ears that she could hardly hear her own voice. "You could...anything could happen to you, even in our own castle," she finished lamely.

Eva only stared up at her, little mouth trembling, and Margerite wondered what she could threaten the girl with to keep her safe. Rape? None of the Burg Falkenstein men would dare to affront her maid, and Eva still had the body of a child, despite the good food she had been getting: her chastity could hardly be doubted.

There was, in truth, little danger to the girl if she walked about at night - except the one Margerite could not speak to her of, the one that could well mean her life. At last she fell back on the threat that had always worked for convincing Gertrude she was serious, even if the maid had never believed it.

"And if I catch you creeping about when you should be asleep, I will have all the skin whipped from your back."

As soon as the words were out of her mouth, Margerite felt guilty, seeing the way Eva cowered back from her as though she really thought her frowe might carry out the threatened punishment. But if that was what it took to keep her out of Ruprecht's hands and alive, it was worth all the terror she could instill in the poor girl.

"Now come. We will go to bed, and forget this happened - so long as you do not do this again."

"Never, Frowe Gräfin!" Eva babbled. "I swear it, I will obey you perfectly in everything. Please, Frowe Gräfin, please do not kill me!"

Margerite's mouth dropped open. What on Earth or in Heaven could have put that thought into the maidservant's mind? Or...the slow realization crept upon her, chilling as an icy bank of winter mist rolling slowly down the side of a mountain...in Hell?

"Have you," she said slowly, "been doing something with Graf Ruprecht?"

"Frowe Gräfin, no! No!" Eva flung her head from side to side, as if a bat had flown, blindly flapping, into her face, and Margerite could bear to press her no farther.

"Calm yourself and go to bed," Margerite ordered. "We shall rise early enough tomorrow, and you shall be needed for the day's work as much as I."

When they broke their fast at dawn the next day, Ruprecht announced that his troops would march out as soon as they could be assembled. "You, Margerite, will see to bringing the Tiefensee villagers, with all their stores, beasts, and valuables, inside the castle's walls. If Heinrich does as I expect, then within three days, we will either be victorious or besieged. If we win, the peasants may complain as they will; if we are beaten back, they will be grateful. As for the rest of us - Bertram, you know what to do. It may be that you will have a chance to sally out and aid us, if we catch them close to the castle: otherwise, hold fast."

"It shall be so, Herr Graf."

"Jochanan, how fast can you move those big guns if you have to?"

Jochanan shook his head, a frown on his swarthy face. "No faster than the carts that carry them, Herr Graf. You know that."

"Then mount them on the outer walls, at either side of the main gates. If we have to get inside in a hurry, they may help delay our foes."

"Herr Graf, you sound worried," Paul said. "Do you know something we don't?"

"It is only prudence," Ruprecht replied. He stood, clapping his hands together briskly. "Now, to work, for there is much to do yet before we can march out."

Margerite rode down to Tiefensee with a small guard, as many men as Bertram thought he could spare. Either they would listen to her, or they would not; and if not, there was little to be done. She reined her horse up beside the linden tree in the middle of the square - thank Christ, the gibbet and its grisly burden had long since been cut down!

"Bring the village Meier to me," she ordered one of her guardsmen. "And bring the midwife Gerhild as well." The man nodded sharply, dismounting and trotting off.

Meier Reinhold of Tiefensee was a short, thin man with a thick shock of brown-gold hair, twitching with nervous energy. He bowed low before Margerite's horse.

"What may I do for you, Frowe Gräfin?"

Tersely, Margerite repeated Ruprecht's instructions, adding, "If Christ and his saints are kind, this will be only a few days of trouble to you. If not, you will have much to be thankful to your lord for."

The Meier glanced at Gerhild, now standing beside him; then his eyes went up past Margerite's shoulder - looking, she realized, at the place where the gibbet had stood. "Frowe Gräfin," he said slowly, "we do not wish to burden the Graf with useless mouths to feed. If you ask anyone in Tiefensee, you will find that we prefer taking our risks here to moving into Burg Falkenstein - we have so much trust," he added hastily, "in Graf Ruprecht's ability to protect us with his sword."

"Stop lying to me!" Margerite snapped. Though her own outburst surprised her, she pressed her advantage through. "The truth is that you fear Graf Ruprecht more than you fear his foe, is it not?"

"Frowe Gräfin!" Meier Reinhold protested, but Gerhild was nodding, her lips pressed together in a tight line.

"Well. Gerhild, you know me well enough. I can promise you that the folk of Tiefensee will be under my personal protection, and you may have my oath on it, by Christ and God and the Virgin Maria. I may have failed once to stay Graf Ruprecht's hand, when he was in the full throes of his hunting fury, but that will not happen again. Will you trust me on it?" She looked Gerhild straight in the eyes, and after a few moments the midwife slowly nodded.

"Reinhold, you may trust her," Gerhild said. "Did she not deliver my child when I, and the babe, should have died? Our Gräfin is a wise woman, and if she thinks it best for us to be within Burg Falkenstein's walls, then I shall stand with her."

Meier Reinhold bit his lip, looking thoughtfully at the midwife. "It will not be easy for us to convince our folk to go into the castle, after..."

"We must," Gerhild insisted. "If you and I speak for it together, with no fear or doubt, and command it in the name of the Gräfin Margerite, I have no doubt that we shall achieve what we need to. Frowe Gräfin, Reinhold will need a little time to call all our folk in from the fields. Then he shall speak, and then I shall speak, and lastly you shall speak: and St. Stefan grant us all eloquent tongues, for we shall need them."

It was past midday when the villagers of Tiefensee at last hurried from the square to their homes, beginning to load their possessions onto their wagons and oxcarts; but at least they were doing it. Some of them, Margerite had no doubt, would flee into the woods the moment her back was turned, but most of them would come to the castle.

Relieved, Margerite rode back to Burg Falkenstein with the sense of a job well-done, only to see that Ruprecht's troops were already riding down the road towards Heinrich's lands. She blinked, and found herself dashing a tear from her eye. And yet I would be as glad to never see Ruprecht again, she told herself.

Bertram was standing on the wall beside the western guard tower, looking out between its stone crenellations with his scarred hands resting on one square gray block. Margerite waved aside the guard at the door, marching up the tower and out onto the wall to join him. Sunk in his own thoughts, he did not seem to notice her there.

"Do you think they will win?" she asked softly.

Bertram started. "I do not know," he answered. "It is not like Graf Ruprecht to prepare for defeat."

"As he said himself, it is only what a prudent man would do," Margerite argued, but she could not even convince herself. "What will we do if...?"

"Most likely, surrender to Graf Heinrich. From all I have heard, he is an honourable man, so that you at least should be well-treated."

Margerite put her hands on the crenellation beside Bertram's. She did not dare to touch him, but this time when he looked down at her, a small sad smile twisted his lips.

"I wish we could have gone back to Maria's shrine," she said. "I know we cannot risk it now."

"No." Bertram looked away, down the road where Ruprecht's men had marched. Then, "I wish we could have, too - Margerite."

Margerite would have stayed with him longer, but the first wagons from Tiefensee were rolling into sight. "I will be needed below."

"Yes." Bertram paused again, and Margerite thought he would say nothing more, but then he spoke again. "Ruprecht does not deserve you, you know."

Margerite did not know how to answer that. She found that she was blushing like a girl, the tips of her ears hot, and to cover her flusterment, she said, "Well, if Burg Falkenstein is prepared well for siege and matters do not go well in the field, we will be able to get better terms from Graf Heinrich if it is a choice between surrender and holding out for some months."

"As I said," Bertram replied. He turned away, staring out over the orchard and the woods beyond, and Margerite went into the guard tower and down to the courtyard.

Nervous as Margerite was, the day passed quickly: shelters had to be put up quickly in the outer bailey for the Tiefensee villagers, their food and goods counted and stored, the weapons and arrows they had brought with them tallied, and arrangements made for feeding them. When she finally got to her chamber at night, for once she found herself longing for one of Cundrîê's draughts to give her easy sleep, but the old woman had stopped bringing them after the night Gertrude disappeared, and Margerite was hardly going to call her back.

The next day dawned dark and ominous, heavy showers of rain sleeting down gray across the ravine and spattering hard against the windows of the castle. Even the fire in the stove did not take the chill from the air of Margerite's chamber. Crouched over her chamberpot, she retched and shivered for several minutes; the only warmth she could feel was Kobolt's furry body brushing sympathetically against her.

Eva, who had grown used to her mistress' morning nausea, was ready with a goblet of wine to clean Margerite's mouth out when she was done. Shuddering, Margerite rinsed her mouth, swallowed a few sips of wine, and washed and dressed quickly, throwing a heavy fur-lined cloak about her shoulders against the cold.

"No word yet?" she said to Bertram when she met him in the great hall, breaking his fast and giving last instructions to his senior guardsmen.

He shook his head. "We are not likely to know until the army rides up to our gates - whichever army it is."

The morning went by in hurried preparation: braziers had to be set about the battlements for lighting fire-arrows in case Heinrich had brought siege-weapons with him, pots of pitch and oil set to heating, empty wine-barrels filled with water and set by the wooden and thatch-roofed buildings against the danger of fire-arrows arching into the keep, and the able-bodied Tiefensee men equipped and given hurried instructions on their part in the defense.

Gerhild was in the kitchens, overseeing the preparation of herbal poultices to stanch the bleeding, keep fever off the wounded, and still their pain, while a couple of the scullery maids were set to cutting up cloth for bandages. Margerite walked about amid the chaos with Kobolt scampering beside her and Eva following at a more respectful distance, overseeing everything. For a midday meal she had to make do with a piece of day-old bread and a chunk of cheese, because she had ordered Berthe to assist Gerhild's work.

She stood in the courtyard as she ate; she had just washed the last dry bite down with a swallow of watered wine when she heard the horns blowing in the distance.

"To arms!" Bertram shouted, his deep voice cutting through the clamour in the yard. "Men, to your posts; women, get back inside."

Margerite drew her cloak about her and gestured grandly to Eva. She was terrified, but she dared not show it, lest those about her pick up on her fear and lose their nerve. "Come," she said. "We shall watch from my room."

Eva scuttled up the stairs behind her. When they were inside Margerite's chamber, Kobolt already sitting in the niche of an arrow-slot with his black tail dangling down the wall, Margerite turned her key in the lock and heaved the thick oaken bolt across the door. If Heinrich's men came up here, they would be delayed long enough - she hoped - for her to identify herself and be able to negotiate her safety and Eva's with the Graf.

"Frowe Gräfin?" Eva said timidly. "Is the castle going to be taken?"

"How should I know?" Margerite asked. "Do you think I can see into the mind of God?"

Eva cringed away. "O, Frowe Gräfin, please do not be angry with me. I meant no impudence, truly I did not."

Margerite's heart softened: she knew she was only snapping at the girl because she was powerless to do anything else. "I know. I am not angry. Eva, I do not know what will happen. But if the worst does come, so long as we do not unbar the door, we will be as safe in here as is possible. And you must not think about going out," she added, for she had begun to think that the child was somewhat simple-minded.

"Even though you are only a child, what men will do during a siege…" She paused, looking more closely at Eva. The girl was standing a little straighter than usual, and Margerite realized that she was wrong. As Eva had put on flesh in the last month, her breasts and hips had grown as well, pressing hard against the tight dress in decidedly womanly curves. How could I not have noticed? Margerite wondered. "You will need new clothes," she said decisively. "We shall see to that as soon as possible." And how can I be thinking of such a thing, with the battle outside and Burg Falkenstein perhaps on the brink of siege or capture?

Margerite turned to the arrow slits overlooking the outer bailey and the castle gates beyond. The army was just coming into view: her heart clenched within her, for they were running hard and she could not see Ruprecht anywhere, though the banner of the Bear's Paw was still uplifted. Then, at the rear of the fleeing host, a banner fluttered free in the rain: it was Ruprecht's white eagle-head on a red field, and behind it, she saw the bright flash of his red and white armour-coat above his dark steed.

But the pursuit was hard upon them, a spearhead of mounted men driving towards Ruprecht. He wheeled his horse, and the knights guarding the rear of the army wheeled with him, ready to meet Heinrich's charge again. Margerite chewed anxiously at her knuckles, her fists balled tight. The castle gates were open, ready to give refuge to Ruprecht and his men if they could make it in. If the mercenaries did not break…but they did not; the Bear's Paw banner began to move towards the fighting as Heinrich's infantry marched into view behind him.

Margerite had never seen battle before, and between the chaos on the field and the drifting sheets of rain misting her vision, she could not make out well what was happening. Once in a while, she was able to see someone she could recognise through the struggling mass of men and horses: Ruprecht thrusting with his sword so that another armoured man toppled from his horse before him; Paul hacking his way steadily through the press of foemen, Jochanan, shielded by several of his fellow mercenaries, jabbing gamely but clumsily with a short spear...but these were only fleeting glimpses.

Faintly, she heard the horns blowing again, and Kobolt miaowed as if to answer them. As well as Margerite could tell, the men at the rear were beginning to break off: the spearmen at the castle gate were marching out behind Bertram, their weapons bristling in a thicket to guard the retreat as Ruprecht's men struggled in across the narrow earthen bridge over Burg Falkenstein's ditch. Ruprecht himself was backing slowly, fighting all the way, but Margerite could tell that he would be the last in, if he made it that far.

"He is so brave," she whispered to herself. "Why..?"

"Why what, Frowe Gräfin?" Eva asked. Margerite shook her head, unable to look away from the fight. Most of the infantry were in now, but the mounted men were harder pressed, their horses' hooves slipping in the churned mud.

Men were running on the battlements: Margerite saw Jochanan's dark figure crouching behind a crenellation and waving his arms, and his handgunners coming up behind him, hastily loading their weapons and pointing them down between the great blocks of stone. An arrow took one of them in the throat; Jochanan dived to catch the weapon falling from his hands, taking his place.

Ruprecht's riders were coming over the bridge now, followed by the spearmen defending their way. Ruprecht was still battling hard, a mounted man fighting on either side of him - Wolfram and Ritter Wilfrid, Margerite thought. She gripped the stone windowsill, standing on her toes as if that would give her a better view.

The two big guns mounted on either side of the gate boomed and flashed, their stones arching far out to crash down among the rear men of Heinrich's army. Where they struck, men and steeds scattered to the ground like broken toys. Why can they not be tilted to shoot near the front, where they would do more good? Margerite wondered. For Ruprecht and his two fellows were at the edge of the bridge now, but they were hard pressed: if they fell and the gate did not close swiftly enough, Heinrich's men would stream over it.

The man on Ritter Wilfrid's left side swung his sword, a hard straight stroke that caved in the side of Wilfrid's helm; the Ritter toppled, his horse bolting from underneath him. Ruprecht was fighting two foes at once now, shielding against the blows coming in from his left and using his sword chiefly to parry the strokes of the man in front of him. Wolfram was faltering badly: it seemed that he hardly had the strength to lift his shield. Suddenly his sword-arm dropped; Ruprecht turned his head to the side as if shouting to his squire, and the Knappe turned his horse, crossing the bridge and in.

Ruprecht will die, Margerite thought: no man could fight three at once, and the rest of Heinrich's army was crowding in fast. But Ruprecht had backed onto the bridge, turning his steed to the side to block the way so that none of the other riders could pass him. The gray-black warhorse kicked out viciously with its rear hooves, forcing the rider pressing Ruprecht from that side to keep his distance. But he cannot hold long: he will die.

Suddenly the roar of guns rose again, seven smaller flashes leaping out from the battlement. The riders who had pressed in behind Ruprecht's immediate assailants scattered, three of them falling to the ground. Perhaps the knight fighting Ruprecht on the bridge faltered in startlement a moment; Margerite saw Ruprecht's sword go into him. Then, in the seconds before Heinrich's men could regroup and close once more, Ruprecht wheeled his steed, galloping the short way across the bridge.

The castle porticullis banged down the moment he had passed through the gate, nearly crushing his closest pursuer. More slowly, the castle gates swung shut behind the porticullis, the heavy oaken tree-trunks that bolted them slamming into place. The siege of Burg Falkenstein had begun.

Margerite hastily unbolted and unlocked her door, running down the stairs and pushing her way through the throng of men in the outer courtyard. Gerhild, Berthe, and the scullery maids followed her with their pots of wound-salve and bandages, for the wounded would need to be treated at once if they were to live.

When she neared the gates, Margerite saw why Wolfram had faltered and turned. The Knappe was already on the ground, Ruprecht crouching over him. A sword had gone between the iron plates of his corselet, cutting deep into his side. Margerite bent and sniffed at the wound, and smelt the unmistakable reek of fecal matter. His guts had been pierced: he might last through several days of agony, but there was no chance that he would survive.

"Gracious and beautiful frowe," Wolfram murmured, lifting a hand to Margerite. The day's worth of black stubble on the Knappe's square-jawed face stood out starkly against his white skin, like grains of earth on chalk. "To see your face before me…makes my wound as nothing." But, though he was trying to smile, Margerite knew that he must be in terrible pain.

She looked sideways at Gerhild. The midwife's glance went down to Wolfram' body. She nodded, a quick jerk of her head, and handed Margerite a phial of dark liquid, a wineflask, and a cup. Margerite sniffed at the phial, then poured half its contents into the cup. It was mandrake and hemlock: it would ease Wolfram' pain, ease him into sleep and, most likely, still his heart. She topped off the cup with wine, swirling it about to mix the draught together, and handed it to the dying squire. Though Margerite could see how it hurt him, Wolfram propped himself up on one elbow so that he could drink.

He raised the cup to his lips, smiling up at Margerite again as the scent reached his nostrils.

"I was not...so ill-advised after all," he murmured. "But it is worth it, to receive the parting cup from your fair hand." He drank.

Ruprecht rose from his side, lifting his bloody sword. "I wish there had been time to do this more fully for you, but the battlefield's honour must be enough. Knappe Wolfram, this day you have done the deeds of a knight. Before the castle's gate, beneath the gaze of the lady you serve, you fought bravely: you did battle beside your knight, you killed your foes, and you bore your wound without fear or flinching. Therefore, I, Ruprecht, Graf von Falkenstein, do dub you this day Ritter Wolfram von Obenheim, in recognition of your courage, without which we could not have held off our foes." He tapped Wolfram once on each shoulder with the blade of the sword, then closed his fist and brushed the knuckles lightly against Wolfram' chin. "Let that be the last blow you take for which you do not give answer. I shall not say arise to you, for the earth on which your blood has flowed is a seat of honour and pride enough."

"Thank you, Graf Ruprecht," Wolfram answered feebly. He raised his hand again to touch the blade of his sword. "I swear...to be a true and faithful knight to you, so long as...I shall live." He slumped back upon the ground. His pupils had already dilated, only a thin ring of blue left about their black depths. His pain was fading; it would not be too long before his heartbeat faded likewise.

"Get Father Hans," Margerite hissed to Eva. "He must have the Last Rites, quickly."

"No!" Wolfram protested, trying to raise himself again. "Noble and radiant frowe...I would not look upon the priest's ugly face as I die, but be blessed only by the sight of you before me, and Graf Ruprecht's words are good enough to guide me into the darkness."

Margerite was about to remonstrate with him, but then she saw what she had never noticed before: that the new Ritter's left forefinger bore a ring like to Ruprecht's, save that its stone was onyx instead of amethyst. He, too, must be a member of the Order - he would not take the Last Rites, because his soul was forfeit already!

But she could not turn away from the enthusiastic youth who had sat hours in the library reading poetry, who had helped her with harvesting and drying the herbs, and who, most of all, had taken his death-wound in her defense. She knelt beside him, praying in her heart that Mother Maria would not let such a good youth fall into the torments of Hell for his errors, and clasped his chilling hands in her own.

"'No, it was not wine,'" Wolfram whispered, so feebly that she could hardly hear him. "'Though like wine to the sight / it was passion without respite / the endless need of the heart.'" He was quoting from Tristan again, from the scene with the fatal drink. Margerite squeezed his cold fingers, though she knew he likely could not feel them by now. The young Ritter's bluish lips moved again, but no sound came from them, and his gaze was fixed glassily on Margerite's face.

Ruprecht, kneeling on the other side of Wolfram' body, reached over to take the youth's ringed hand. Margerite could hear the tears choking in his throat as he spoke. "Ritter Wolfram von Obenheim, go thou into the darkness like a star, burning with unquenchable fire, until thou art received at last by the fair Lord of Knowledge. Pass through ignorance to wisdom, through death to life, through Night to Morning: Ex Tenebrae, Lux."

Wolfram' eyes drooped closed. Margerite could barely see the breath moving his chest: soon enough the hemlock would reach his heart, and that, too, would stop.

"How long?" Ruprecht said quietly.

"Not very."

"Then go you on, for there are many other wounded to be seen to."

"Farewell, Wolfram," Margerite murmured to the unhearing youth, and rose, her gaze darting quickly about to see where the next most desperate case - pray Christ, not so desperate! - might be.

There were few men on the brink of death inside the castle, for the simple cause that the worst-hurt had not been able to get inside. Now and again a man's despairing scream could be heard from beyond the walls, as Heinrich's troops put paid to one who was not quite a corpse: Margerite tried to block her ears to the sound, but she could not. The battle had taken a heavy toll: from what Margerite could gather from the snatches of conversation she overheard, if not for Ruprecht's foresight, his army would have been destroyed utterly.

And what of evil means turned to good ends? Margerite wondered, taking another bandage from the basket Eva was carrying and wrapping it tight to stanch the bleeding from a castle guardman's leg. Have Ruprecht's demons saved us from plunder and rapine - and, if so, are our souls in worse peril? But there was more to think about than that: gaping, bloody rifts in flesh that had to be sewn shut, as the wounded soldiers gritted their teeth beneath the needle and thread drawing their skin together; broken arms and hands to be splinted; men who had taken hard blows to their helms to be marked and watched, lest what seemed to be a simple bruise suddenly lead to faintness and delirium, even death.

Kobolt followed her about, often rubbing against a wounded man or putting a paw gently upon his knee; and to Margerite's surprise, the men tolerated it, some of them even reaching out gingerly to pet the cat as she tended to them.

"There's luck in your beast, Frowe Gräfin," one grizzled old veteran said as she washed out the deep slice through the muscles of his shield-arm. "Ugh! Easy, now...Priest wouldn't like to hear me say it, if he could hear anything through the walls of his wineskin, but I'll say it again: that cat's lucky. I bet the lads he sees to heal faster than those he doesn't, just you watch it."

Margerite opened her mouth to berate the man for his superstitions, but closed it again. She knew full well that a wounded man's heart could make as much difference as any tending he got, and her father had told her at home that if one soldier carried a black stone for luck, or another knocked thrice on the castle door before marching off to battle, it was best to say nothing, for Christian or not, a man's trust in his luck could be the difference between his life and death in a fight.

So she answered only, "He seems to like you," and went on with her work.

With no warning, a black cloud dropped over her sight. Vaguely, Margerite felt herself falling, then nothing.

She awoke lying on her back, Gerhild's triangular face hovering closely above her, with Ruprecht's head a golden blur behind. Kobolt was sitting on her stomach, kneading her womb with his paws and purring so richly she thought his throat would split.

"Margerite?" Ruprecht was saying anxiously. "Margerite, speak to me. Woman, is she all right? What has happened?"

"Be easy, Herr Graf," Gerhild answered calmly. "I will need to examine the Gräfin more closely in private, but I can tell you that she has no fever. Perhaps she has simply swooned from exhaustion, and perhaps I will have better news for you in a little time." She lifted Kobolt from Margerite's stomach. The black cat hung limp and purring in her arms, drooping his head back to look lovingly into her eyes. "Eva, help your mistress to her bed. I shall come up anon, when I can leave these men."

"Go with her now," Ruprecht commanded. "The worst cases have been seen to...one way or another," he added painfully, "and, between myself and a few others, we have enough skill in treating the wounded to take care of the rest." He gestured towards Jochanan, pouring something dark over the wounds of a Bear's Paw man who jumped and swore beneath the medication; Paul, tying a splint onto a guardsman's broken arm, and Bertram, carefully stitching together the gash in another warrior's shoulder.

Now and again, as if against his will, his eyes flickered towards Margerite, but he did nothing more to show his concern. "I was glad enough to see Bertram's mercenaries, but I would never have guessed how useful they would be," Ruprecht added quietly, as if shaken enough to let his private thoughts come to his voice. "Can you stand, Margerite?" He reached to help her up. Margerite would not have let him, save that, not an hour ago, his hands, like hers, had been clasped about those of Wolfram: his kindness to his dying companion did not wipe out the horror of her memories, but neither could she pull away from him in terror.

Ruprecht lifted her easily to her feet, draping her arm about Eva's solid shoulders. "Go on, my beloved," he said to her. "You must rest: you have done more than your part."

The serving maid supported Margerite up the stairs with surprising strength, for which Margerite was glad: her legs were still weak beneath her, and it was a long way to the top of the castle. When she reached her chamber, she lay down willingly, and Gerhild set Kobolt down beside her.

"Frowe Gräfin, have you been puking in the morning?" the midwife asked her bluntly.

"Every morning, for a good month now," Margerite answered. Gerhild nodded, pushing back a few wisps of brownish-blond hair that had escaped from her braid. Her fingers left a smear of blood on her temple; she glanced down at her besmirched hands.

"Eva, bring me water for washing, and help your frowe to take her dress off."

When Margerite had undressed, Gerhild probed gently at her breasts. "Nipples a little swollen - have your breasts been tender?"

"Yes."

Gerhild felt Margerite's stomach gently, her lips curving into a small smile as she did. "There is little doubt of it, Frowe Gräfin. You are with child. You need not be worried about having fainted: that is not unusual in a woman who is bearing. Eat well, and be sure you get plenty of cheese and milk, so long as there is any to be had, for that will help keep you from losing your teeth, though they say that each child will cost one tooth, no matter what you do."Absently she stroked Kobolt. "If this gentleman keeps up his work, we shall have little trouble finding a bearing she-cat to put in the birthing chamber with you. My own red puss made six black tuft-eared kittens only two weeks ago, which look just like every cat born in Tiefensee since the middle of July; and I do not think there is another tomcat left within a day's ride of Burg Falkenstein, nor a queen who is not pregnant."

"Have you been doing that, sir?" Margerite asked Kobolt. He looked up at her smugly, purring as if he understood her words, then putting a soft paw upon her stomach.

"Aye, and no doubt he thinks he made the child inside you as well. You will have to be careful of him when it is born, to make sure he does not overlay it, since he is twice the size of a newborn babe and could easily do a child a mischief without knowing it. Well, Frowe Gräfin, there is nothing much I can do for you now, so long as all goes well. Rest and eat well, and do not feel guilty about feeding when we are under siege, for you have a second life within you, and the Graf's heir at that. A cup of weak peppermint tea when you wake in the morning should help to settle your stomach - Eva, can you make sure your frowe has that?"

"I can," the serving girl said.

"Stay here and rest a little longer. Eva, get the Gräfin some bread and meat, and a little ale to wash it down with. Ale is better than wine for a bearing woman. Now, I shall go back down to the wounded. Would you like me to bear the good news to the Graf, or would you prefer to tell him yourself?"

"You tell him," Margerite said weakly, sitting up and motioning to Eva to help her dress again. It still ached a little in her heart that Bertram had not come over to her when she fainted, though she knew full well that it would not only have looked strange, but been a betrayal of those men he should have been tending to. Yet she had to speak of him, if only to hear his name in her mouth, and so she said, "You were right about Bertram, you know. He is a far better man than I had thought him."

Gerhild stroked her hair lightly, as she would stroke the head of a child. "Yes, of course," she said soothingly. "Lie here and rest, for I think you are still faint, and it is not good for a pregnant woman to suffer such strains as you have just done."

It was not long after when she heard Ruprecht's light tread dashing along the corridor, and the door of her chamber flung open. Ruprecht's golden hair looked windblown and disheveled, his face flushed, as though he had run without stopping to the top of the tower. He held one hand behind his back.

"Margerite!" he cried. "Gerhild has just told me that you are certainly with child. This has turned a dark day into a bright one for us."

"It has," Margerite forced herself to say. If only she could have seen that look of joy on Ruprecht's handsome face before…if only she could be sure that the child, whether Ruprecht's or Bertram's, bore no taint of whatever had come to her that night!

Then Ruprecht sobered abruptly, looking down at her with a great tenderness in his blue eyes. "If our child is a son," he said, "we shall name him Wolfram, in honour of my brave Knappe, who died knowing that he was defending you. What do you say to that?"

"I had thought of Hubert, after the patron saint of hunting," Margerite answered. "But...yes. Wolfram would be a fitting name for our son." She had also thought that, if the child were a daughter, she would name her Herzeloyd, heart's suffering, after Parzival's mother; but she was sure, in a way that went deep beyond thought or understanding, that she bore a son in her womb.

Ruprecht brought his hand out from behind his back. In it sparkled a beautiful necklace: beads of ruby, amethyst, and crystal, from which hung a gold pendant in the shape of a falcon, a clear drop of adamant gripped in her claws and her eye set with a deep blue sapphire. "I have been waiting for this day to give this to you," he said. "Put it on, my beloved."

Margerite took the necklace from him. It tingled oddly in her hands, so that she found herself curiously reluctant to put it about her neck; but Kobolt purred and batted at it, then stood up with his paws on her shoulder, butting his head against her cheek as if to encourage her. Carefully she draped it over her head, then suffered Ruprecht to kiss her.

"A fair gem, on a fairer woman," he said. "I only wish that we could afford to hold a proper feast of celebration now."

"The celebration may wait until Wolfram is born," Margerite said. "I do not mean to dampen your joy, my husband, but you must know that a child's birth is not certain until it has drawn breath, and much may happen between now and then."

"Of course," Ruprecht answered. "Yet I feel that we have nothing to fear for little Wolfram."

He stayed there talking for a little while, then said, "Well, I must go down to see how things are getting on with our men. You stay here and rest."

"No, I am well enough now," Margerite answered, standing up. "I shall come with you."

Ruprecht frowned. "If you are certain. Eva, stay close to the Gräfin, lest she should faint again."

All the wounded had been sorted out by the time they reached the courtyard again, those who were grievously hurt put to bed in the soldiers' barracks or the peasants' shelters and the rest turning their hands to whatever they were able to help with.

"How badly did things go with your men, Paul?" Ruprecht asked the Bear.

Paul shook his head. "We lost a lot, Herr Graf. I do not think I have more than sixty left in fighting condition. Thirty-eight badly wounded, though the most of those should recover if they do not take fever, and Jochanan has some wonderful potions against those. He says he can make more, too, if you have the glassware for him to set up a still."

"He shall have that. You have done well, and I shall not forget it when the time comes to give you the last of your pay."

"Much appreciated, Herr Graf," Paul said, bowing clumsily.

"'Ware arrows!" someone shouted. Margerite glanced up; but the black dart was arching too high for it to have been shot with any hopes of finding a lucky target. As it began to drop downward, the courtyard cleared beneath it.

Ruprecht walked forward to pick the arrow up. A piece of parchment had been rolled tightly about the shaft and tied. "Now we shall see." He untied and unrolled the parchment, reading it quickly, then threw back his head and laughed, raising his voice so that all those around could hear him. "Heinrich offers us easy terms if we surrender now. He shall let Margerite and I go unharmed, and even leave us Burg Falkenstein, if only we will renounce claims to Burg Düsterstein, give him Burg Eichenwald and all the land on our side of the border for a half-day's ride around, and repay him for all the damages he has suffered in the war, which he has calculated most precisely. Well, let him break his teeth on Falkenstein: we can hold out within longer than he can without. Winter is coming on, and we shall eat good meat by warm fires while Heinrich and his men are freezing their... fingers off and chewing on dead grape leaves outside."

A few men cheered raggedly. Ruprecht looked around, smiling at them, and snapped his fingers. "Wolfram!" he shouted, then closed his mouth, his face twisting in a smile of pain. "I was too used to him," he murmured, so softly that only Margerite could hear. Louder, he said, "Someone bring me quill and ink, so that I may give Heinrich the reply he deserves. Burg Falkenstein shall never surrender!"

Chapter Seven

Busy as the days before had been, the first days within the walls of the besieged castle were even more frantic. Margerite ordered guards put on the food stores at once, lest any of the more forward-thinking villagers should try to start hoarding food early. There was no way to feed most of the beasts the Tiefensee folk had brought with them, for little grass grew within the castle walls, and the villagers were hard enough put to it to keep the cows and sheep out of the vegetable garden - most of the crops were harvested, but there were still some leeks, onions, and garlic in the ground, as well as turnips, mangolds, and carrots. Burg Falkenstein had a good store of hay, but that would have to be saved for the horses.

Thus the animals had to be slaughtered, with only a few ewes and cows left for milk to be carefully rationed out to those women who were with child. The first morning frosts were already leaving their white traces upon the courtyard's hard-packed earth, which was well enough for the slaughtering, but reminded Margerite uncomfortably that there was no way for Burg Falkenstein to renew its fuel supplies while the siege lasted, and she directed that there should be no fires save those needed for cooking and those in the rooms where the most grievously wounded lay. The constant strain of keeping track of each day's supplies and allotments was already telling on Kai's nerves: the seneschal grumbled and muttered to himself, his normal morose demeanour sinking into a deep depression.

"At least," he said to Margerite as the two of them stood tallying bales of flour in one of the castle's storage rooms, "there has been little loss from rats and mice since you brought that creature of yours here, whereas it was always grievous in earlier years. I wish we had ten more like him, and I never thought I would say that."

"From what I hear," said Margerite, bending down to stroke Kobolt, who arched his back and purred beneath her caress, "you should have no trouble in finding plenty of his sons and daughters."

Kai raised an eyebrow. "Perhaps so. I shall tell Berthe not to drown her kitchen cat's latest litter when she finds it. Frowe Gräfin, I wish you had brought more salt from Freiburg. I thought it too much, but with all the meat we have had to salt down and pickle, I do not think it will be enough for our needs. And we have lost this year's harvest of grapes as well, and our good apples are still hanging on the trees for Heinrich's men. Thanks be to Christ, at least the siege did not begin until all the grain was in, although only He knows how we are going to grind it into flour for baking. I suppose much of it can be malted for ale, much as I hate to think of the fuel that will take."

"Paul the Bear and his Company will not complain if they find themselves living on ale before this is over," Margerite said, hoping to cheer him. Kai rewarded her jest with a sour smile.

"I am sure. I do not know whether to pray for an early snow, to preserve our meat, or for the weather to warm again, to preserve our coal and wood."

"Pray that Heinrich finds himself forced to give up and go away soon enough," Margerite advised. "I know that I shall."

"Aye, and hope that God's ears are not deafened by the voice of Father Hans whining that I have cut his daily allowance of wine to no more than the three cups everyone else is getting," Kai said in disgust. "He came to me yesterday, saying that the cold had settled deep in his chest and that he had to have more wine to warm him so that he could speak the words of Mass. If he is sick with anything, it is no worse than a hangover. And I am sure that he has a private stock of wine that he will not report to me."

"He did not seem well when he was holding the funeral Mass in the courtyard," Margerite mused.

The priest had found himself forced to consecrate the southwest corner of the outer bailey for the bodies of Wolfram and the three others who had died shortly after the battle, and he had been coughing and sneezing as he hoarsely spoke the words over the hastily-dug graves.

But Margerite had much more to worry about than the state of Father Hans' health. From her window, she could see Graf Heinrich's pavilion, pitched at the edge of the woods just beyond bowshot: though the Graf and his sons were sleeping warm in the houses the Tiefensee villagers had abandoned, they marched out early every morning to direct their men.

The Graf was easy to recognise by his rich clothes and gilded armour, yet - as well as she could tell over the distance - there seemed something else familiar about his blocky build, his grizzled hair and beard, as though she had seen him before, though she could not guess where. With him were two young men who had to be his sons: Nikolaus she recognised at once, from the dinner in Freiburg, yet the other, a little taller and with less belly hanging over his gilded belt - Christoph, that was his name - seemed familiar as well.

Although they were too far away for Margerite to see their faces, it seemed to her that she knew Christoph's look, with uptilted nose and pale gray-green eyes, as well as she remembered Nikolaus' sullen expression. Christoph had his left arm in a sling: he must have been wounded in the fighting, but it did not seem to be bothering him at all. Often he gesticulated violently towards Burg Falkenstein, and Margerite guessed that he was arguing in favour of assaults on the walls.

She almost hoped that his father would listen to him: the ground was clear around the castle, so that anyone coming near would be a good target for the archers on the battlements, and the combination of the land's sharp upward slope with the deep ditch about the walls would make it very difficult to bring up siege weaponry.

Michelmas came almost without notice in the besieged castle. Father Hans managed to rouse himself from his sickbed to choke out the words of the Mass for Margerite and the few Tiefensee villagers who came to the little chapel in the guard tower, but there was no breaking the stern rules about food distribution to have a feast. Even for Margerite and Ruprecht, the midday meal was no better than cold pickled venison and bread made with soaked peas mixed in to stretch the flour, and afterwards Margerite felt heavy in the stomach and went up to lie down in her chamber for a little while.

It was as chilly there as everywhere else: though the sun was shining brightly, it shone down upon the last white traces of a hard frost, and though Gerhild had ordered a fire in Margerite's stove at night, seeing how everyone else shivered made her feel too guilty about using extra fuel for her to allow herself any heating by day. Shivering, she crept beneath the blankets, letting Kobolt snuggle close to her.

"Frowe Gräfin?" Eva asked tentatively. Margerite turned over, blinking at the girl, who had unshuttered one of the arrow slits and was looking out, squinting against the cold draft. We must make new clothes for her, she thought again, for a good inch of Eva's thick wrists showed beneath the gray hems of her sleeves.

"What is it?"

"There is a man riding up to the castle gates. I think he is a priest of some rank, for he is wearing a black robe over his clothes and has a large gold cross about his neck, and there is an amice upon his head. Do you know who he is?"

Margerite sprang out of bed, peering out the narrow window. Alarm shocked through her body as she saw that the gates below were swinging open, the porticullis lifting. But Heinrich's men were staying well back, leaving the ground clear: whoever the rider was, he was coming alone. "He must be important," she thought aloud. "Else Heinrich would not let him pass, nor would we open our gates to him. I do not know any such priests, but I am going downstairs to see who he is."

Ruprecht was sitting at ease in the great hall, a goblet in his hand and his two mastiffs thumping their tails beside him; Bertram was there as well, and the castle minstrels were playing quietly in the gallery overhead.. The Graf waved Margerite to join them.

"We shall be receiving a visitor in a few moments," Ruprecht said. "Seat yourself and be ready to look your best for him, my wife. We do not wish him to think that we are suffering from this siege."

Margerite sat down, accepting the goblet of wine one of the servitors handed her. She did not start when she heard the footsteps on the stairs leading up from the main door, only turned her head, smiling slightly. Ruprecht gestured the minstrels to silence.

The man who entered wore, as Eva had said, a black cassock, a large gold crucifix around his neck, and a canon's flat black headdress with its rolled corners. He was quite tall, a little taller than Ruprecht, but very slender beneath his thick robes. His thick wavy hair was deep brown, with gray wings at the temples, and his close-cropped brown beard had a tuft of white beneath the lower lip.

He was handsome in an ascetic manner, the bones of his face standing out over slightly hollowed cheeks and deep-set blue eyes, and he moved gracefully, but with great dignity: Margerite guessed his age at about forty, or perhaps a little less. At his side hung a sword, not the heavy weapon of a knight used to fighting foes in armour, but a long slender blade, such as a man of his light build could easily wield if set upon unexpectedly.

"Greetings, Graf Ruprecht and Gräfin Margerite von Falkenstein," the priest said. His voice was a hollow baritone, a little monotonous, but not unpleasing to Margerite's ears, its tones smoothed by a slight French accent. "I am Canon Etienne de Dion." He bowed.

Margerite sensed, more than saw, Ruprecht's muscles tightening beside her, as if he recognised the name. If he did, though, he gave no sign of it, only nodding his head in reply to the priest.

"Greetings, Father Etienne. I understand that you have been sent to speak with Graf Heinrich von Fürstensee and myself, in hopes of finding a resolution to our war?"

"As you say," the priest replied. "You must know that the Kaiser is very much against such private feuds between his lords, and the Bishop of Augsburg, who sent me here, is of the same mind. A resolution, and peace henceforth, will be the best for all concerned."

"And what terms do you bear from Graf Heinrich?"

"The same that he offered you before: for surrender and repayment of damages, he will leave you be. He adds, however, that he will not hold this offer open to you past the first day of October. Thereafter, though you may surrender and keep your lives, he will take possession of Burg Falkenstein; and if - his words, not mine - you are foolish enough to hold until after the first day of November, he will allow your women and children to leave, but your life and those of all your men will be forfeit."

"My reply is the same as it was," Ruprecht answered. "You may stay with us as long as you please: Burg Falkenstein will not surrender."

"Graf Ruprecht, I would advise you to send Graf Heinrich a counteroffer regarding what you are willing to repay him in damages. I believe that he is willing to treat with you, and to accept a reasonable offer which will salve his pride and assure him of quiet on his western border hereafter. But you must know that his army is well-stocked, and can easily reprovision itself from the villages of your land without sending too great a part of his force away from the siege here. I do not think that you can hold out against him forever, and the longer he waits, the more brutal his revenge on you will be."

Bertram's lips were pressed hard together, and the green streaks in his brown eyes glinted, as though he were forcing himself not to speak. Margerite guessed that Ruprecht had already told his mind to his Hauptmann, and ordered Bertram not to argue with him. Her eyes met Bertram's for a moment before he looked away, and it seemed to her that she could read the concern and doubt in his thoughts: if he were ruler in Burg Falkenstein, he would surely be preparing to come to terms with Heinrich, for her sake if not for his own. Suddenly she longed to touch him, at least to lay her hand upon his; but he was too far away for her to reach him, even if Ruprecht and the priest had not been watching.

"Heinrich will have to reach us before he can carry out any revenge, brutal or otherwise, and that he shall not do. But I am remiss in my hospitality. Wine for our guest!" Ruprecht said to the servitor by his shoulder. "Have you eaten your midday meal, Father Etienne? We have finished ours, but I believe that we can find something fit to offer such a distinguished guest."

"I have eaten today, though I thank you for the offer," Etienne replied. "By your leave, though, I shall guest within this castle for a little time, and hope that you will come to more sensible thoughts."

Ruprecht glanced upward, making a small motion with his hand, and the minstrels began to play quietly, the lead singer's tenor voice wafting out across the hall, as the priest was given his wine.

Etienne sipped slowly. "Is this wine from your own vineyards? It is very fine for a German vintage, though I am more used to the wines of France."

"The grapes grow well here," Ruprecht told him.

"Indeed."

"But if French wine is more to your taste, we have a certain stock of it here, both the red and the white."

The canon waved his hand in negation. His pale fingers were very long and slim, the index pad stained with a shadow of ink. Margerite found that she was looking at his hand for an Order ring, but, to her great relief, saw none. The sole ring he wore was a massive gold family signet, graven with arms of a winged hammer above a rising sun. "This suits me well, Graf."

Etienne stayed talking with the Graf and Gräfin for some little while more, but at last pleaded tiredness from his ride. One of the servants showed him up to a guest-chamber at the western end of the castle's top floor. The chamber had already been prepared for him, fresh linen on the bed, strewing-herbs scattered across the floor, and his chest carried up and set beside the table under a wide window overlooking the courtyard.

After his long ride in the cold, Etienne had hoped for a tub of hot water, but, despite Graf Ruprecht's bold words, that was evidently too much luxury for a besieged castle with limited stocks of fuel: Etienne had also noticed that the fires of the great hall were not burning. At least the stove was heating the room, and there was a pot of water for washing upon it. Carefully he sniffed at the steam, to be sure that no herbs beyond the ordinary run had been steeped in it, then closed his eyes for a moment, breathing deeply and letting his spirit calm to the depths of an untroubled pool - waiting to see what disturbances might ripple across it.

His chamber was clean: Ruprecht had gotten little warning of his arrival, either by earthly means or - because Etienne had been very careful to hide his path from the eyes of such messengers and spies as the Order of Light-Bearers used - unearthly. When Etienne tentatively felt farther, though, he could sense the taint of Order magic. He could almost see it, the starlike glow in the darkness at the eastern end of the corridor, fading and brightening again towards the northern wing...and then the shimmering light of the shields beyond, shields that he dared not try to breach, any more than a knight given guest-right in the castle of a foe dared draw his sword to pierce another's armour without direct provocation.

For a moment he wondered if it would be wiser not to set such shields of his own, which would confirm to Ruprecht that his guest was as accomplished in the subtle arts as he himself, if not more so. But the chances were good that the Graf had already recognised the name of Canon Etienne - Etienne the Exorcist - for even as the canon knew the Order, so was he known to them. And the analogy of a knight guesting among his foemen only held good for a little way, for unlike that hypothetical knight and his host, any harm that either he or Ruprecht did to the other would not be seen by other human eyes, save perhaps those of the Gräfin, if...

Etienne put the thought from his mind, stilling his spirit again. From his chest, he drew a gilded censer, a bag of incense, a yellow candle inscribed with a cross, a battered leaden pilgrim-phial of holy water, a small box of salt, and a tinderbox. On the top of the stove he kindled a tiny fire and lit the candle from it, murmuring, "I exorcise thee, O Creature of Fire, by Him through Whom all things have been made, so that every kind of Phantasm may retire from thee and be unable to harm or deceive in any way, through the Invocation of the Most High Creator of all. Amen."

With the consecrated candle, he lit the censer's charcoal, saying "Bless, O Lord All Powerful, and All Merciful, this Creature of Fire, so that being blessed by Thee, it may be for the honour and glory of Thy Most Holy Name, so that it may work no hindrance or evil unto those who use it. Through Thee, O Eternal and Almighty Lord, and through Thy Most Holy Name. Amen."

Etienne sprinkled the incense upon the charcoal, a fragrant cloud of smoke streaming out of the holes in the censer's top and sides as he walked about the room, swinging it in slow circles about himself and saying, "I exorcise thee, O Creature of Air, by Him Who hath created thee, Who moved upon the waters before the beginning of time. Let all malignity and hindrance be cast forth from thee, and drive forth all the deceits of the Enemy, all the impurities and uncleanness of the Spirits of the World of Phantasm, so they may harm me not, through the virtue of God Almighty Who liveth and reigneth unto the Ages of Ages. Cleanse this room, that no creatures of ill may stay here or come within, nor the wiles of the Enemy assail it. In the Names of Father and Son and Holy Ghost, Amen."

He repeated the prayer for water, sprinkling the chamber all about with the holy water, and likewise for earth with the salt. Lastly, Etienne faced east, clasping his hands over the gold crucifix on his bosom. "ATOH MALKUTH, VE-GEBURAH, VE-GEDULAH, LE-OLAHM, AMEN. Before me Raphael, behind me Gabriel, on my right hand Michael, on my left hand Uriel, in the holy Names of God YOD HE VAU HE, ADONAI, EHIEH, AGLA. Be this chamber warded against all ill, shielded from the eyes of mine enemies and from all foes of the Kingdom of Heaven, a fortress unassailable and impervious, defended by the powers of the angelic hosts and the strength of the Lord God ADONAI. Amen."

Etienne quenched his candle with the prescribed blessing, leaving the incense to burn itself out on top of the stove, and sat down, looking out thoughtfully over the thronged inner courtyard. Burg Falkenstein was surprisingly well-prepared for siege, given what the Bishop of Augsburg had heard about the course of the war previously.

A reconciliation was hardly to be looked for - but then, despite what he had told Ruprecht, negotiation between the two quarreling Grafs was not his chief reason for coming to Burg Falkenstein. He was looking for a young orphaned noblewoman who, put into a convent, had disappeared before taking her final vows: until she had made those vows, her cousin could not claim her lands with full right.

When the Abbess in whose charge she had been put proved unwilling to answer questions about her whereabouts, the cousin had appealed to the Church - and Etienne, who knew the allegiances of the Abbess of the Holy Cross, and was sure the child had been sent away for Order purposes, had taken the opportunity to offer his services.

Two fortunate meetings had led him to Burg Falkenstein. On the road, Etienne had met his old acquaintance Damiano, who had casually mentioned what a dreary journey he had just endured as nursemaid to a child being sent from a Passau convent to supply an Order member with a maidservant, complaining that the Order should send women to do women's work: that chance had directed Etienne to Burg Falkenstein.

Then, while guesting with the Bishop of Augsburg on his way, Etienne had mentioned his destination, and the Bishop had seized upon the chance to gain credit for the reconciliation of the two feuding Grafs at no cost to himself. And thus he was here: but now he would have to tread carefully. He already believed that the little maid who stood cringing behind the Gräfin's shoulder was the girl he sought, Eva von Bärenberg, but he was also sure that there was more going on in Burg Falkenstein than a simple siege, so that he was loath to let any hint of his true purpose slip before he was ready.

The canon sighed, taking a bottle and a tiny silver cup from his chest. He poured a small measure of aqua vitae into the cup, swirling the dark amber liquid about and sniffing pleasurably at the rich fruity scent that rose from it. It was his habit to drink lightly, but regularly, of the medicinal cordial, for its hot and dry nature was proof against all the diseases and corruptions that arose when a body's balance of humours was allowed to swing too far towards cold and moistness. Letting a few drops run over his tongue, Etienne settled himself to reviewing the situation.

The previous night, Graf Heinrich's younger son Nikolaus, whose ring showed him to be among the Light-Bearers' lowest-ranking members, had been persuaded by a good dose of aqua vitae and the mention of certain things implying Order connections to tell Etienne all that he knew about Graf Ruprecht and his young wife.

Nikolaus was convinced that the Gräfin Margerite was an initiate, for she had been sent to Freiburg to oversee Ruprecht's Hauptmann on Order business; Damiano, though more close-mouthed, had implied something similar in the middle of his grousing. It was plausible enough: from all Etienne knew, Bertram had worked for the Order as mercenary leader and then castle guardsman for several years, but his name had never come up in connection with their more secret affairs.

Until proved otherwise, then, Gräfin Margerite was to be regarded as an enemy and a danger, which would not help Etienne in confirming the identity of her serving girl, nor in watching and protecting the maiden until he was ready to take her away. In fact - Etienne frowned at the thought - there would be very little he could do directly if the Gräfin decided to sacrifice her maidservant in the near future, save watch and pray that he would manage to be alerted in time.

Etienne sipped again at his aqua vitae, considering. At first he did not notice the scratching at his door; his mind passed it off as the scuffling of a rat. But it was too loud for a rat, and - he sniffed - there was no smell of rat or mouse in the room, though he would have expected it if the creatures were bold enough to run about in full daylight. Cautiously, hand on the hilt of his sword and the first words of a prayer of banishment ready in his mouth, he went to the door and opened it.

A huge black cat leapt straight into the air, then bounded away down the corridor. Etienne wrinkled his nose as the stink hit him, looking down at the dark stain on the stone door-jamb and the puddle spreading below it. He closed the door again, glad that he had been so quick to ward his chamber.

"I would have thought," he murmured to himself, "that an Archbishop in the Order would be more subtle."

When the priest had gone at last, Ruprecht retired to his own chamber, sitting on his bed and stroking the rough heads of Mark andBrangæne until the beating of his heart had calmed. The arrival of Father Etienne was a blow to the Order's plans: the Bishop of Augsburg would undoubtedly report to all concerned that he was directly intervening to bring the matter to a peaceful end, and, with Ruprecht mewed up in his castle, there was no chance of spreading the war's effects further.

And a real priest might notice many things that Father Hans had missed in his drunkenness: Ruprecht would have to be very careful, lest he give something away that he ought not. Resignedly, Ruprecht stood. Whether he reported failure or success, Günther would still need to know what was taking place, that the Order might change its plans accordingly. He pulled aside the heavy hunt-tapestry on his northern wall, unlocking the door behind it. Beyond the door, the narrow spiral of dark stairs reached down into blackness: he trod the spiraling path, down and down and down to its end.

The corridor at the foot of the staircase was very warm, for it lay concealed in the back of the castle's smithy, and the glowing fires of the forge kept heat in the walls. Beyond that corridor was Ruprecht's sanctum; again his keys clicked quietly in the lock, and the door swung open. The candles were lit inside, casting a pale light over the small antechamber. Two shadows detatched from the walls, one holding a robe, the other a basin of hyssop-scented water. Ruprecht glanced between them, quelling the tiny shudder that the sight of their faces always brought him.

Ruprecht stripped his robe off again, handing it to Clingschor. Dipping his hands into the basin Cundrîê held, he poured great double-handfuls of water over his head, murmuring as it dripped down, "Asperges me, Domine, hyssopo, et mundabor;Lavabis me, et super nivem dealbabor." He took the garment Clingschor held - another robe of pure silk, but of deep ebony-purple, like a bishop's robe washed in black, and slowly lowered it over his head, fastening it at his waist with the lionskin girdle, whose clasp was a gold lion-head.

Cundrîê set down the basin, offering him in its place a pot of sweet anointing oil, and he dipped his fingers into it, touching his temples and eyelids. From Clingschor he took the gold Pentagram of Solomon, settling it around his neck; he reached down to be sure that the cord that held the cover of the Hexagram of Solomon at his vestment's hem would fall away properly, so that, if he needed to, he could force the thing he summoned to take human form. Lastly, he accepted the Ring upon his finger: its emblem would shield him from the flaming breath of the spirit he called, if it chose to struggle against him.

"In the mystery of these vestures of the Holy Ones," Ruprecht said, "I gird up my power in the girdles of righteousness and truth in the power of the Most High. Ancor: Amador: Amides: Theodonias: Anitor: let be mighty my power, let it endure forever, in the power of Lucifer, to whom the praise and the glory shall be, whose end cannot be."

Ruprecht opened the second door, striding forth into his sanctum. The candles were already lit, burning in the hearts of the four pentagrams traced around the great circle in the centre of the floor. He had painted the pentagrams, the circle of protection, and the invoking triangle himself, going over the paint layer by layer until it lay thickly enameled on the stone paving to make sure that no weakness in the mortar would crack it and allow one of the things he summoned the freedom of the outside world - or let it in to get at him.

The great snake coiled thrice within the rim of the circle, the Hebrew letters written along its body shining deep black like twisted scale-marks against its yellow brightness; inside its coils were the four hexagrams, golden-pointed and green-centred flowers with the names of power written within them, and in the heart of the circle was the single red square embossed with the simple word "Master".

Opening the chest that stood in the far corner of the room, Ruprecht took out his sword and wand, girding the sword about his waist and lifting the stave in his hand. Carefully he rounded the circle, stopping in the East before the head of the serpent and knocking thrice against the air before he stepped in, closing the ring again with three strokes of the wand behind him. Taking his place in the centre of the red square, Ruprecht stopped, breathing deeply to make sure that his heart was clear, that no weaknesses or worries dogged his mind.

This summoning of demons was like battle against a slightly better opponent: the endless worrying, watching for subtle tricks, or the turns that might hide behind them; the nerve-grinding alertness, the wearing need to do the foe's work for him, watching for weaknesses until one became weak from watching...Ruprecht struck himself on the side of the head with his wand, the sharp pain catching him away from his dark thoughts. Here in the circle, the gates between Heaven and Earth and Hell gaped wide; standing here, he might as well have wandered into a wood where an old boar lay in wait in a thicket, ready to open his body from thigh to navel...

He struck himself again. The boar might lie in wait, he thought in the sharp lightning of clear pain, but he was the hunter; the demon who was close was all the more easily caught.

"I invoke and move thee," Ruprecht cried, lifting his wand. "O spirit Malphas, I conjure thee by all the most glorious names of Our Master Lucifer, to come quickly and without delay from all parts and places of the world where-ever thou may be, to make rational answers unto my demands, and that visibly, and affably, speaking with a voice intelligible to my understanding. I conjure and constrain thee, O spirit Malphas, by all the mighty names of the Light-Bearer, and likewise by those seven great names with which Solomon the Wise bound thee and thy companions in his vessel of brass. ADONAI, PRERAI, TETRAGRAMMATON, ANAPHAXETON, INESSENFATOAL, PATHTUMON, ITEMON! Appear here, before this circle, to fulfill my will in all things that seem good unto me. And if thou be still so disobedient, and refuse still to come, I shall in the power and by the power of the name of LUCIFER, SATHANAS, STAR OF THE MORNING, created brightest of angels, ruler of Hell, curse thee and strip away thy office, joy, and place, and bind thee in the depths of the Bottomless Pit, there to remain until the Day of Judgement. And I shall bind thee in the Eternal Fire, and into the lake of Flame and of Brimstone, unless thou come quickly and appear here before this Circle, in the Triangle prepared for thee, to do my will. Therefore, come thou! in and by the holy names ADONAI, TZABAOTH, ADONAI, AMIORAN. Come thou! for it is LUCIFER who commands thee!"

Ruprecht waited, watching the triangle. In the corners of his eyes, the candle-flames flared into haloes of coloured sparks against the darkness; it seemed to him that he felt the air thickening, thunder-charged against his skin so that his silken robe sparked against every hair with each slight shift of his body. Already the darkness was clotting into the centre of the triangle, a faintly glowing fog like a patch of mountain mist, shaping slowly into the form of a great black bird.

Ruprecht reached down, dropping the cloth that revealed the Hexagram of Solomon. The crow opened its beak, hissing in a disappointed way. Slowly its form melted, rising up like a curl of heavy smoke from green wood, and shifted into the shape of a black-haired man.

"Welcome, spirit Malphas, O most noble president!" Ruprecht said quickly, before the demon could address him. "I say thou art welcome to me, because I have called thee through Him, who knows Heaven, and Earth, and Hell, and all that is in them contained, and because also thou hast obeyed. By that same power which has called thee forth, I bind thee, that thou remain affably and visibly before this Circle and in this Triangle, so constant and so long as I shall have occasion for thy presence, and not to depart without my license until thou hast duly and faithfully performed my will without any falsity."

Ruprecht stretched out his wand in a gesture of command, breathing deeply, and thundered, "By the Pentacle of Solomon I have called thee!" He paused to order his thoughts: it was never safe to speak to a demon at once, lest a hasty tongue betray the magician to his own undoing. "As I command you, doing no more and no less than I order," Ruprecht said slowly, "You shall appear to Günther von Hohenfels, Princeps of the Order of Light-Bearers, in an affable and benevolent form, invisible and inaudible to all others, speaking in a voice and language intelligible to his ears, without doing harm to any being or thing, and you shall tell him this, without changing or altering anything that I say. The siege of Burg Falkenstein continues: with care, we may still have enough food for three or four months, but our stocks are lessening daily. The Bishop of Augsburg has sent an emissary, one Father Etienne, to speak to us of truce. I have refused that, but Father Etienne will not leave. Margerite is well in her pregnancy, carrying the child whose conception I told you of. Though her inborn power has grown greatly since she came here, and promises so well, while she is with child - most particularly, this child of Power on whom so many hopes of the Order rest - I dare not send her soul out, as I have before, to spy out Heinrich's forces or listen to his plans, for all her strength must go to nurturing the babe in her womb. Nor has Heinrich's son Nikolaus achieved the rank and skill whereby I can safely communicate with him as I do with you. I ask your advice and aid. Malphas, go to Prince Günther with those words, and return to me without delay when you have delivered them, remaining in this form to which I have summoned you, affable and benevolent, without alarming or endangering me or those about me in any way."

The spirit vanished; Ruprecht waited within his circle, the sweat slowly cooling to clamminess within his silken robe. The sudden weird shimmering within the triangle forced him to blink; and then the figure of Malphas was suddenly there before him, the black eyes peering from beneath the thick brows in weird amusement.

"Prince Günther bids me tell you that you are doing well with Margerite. Teach her what lore she can learn, but do not let her turn her hand to magic before the child is born. Both she, and it, are too great in potential power and usefulness to risk damaging either for a moment's advantage. He bids me tell you that he is disappointed in your other news, but the Order's purposes will have been served well enough here when he and you together have removed Heinrich and his eldest son Christoph, who is of his father's mind in all that matters to us. And that must be done in battle, if you can, rather than leaving it to Nikolaus, who cannot safely dispose of his kin without facing investigations afterwards, though whether it is Nikolaus or you who holds Burg Fürstensee is of little concern to the Order. What matters now is that the Order gains the Fürstensee lands, to strengthen its stronghold in the Schwarzwald without threat or hindrance and to clear the path for its business associates in the Free Companies. He bids me tell you to beware of Father Etienne, elsewise called Etienne the Exorcist. Etienne is a foe of the Order, but one of great power, both spiritual and secular. If you could make him disappear without drawing attention, it would be well, but Prince Günther cautions you that this cannot be done easily, for Etienne the Exorcist has many friends of high influence. Prince Günther says that he will come to your aid when it is time."

"Did he say any more? I bid you tell me truthfully."

One corner of Malphas' mouth curled up in amusement. "He said, 'O thou most wicked and disobedient spirit Malphas, because thou hast rebelled, and hast not obeyed nor regarded those words which I have rehearsed...'"

"I know the conjuration," Ruprecht broke in. He gripped his wand more tightly to keep his hand from shaking - because he had not thought to tell Malphas to inform Günther upon appearance that Ruprecht had sent him and held him in thrall, his demon might have been locked away before the message was ever delivered. A slight error, one that endangered Ruprecht little...but a chance little worse might have had his bowels twisted from his body around a white-hot poker. "Had he any other words for me?"

"No."

Although Ruprecht wished to send the demon away as soon as possible, he knew that he must not miss any detail, lest it be the one that trip him up. "Tell me the whole of your conversation with Prince Günther von Hohenfels."

Malphas grinned, and spoke in Günther's voice. "O thou most wicked and disobedient spirit..."

Ruprecht listened silently. Malphas had delivered his words as ordered; Günther's reply was as the spirit had said.

"Now," Malphas added, "you commanded me to fetch for your wife Margerite von Hirschenberg a fitting familiar, to be her helper in all things, and serve her faithfully in all her magical works and powers, one that must appear to her in a manner pleasing to her, that she never be alarmed or distressed by it, in the shape of an animal natural to man's earth and not unusual within your castle's walls, and not unfitting or unpleasant for the Gräfin to have with her wherever she goes. Behold, I fetched unto her a familiar in the form of a cat, and she has taken it to her, and given it a fitting name. Are you satisfied with the work that I have done and the spirit that I have found?"

Ruprecht lifted his wand again, his thoughts flickering through his brain. The cat seemed to be serving as he had meant it to, but to admit full satisfaction would be to lay himself open to the demon's power, if there were some fault which might yet harm either of them concealed beneath Kobolt's black furry hide. Yet if he voiced dissatisfaction, Malphas would use the opportunity to whisk the cat away and subsitute some other creature, and he had phrased his order as carefully and perfectly as he could - and Margerite would be heartbroken if she lost her beloved tom.

"I have not yet found fault with it," he said slowly. His nerves tingled as though a host of flies were crawling over his body, as they had every time he summoned a demon to do some work in the world of men, but he held tight to his wand, and its sure solidness seemed to draw his thoughts in to a single core of strength. Now, his work was done, and the best demon was one that had been dismissed.

"O thou spirit Malphas, because thou hast diligently answered my demands, and been ready and willing to come at my call, I do here license thee to depart unto thy proper place, without causing harm or danger unto man or beast or thing. Depart, I say, and be thou ready to come at my call, being duly exorcised and conjured by the sacred rites of magic. I charge thee to withdraw peaceably and quietly, and the peace of LUCIFER and the Abyss be ever continued between thee and me. Amen."

The shape of Malphas thinned as Ruprecht spoke, and by the time he had voiced "Amen", not even the faintest haze of whirling sparks was left within the triangle. Yet Ruprecht waited a few moments before he began the final words of exorcism that would make sure of his safety when he stepped outside the circle again. Now the stakes were higher than ever, for now the Order's plans were drawn up for the child his wife bore - the child that would be his to raise and teach and initiate, born of Margerite's incomparable, if yet untrained, magical strength and his own body as the vessel of Infernal power.

O, Margerite, Ruprecht thought. Once the war is over, then there will be time for you to learn of the deeper delights our marriage has to offer you It will be more than worthwhile in the end, once you know all that has come to pass, and find your true worth known and hailed by the highest and greatest of men...Once the child was born Ruprecht could share the hidden worlds beyond man's sight with Margerite, and at last make her his partner and helpmeet in all his magics, as he had longed to do since shortly after he wedded her.

If all went well, it would not be long after the birth that he would be elevated to the rank of Princeps in the Order. Then there would be but one who could command him - Satan's Viceroy on Earth, who wore the adamant ring of the Order's head - and with Margerite and their child by his side, even that one would find it difficult to confront the three of them. But first, he would have to win his war, or at least hold out until Günther's aid came.

Ruprecht knew that it was probably wise of Günther to leave cold and the rigors of besieging a castle to gnaw on Heinrich's forces as long as he could; but that would do little to ease those inside while they waited, and in the meantime, he still had Etienne to contend with. As the days under siege wore slowly on, Margerite marked that everyone's temper was growing less even. Often she found herself on the verge of slapping Eva, her hand stayed only by the memory of the unlovely sight of the maidservant's cringing and whimpering.

The confinement was wearing harder on Ruprecht: though he had not flown into one of his murderous rages yet, Margerite often heard him shouting at servants who had the misfortune to move a little too slowly to his summons, or not to guess exactly what was in his mind. When the Graf was not pacing about the courtyard with his mastiffs by his side, or reordering the wall's defenses, he often disappeared into his chambers for hours on end, or stood brooding by one of the large windows across from the fourth-floor opening to the well shaft, staring out at the rain whipping across the ravine.

Margerite had to pass him then on her way to and from her chamber: she could not bring herself to go to him, but it was painful to look at him fretting and pining like a new-caught eagle in captivity, desperate for the sky. Although he was polite to Father Etienne at mealtimes, neither Margerite nor - she was certain - anyone else could fail to notice that he wished the priest to depart. Etienne, however, refused to notice any of Ruprecht's hints, no matter how firmly they were phrased, only repeating his observation that Graf Heinrich could and should be negotiated with, even though his stated deadline of October first had passed without any sign of compliance from Ruprecht.

Outside, Heinrich's men lit their fires and waited. They had tried to strip the orchard of apples, but a hail of arrows and a blast from one of Jochanan's cannon had driven them back: now the bird-tattered fruit were falling rotten into the untended grass below the trees, scattering down onto the frozen ground like heavy drops of dew whenever a strong gust of wind shook the branches. Margerite did not look out over the orchard often, for it saddened her unreasonably to see the waste of fruit that had bloomed and ripened with such promise.

Only Bertram seemed unaffected by the strains of the siege. Calm as ever, he drilled his guards and the Tiefensee men with the Bear's Paw soldiers in the courtyard; and if his tongue was often rough with them, it was no worse than it had ever been. Margerite found herself making excuses to speak with him, even if it was only a few words concerning supplies and requirements. Though he was always perfectly formal and correct with her, sometimes she would find herself gazing into his eyes for a little longer than their speech needed, and sometimes he seemed reluctant to leave her, breaking off their conversation only when it was clear that there was no more they could say to each other in the sight and hearing of everyone in the courtyard.

However, with the siege, Ruprecht had offered Bertram and Paul both rooms within the castle - the chamber that had belonged to Wolfram and the one beneath it - saying that he wished his commanders to be in his immediate reach, and the two of them had assented quickly enough. And thus it was that, one frosty night in mid-October, Margerite told Eva that she was going to the kitchen to prepare herself a posset, and the girl should stay where she was. Gertrude would have argued, but Eva only cowered back, saying, "Yes, Frowe Gräfin."

As Margerite was passing down the corridor towards the western staircase, the door of the chamber beside hers opened and Gerhild stepped out, clad in her white nightshift, with her long gold-brown hair flowing about her shoulders like a river of grain. Margerite silently cursed her own forgetfulness. Ruprecht had also ordered the midwife into the castle, so that she would be at hand immediately if Margerite had any difficulty: of course Gerhild would be alert for any unusual sounds from her chamber, and come out to see if anything was the matter with her.

"Frowe Gräfin?" Gerhild asked. "Is all well with you?"

"It is," Margerite replied. "I only..." She had been about to give Gerhild the same story she had given Eva, but realized that the midwife would insist on brewing the posset and bringing it up to her. "I felt suddenly faint, and wished to have a piece of cheese, or perhaps a cup of beef soup, as you told me I should do."

"Then you should not be up and about," Gerhild said decisively. "What is the matter with that serving maid of yours? Have her legs suddenly dropped off from St. Anthony's Fire?"

"Eva is asleep, and I did not wish to wake her. You know how tired a growing child can become at that age."

"She is hardly a child now, but I will grant you that she is growing, at a rate any boy would envy. She must have been piteously starved before, to put on size and flesh so quickly on siege rations. In any case, you should go back to bed, and I will bring you up something nourishing."

"No. My room is stuffy, for I have not been able to open the shutters for days, and the walk to and from the kitchen will do me good."

"Hmm. Have you had any unusual pangs? Any tightness of the belly?"

"No, and no. Gerhild, I thank you, but truly, there is nothing wrong with me. I will call you if there is, but now I want to be alone."

The midwife shook her head. "You are - two and a half months along, or so? Well, you may find yourself taking such fancies now and again. All I can say to you about it is, be careful. And do not let the vapours from your womb disorder your good sense." Gerhild looked straight into Margerite's face, the candlelight pooling shadows about her luminous gray eyes, and Margerite had the sudden disquieting feeling that the midwife knew exactly what she was about.

"Goodnight, Gerhild," she said, and continued towards the staircase, relieved to hear Gerhild's door shutting behind her.

Her relief was short-lived, though. She had not reached the stairs yet when Father Etienne's door opened at the end of the corridor, the priest's tall slim shape dark against the warm glow of the candles within his room. At the sight of him, Kobolt arched his back, hissing and spitting. Margerite had noticed before that her cat did not seem to care much for Etienne, but Kobolt had never reacted so strongly to him before. Perhaps it was the priest's scent: as he came closer, Margerite could smell the faint sweetness of incense wafting from the rustling folds of his black velvet cassock.

"Good evening, Frowe Gräfin," Father Etienne said, his accented voice cooly polite. "It is a late hour for you to be up."

"And you as well, Father," Margerite answered just as cooly, though her heart was beginning to beat faster and she could feel the faint damp warmth of sweat breaking out upon her palms. "I trust all is well with you, and that you do not find anything lacking in our hospitality? If there is anything you need, I shall be glad to find a servant to see to it."

"Strangely enough," the priest said with a small smile, "I was only coming to see if there was anything with which you might need my help. May I be of assistance to you?"

A low growl sounded from the darkness. Margerite started, glancing about, but it was only Kobolt, his eyes reflecting the candlelight greenly as he bristled and stared at Father Etienne. "Silly cat," she said unthinkingly, then, to the priest, "No, thank you. I was only on my way to the kitchen, for Gerhild Midwife has ordered me to eat a last small meal before bed, to nourish the child within me while I sleep. You are kind to offer help, but I do not need anything now."

"I shall accompany you then, if you have no objection," Father Etienne declared. Margerite's heart sank, but she could not back out now, nor could she bring herself to plead any of a bearing woman's weaknesses to a man, even a priest - especially this priest, with his air of cool aristocratic superiority that still made her feel very much like the daughter of a simple border Ritter.

"Of course not," she lied, trying to quiet her heartbeat and her disappointment together.

Father Etienne followed her down the two flights of stairs and into the kitchen, where a couple of scullery maids slept beside the coals glowing in the largest hearth. Even here, in the warmest room in the castle, the icy night chill was already beginning to creep in through the glass panes of the wide windows and around the wooden shutters blocking the arrow-slits. The kitchen cat, a huge fat calico, stood up, stretching delicately, then gave a little chirp of welcome as Kobolt slunk up to her, rubbing and nuzzling at him shamelessly while he licked her face.

"Wake up," Margerite said, touching one of the maids in the ribs with a toe. "Bring wine and bread and a little cheese or beef soup to the great hall for the Father and myself."

"Yes, Frowe Gräfin!" the girl said, springing to her feet at once.

Father Etienne and Margerite proceeded into the hall. The priest did not take his usual place by Ruprecht's chair, but sat beside Margerite instead. The flickering light of the two candles shadowed his face, so that his prominent cheekbones and brow-ridges stood out more bluntly than usual; their gleam also emphasized the tuft of white in his short beard and the white wings over his ears, so that he looked both older and more somber than by daylight.

Margerite was afraid that he would address her again on the subject of negotiations with Heinrich, but instead he only swirled the wine in his glass, saying, "It was wise of you not to send your serving maid running about so late at night, when she is nearly of a woman's years."

"So she is. But there is no need to fear for her chastity," Margerite went on hastily. "She is far too frightened of everything to be making up to our guardsmen." She bit her tongue then, as if the pain could drive away her memory of Gertrude, summoned unexpectedly to her mind by her hasty words.

"It may well be so. Do you know why she is so fearful?"

"No. She was like that when she came here, and has gotten little braver with time."

"Where did she come from?"

"From..." Margerite racked her brains to remember what Eva had said. "The Convent of the Holy Cross in Passau, I believe. One of the Graf's friends brought her, after my own maidservant had...disappeared."

"Disappeared?" Father Etienne arched an eyebrow. "How did that happen?"

Margerite nearly opened her mouth to tell him everything, but the scullery maid's candle was flickering closer, her feet scuffling heavily through the dry reeds, so she said only, "She was gone one morning when I awoke. Her betrothed was executed that same day."

"For her murder?"

"The Graf caught his grandfather poaching," Margerite answered flatly. The scullery maid put her bread and soup down before her, and she stirred the steaming broth, watching the candlelight swirl on its dark surface.

The ache of Gertrude's loss and her own failure to save Eckhardt was pressing harder on her heart with each word, and so she sought to turn the conversation away, as she would have turned a horse from the rushing waters of a ford flooded too deeply to cross. "I asked Ruprecht for a new maidservant, and he gave me Eva. For all her whining and cringing, she is a good girl, and skilled enough in her duties."

"Yes, I can see that she well knows how to dress you in the latest fashions...for this country," Father Etienne added, the corner of his mouth twitching as though he could not quite rein in the French barb of his wit. But the spark of humour in his blue eyes died quickly as he continued. "She may have learned such things in a convent, since the title of Abbess is no guarantee against the sins of pride and vanity. But do you have any idea where she came from before that? As little as I have heard her speak, she does not sound like one who was raised in a peasant huts or on the streets of the city."

"She is well-spoken enough, when she is not too afraid to say anything," Margerite admitted. "But she has never said anything of her family, so I assume she was raised in the convent."

Father Etienne nodded, sipping at his wine. Although Margerite had not thought herself hungry, she found that she had finished her bread and broth almost without noticing it, and, had she not been so mindful of the castle's stocks, she would have been sorely tempted to call for a larger meal.

"Well, Father, it is growing late, and I need my rest," she said when she had downed the last swallow of her wine.

"Of course," Etienne said dryly, inclining his head to her as if she had scored a point of some sort. He rose gracefully, picking up his candle, and gestured for her to precede him out.

When Margerite had seen the priest to his room, she did not return to her own chamber, but went on, somewhat nervously, down the corridor towards the northern staircase. She could see the faint glow through Ruprecht's keyhole and about the edges of his door; for a moment, though she knew it was foolish, she found herself pausing to see if he would come out.

But she heard only the low sound of his voice, murmuring, "Good Brangæne, good Mark...up, my sweet hounds. Tonight you shall sleep on my bed to keep me warm, my fine grey ones. There, lie down now..." and then a soft thumping, as of an mastiff's tail beating against a bedpost.

The guard standing at the head of the staircase looked at her with a slightly puzzled expression on his broad face, but said nothing: if the Gräfin wished to walk about at night, it was not his place to challenge her. To reach Bertram's room from this side of the castle, Margerite had to pass through the great hall once more, then past the kitchen and down the western corridor to the same staircase she had come down with Father Etienne. Walking through the hallway, she stopped in alarm at the sounds she heard: the banging of wood on stone, a woman's muffled cry...

Margerite put her fist in her mouth to quiet a sudden fit of giggles. The room from which the noises were coming was the chamber Ruprecht had given to Paul the Bear, and what was going on in there might be unchaste, but it was none of the unholy things she had feared. If Berthe could not keep her scullery maids out of the mercenary captain's bulky embrace, it was she who would have to answer for it when the belly of one girl or another began to swell. Margerite hurried swiftly on.

Bertram's new chamber on the third floor was between Kai's room and the library. There was no sign of light from either Kai's keyhole or Bertram's, but when Margerite knocked softly on Bertram's door, it opened almost at once.

Bertram's tunic was askew and unbelted; he held a sheathed sword in one hand and his helm in the other, as if she had sounded an alarm. "What is it?" he asked in an alarmed whisper. "Is Heinrich making an assault?"

"Nothing of the sort," Margerite whispered back. "May I come in?"

Bertram stepped aside to let her through the door, Kobolt slipping softly past her legs. His room was icier than hers, for one of his arrow-slits was unshuttered, the distant hoot of an owl sounding clearly through the narrow gap into darkness. Despite her heavy cloak, Margerite began to shiver almost at once.

"Is all well, Frowe Gräfin...Margerite?" Bertram asked, laying aside his blade and helmet. "What brings you here at this hour?"

Now that she was here, Margerite did not know what to say to him. Instead she grasped his big calloused hand, holding it tightly in both of her own as a warm tear ran down the chilled skin of her face.

"Has Ruprecht done something to you?" he asked, and Margerite shuddered again, for she could hear the grim deadliness beneath Bertram's quiet words.

"No. It is...oh, there is nothing wrong, but I had to speak to you, for there is no one else here whom I trust fully. I..." Unexpectedly, she found herself sobbing, huddling against him for warmth. "Why is it," she said, gulping back tears, "that I am always weeping when I come to you?"

"You have endured much," Bertram answered, his low voice warming. "I have seen soldiers hold up less well than you have in a place besieged, and that without the other burdens that you bear. Do not fear that I will think the less of you because you weep." He put his arm about Margerite's shoulders, letting her lean upon him.

"I do not know what will become of us, or of the child I bear," she said. "Maria help me, I do not even know who the child's father is - you, or Ruprecht!"

Bertram pulled back a little, looking down at her in astonishment. "Do you mean... Margerite, could it be mine?"

"It could. May Christ forgive me," she added softly, "I hope that it is."

Bertram's face tightened in pain. "Ah, Margerite. If it were, it would be a bastard, conceived in the most grievous sin. I would not wish that on any child of yours, and yet..."

"All children are conceived and born in sin, save the Virgin and Her Son. And I would rather bear your seed beneath my heart than Ruprecht's, even at the risk of being found out when it is born." She knew how foolish her words were: if Ruprecht took dreadful vengeance for trespasses against his woods, what would he do with the wife and man who had betrayed his marriage bed? And yet, senseless and daring as her feelings might be, they were the true thoughts of her soul.

"There is little chance of that," Bertram said absently. Margerite reached up to touch his hair, winding one of the thick black locks about her finger. "No, my child would not be born with black hair. I only dyed mine so that I would not be recognised by anyone who might have known me."

The tightness in Margerite's chest eased a little, for Bertram had just allayed one of the fears that had been gnawing at her over the past two and a half months - even as it confirmed the truth of her dream; and that gladdened her heart, for now she had no doubt that Mother Maria had sent her the vision, that she might be sure of Bertram as her help and comforter. "What colour is it?" she asked, staring at his face as if to see through the illusion that covered it.

"Light brown, a little darker than yours - much the same colour as Gerhild's. And it was white when I was a young page."

Whoever his father, then, little Wolfram would be fair, bearing no sign that he was not Ruprecht's. Unless... Margerite felt the uneasiness turning within her like worms in the belly... he were the child of that Other: who knew what monstrousness might spring from her womb then? Shuddering, she remembered the words of the mad friar she had seen in Freiburg. I saw a beast rise up out of the sea, having seven heads and ten horns...And the beast which I saw was like unto a leopard, and his feet were the feet of a bear, and his mouth as the mouth of a lion...

"There will be no sign, then," Margerite said with a firmness she did not feel. "That lightens my heart to know."

Bertram embraced her, holding her as tenderly as if the small child were already cradled in her arms. "I wish we had spoken before. I would not have had you in fear of such a thing, nor bearing this burden alone. Maria forgive me for laying it upon you: if not for my weakness, you should not have had to bear it."

Margerite gazed up at him. The glow of the candles seemed to make his beard and wild tangle of hair insubstantial as shadows, and, as sometime happened, it seemed to her that she could really see Bertram beneath his disguise: straight nose and blunt cheekbones, the flesh drawn over them by the strains of the siege; the slant of his jawline and firm set of his chin...

She could almost see the younger Bertram overlaid upon the older, the clean-shaven, well-favoured knight with thick brown-gold hair curling upon his shoulders and the green streaks in his eyes glinting with eagerness. Then the vision passed, and she found herself ready to weep again at the deep lines of pain that had scored the corners of his eyes and graven their scars about his mouth.

"That I lay with you," she said, "has been my only comfort and hope through these months. Though I may confess the sin, I shall never regret the love."

Margerite could feel Bertram's powerful body trembling, his heavy arms shaking on her shoulders as if he were wrestling with an unseen foe in her place. She feared that he would pull away from her, racked by one of his fits of contrition and self-hate. But slowly Bertram seemed to master himself...and then he leaned forward to kiss her. His lips were rough against hers, chafed by frost and wind, and his beard scratchy against her face, yet she met his mouth eagerly with her own, and it seemed to her that she could feel a stream of golden warmth pouring from her lips to his like a draught of strong wine.

"Margerite, I love you," Bertram said. His words lay there for a moment, warming the chill silence like hot stones taken from the fire and wrapped in cloth to warm an icy bed. But when he next spoke, there was an unexpected note of plaintiveness in his voice. "What shall we do?"

"I do not know," Margerite replied. "I have little hope of parting from Ruprecht while he lives. And Burg Falkenstein is still under siege: it may be that none of us have much longer for life."

"That may be. But Ruprecht was right in this, at least: the winter will be much harder on besieger than besieged. Even with our villages undefended, Heinrich will not find it easy to provision his troops as well as we are supplied, and though he and his knights are warm in the Tiefensee houses, the cold and waiting will wear worse upon his men in their tents than upon ours in our castle. I wish," Bertram added, a sudden sharp passion in his words, "that Ruprecht had been killed before the castle gates."

"So do I," Margerite admitted, her tongue heavy in her mouth. "We might have negotiated then, and it might not have been so bad to come under Graf Heinrich's protection. Except from Ruprecht, I have heard little ill of him, and I think..." She did not know why, but she was suddenly as certain of it as she was of the child within her... "I think that Heinrich, and his eldest son at least, are good men."

"That is so, from all I know of them."

"But Heinrich's younger son Nikolaus is a member of the Order as well."

Bertram closed his eyes for a moment, shaking his head. "He is. And yet..." He took Margerite's hands in his, his touch warming her icy fingers. "I had thought of killing Ruprecht by stealth, several times. It came to my mind that if he were to disappear, you would have rule alone over Burg Falkenstein, and perhaps the Order's intentions could be thwarted. But they were willing enough to risk his life in this, and who could say whether slaying him and surrendering to Graf Heinrich would not help to deliver their desires to their hand?

For all Ruprecht's evil, he still shows himself to be bound by honour in certain things. Not all members of the Order are so constrained: I do not believe Nikolaus is. And if Ruprecht died, you would be a widow - free in law, but it would not be long before Graf Günther, or someone like him, made suit to Kaiser Karl for your guardianship; while Heinrich is a widower and has two unmarried sons, one of whom is Nikolaus.

How should I, a guard Hauptmann who was once a man of the Black Sword Company, be able to stand against the power of such men - to press my suit for marriage?" The candlelight glinted off Bertram's hazel eyes, their green streaks and speckles shining like the mottling of a stone beneath the waters of a clear stream.

Margerite drew in her breath at his last words. To be free of Ruprecht...to be married to Bertram...the thought seemed a delirious dream. "If we could flee together..." she murmured, her voice trailing off.

Bertram smiled sadly. "Margerite, you know nothing of the life we would have to lead if we tried it. A man alone, who can sleep in the wild and live as rough as an animal or bandit, who does not care overmuch what he does or what becomes of him: yes, he can survive as an outlaw. A woman, with a babe in her belly or at her breast?"

Bertram did not have to speak any more brutal words: Margerite could hear them for herself, as clearly as if he had stopped halfway through reciting a poem she knew well. All the life Bertram knew was fighting: she would be barely better than a camp follower, and if any ill befell him - if he were wounded or fell sick - there would be no choice in what she had to do to survive.

"I know enough to be sure that you are right. And yet, if we stay here and all goes as it has, then what shall we be able to do?"

"Watch, and wait. I have seen this often enough in the field. Two armies will skirt each other for days, months even, with both commanders seeking to gain a clear advantage before they join battle. At last something always happens, even if it is one leader's nerve breaking, and then the outcome of the combat waits upon strength and skill - and the wit with which the forces were manuvered beforehand."

"The forces," Margerite murmured. "Bertram, if we were to strike against Ruprecht - if it were to come to fighting within Burg Falkenstein - who do you think would stand with us?"

Bertram blinked, his thick black eyebrows drawing down in thought. "It is a good question you ask. The older castle guardsmen would defend Ruprecht in any struggle, certainly; but many of the younger ones would be with me, particularly since Eckhardt's death." A shadow of pain passed behind his eyes at those words, but he continued. "I do not know about the Bear's Paw Company. When Paul's loyalty has been bought with a contract, he does not sell it again, and he thinks Ruprecht to be a great leader and a fine employer. Yet he trusts me well, from long acquaintance, and he and Jochanan both think very highly of you: I believe that neither of them would see you harmed for anything, else the Bear might have ordered his men rather more for their own safety and less for Burg Falkenstein's in the battle before the gate."

"And Father Etienne?" she asked. "What do you think of him?"

"I do not know," Bertram confessed. "I do not believe him to be an Order member: Ruprecht seems to have little love for him, and I do not think that is feigned. And yet I should be reluctant to tell him of the Order and such part as we know it has played in matters here."

Margerite thought about the conversation she had held with the priest earlier that evening. It would be difficult to tell Father Etienne part of the truth: he seemed a man to whom asking searching questions came as naturally as breath. "As you will. I shall trust your judgement in this…my love."

"My love," Bertram breathed, almost as if he were praying. He kissed Margerite again, holding her to him. As before, his embrace calmed her shaking as if he were steadying a statue on an unbalanced pedestal, strengthening her and driving the fear from her heart. "You should go back to your chamber, Margerite," he said abruptly. "We have already risked too much."

"Aye," she admitted. "We have. And yet…"

"I know." Bertram stroked her unbound hair. "I know, Margerite. If you can bear the mess Father Hans has made of the chapel - go and pray for all of us."

"I shall."

Margerite did not dare go straight up to the top floor from Bertram's chamber, for to do that she would have had to pass the doors of Etienne and Gerhild again. She retraced her steps, passing the guards silently. By the time she was back in her room, she was trembling violently from the cold, though the low coals in her stove made it the warmest place in the castle. Eva was snoring on her pallet in the corner, head thrown back and mouth open. Her throat glowed white in the candlelight, her fair hair shimmering like a fall of flax upon her pillow. Plain as she was when awake, the serving maid was almost beautiful in her sleep, her generous, well-balanced features no longer pinched by terror; and the hills and valleys of her blossoming body stood out even beneath the thick blankets.

I wonder where she did come from before the convent? Margerite thought. It is as well that she got out, though. A young and pretty nun, who did not take the habit from vocation, is as likely a cause of trouble as I can imagine.

Calmed by the ordinary thoughts, Margerite blew out her candle and got into bed, still wrapped in her fur-lined cloak. Kobolt curled up by her head, kneading and nuzzling at her hair until she pushed him away. "I cannot sleep with you pretending that you are a kitten nursing at your mother's breast, sir," she told the cat. "Be quiet, or go chase mice." Kobolt rolled over and settled himself, and Margerite settled herself as well.

Still, sleep did not come to her until she let her mind wander into the paths of what could never be - of Bertram, trimmed and neatly dressed, with the black dye washed from his hair; of the two of them sitting side by side at table, her hand in his; of embraces without shame and kisses with no salt taste of tears in their mouths...

Cold as it was, the first snows did not begin to scatter down until the beginning of November, a white dusting over the frozen earth. Although Father Etienne still took his meals at the high table with Margerite and Ruprecht, Ruprecht was barely speaking to him, and when he did, it was to deliver pointed hints that the priest would be welcome to depart whenever he chose, the sooner the better.

Margerite hardly blamed her husband, for as long as Etienne was present and making observations on the wisdom of negotiating with Heinrich, the food and drink served to three of them had to be at least of a quality and quantity to impress the priest with the fact that Burg Falkenstein was not yet on the brink of starvation.

Though Margerite felt foolish admitting it to herself, there was something that made her profoundly uneasy in the way Kobolt hissed and spat, hiding behind her skirts whenever he saw Father Etienne. Perhaps it was wicked, even sinful, to trust the judgement of a cat in such matters, but Margerite could not help wondering if Father Etienne harboured some dark thoughts or intentions beneath his polished and sophisticated surface.

He was a charming enough dining companion, widely traveled and well-read, with a dry wit that even brought an unwilling smile to Ruprecht's lips now and again, but she thought she might be relieved herself when he was gone.

Early on Martinmas morning, Margerite was in the outer courtyard, watching one of the kitchen maids toss a bagful of burnt crusts and scraps into the snow for the geese and chickens, holding Kobolt in her arms to keep him from stalking the fowl and wondering if she could order at least one of the geese slaughtered for the high table's Martinmas dinner when Eva ran up to her, nearly stumbling over the huge skirts of one of Berthe's cast-off dresses that had been newly given to her.

"Frowe Gräfin, Father Hans is lying in his room above the chapel and will not move. I think he is dead," her maidservant gasped breathlessly.

Margerite sighed. "That one," she said to the kitchen maid, pointing at a gray goose which had just driven two black hens from a large crust. "Kill it and tell Berthe to serve it up tonight."

"Yes, Frowe Gräfin," the girl answered, running at the goose to chase it away from the others. Kobolt, seeing the game, leapt from Margerite's arms and went after the same bird, so that it veered from its path, its big webbed feet scrabbling helplessly on a patch of ice for a moment before the frantic beating of its clipped wings could restore its balance. The maid dived, grabbing the goose about the neck even as Kobolt pounced at it; Margerite gathered her heavy cloak about herself and followed Eva to the chapel.

The room beneath the one Bertram had lived in was a mess, reeking of spilt wine, urine, and the unwashed body of Father Hans; the straw on the floor had half-rotted into heaps of muck. The priest himself was lying on the bed, his blankets on the floor beside him and his filthy cassock rucked up to show bony ankles and bare blue feet. His eyes were open, staring sightlessly at the stone wall. Margerite reached down to touch the clawlike hand protruding from Father Hans' sleeve. His flesh was cold and hard: he had been dead for some time.

At least with the icy weather, there were not many flies in the room, or else, Margerite knew, the sight there would have been much more unpleasant.

"Go fetch Father Etienne," Margerite ordered. "If he is not in his own chamber, you will likeliest find him in the library." Eva fled, and Margerite walked outside, looking about for able-bodied men whom she could set to digging another grave in the hastily consecrated corner of the outer bailey.

Berthe, delighted to have a chance to show her skill after the months of siege rations, had roasted the Martinmas goose magnificently in time for a late midday meal. Margerite's mouth began watering the moment she walked into the great hall and scented the aroma wafting out from the kitchens: although there had been plenty of smoked and cured meat, she was as hungry for fresh as if it were the end of the Lenten fast. Rather than doing the goose up as an elaborate subtlety, the cook had wisely chosen to enhance its nature, trusting in the hunger of her eaters to sharpen their appreciation of the large bird.

The crackling brown skin, gilded with drippings of its own fat, could not have been finer if the goose had been dressed in the shimmering-feathered skin of a peacock. Though the apple harvest was lost, there were plenty of dried sour cherries, and with those Berthe had made a deep scarlet honeyed sauce, served in little silver bowls on the side with a few ladlefuls poured over the goose's platter so that it might have been lying in its fresh blood. There were cherries in the stuffing as well, and dried plums steamed back to rich succulence by their long roasting inside the goose.

With it, Ruprecht ordered the last of their red French wine served, the dark wine's dry fruity flavour complementing the savoury sweetness of the goose perfectly. Kobolt sat by Margerite's feet: every so often he would stand up on his hind legs to put a soft black paw on her wrist, and sometimes, though she knew it was a waste to give such good food to a cat who could catch his own meals, she would pass a small bite down to him.

Berthe had set the goose's liver aside, mixing it into a smooth paste with herbs and a little milk for Margerite. She began to eat it with only a slight qualm about taking more food than her share, and it was delicious. Yet to her horror, by the time she had reached the last bites, not only did the liver paste seem too smooth and mild on her tongue, but she found herself wishing that she could have had it raw and warm, with the goose's blood still hot on it.

Yesterday she had visited the mews, and caught herself reaching for the raw meat on the platter Johann had prepared for the birds. Margerite knew that pregnant women often had strange cravings, but hers seemed more than passingly strange: more than once, she had found herself daydreaming about her hunts with Ruprecht, her mind dwelling on the memory of the torn and bloodied flesh of the beasts they had brought down, and realized that her mouth was watering horribly.

I will speak to Gerhild about it¸ she said to herself ; and resolutely, bland as the dish now seemed to her, she wiped up the final bits of liver with a piece of bread, forcing herself to chew and swallow. Father Etienne praised the meal in his usual courtly and witty manner. Though Margerite knew his compliments were largely made for the sake of conversation, the Martinmas goose deserved his praise, and for once she felt that she could receive it without embarassment.

"I shall perform the funeral Mass for Father Hans when they have finished digging his grave outside," Father Etienne declared after a little time, dabbing a drop of cherry sauce neatly from his white beard-tuft with the corner of his napkin. "He was the only priest near Burg Falkenstein?"

"Yes," Ruprecht said forbiddingly.

Etienne cut a small, juicy chunk of white flesh from the half-breast remaining on his silver platter, fastidiously dunking it in the puddle of sauce on the plate and lifting it to his mouth. He chewed quietly for a moment, washing the bite down with a sip of wine before he spoke again.

"You will need a priest here at least until you have reached terms with Graf Heinrich or the siege is broken, and I am willing to offer my services."

"We only need a simple priest, not a canon. I thank you for your offer," Ruprecht managed to get out, though by the look of distaste on his face, the words tasted worse than a maggoty fruit. "But there is no need for you to remain longer, when I am sure you have pressing business elsewhere. There is certainly none for you to conclude here, unless you wish to put on armour and take a place defending my walls."

"I would be remiss in my duty as a priest," Father Etienne answered smoothly, "if I abandoned the folk of a castle and its village without spiritual solace, most of all in the middle of a siege, when both their souls and bodies are in the greatest peril. I shall stay with you, Graf Ruprecht, and serve you and your people as the Church requires until you can send for a parish priest of your own."

Ruprecht's left fist clenched, and Margerite almost fancied that she could see the purple glow of the amethyst in his Order ring darkening like an angry eye. She held her breath, waiting for an explosion more violent and dangerous than any Jochanan could make with his gunpowder. As if in sympathy, Kobolt miaowed, the harsh cry of one tomcat challenging another.

Father Etienne sipped casually at his wine, his long slender fingers twirling the goblet's gilded stem as if he were waiting for one of his fellows to answer the point he had raised in a friendly theological discussion. At last Ruprecht muttered something that sounded like a bitten-back curse, then lifted his own goblet and knocked back a good draught of the red wine.

"You may stay," he acknowledged grudgingly. "I suppose I cannot really force you to go."

"This is your castle and your land, Graf, but these people are also my flock," Etienne insisted. His voice was still even-toned, but his French accent was coming out more markedly, as if his native thoughts were forcing their way past his mask of calm.

The amethyst on Ruprecht's forefinger gleamed dark as he waved his hand in irritation, as if brushing away a cloud of midges. "Stay, then, but if Burg Falkenstein falls, do not think your cassock will save you. If you choose to live with us now, then if we perish, you shall surely die too - whichever side cuts you down."

"I shall take that risk," Etienne told him, the aristocratic calm of his ascetic face still unruffled. Margerite let her breath out in a long silent gust, reaching down to scratch Kobolt behind his flattened ears. The cat looked at her, then stalked away, sitting down with his back to the diners and his tail curled tightly about him, as if to inform Margerite that he was no longer recognising the right of humans to live in his castle.

Out of her sense of duty, more than anything else, Margerite stood by the graveside as Father Hans was lowered in, drawing her hood low against the grainy scatters of snow stinging her face and eyelids. Most of the Tiefensee villagers, at least those who could be spared from manning the walls, were gathered about, their heads bowed in respect for the dead - and, perhaps, for the tall priest who stood bare-headed as if he did not notice the icy drops catching in his thick gray-shot hair, intoning the funerary words in a voice that carried easily over the sound of the wind and the faint clattering of the prayer-beads in several of the villagers' hands.

The icy clods rattled hollowly on the top of the makeshift coffin, and Margerite blinked hard, no longer able to look at the box of uneven and crooked-nailed planks - she had seen too many coffins quickly cobbled together, dropped, like this, into graves dug shallower than their full six feet. Poor Father Hans, she thought. A drunk and a half-hearted priest; but Ruprecht says he was a good man once, and he did not fail in bravery when his flock needed him. With that thought, Margerite realized that the heavy feeling in her chest was guilt: had she not often thought badly of Father Hans, and paid little attention when she was told that the priest was ill?

She had not even made Confession to him, not once since coming to Burg Falkenstein.

When Father Etienne turned away from the grave, Margerite followed him, catching up with him outside the castle door. "Father, excuse me."

"Yes, Frowe Gräfin?" Etienne said, looking down his slightly crooked nose at her. Although his tone was polite, it was also that of a man who really had little time for trivial distractions, and doubted that she would have anything of importance to say. Well, he had protested the importance of serving the folk of Burg Falkenstein and Tiefensee; and Margerite was quite certain that he would have to count her within his temporary flock.

"Father, I would confess to you, for I have sinned."

"Come along, then," Father Etienne told her. "It is cold out here, and the chapel will require cleaning before it is used again. We shall go to my chamber."

As Margerite stepped into Father Etienne's room, she felt a wonderful quiet peace coming over her. Perhaps it was the scents that filled the room, the sweetness of frankincense and myrrh mingled with the cleanness of hyssop, rosemary, and rue. It might have been the light as well, for although the arrow slits on the southern and western walls were closed, there were three large windows - one more than in her own chamber - overlooking the inner bailey. Or perhaps it was only the relief of knowing that, at last, she could unburden her soul of the weight of sin that had been gathering on it since her marriage to Ruprecht like snowflakes settling on a tree branch until it bent beneath its load.

Father Etienne seated himself beside one of the windows, and Margerite knelt before him. "Forgive me, Father, for I have sinned."

"Tell me your sins, my child," Etienne said, his voice quiet and resigned.

"Father, I often thought uncharitable thoughts about Father Hans, and did nothing for him while he was dying."

"Tell me more of this, Gräfin."

Under Father Etienne's questioning, Margerite gradually unfolded her feelings, spreading out her sins like dirty laundry on a streambank - most of all, her contempt for the priest's drunken state, which had kept her from making Confession to him, and, too often, made it easier for her not to attend Mass in Father Hans' chapel.

"You were remiss in not going to Father Hans, if you knew he was dying, and hence you bear some guilt for his death and must do penance for it. Confession, as you know, is only required before Easter for the layman, but it was lack of charity that kept you from doing what you knew you ought to. Do you repent of that?"

"Father, I do. Please God, I shall not ignore another's ills because I think little of the one who is sick again, nor shall I neglect my duties to Christ out of fastidiousness."

"Is that all?"

"Father, I am often angry with my maidservant."

"Why? Does she not do her duty well?"

"She does. But she cowers before me and cringes and whines until I am nearly driven mad with it, and then I am tempted to slap her."

"Have you ever struck her?" Etienne was leaning forward now, the gaze of his blue eyes more intense above his slight frown.

"No," Margerite answered honestly. "But sometimes I have lost my temper and offered her threats that terrified her."

"Do you remember the words of Christ to His disciples? 'Blessed are the poor in spirit, for theirs is the Kingdom of Heaven...Blessed are the meek, for they shall inherit the earth... Blessed are the merciful, for they shall obtain mercy.' And remember also the epistle of St. Paul to the Hebrews: 'Let brotherly love continue. Be not forgetful to entertain strangers: for thereby some have entertained angels unawares.' Do you honestly regret your ill temper?"

"I do."

"As well as the penance I shall give you, you must apologise to Eva and tell her that you did not mean your threats and shall not do whatever it was that put her in fear of you."

"I shall do that."

"Is that all?" This time Margerite was certain that she could hear the sigh in his voice, and it made her indignant: it seemed to her that he was treating her sins as if they were mere annoyances. And I do not know what important thing I might be keeping him from, when he is as trapped here as the rest of us - and that by his own choice! The thought unloosed her tongue: she found that she was speaking freely, as she had feared she would not be able to, using her words as siege weapons to try to break through Father Etienne's impervious dignity.

"Father, I have committed adultery."

The French priest's long eyelashes fluttered, as if he had just stopped himself from blinking in surprise. "This is a most serious sin. The man with whom you committed it - was he also married?"

"No, Father," Margerite replied meekly.

"Is the child you bear your husband's, or is it the fruit of your adultery?"

"Father...I do not know." Margerite wished she could bite the words back, for she knew they showed her to be a careless slut. She wanted to wail, It was not like that, it was not like it sounds! but she knew saying such things would only make her seem the worse.

"You do not know," Father Etienne repeated. Although his tone did not change, there was something in his slight French accent that made the words sound mocking, scalding against Margerite's ears. "Have you told your husband of this adultery?"

"No, Father."

"So Graf Ruprecht expects to raise the child as his own. You are aware that if you do not tell him, you will add the sin of deliberate deceit to lechery and the breaking of your marriage vows?"

"Father...I am aware of that." Margerite's voice was distant and tinny in her own ears, her head beginning to spin. Vaguely she wondered if she were going to faint.

"Do you regret your adultery?" Father Etienne pursued. Margerite could not answer. "Can you honestly say that you would not do it again?"

Again she was mute. Father Etienne leaned forward, his blue eyes shining cold and piercing from his ascetic features. "Margerite, do you love your husband?"

Where the other questions had reduced her to baffled terror, this one seemed to tauten her backbone as if it were drawing a slack lutestring twangingly into tune. Margerite rose from the floor, dusting her skirts off. "That," she said haughtily, "is hardly a priest's concern."

"I cannot offer you absolution until I know that you are truly sorry for what you have done, and do not intend to sin further. Go to the chapel and meditate on what you have done and on the deception that you are contemplating. But do not come back to me until there is genuine repentance in your heart."

Father Etienne rose as well, walking to the door and opening it for Margerite. She did not trust herself to speak: straight-backed, she swept past him and out. When the Gräfin was gone, Etienne sat down with a deep sigh. The woman was subtle - too subtle to be playing such games with him, he added to himself. He had seen members of the Order of Light-Bearers mock Confession before, pretending contrition while eagerly embellishing their alleged sins in whatever manner they thought would most provoke the confessor.

The Gräfin's lengthy description of the self-incapacitation of the Church's representative in Burg Falkenstein, and of how she had passed over his dying illness through contempt and carelessness - smacked very much of that same gloating mockery to him: she was telling him, very nearly in plain language, how useless and foolish the Church was, and how she hoped to gleefully watch its power sicken and die within Burg Falkenstein's walls.

Of her confession regarding Eva, however, he was less certain. He did not know if she had any idea who her maidservant might be. As far as he could tell, Eva's cousin had kept her precise identity even from the Abbess of the Convent of the Holy Cross, in order to make sure that no other could seize on the opportunity to champion the girl towards her inheritance with an eye to personal gain thereby. However, the Gräfin could well have interrogated the girl, either by arcane means or simple threats.

But it was the Gräfin's last confession that Father Etienne found most disturbing. He knew, full well, that the Order of Light-Bearers practiced sexual magics of various perverse sorts, from the many forms of sodomy to intercourse with demons, and often their rituals of lust called for more than one partner. Was the Gräfin boasting to him of having gotten her child in such a ritual? Etienne called her words before his mind again.

That she did not know which man the father was - how else could he read that? She said she had not told the Graf:because he already knew, because he had taken part in the rite? Yet she had seemed genuinely distressed when he had questioned her further. The paleness of the Gräfin's cheeks, washed away almost at once by the bright flush of red blood to her face; the way her eyes had widened and the muscles of her delicate jaw clenched, as though she were trying not to be sick...

If Etienne had not had the words of two Order members and the proof of the Gräfin's black familiar as evidence of her allegiance, he would have been willing to swear then that she was no dark magician, but simply a very young woman who had gotten herself into the same predicament that so many of Eve's daughters had faced before her - for even the Blessed Virgin had needed to tell St. Joseph that she would bear a child who was not begotten of his seed.

Still, Etienne knew what he knew about the Gräfin. To confirm the other evidence, he had tried - very carefully, to avoid alerting her - to scry Margerite, gazing into an unblemished crystal for almost an hour. But she had warded herself well indeed: he had been able to see nothing but a golden glow, centering upon the image of a falcon which she wore as a pendant. And there was something about the style of the enchantment about her which was most certainly Order work: Etienne could read it in the shape and feel of the magic just as surely as one master sculptor could recognise the chisel marks of his greatest rival.

So, if Etienne could not fathom the Gräfin's game, he would wait, and watch. That he would be able to stay in Burg Falkenstein without open opposition was well, but hardly to be counted as a triumph. In fact, it reminded him of something his own teacher in the secret arts, Stefan von Hauenstein - another German, oddly enough, but dwelling in a mountain retreat in the Pyrenees - had been wont to say to him when he was young.

"Sometimes you must put your hand in the wolf's mouth, and that may seem hard, for it takes bravery." Stefan had smiled rather wolfishly himself there, looking up at the apprentice who already towered over him by half a head. "But the real challenge only begins there, for to get your hand out of the wolf's mouth again calls for wisdom, which is far harder to exercise."

Well, Meister Stefan, Etienne thought, my hand is well and truly in the wolf's mouth, all right, but I have put it in and pulled it out again a fair number of times since you said that to me. I believe I can do it once more, and, as my will and wit hold, pull little Eva out as well, and put a spike in the maw of the beast to finish with.

Margerite went at once to the chapel, sorely disordered and distressed of heart. Surely enough, Father Etienne had touched her trouble at the root. She knew that she had sinned, and was compounding her sin by not telling the truth to Ruprecht - but she did not know that she would ever be able to repent of what she had done. Though her mind only seemed to be wobbling in circles, she lingered in the chapel until the candles that lit it had burned down a full fingerlength.

After the evening meal, Margerite summoned Gerhild to her room. As she stitched on her embroidery, Gerhild's fingers twirled on her spindle, and Eva diligently snipped and stitched at one of Berthe's oversized dresses, Margerite described her strange craving for raw and bloody meat. The midwife nodded wisely.

"That is not uncommon. As you are making flesh within you, so your body desires flesh to eat. Nor is it strange that you want it raw: I have seen women who have given birth hunger after the afterbirth as any cat or dog would. Our bodies are a mystery, save to the great Lord who made them."

"That is so," Margerite said, relieved.

Although she had thought the door closed, it was swinging slowly open. Margerite whirled, expecting to see Cundrîê or Ruprecht there, but it was only Kobolt, trotting briskly in with something large and dark in his mouth.

"Kobolt, keep that rat off my bed!" Margerite said sharply. Golden eyes fixed on Eva, the cat barely twitched an ear towards his mistress. The girl sat in her chair as if paralyzed as Kobolt stood up on his hind legs with his paws on her thigh, dropping his booty in her lap, then walked away, tail high with the air of a job well done.

Eva gasped; at the same time, Margerite heard the small mew from her skirts. "It's a kitten!" the maidservant squeaked. The little creature was already scrambling up onto her leg, mewing indignantly. "Frowe Gräfin, what shall I do?"

Margerite laughed, going over to her and picking the kitten up. Its pearly little claws were stuck in Eva's skirt; when she disentangled it, it immediately twisted in her hands, clinging to her sleeve. It might have been a month or two old - Margerite would have been able to tell at once with a puppy, but she had never paid attention to the breeding of cats - and already had Kobolt's tufted ears and powerful back legs, but rather than being solid black, the kitten had a red-gold mark on its forehead, one red-gold back paw, and a shimmer of golden hairs throughout its fluffy pelt. The little cat's slanted eyes were just brightening to a greenish yellow, but had not quite lost their bluish cast.

"It must be one of the kitchen cat's kittens," Margerite said thoughtfully. "Kai said something about Berthe drowning them...Strange that Kobolt should bring it to you; I thought that toms would kill kittens when they found them."

"He did when he first came to Tiefensee," Gerhild put in. "But even a tomcat often knows his own. Let me see that." She lifted the kitten's tail, looking closely. "Good, it is a queen. You would never be able to keep another tomcat with Kobolt about, for he is sure to drive off all his sons by the time they are a year old, unless one of them can defeat him."

"Well, Eva? Do you want to keep her?"

Eva's hands trembled as she cupped them for Margerite to set the little cat in, and Margerite thought she saw the girl's lower lip quiver. "Frowe Gräfin? What would I do with her?"

Her afternoon Confession still sharp in her mind, Margerite reminded herself to be gentle with the girl. "Pet her, perhaps, and play with her, and mayhap she will grow up to be as good a companion to you as Kobolt is to me."

Eva looked at the kitten again. It yawned, tiny white teeth spiky against the bright pink inside its mouth, then curled up in her hands and began to purr. "Frowe Gräfin, I know nothing of cats. The Abbess had one..." She tried to bring her hands up to cover her mouth, realized they were full of kitten, and started to snuffle in consternation.

"Well," Margerite said kindly, "this is a very young cat. If Berthe is drowning the litter and will not promise her safety, so that she cannot keep suckling her mother, she must have..." Margerite paused. Kittens could not be that different from puppies; what was good for a valuable hunting dog should not hurt a cat too much. "A little bread in meat broth, several times a day, and a warm basket to sleep in. And you might give her a name. What would you like to call her?"

Eva lifted the kitten up, holding her close to her face. The kitten nuzzled against her as if seeking to nurse on her cheek, and she giggled. "She is very pretty," Eva said, as if surprised. "But she also looks as if she could be wild and fierce. I shall call her Kriemhilt."

"Kriemhilt she is, then. And you may set your sewing down, if you like, and drag a straw across the floor to see if she will chase it."

Incredulously, Eva did, though at first she still kept glancing up as if she expected Margerite to turn upon her and berate her. But little Kriemhilt seemed to enchant the girl quickly, and soon Eva was paying no attention to anything but her kitten and Kobolt, who joined the game before long.

The three women stayed there for some time, sewing, spinning, and playing with the cats. The wind had grown much stronger, howling through the ravine and rattling the wooden shutters over the arrow-slits. One of the shutters had not been fastened properly, and a gust flung it open, scattering a few flakes of snow into the room before Gerhild could spring up and close it.

The midwife shuddered, crossing herself. "I think Wodan and his host are riding tonight," she said.

"What do you mean?" Margerite asked.

Gerhild did not look directly at her, but the candle's flame underlit her gray eyes so that they seemed strangely luminous. "It is a prayer we have here, a night-blessing for such stormy winter evenings. 'Against witches and unholy spirits, against Wodan's host and all his men, may Christ protect me.' Wodan is one of the old demons who used to live here, and they say when the wild winter winds blow, he leads the heathen dead and the souls of the wicked forth from Hell to hunt the living. I am glad that we are within and Graf Heinrich's men without."

Margerite was about to rebuke her for her superstition, but then Eva spoke up from the floor, also crossing herself. "I have heard that as well," the maidservant said in a small voice, her face very pale. "In Passau we say that it is der grimme Hagene, Hagen von Tronje, who leads the Wild Hunt. I knew a girl who said she had seen him riding through the stormclouds, a one-eyed man in a dark cloak, holding the spear he slew Sîvrit with."

"I have never heard such things," Margerite declared stoutly. "Eva, if you have nothing better to think about than unChristian fancies, perhaps you had better put your cat on your pillow to sleep and get back to your sewing. Gerhild, you should not tell Eva things that will frighten her."

The midwife raised a slanted eyebrow at Margerite, but did not argue with her. Gerhild went on spinning in silence, as Eva contritely deposited Kriemhilt on her pallet and went back to her sewing. Margerite tried to apply herself to her embroidery, but the shrieking of the wind outside and its noise through the shutters was beginning to unnerve her, as it had not before.

"I am tired," she said aloud, more in hopes of convincing herself than the other two.

But in spite of her words, Margerite found herself lying awake late into the night, her thoughts swinging from one pole of distress to the next. Ruprecht and the Order... the child she bore...Father Etienne, "Do you love your husband?"...Heinrich's host, Wodan's host, the Wild Hunt outside... When her eyes closed, it was only to toss and turn in half-dozing exhaustion, until at last the gray light of dawn began to glimmer over the still whiteness of the night's snowfall, and Margerite felt her limbs relaxing into true sleep.

Chapter Eight

The winter settled in hard and sharp after Martinmas, gray clouds drifting low over the peak of the mountain behind Burg Falkenstein to drop their heavy burden of snow on the castle and the lands about it. The mountain had taken on a stark beauty, the branches of the pines showing black through their thick coat of snow; the crags of the ravine glinted icy and treacherous above the frozen river below. Around the castle rose little plumes of smoke from Heinrich's fires, their gray trails thinning swiftly into the white swirls of snowflakes on the wind. Between the winter storms, the sun glared brightly from an ice-blue sky, glittering off the snow as if from a thousand fragments of a shattered silver mirror.

Those clear days brought no warmth, but only a sharper frost that sliced through the heaviest furs and wool, and by night the bitter silver light of the stars cut like tiny knives of ice. Ruprecht's prediction had come true, at least in part: as far as those within Burg Falkenstein could tell, the besiegers were suffering worse than the besieged, and, if the winter weather held, it was anyone's guess as to whether Heinrich could keep his army there past January.Deprived of hunting and hawking, forced to share his castle with the watchful Father Etienne, and unable to go to Margerite's bed lest he endanger the precious child in her womb, Ruprecht retreated more and more to his secret quarters beneath Burg Falkenstein.

There, among his alchemical retorts and bubbling stills, his books and the tools of his magic, he found enough to occupy his mind. He was proud of the falcon-necklace he had made as a protection for Margerite, for it was the culmination of several experiments that involved ritually stirring certain herbs and fragments of bone into molten gold, directing their sulphur and mercury, their essence, into the metal along with the little bursts of power released as the salt of their base matter flared up on contact with the hot gold, the last impurities sloughing off into the casting sprue when the melted metal was poured into the mold.

That necklace would serve his wife well, for it would protect her and her child from any beings of the spirit world, whether they stemmed from Above or Below, and also keep her from being scried too closely or influenced by the workings of either Graf Günther, against whom Ruprecht had originally conceived of the gift, or, now, Etienne the Exorcist. Thinking of Father Etienne, Ruprecht shook his head. There was no question that Etienne was a foe of the Order, but he was not one of whom it would be easy to be rid. Ruprecht had several times contemplated the murder of the French priest, and regretfully discarded every plan.

Simply killing him and disposing of his body in the ravine would not have been wise, even in summer when the river, flowing free of ice, could carry a corpse down to sink forever in the Tiefensee. Etienne had too many powerful friends, both in the spiritual and secular worlds, for him to disappear like that, especially when the Bishop of Augsburg had sent him on an official mission of reconciliation. If Ruprecht claimed that the priest had died of sickness, he would have to have witnesses, and that meant magic or poison.

But poison was a chancy thing: even if Ruprecht could get into his own kitchens without arousing suspicion, and order a servant to give a certain dish to Father Etienne, it would be too easy for something to go awry - especially with everyone's bellies half-hungry from siege rations: what if the priest courteously offered Margerite a portion from his plate, as Ruprecht often did when he noticed the beginnings of the drawn grey look of hunger on her face?

If Etienne were an ordinary annoyance, Ruprecht could have directed Cundrîê to bring him one of her evening possets, but he had ordered Cundrîê and Clingschor to stay out of the priest's sight, for the less Father Etienne knew about Ruprecht's resources and connections, the better. As for magic, Father Etienne was as well-warded as anyone Ruprecht had ever seen.

Ruprecht might be able to get through to him, might even be able to destroy him, but it would take a magical battle such as was seldom seen, within or beyond the Order's ranks, and the demons on whom Ruprecht would have to call would endanger himself as much as, or more than, they endangered his foe - not to mention everyone else in Burg Falkenstein.

For a moment Ruprecht toyed with the thought of forbidding Margerite to speak with the priest, perhaps claiming that he suspected Etienne had taken bribes from Graf Heinrich. He doubted, however, that his words would have any effect on her in that regard. On the other hand, she had seemed much colder towards the Frenchman since poor Hans' death: Ruprecht wondered if the two of them had exchanged hard words over that.

The oil in the bronze pot above his brazier's flame was hot now: Ruprecht dropped a tiny piece of dried vervain into it, and the little brown stalk bubbled furiously, skittering from side to side of the pot. Slowly he added the rest of the herbs he had prepared, stirring them in with a long-handled spoon of hazelwood and murmuring an incantation as he stirred. Without Wolfram, he had to do much more of the simplest preparation work for his magics - everything, in fact, that could not be left to Cundrîê and Clingschor.

But that was not altogether ill, for the discipline and concentration it called for made it easier for him to still his mind, silencing the clamour of all the earthly distractions that nagged at his mind. Ruprecht came back to his hidden chambers after the evening meal. Clingschor had strained, bottled, and labelled his oil while he was away. The little bottles gleamed dark on the shelf beside the many other such preparations lined up there, the torchlight glowing amber and ruby and deep green or azure from their depths.

"Bring me shards of lapis, powdered tin, dried hyssop, and my mortar and pestle," Ruprecht commanded Clingschor. "As it is Thursday, I shall work on matters pertaining to Jupiter."

"As you will, Master."

Ruprecht settled himself to his work, crushing the gold-glinting nuggets of deep blue stone between pestle and mortar, then grinding their gritty fragments down further. As he did, he silently meditated on the names, spirits, and correspondences of Jupiter: Bethor, its ruler; tin, its metal; lapis, its stone; hyssop and saffron, its incenses; blue, its colour...with power over honour, over things desired, over riches and apparel, over rulership...

Intent on his work, Ruprecht did not look up until the pigment had been completely ground. When he did, Clingschor was standing before him, waiting patiently.

"Master," he said, his deep bass voice resonating through the stone walls, "Graf Günther's messenger waits outside the door."

"Bring him in at once. When you have done that, fetch him hot spiced wine and prepare the private guest chamber for him with hot stones for his hands and feet, for he will be frozen from his journey." Fires could not be kindled in the hidden guest room lest their smoke be seen by the guards on the walls above the tower, but Ruprecht's lower chambers vented alongside the smithy's fires, where the smoke and smells of his alchemical workings passed unnoticed.

Ruprecht rose, setting his mortar and pestle aside, and followed Clingschor along the stairway that led downward through the lowest chambers and to the door beyond, which opened onto the secret pathway down the ravine. Graf Günther's messenger was muffled up in a hooded cloak of white fur; streaks of wet dirt on the pale fell showed how difficult it had been for him to scramble up the icy ravine path.

Although the way over the crags was not quite as bad as Ruprecht had told Margerite it was, nevertheless it was a hard and perilous way at the best of times, let alone in winter with the snow and slick patches of ice making foot- and hand-holds difficult. The messenger's cloak was humped up over his back, his small pack giving an impression of deformity.

He did not take off the wet furs at once, but stood shivering within the room, blue eyes glancing about at Ruprecht's magical paraphenalia. His face was white with cold, save for the straight scar on his left cheekbone, which stood out pink against the grayish skin.

Cundrîê appeared with two steaming goblets of wine. "Come," Ruprecht said to the messenger. "It is warmer above, and you can sit there in comfort." He led him up to the round room halfway up the guard tower, where Clingschor had already piled thick blankets onto the bed as Ruprecht had ordered. "You must be quiet here, however, for the tower rooms above are manned from the walls: as far as anyone else here knows, these lower rooms are filled with rubble from the building."

"Your welcome is kind, Archbishop," the messenger said, accepting a cloth-wrapped stone from Clingschor and clasping his gloved hands about its warmth. "The way here is not easy."

"If it were, you should not have been able to get in. Now tell me: what tidings do you bear from Order Prince Günther that he could not send me by other means? Is his army marching to break the siege of Burg Falkenstein?"

"His army will march out as soon as it may, for he is mindful of the oaths that lie between you and the fealty that you swore to him, your Prince in the Order. But he says for you to hold out as best as you can, and not expect him too soon, for it will not be an easy journey in this weather."

Ruprecht exhaled thoughtfully, trying not to show any sign of the relief he felt. Yes, Günther had promised him rescue if he needed it, but a man as used to dealing with demons as was the Prince of the Order would be likely to find a way to squirm out of even the most unambiguous oaths, if he so desired.

"That is well. But why did he choose to risk sending a man in person? I know that he does not hold your life to be something easily cast away." Ruprecht knew nothing of the sort, save that Günther would have to look on a messenger of such skill and speed as this man possessed as valuable; but it would not hurt if Günther's servant thought him to be more deeply in the counsels of the Prince than he was in fact.

"Because he has something else for you, which required human hands to deliver." A scatter of melting snow fell from the messenger's furry hood as he cast it back and raised his head, looking about himself like a leithund sniffing for a track. "Are we alone?" He took no notice of Clingschor and Cundrîê, quietly heating water and draping hangings about the walls to block their stony chill.

"We are."

The messenger shrugged off his heavy cloak, wriggling out of his pack. Opening it, he dug through the layers of folded clothes until he found a black silk bag the length of Ruprecht's forearm. "This is the tool which Prince Günther has prepared for the working you must do. He bids me say to you that, since all our efforts to hold back Kaiser Karl from his visitation to Avignon and the campaign he and the Pope are furthering against the Free Companies have failed, there is no choice now but to bring about the Kaiser's death.

For this purpose, a Great Offering must be made precisely at midnight of the Day of the Light-Bearer, when the full depths of the Powers of Darkness can be loosed upon the earth: and to this end all those who wear the rings of amethyst and ruby will be joined in the same rite. Here is the text of the ritual - " he handed Ruprecht a rolled parchment scroll - "and within that bag are the dagger with which you are to make the Offering and a tunic which the Kaiser has worn, to put upon the Offering's body. Your Prince hopes to be with you upon the night, but he warns you that, if he cannot, you must carry out your part yourself successfully, for if any of those who begin the ritual do not complete it properly, the whole will be sure to fail."

"That I still stand here is proof that I do not bungle rites," Ruprecht replied, taking the bag from the messenger. Even through the insulating silk, he could feel the power dormant within, like the germ of life hidden beneath a seed's dark hull. He had not yet taken part in an Order working of such great delicacy and importance, for the difficulty and risk involved in coordinating a far-flung number of magicians so that they could all perform exactly the same rite at exactly the same time was such that the Order only tried collective workings when there was no other choice.

And simply from handling the silk-wrapped dagger, Ruprecht could tell that there would be much preparation needed, both of his chambers and tools and of himself, if he were indeed to carry out the rite successfully - for the least flaw in his working would certainly mean his own death, and worse beyond.

The Advent abstinence began with little notice in Burg Falkenstein. At Gerhild's advice, Margerite had gone to Father Etienne and requested a dispensation from the general abstinence and the Wednesday and Friday fasts on the grounds of her pregnancy, which the priest gave her without question.

Indeed, there were few who had not gotten similar dispensations: as well as the usual exemptions for those performing bodily labour, Father Etienne could not have helped marking that a good portion of Burg Falkenstein's stores consisted of the smoked and salted meats they had put up earlier, while there was little dried fish remaining.

Father Etienne himself, however, kept to the Advent diet, as did Bertram and Eva - and, to Margerite's surprise, Ruprecht: she could only imagine that either his pride or some rule of the Order of Light-Bearers kept him from asking for a dispensation, and he had already shown himself unwilling to overrule Margerite's orders to the kitchen regarding abstinence-foods.

Ruprecht's cup even held water instead of wine, though this he had made a jest of, saying that he was not drinking wine now because he would wish to drink deeply at whatever they could manage for a Christmas feast. Other than his lenience on the matter of diet, Father Etienne's handling of the season was as proper as Margerite had seen.

The Advent wreath in the chapel was a simple twine of ivy pulled from the castle's walls, but its ring of four candles around a central taper was set up as it ought to in the newly cleaned and freshly censed chapel, with one more light to be kindledeach Sunday. Margerite attended not only the Sunday Masses, but those of the saints' days, with a faithfulness sharpened by her guilt about avoiding Father Hans' services.

Even though she could not take Communion, nor meet Father Etienne's eyes when the time came for him to share out the cup of Christ's Blood, it was comforting to her simply to be in a consecrated place and hear the holy words spoken. St. Lucia's Eve, the eve of the longest night of the year, was also the day of one of the worst storms yet. By the time Mass was over, the snow was blowing so thickly across the courtyard that for a moment, Margerite was almost afraid that she would be lost on her way back to the castle door.

Between the storm and the time of year, the day grew dark unnaturally soon; the evening meal was served a little after sunset, and Ruprecht did not even bother to come into the great hall for it, as if he found the bad weather and the uncomfortable company too much to bear.

When she had finished eating, Margerite hurried up the stairs to her own chamber - she was beginning to move more awkwardly now, for she could no longer wear the tight-bodiced dresses from Freiburg and the weight of the child in her swelling belly already threw her balance off slightly.

Eva walked before her, holding the doors open for her. But at the door to Margerite's room, her grip faltered. With a nervous glance towards Margerite, she dived in ahead of her mistress to where Kobolt and Kriemhild were playing with something amid the blankets of her pallet.

At first Margerite thought that the two cats had a mouse or a bug. She was about to tell Eva to leave it alone, and would have if she had not just caught the flicker of the girl's hand hiding something in her skirts.

"What is that you have there?" she asked sternly.

"Frowe Gräfin? It was only the cats."

"You picked something out of the blankets, and I saw you conceal it. Show it to me."

Quailing, Eva brought her hand out again. She held a silver crucifix on a broken chain - the same that Eckhardt had given Gertrude, which Margerite had hidden at the bottom of her own clothes chest, wrapped in a shift, so that nothing more would befall it. But, of course, Eva had plenty of chances to go through the materials there, searching for her mistress' daily wear.

"You stole that from my chest," Margerite accused bluntly.

Eva burst into tears, sinking to her knees. "Please, Frowe Gräfin! I did not mean to steal it, but, but..."

"But you were taking one of my dresses out and it just fell into your bedding."

Eva nodded, blue eyes wild and stricken in her tear-stained face. Coldly angry, Margerite realized that she would be well within her rights to order the girl whipped or branded, and she probably ought to. She snatched the crucifix from Eva's hand, fighting back an urge to strike her across the face with it.

The keen memories of Gertrude that flooded back to Margerite as she held her dead maidservant's treasure should have mollified her wrath, but instead she found that she was only growing angrier. Eva had taken Gertrude's place and her clothes; should she then steal the most precious thing Gertrude had owned?

"Go to Father Etienne, right now!" Margerite ordered. "Find him and confess everything to him - not only your theft, for which you had better be repentant or you will suffer worse punishment than any penance he can give you, but everything you have done since your last Confession."

"Everything, Frowe Gräfin?" Eva asked, her lower lip trembling as though she were about to start weeping again.

"Everything! From the least sin to the greatest, I want you to confess every single thing you have done that keeps you from taking the Sacrament, for your soul had best be clean next Sunday." Even as she spoke, Margerite felt like a hypocrite, for she knew she would not be able to share in Holy Communion alongside her maidservant. But the words were out, and perhaps this would serve as atonement in place of the apology she had never made time to give Eva.

"Now, Frowe Gräfin?"

"Yes, now!"

Eva scrambled to her feet and ran from the room, still weeping. Exhausted as if she had just finished a wild gallop on horseback, Margerite sat down heavily on the bed, folding her hands over the slight bulge of her belly. As Gerhild had predicted, she was feeling better now than she had in the first months of her pregnancy.

Though the craving for raw meat was still upon Margerite, and she grew tired more easily, she was no longer sick in the mornings: in fact, even with the dispensation freeing her from the Advent abstinence, it was a struggle to keep herself from grossly outstripping her fair share of the daily food ration whenever she had the chance.

"You are a hungry little creature, Wolfram," she said to the child within her. It seemed to her as though she could feel her son moving within her, perhaps pressing against the wall of her womb with a little hand or foot. "Perhaps I shall lie down and rest for a while."

Margerite settled herself under the blankets, but the two cats were of a different mind. Kriemhilt dug her little claws into the coverlets, pulling herself up onto the bed and walking up to start licking every bit of Margerite's exposed face she could reach. When Margerite groaned and turned over, pulling the blankets over her head, the wind was nearly driven out of her by Kobolt landing hard on her ribs.

Sighing, she got up again, picking up one cat under each arm. "Go catch mice in the storeroom, or do something else useful, but leave me alone," she said to them, putting them outside the chamber and closing the door firmly, then locking it. It would do Eva no harm to meditate on her sins for a little while when she finished her confession, and Margerite was tired of being bothered.

Father Etienne sat at his table beneath the window, ink, pens, and a piece of parchment before him. He rubbed his thin hands together to warm them, glancing regretfully at the cold stove. After he declared that he was staying, the Graf had ceased sending servants up with fuel for it: a sensible enough decision, since only the Gräfin, by virtue of her pregnancy, was allowed a personal fire, but one that still grated a little, since it seemed to have been made out of spite rather than prudence with the besieged castle's supplies.

Etienne tried to dip the point of his pen into the ink, then frowned again. A film of ice had formed over the dark surface, cracking away in watery blue shards. He put the top back onto the bottle, and was shaking it vigorously when he heard the tap at his door.

Eva was outside, her eyes red and swollen and a smudge across her left cheek as though she had been trying to wipe away tears with an unwashed hand. "Father Etienne?" she whispered, trembling violently.

"Come in," Etienne told her. "What do you wish, my child?"

"Father, she...the Gräfin, she told me to come to you and confess."

"What do you have to confess, child?"

"Everything," Eva whimpered. "She told me to confess everything, and the Graf told me that I must obey her."

Father Etienne settled himself in his chair. After a little hesitation, Eva knelt in front of him. "What are your sins, Eva?"

"I stole a silver crucifix from her clothes chest!" the girl wailed. "I would not have taken it, but I was so afraid of what she would do to me, and the Graf...It was just silver, like a rich peasant might have, and I thought it would be nothing to her, when she has so much gold to wear. I only took it last night, because I had gotten so frightened. I had it hidden in my bedclothes, and the cats found it."

"Why did you think you needed the crucifix?" Etienne asked patiently, his heart already beating faster within his breast. If he were right, this might be the moment of crisis: if he could get Eva to confide in him, tell him what the Graf and Gräfin were doing with her, he might have enough knowledge to do something. Thought Before Action, Father Etienne reminded himself, glancing at his signet ring: it was his family motto, and one that had always served him well in his career as an exorcist.

"Because of them! They threatened me with demons; he said his demons would crawl inside my ribs and eat my heart, and she said that she would have my skin whipped from my back. And he said last night that he wanted me to fast completely today, and he makes me take a bath prepared by that woman every night, and I am afraid of what they are going to do to me."

Father Etienne breathed deeply, trying to make sense of Eva's blurtings. "The Gräfin prepares a bath for you?"

"No! That woman Cundrîê, the Graf's servant, and her brother Clingschor. They are frightful creatures, and they are always watching me when I am down below the castle. He told me not to speak of it to anyone, but she ordered me to confess everything, and he said that she is higher in the Order than he is."

Etienne rose, taking his bottle of aqua vitae and pouring a small cupful for Eva. He did not pour any for himself, for he wanted to have his head clear, and the Advent diet was not the best grounding for strong liquor.

"Drink this," he told her. "Sip carefully, for it may seem very strong to you, but it will calm you down."

Eva brought it towards her mouth, then shook her head as the fumes hit her. "He says I am not to have wine, nor even ale, until he says so, for we must purify ourselves. And if I do, Clingschor and Cundrîê will smell it upon me, and then the Graf will kill me. And he told me to fast today," she repeated.

Father Etienne nodded: as soon as he had noticed that Ruprecht was no longer eating meat, he had suspected that the Graf was preparing himself for some potent rite. Eva might be helper, or sacrifice...but why was the Gräfin not abstaining as well? Did her pregnancy simply disqualify her for whatever work they were performing? The day of total fasting suggested to him that the ritual, whatever it might be, would take place that night - and it was the eve of St. Lucia, the Lightbearer, which the Order held to be the night on which their power was strongest.

"What are you purifying yourself for?"

"I do not know," Eva confessed. "He has taken some of my blood for it, but I do not know why, or what he is doing with it. The Abbess never told me either."

"Tell me about this," Etienne encouraged softly.

Under his gentle prodding, Eva's tale slowly emerged. The Abbess had been using her as a virgin disciple in her magics - virgin in that she had never had congress with men, nor had her maidenhead been breached, though the Abbess had taken advantage of the maiden in some of the other ways practiced between female Order members. Eva told Father Etienne of the hidden staircase running from Ruprecht's chamber to his magical study below, repeating the words the Graf had spoken to her upon her arrival at Burg Falkenstein - from the way her low voice changed as she spoke, approximating Ruprecht's tone and timbre as well as a maiden's could, Etienne had little doubt that she was remembering accurately.

"Then you should know that the Gräfin is set higher in the Order than I, though that is known by only the fewest, and she wears no ring for the sake of secrecy. She is cold-hearted and cruel, and would have no qualms about having you slowly torn to pieces with red-hot irons if she so chose."

"Is that true?" Father Etienne asked. If Ruprecht had lied to Eva, if Margerite were not one of Lucifer's willing servants, but an unknowing pawn of her husband...suddenly a number of the small strangenesses he had noticed about the Gräfin were beginning to fall together into shape, like a disordered collection of coloured glass beginning to form a saint's image under the hands of a cathedral window-maker.

"Father, I do not know. The Gräfin often speaks sharply to me, and she threatened to whip me once, but she has been kind otherwise. She even gave me one of Kobolt's kittens for my own. I was afraid of the kitten at first, because the Graf told me that the Gräfin's cat was a demon familiar like the Abbess', and I thought it would steal my soul, but she is the sweetest little kitty. And I think Kobolt is not much like the Abbess' black cat, because I have to clean it up when he empties his bowels in the corner or sprays, and the Abbess' cat never did that."

Father Etienne thought about that a moment, then put it away for further consideration. "While you are making your confession to me, Eva, have you any other sins burdening your soul?"

"I used to steal food in the convent, because the Abbess kept me on an abstinence diet all year 'round, and there were many weeks when I was supposed to fast before her workings. I would not have done it, but I was so very hungry. At home I was allowed to eat when and as I pleased, and then the plague took my parents, and my cousin Wachholt sent me…there, and I did not have another decent meal, except for what I stole, until I came to Burg Falkenstein."

Eva's back had straightened unconsciously as she spoke, shoulders squaring and head held more proudly. For the first time, Etienne could see the young noblewoman beneath the frightened-rabbit display of the maidservant; and for the first time, as well, he noticed that Eva was not the child he had thought her to be, but a solidly built and swiftly-growing young woman.

"Do you repent of your thefts?"

"Oh, yes. I did not want to do it," Eva insisted. "Father, am I guilty of gluttony as well?" She cowered down again, as if she had just noticed her own change in demeanour, and Etienne raised an eyebrow to himself, for now, though he was looking straight at her, he would almost have sworn again that she was an undersized girl of eleven or twelve whose breasts had not yet budded. But no wonder she has learned to hide her womanhood, after her time with the Abbess, he thought.

"Gluttony is the excessive love of food, not the feeding of a natural hunger. Theft is both a crime and a sin, for which restitution ought to be made, but you can hardly pay the convent back for the food you took, and the Abbess is at least partly to blame, for placing demands on you that you were not fit to fulfill. As your penance, when the Gräfin will allow you time to yourself, you shall spend it in making sure that the Tiefensee folk are getting their share of the daily rations, and helping those who are infirm to claim and prepare their food. As for your theft from the Gräfin..." Etienne paused. "How did you say she discovered the crucifix?"

"Kobolt and Kriemhilt had found it in my blankets and were playing with it."

"She has lost nothing, save her trust in you, if she has it back now, and by following her orders, you have made the restitution she required." And perhaps a far greater one, Etienne thought to himself, for a fragile bud of hope was beginning to green in his heart. "For the other things you have done...do you truly regret them?"

"I do." Eva straightened her shoulders again. "If I did not, I would not have sought a crucifix to protect me."

"And you will not willingly engage in black magic again, if you ever did it by choice?"

"Not willingly, Father."

"Then I absolve you of all your sins. As your penance, you shall do what I have prescribed for you already, and you shall also help in the daily cleaning and ordering of the chapel, that you may do willingly for Christ what you did unwillingly for His Enemy."

"Gladly, Father."

"Then go forth, and sin no more. And be careful tonight, above all nights: do not go anywhere at the Graf's bidding. Wait." Etienne paused. "There is one more thing I want you to do for me. Can you catch the Gräfin's cat and bring him to me - preferably in a closed basket or box - without her knowing?"

"Yes, Father. You are not going to harm him, are you?"

"If he is a demon, he must be exorcized from this place before he can cause more harm."

"I suppose so," said Eva, but she sounded unhappy.

"Eva, keep in mind that evil often seems harmless, even fair: otherwise few would fall to temptation. If a demon appears well-tempered and friendly, it is merely concealing its nature in order to deceive and destroy those mortals with whom it deals."

Eva nodded. "Yes, Father. I will bring Kobolt to you. Do you want my little Kriemhilt as well?" she added bravely, though her voice was trembling.

"It will depend on what passes with her father. If the one cat is a demon, the other is likely to be as well."

"Poor little Kriemhilt, who suckles broth from my fingers... Yes, Father, I know. I will give her to you if you say I must."

"Perhaps it will not be necessary. Go on, now. I would carry out my examination as soon as I may."

By the time Eva returned with a yowling basket over her arm, Father Etienne had cleared away the straw and strewing herbs from the middle of the floor and chalked circle and triangle upon the stones, the protective names of God lettered within in his finest Hebrew calligraphy. Inside the circle, he had all his exorcist's paraphenalia - censer, bell, book, and candle, and holy water - as well as his scrying crystal, wand, and dagger.

"Put the cat there, and withdraw," Etienne ordered the girl. As Eva bent to deposit the basket, a black paw snaked out from under the lid, clawing the fastening open. The cat sprang out, tufted ears laid flat against his head and golden eyes blazing. He ran frantically about the room; leaping onto the table and from there to the bed, the kick of his powerful back legs sending the bottle of half-frozen ink flying to crash against the wall. Standing on Father Etienne's pillow, he crouched, his tail jerking, and stinking yellow liquid spattered the bedclothes.

Father Etienne did not curse, for he knew the power of careless words, but he grabbed the tomcat by the scruff of the neck, avoiding the raking of his hooked claws. Stuffing the cat roughly back into the basket, he plunked the basket down in the middle of the triangle. "There," he panted. "You shall not get out of that."

The cat yowled, and the basket's walls shook with the violence of his struggle within, but Etienne ignored it. "You might take those..." he gestured at his fouled bedclothes... "to be washed, and see that new ones are brought to me this evening, though not before, for this may take some time."

When Eva was gone, Father Etienne spent a little time collecting himself before he stepped into his circle, closed the ring with his wand, and began to pray and cense about himself. As he was doing that, the lid of the basket flew open again, the cat standing up on his hind legs with his paws on the rim and hissing at the priest.

His preliminary prayers and invocations completed, Etienne lifted the crucifix from about his neck, holding it before the triangle. "If thou art a spirit unclean, owing allegiance to Lucifer or any beings of the Infernal Depths, let this holy sign constrain and compell thee to depart."

The cat glared at him.

"O thou creature, as thou hast come here from Hell, and labour in the service of those who dwell there, I conjure thee by this curse. That thou shalt be accursed, damned, and eternally reproved, and tormented with perpetual pain, so that thou mayst find no repose by night nor by day, nor for a single moment of time, if thou obeyst not immediately the constraints of Him Who maketh the Universe to tremble; by these Names, and in virtue of these Names, the which being named and invoked all creatures obey and tremble with fear and terror, these Names which can turn aside lightning and thunder; and which will utterly make you to perish, destroy, and banish you. These names then are ALEPH, BETH, GIMEL, DALETH, HE, VAU, ZAYIN, CHETH, TETH, YOD, KAPH, LAMED, MEM, NUN, SAMEKH, AYIN, PE, TZADDI, QOPH, RESH, SHIN, TAU. By these secret Names, therefore, and by these signs which are full of Mysteries, I shall curse thee, and in virtue of the power of the Three Principles, ALEPH, MEM, SHIN, I shall deprive thee of all office and dignity which thou mayst have enjoyed up till now; and by their virtue and power I shall relegate thee into a lake of sulphur and of flame, and unto the deepest depths of the Abyss, that thou mayst burn there eternally forever. By this power I conjure thee: depart now, returning to that place from whence thou camest, and return never again to this world, lest thou be cast into the lake of unquenchable fire and destroyed altogether. By the holy names of God: YOD HE VAU HE, SHADDAI, ADONAI, EHIEH ASHER EHIEH! I command thee, spirit of Hell, to obey me and depart without doing harm to any."

The cat's head disappeared beneath the rim of the basket. Peering closer, Etienne saw that, rather than sinking away as he had expected, the tom had lifted one leg and was diligently licking his substantial privates.

Etienne swung the censer towards him, sending a cloud of smoke into the triangle. The cat sneezed twice, then hissed again, flicking his ears as Father Etienne sprinkled a few drops of holy water over him.

The priest paused, nonplussed for almost the first time in his long career as an exorcist. He had never seen a demon who, captured and constrained as the black tomcat was, could ignore all the things he had done so blithely.

"What are you?" Etienne said softly. "What is your power?"

The cat looked up and yawned at him. For a moment, Etienne almost wondered if it were an ordinary cat - but an earthly beast would not have been held by the triangle. And a demon would be gone by now, or at least struggling against him, and would not have played blithely - if Eva's account were correct - with a crucifix.

"We shall see," Etienne said, as much to himself as to the cat. Again he remembered the words of Meister Stefan, from one of his earliest lessons. Etienne, you know of the spirits of Heaven and Hell. But do not forget that there are many others, who serve neither your God nor your Satan; there are other gods and other beings in the universe. Some of the mightiest of these are remembered only in legends of early days and old women's stories.

Though they live in their strength yet, they wait, half-hidden, for another turning of the world, when they may be honoured as they were before; but it will be long before that comes to pass. And some are spirits dwelling in earthly homes, in trees or rocks or springs; and these are often fed and worshipped under the names of saints. The Elements have their own powers: Salamanders of Fire, Sylphs of Air, Undines of Water, and Kobolts of Earth...

"Kobolt!" he said aloud: Eva had given the cat that name. The tom looked up at him, his flattened ears pricking up again.

Slowly Etienne raised his scrying crystal, gazing at the cat through its glassy-clear facets. At first he saw only the dark shadows inside the half-uncovered basket, and the pair of golden eyes looking out of the blackness. Then his sight began to blur in the familiar way that meant the vision was coming on him. As always, he had to discipline himself not to beat down the dizzy spinning in his head or let it overwhelm him, but to let it lift him up, to ride on its power without being overcome.

Although it was still a cat in shape, Etienne could see the deep green glow around the Kobolt now; its eyes gleamed like gold on black earth, and it seemed to him that a faint shimmer of pale green, like a shadow of leaves budding and unfolding, overlaid its form. As he looked at it, his sense of space seemed to shift: the creature might have been three times his own size, or small as a housefly, or both at once.

It did not speak to him in words, as a conjured elemental might have, but the sense he felt from it was clear. His prayers and incantations were an annoying jangle in its ears; the consecrated incense made it sneeze; and it hated being confined here when...vague sense of a mouse's guts laid bloodily open, the sweetness of a saucer of milk, and a hot urgency of the loins that made Etienne blush, thankful that he had sent Eva away.

"Kobolt," he said, "how did you come here?"

Another vague impression: Ruprecht holding the leash of something black and stinking that pulled aside the bar of a heavy door; a shaft of light through a clear passage; and then, as brightly as if she stood before him, the face of the Gräfin. That last vision broke into another cascade of senses - sweet milk suckled from a furry breast, the feeling of his head and back being stroked, and again, the overwhelming urge pounding in his loins.

Etienne threw back his head and laughed, both to break the link and because he had realized what had happened. There were many demons who could bring familiar spirits: Ruprecht must have summoned one, hoping to corrupt Margerite. But the demon had been cleverer than the Graf, and deliberately fetched, not another servant of Hell, but...a Kobolt, who could serve as Margerite's familiar, but might not do the will of Ruprecht or his superiors in the Order.

The Kobolt climbed out of the basket, miaowing plaintively and pawing at the inner line of the triangle that held him. Etienne reached in, lifting him through the barrier. He hung limply in the priest's arms. To his own surprise, Etienne found that he was scratching the Kobolt behind his ears, and the creature was purring raspily to him.

"Come, sir," he said to it. "We have much to explain to your frowe." For the priest was sure now that the crisis would soon be cresting, and Margerite, and the child beneath her breast, were in at least as much danger as Eva - if not physically, then spiritually.

Father Etienne knocked on Margerite's door. "Who is it?" the Gräfin's voice came weakly from within.

"Canon Etienne. I must speak with you at once."

Etienne heard the sound of the key turning in the lock, then the door opened. The Gräfin's face was very white, little wisps of hair sticking up from her crown of braids. Although her belly was just beginning to swell noticeably beneath the dark velvet folds of her skirt, she had the puffy look about the face and swollen shadows beneath the eyes that pregnant women often got when their carrying was going hard.

"Come in, Father," she said nervously. "Is this about Eva's confession?"

"Eva's confession is a matter for herself and God." Etienne lifted up the Kobolt, who squirmed until the priest settled him into a more comfortable position. "Do you know what this is?"

"A tomcat. Father, he did not soil your room, did he?" By the anxious note in her voice, Etienne guessed that the Kobolt had done such things before.

"He did, actually. But he is not a cat. How did you come by him?"

"He was there when I awoke on the morning after my wedding. Everyone here seemed to think that I had brought him with me, and I was happy enough to keep him by me, for he loves me dearly and there have been times when he was my only comfort."

"I am sure of that," Etienne said, remembering the feelings that had come along with the Kobolt's vision of Margerite.

"What do you mean by saying he is not a cat?"

Etienne held up a hand to forestall her recitation of the Kobolt's catly behaviour. "You need not fear, for he is not a demon either, though it is only by the malice the servants of Hell bear to one another that you have been spared that. He was brought by a demon to be your familiar in your magics, but he is an earth spirit - a Kobolt, just as you have named him."

"My magics? What do you mean, Father? I practise no magic."

"Never? What of that necklace you wear?"

Margerite's hand went to the gem-eyed falcon upon her breast. "It was a present from Ruprecht when he knew that I was with child. I thought he had chosen it because I love falconry, and because..." The Gräfin's eyes widened, her face paling further. It seemed to Father Etienne that she was not looking at him, but past him, into some abyss of misty memory.

"Father, I have not practised magic, but I have dreamed. I dreamed of being a falcon." She stopped, taking the Kobolt from his arms with the slow movement of a sleepwalker as she looked deeply into its golden eyes. Father Etienne could not sense what was passing between them, but he knew that something was. He waited, silent, until Margerite drew a long shuddering breath and spoke again. "I had forgotten my dreams until now: but I flew forth from here, with Ruprecht whispering in my ear, and in those flights I looked down to see where armies were camped and where they were moving - I even overheard Graf Heinrich and his sons speaking within Burg Fürstensee. And in the last dream, I saw..." She went on to recount her vision of the death of her former maidservant, in detail that left no doubt in Father Etienne's mind as to what she had seen. As to the ritual Ruprecht had performed there, that would be of grievous moment later, but for now there was no time to waste, if he were to be stopped from doing whatever he had planned for that night.

"This is to do with the Order of Light-Bearers, is it not?" Margerite asked. Etienne almost smiled, for she had saved him a great deal of explanation. Still, it left another question.

"How do you know about the Order?"

"Bertram told me. He is their foe, and has been watching them in disguise for some years."

Another piece fell into place within Etienne's mind, and he did smile now, though sadly. It would be well for Margerite if the child whose father she did not know had been begotten by Bertram, bastard or not. But the matter to hand was more important, and it would be well to have a proven fighter beside them, if they were to beard Ruprecht in his lair: as a youth, Etienne had gotten the schooling in arms that every young man of noble birth had, and he could defend himself well enough with the slim sword at his side, but he knew better than to think that he could stand against a fully-trained knight.

"I shall bring Bertram here. Eva has taken my bedding away to have the Kobolt's blessing washed from it, but when she comes back here, do not let her leave again. And take that necklace off, for I do not know what charms Ruprecht might have laid into it besides the one that protects you from being scried, and I cannot tell without more time to look at it."

But when the Gräfin tried to lift the strand of gleaming beads from her neck, the Kobolt miaowed, hooking it with one paw and tugging it back down. Father Etienne wavered for a moment, then shrugged. "Perhaps it were best if you left it on for now, then. But be careful, and ready to remove it swiftly if you must. Wait here: I shall be back with Bertram shortly."

Margerite paced about her chamber for a few moments, twisting her hands together. She was frightened, but also beginning to feel a rising tingle of excitement: the priest had given her her first hope of being able to do something about the horrors that had haunted her since Gertrude's death. As she walked, Kriemhilt scampered behind her, pouncing at the hem of her skirt, then sinking her claws into the velvet and beginning to scramble up Margerite's leg. She stopped, disentangling the kitten and lifting her up.

Kriemhilt squirmed in her hands, then began to miaow pathetically. Margerite put the kitten down on the bed, but she kept crying, crawling about on the blanket and raising her head as though she were looking for something.

"What is it?" Margerite asked her. "Is it Eva? Has something happened to her?" Kriemhilt let out a piercing cry, a sound that seemed too loud to come from her small furry body.

Margerite strode out into the corridor and opened Gerhild's door. The midwife was bent over mortar and pestle, muttering something under her breath; the wiry muscles of her forearms bulged in narrow cords along their bones as she crushed the hard pieces of dried root in her bowl. "Gerhild," Margerite said, "will you do something for me? Eva has taken Father Etienne's bedding to be cleaned, and she is being rather long about it. Would you see if you can find her?"

In the shadows of the candlelight, Gerhild's triangular face looked much older, the slanting planes of her cheeks and narrow jaw hard as polished wood. "Have you no other servants that you can send on such a mission?" the midwife asked.

"Call it a pregnant woman's fancy, if you will, but, with this storm raging and all, I am frightened for her."

Gerhild muttered something under her breath that Margerite could not quite hear, although it might have been something like, you will not speak so scornfully of unChristian fancies another time. "I will look for her, then," she said, getting up. "Perhaps you should go back to bed and sleep, if you have nothing better to think about."

Margerite did not argue with the rebuke, but only nodded meekly and went back to her room, where Kriemhilt was still mewing piteously, in spite of Kobolt's attempts to quiet her by holding her down with a big paw and washing her ear.

Thankfully, it was not long before Bertram, fully armed and armoured, came in, with Father Etienne behind him. Bertram's steel cap and chain-mail coif hid most of his face, but his hazel eyes gleamed from the shadows beneath his helmet-rim, bright with an excitement that Margerite had never seen in him. With his beard pressed down and largely covered, he looked younger, as well - almost like the image of himself Margerite had been cherishing in her memory. She longed to run to him and embrace him, but this was no time for such things.

"Eva is not back yet?" Etienne said.

"No. I have sent Gerhild looking for her, because…" Margerite felt stupid saying it, but she thought she must. "Because the kitten Kobolt gave her is so agitated, I became afraid."

Father Etienne's dark brows lowered, his face growing stern. "You were wise. It is still some time until midnight, but we must find Eva and confront Ruprecht before then, for - I know enough of Order magic to be sure of it - that is the hour at which his working, whatever it may be, is sure to be consummated."

"We will need someone else with us," Bertram said bluntly. "Even if Ruprecht is fully armed, I believe that I can meet him, but there are those two servants of his, Cundrîê and Clingschor, and he may be able to summon other aid as well."

Father Etienne touched the hilt of his sword, frowning, then nodded. "Who do you trust? Wait: although Jochanan the alchemist is not of our faith, I think we may ask him to stand by us in this. He is not much of a warrior, but his knowledge may be of use."

"And if Jochanan is with us, I think Paul the Bear will stand beside us as well," Bertram told him. "I had thought of him before, and if you are right, the need is great enough to take the risk. At worst, he can only refuse."

"Yes: if Ruprecht has gone to his hidden chambers already, Paul will hardly be able to warn him, unless we have all seriously misjudged the man. So be it."

A knock sounded on the door. All three of them jumped.

"Frowe Gräfin?" Even through the heavy wood, Margerite could hear the strain in Gerhild's voice. "Eva is nowhere in the castle. Would you like me to search for her outside?"

Margerite glanced questioningly at Etienne, who shook his head, making a sharp, palm-down gesture as if to suggest she should order the midwife to stay.

"No. Wait in your chamber, and listen for her coming back. If she does, do not let her leave again."

"As you wish, Frowe Gräfin."

There was no answer when they knocked on the door of Paul's chamber. Margerite searched through the keys on her belt, unlocking it. The room was dark and cold, as though no candle had been lit there that evening; and, thinking back to supper, Margerite thought the mercenary commander had been talking with his gunner when they left the great hall.

"They may both be in Jochanan's tower," she said. "Let us hurry there."

The storm had grown worse since nightfall. Margerite clung to Bertram's arm for support against the driving winds, secure in the knowledge that, between the darkness and the howling whirls of snow, no one would be able to see her holding onto the Hauptmann. Their trek across the courtyards seemed endless, slipping on the hard-packed snow beneath the drifts of fresh fall that reached as high as Margerite's knees, finding their way through the blinding darkness, between the Tiefenseers' lean-tos and tents that ringed the inside of the wall, by memory and touch alone, until at last they came to the guard-tower where Jochanan lived and made his gunpowder.

The door was locked; Bertram banged on it with his fist in frustration, roaring, "Let us in! Paul, Jochanan, God rot your black arses, let us in! Forgive me, Margerite," he added swiftly, as if he had just heard the sound of his own words. "I am so used to talking to soldiers in a certain way…"

"I understand," Margerite answered, smiling fleetingly up at him. The door opened.

"What brings you out tonight?" Paul asked, looking quizzically at the three of them. "Have you come to celebrate St. Lucia's Eve with a drop from Jochanan's still?" He lifted the goblet in his hand as if to demonstrate.

"There is a much graver matter at hand," Father Etienne said, stepping forward. "Let us in, and we shall tell you about it. Is anyone besides Jochanan in there with you?"

"No."

They followed Paul up the stairs. Passing the first level of the tower, the reek of gunpowder was so strong that Margerite could hardly breathe, its sulfurous stench overlaid with the sharp scent of alcohol and other things that Margerite could not identify. But Jochanan's quarters above were warmer, heated by the charcoal fire burning beneath the bubbling copper- and glassware of his still and by the small enclosed oven under a shuttered arrow-slit, from the vent of which steam was gently rising.

On Jochanan's table was a seven-branched candelabra, though only two of the candles were lit. The alchemist's stained clothes were scattered over the floor like heaps of strewing herbs, interspersed with battered and much-scraped and -inked pieces of parchment, and the wooden plate in front of him was crusted with what looked like the remains of several meals.

Jochanan himself was dressed in his dark blue robe and a stained and tattered pair of fur-lined boots. His clothes were smeared with soot, and he had a dark smudge along one heavy cheekbone, as though he had absent-mindedly wiped a dirty hand across his face. Nevertheless, despite the mess and the smells from gunpowder and whatever alchemical concoctions Jochanan was working on, Margerite felt comfortable at once in the chamber - more so than she had felt anywhere in the castle except for Father Etienne's room. Margerite had not seen Kobolt come in, but the cat leapt onto the table in a shower of melted snow, sticking his muzzle into the little mug in front of Jochanan and lapping enthusiastically at the contents. Jochanan backed away, flapping his sleeves at Kobolt.

"Get away, cat! That is freshly distilled medicinal Branntwein, and not for you."

"Nor for you this night," Father Etienne said grimly. Jochanan stopped his futile effort to drive Kobolt away, his craggy features going serious as he heard the tone in the priest's voice. "Paul, put your cup down, for there may soon be fighting."

Paul banged his goblet down on the table and scooped his helm up from the floor. "What is it? Heinrich cannot be assaulting in this weather."

"No. It is a battle within the castle, not without."

"Traitors?" Jochanan asked.

"Quite possibly," Etienne said, almost smiling at his own irony. "Ourselves - for the life, and perhaps the soul, of a well-born maiden."

"What do you mean?" said Paul.

"Graf Ruprecht is a pracitioner of black magic. At midnight tonight he will carry out a ritual which may well cost the Gräfin's maidservant her life, unless he is stopped. The three of us mean to stop him, and we want your help, for we know that he is not alone and we do not know what else he may be able to call to aid him."

The Bear's eyes bulged comically, but Jochanan's dark face only grew graver, as though Etienne had simply confirmed his own suspicions. "I thought there was something..." he murmured, then pointed. "Straight north of here, on the far side of the castle, isn't it?"

Father Etienne nodded.

"I knew there was a disturbance to the north because nothing from that quarter would work quite right for me since I came here," Jochanan explained. "I tried to scry it, but..." the colour of his cheeks darkened slightly... "I had not gotten past the smithy when I bumped into the bowl I was using and spilt all the water. Things like that happen to me all the time," he added apologetically. "Rebbe Avram never really wanted to teach me, for fear I would bungle a word at the wrong moment."

"Sensible enough of him," Etienne snapped impatiently. "Nevertheless, you are here, and there is not more time to waste. Will the two of you come with us, or not?"

"Against our employer?" Paul said.

"I am your employer as well," Margerite broke in. "And if Eva dies, and you could have helped but did not, I will hold it to your account."

The Bear put his helmet on. "I must be mad," he muttered, shaking his head. "But for your sake, Frowe Gräfin, and because I trust Jochanan and Bertram, I will fight for you."

"Thank you!" Margerite said, clasping one of his calloused hands in both of her own. Paul patted her awkwardly on the shoulder, as he would have patted a young soldier. "I must be mad," he mumbled again.

After a flury of frantic rustling, Jochanan finally found his helm, falchion, and cloak. He picked up the short spear standing by the door as well, and the five of them trooped out.

The path Etienne, Bertram, and Margerite had broken from the castle was already hidden in the drifting snow. The wind was blowing straight into their faces as if to drive them away from Burg Falkenstein, flinging Margerite's hood back from her head and tearing at her braided crown. She could feel the wind-tears trailing into ice at the corners of her eyes; the rest of her face was numbed beyond pain. If it had not been for Bertram supporting her on one side and Jochanan bearing her up on the other, she would have fallen into the snow a number of times; but she would have crawled through the drifts on hands and knees before giving up now.

The guards at the castle door, seeing the three armed men, sprang to attention. "Is an attack under way, Hauptmann?" one asked. "Should I sound the alarm?"

"No. Stay, and guard."

The five of them hurried up the dark stairs to the top floor. The guard at the head of the staircase stepped forward to block them, then, recognising Margerite, stepped back with a salute.

"Go downstairs," Margerite ordered him. "There is no need for you here tonight." He looked at her dubiously, but did as she commanded.

Kriemhilt was sitting before Ruprecht's door, yowling as if her little heart were breaking. "Wait," Etienne said breathlessly. "I must fetch something." He ran down the corridor, was back almost moments later with a clattering bag and a large yellow candle in his hand.

The door to Ruprecht's room was locked. Margerite fumbled desperately through her keys, realizing in a moment that there was none on the iron ring that would fit his lock.

"Let me, Frowe Gräfin," Jochanan said. He drew a piece of stiff wire out of his belt-pouch and crouched down; Etienne held the candle to light his work. The lock clicked softly, and the door swung open.

Ruprecht's chamber was almost severely tidy, save for the book open on the table and the two mastiffs sprawling on the bed. Margerite held her breath in fear lest the hounds should attack. Paul and Jochanan must have been thinking the same, for Paul's sword was halfway out of his scabbard and Jochanan held his spear ready to jab; but Mark only raised his head to greet Margerite with a quiet woof before he dropped it onto his paws again.

"Where is the passage?" Bertram asked. Father Etienne bit his lip, his face paling.

"The seal of Confession..." he murmured, as though he had just remembered something dreadful. And if Eva had told the priest how to get to Ruprecht's chambers in her Confession, he could not reveal what he knew!

Margerite glanced about the room. The horn she had given Ruprecht hung above his bed; other than that, the only ornament was the large hunting tapestry covering the northern wall. As she looked at it, it shivered suddenly: Kobolt darted out from behind it, then stood up to sharpen his claws on the thick-woven fabric. Quickly Margerite pulled the tapestry aside, sighing in relief when she saw the door behind it. "Jochanan?"

Jochanan set to work on this lock as well, but it proved harder: his wire and the small pick he produced from his bag twisted and bent beneath the iron curves within, and the lock did not yield. At last he straightened, putting his tools back and muttering, "I hope this works."

The gunner set both his hands on the lock, staring intently at it. Margerite did not understand the words he spoke - she supposed they were Hebrew - but when she looked out of the corner of her eye, it seemed to her that she could see a faint orange glow shifting about the lock.

Something clicked within the door, then clicked again. Jochanan pushed, but the door was stuck tight.

"Try your picks again," Father Etienne ordered. This time the door swung open, revealing a staircase spiraling down into darkness. The priest handed Margerite his candle. "This should keep you safe, as much as anything may," he murmured.

Bertram and Paul, their blades drawn, took the lead, with Jochanan and Margerite behind them; Father Etienne, his slender sword in his right hand and a pale rod of polished wood in his left, guarded the rear. The candleflame quivered in Margerite's hand. She felt all her nerves drawn up within her like the strings of a lute tuned near to breaking point; she knew that she was moving clumsily, for she could feel the weight of her child swinging within her belly as if she were only days from birthing, throwing her off-balance. Once Jochanan's foot slipped on an uneven step, the butt of the alchemist's spear clattering loudly on the stairs as he recovered his balance, and Margerite nearly screamed at the sound.

"Quiet!" Etienne hissed from behind.

The staircase led down into a long corridor. Margerite sniffed: she thought she could smell smoke and scorched metal. They must be...behind the smithy now: the stairs had not gone far enough to take them underground.

A light suddenly flared up in the darkness ahead of them, the torch's flame shining from an ugly pale face. Clingschor or Cundrîê: Margerite was not sure which until the dark figure stepped forward, speaking in Cundrîê's clear soprano voice.

"What do you wish here? The Graf is not to be disturbed."

Bertram pressed on towards her, Paul keeping pace at his side. "Stand aside, old woman."

With a horrible shriek, Cundrîê sprang towards him, thrusting with her torch. The curved blade of a knife glinted in her hand. Bertram kept his blade beween them: Margerite thought Cundrîê would spit herself upon it, but the sword glided harmlessly past her black silken robes as she swung the torch at Bertram's helmet, thrusting underhanded with her knife in the same motion. Bertram's sword blocked the torch, knocking it flaming from her hand; the tip of her blade shrieked across an iron plate.

Bertram brought his sword down again in a stroke that should have cleaved neatly between Cundrîê's neck and shoulderblade. The old woman staggered beneath the force of his blow, grunting again as he drove the point of his sword in beneath her ribcage. Bent forward over Bertram's blade, Cundrîê's bony arms gleamed white beneath her sleeves: she struck again, her knife slicing into the leather between the iron plates armouring Bertram's body.

Bertram's sword hit her knife-arm, knocking it aside; but no blood showed on Cundrîê's pale skin. He dropped his blade, leaping forward and trying to grapple with her. She evaded him, dodging back with the unnatural agility of a cat.

"After her!" Paul shouted, pounding down the corridor with Bertram beside him. Cundrîê backed up swiftly, dodging beneath a narrow stone archway. Paul was in behind her in a moment, Bertram following. Margerite snatched up Cundrîê's fallen torch before it could gutter out, running heedlessly in after the combatants.

The flames of torch and candle swung wildly in the winds of running and fighting, their flickering, distorted shadows showing a battle out of nightmare. Paul was fighting Clingschor, but the old man had gotten in too close for the Bear to swing his sword; Paul's arm was drawn back, and he was jabbing frantically at Clingschor's dark-robed body, trying to fend off the vicious swipes of the old man's sickle-bladed knife with his left hand.

Bertram was trying to come to grips with Cundrîê, who kept dodging his grasp and swinging at him with her own knife, her blade-hand blurring in the torchlight. Jochanan elbowed Margerite roughly aside, thrusting at Cundrîê with his spear. She avoided the point easily, darting past Bertram's side, and again Margerite heard the screech of knife on iron.

A hoarse rattle followed, and Margerite's eyes flickered over to Paul and Clingschor. The old man was collapsing, the tip of Paul's blade glinting dark-blooded from his back. Paul pulled his sword out of the falling body, dashing towards Cundrîê and Bertram, but Father Etienne had gotten there first. The priest's slim blade flashed red, sliding past Cundrîê's black knife to score a deep wound across her forearm.

Cundrîê backed up, licking her lips and spitting towards them. The tip of Etienne's wand moved in a pattern that Margerite could not quite follow as the priest stalked towards her. Her attention on Father Etienne, Cundrîê did not even see Paul's sword coming up to stab in beneath the side of her ribs and up into her chest. Pale lips rucking back into a snarl, she half-turned, her knife-arm swinging in a wide circle towards the Bear, but sagging downward before it reached him.

The blade dropped from her fingers, clattering onto the floor. Paul let the hilt of his sword fall from his hand as the weight of her body dragged it down. He was swaying where he stood, and the flickering light of her fires showed Margerite that his ruddy face had gone a shocking gray.

"So your alchemy worked on my sword after all, Jochanan," he murmured. "I thought you had only half-ruined the temper..."

Jochanan moved in swiftly to support his commander. Clingschor's knife had torn deeply through the Bear's leather jerkin, and Margerite could see the blood dribbling down from the deep slice across his chest. "You are not too badly hurt," he said, but Paul shook his head.

"I feel faint. I will sit down now," he said, thick legs folding up beneath him. Father Etienne moved in swiftly, shaking his head.

"Those knives may have been poisoned. But God willing, and if you are strong, you may yet pull through."

Paul closed his eyes. His head leaned back, then jerked forward again. "Bertram. The first law of winning a battle..."

"Make sure the dead are really dead," Bertram and Jochanan said together. Bertram jerked Paul's sword from Cundrîê's body; Father Etienne lifted the old woman's head by the hair, and Bertram brought the blade down across her neck. Two blows severed Cundrîê's head; they did the same for Clingschor.

"Margerite, you stay here with Paul," Father Etienne said. "We will go on."

Jochanan shook his head. "No, I will stay. I cannot leave him like this, and if something else comes - I may know how to fight it."

"Christ preserve me from half-trained Qabalists," Etienne muttered. "Perhaps it is just as well if you are here, rather than where you might have to battle with arcane skills and risk destroying us all. Come then, if you are coming, Margerite. Bertram, take Paul's sword; but I will go in the lead from here on. Bertram, are you unscathed?"

"She scratched my hand, only," Bertram replied. "I am a little faint, but I can still fight."

Father Etienne, Margerite, and Bertram went on down the stairs to a second round tower room. As they passed through, Margerite noticed the books and bottles that lined the walls, the bunches of herbs hanging from the ceiling - so this was where Cundrîê had kept them! There were two doors in the tower room.

The wood of the western one was chill to her touch, as if it opened to the outside; but Father Etienne went on to the second with hardly a glance to the other. To Margerite's relief, it opened easily at the touch of his hand. The room beyond was lit by several small fires, charcoal-laden braziers glowing beneath bubbling retorts.

The hairs were standing up along Margerite's back and arms now: it seemed to her that she could feel something gathering like the muscles of a great serpent bunching to strike, the air about them growing thick and viscous with the power that prickled painfully through her nerves.

Through the curtain closing the doorway at the far end of the chamber, she could hear the low sound of Ruprecht's voice, rising and falling in a terrifyingly familiar cadence - just as she had heard it in her dream on the night of Gertrude's death.

A cold sweat sprang out on her brow, but she grimly forced herself to keep walking behind Etienne, candle and torch held high in her damp palms. Father Etienne pushed the curtain aside with the tip of his wand, and Margerite and Bertram followed him through. Ruprecht stood in the center of a serpent-wound circle painted on the floor, four candles burning in the hearts of the four pentagrams around it.

He wore a robe of deep violet silk girded with a silver-hilted sword, his golden hair streaming brightly about his shoulders; his right hand held a wand, and his left hand a dagger, its blade so black that it seemed to draw in all the light about it. Eva lay at his feet, clad only in a large white silken tunic that pooled about her prone body.

For a sickening moment Margerite thought they were too late, until she saw that the girl's breasts were still rising and falling.

His eyes fixed upon a point above the triangle painted to the east of the circle, Ruprecht did not so much as twitch to show that he had noticed their presence. His mouth opened and closed, and the voice issuing from it seemed to shake the stones about them.

"Thamiel, Satan, and Moloch!" he cried. "Chaigidel, Beelzebub; Satariel, Lucifuge; Gamchicoth, Astarte!"

With a roar, Bertram charged at Ruprecht, his naked blade flashing. When he reached the edge of the circle, however, he stopped as though he had run into a stone wall, crying out inarticulately as he struggled to pass it.

"Golab, Asmodeus! Tagaririm, Belphegor; Harab-Seraphel, Baal!" Ruprecht intoned, as though there were nothing that could disturb his working.

Margerite let out a soft moan of despair, for she was sure that they had failed. She stood, frozen, until the sharp blow of a slender rod cracked across her shoulder.

"Try to break the circle!" Father Etienne shouted, lifting his wand again. He ran past Bertram to the eastern side, standing between Ruprecht and his triangle and striking alternately with wand and sword at the unseen wall that seemed to ward the magician. Unsure what to do, Margerite wavered a moment. Then she saw that Kobolt was already at the north of the circle, standing up on his hind legs and clawing at the air with a sound like fraying silk. She ran to her cat, reaching above his head to press inwards.

"Eva, Eva!" she screamed, hoping that her voice would wake the girl. "Mother Maria, help me!"

"Samael, Adramelech! Gamaliel, Lilith!" Ruprecht called."Hear ye my invocation, ye five accursed nations; ye Amalekites, ye Geburim, ye Raphaim, ye Nephilim, ye Anakim!" Standing so, with his golden hair floating about his dark-clad shoulders and the blasphemous words pouring from his open mouth, he was still beautiful: gazing at the triangle, his blue eyes shone with the brightness that Margerite had seen in them when he had gazed upon her in her father's sunlit meadow, as they rose with hawk in hand.

And the pain of that memory stung Margerite more deeply than her fear or horror, for now she stood living to gaze upon her love's betrayal. She had come to Ruprecht as falcon trusting her falconer, and thus he had used her, turning her love and all her skills to his own will, even making her own body a sacrifice to his dark magic, as he had sacrificed Gertrude's life...

"Ruprecht!" Margerite shouted, a despairing cry of anger and sorrow wrung from the depths of her bowels, its high note cutting through his clear baritone chant. "Ruprecht, turn and face me - for I loved you! How could you do this? How could you have treated me so?"

Ruprecht stopped in mid-word, standing stunned as if she had struck him with a mace. Then he did turn to face her, his eyes widening in shock. "Margerite! Run, you do not know the danger!" he shouted.

The muscles of his shoulders and arms strained and quivered beneath the purple silk of his robe, as though he were upholding a great weight with the last of his strength, and his face was as white as if he had taken a deep wound in his bowels. But all the terror and fury Margerite had leashed within herself in the past months had found its outlet, and she could no more have held it back than she could have stilled the storm outside in its full strength.

"I loved you, and you betrayed me! You killed Gertrude, and you brought...that...to my bed in your shape. You never loved me; you were lying, all the time, because you could use me. But I will not be used or deceived any longer, for I have learned the truth!"

"Margerite," Ruprecht whispered. The wand and dagger in his hands were shaking harder with the trembling of his arms now, but the circle yet barred any crossing: though, even now, Margerite did not know whether she was trying to break through Ruprecht's fortress or reach out to him, she could not stir a finger's width past the outer line of black.

"Margerite, I have wronged you, I know, but I would make it up...I do love you, Margerite, believe me - but for your life's sake, if you will not run now, step inside the circle, where you will be safe!" He stretched out his right hand towards her, striving to lift his wand a little higher.

"I will not come to you!" Margerite cried. "We will put an end to this!"

Ruprecht's gaze flickered from side to side, from Father Etienne to Bertram, then back to Margerite. His face twisted, and Margerite saw her own heart reflected there: the realization of betrayal, the sudden knowledge that love had turned like a treacherous knife in the hand. Ruprecht's straining fingers gave way: the wand dropped to the floor, and the unseen wall that had kept them from him was gone, like a bubble bursting in a stream. Unbalanced by her swollen belly, Margerite fell forward, barely catching herself in time to keep her head from cracking on the floor; but Father Etienne cried out in triumph, stepping over the circle's edge.

His fair face twisted in fury, Ruprecht drew his sword and flung himself at the priest. Father Etienne caught the blow on his slender blade, parrying it to the side, but before he could stab inwards, Ruprecht's sword had come down again, hammering the priest's weapon from his hand in a ringing stroke; Etienne's sword crashed against the wall, falling bent to the floor.

Bertram charged in low, his blade cutting deep into Ruprecht's left shoulder. The blood sprang out bright, spattering over Ruprecht's violet robe and the painted circle. Ruprecht whirled away from Etienne, lashing out at his new assailant. The tip of his sword bit between the iron plates sewn over Bertram's jerkin, and a spray of blood followed when he jerked it back, but Bertram did not seem to notice, beating grimly at his enemy.

Crouched helplessly on the floor, Margerite stared at the two fighters with her heart choking in her throat. Though Ruprecht had neither armour nor helm and Bertram was fully armed, Ruprecht could move much faster than his foe, dancing away from most of Bertram's sledgehammer blows. The clashing of metal on metal filled the room, ringing over the two warriors' harsh breathing and the muttering of Father Etienne as he bent over Eva's unconscious body.

Another of Ruprecht's snake-swift strikes sliced through the leather over Bertram's left shoulder, his sword cutting deep. Ruprecht twisted away from the return blow, which tore a great flap from his dark silken robe, baring his pale chest and leaving a thin line of red droplets across it, but doing him little harm. Grunting in pain, Bertram stabbed again, and though Ruprecht was able to deflect the killing force of his stroke, it left a deep gash above the Graf's left hip.

The two of them fought on, battering grimly at each other. Twice Ruprecht's sword rang from Bertram's helmet, blows that dented the metal and would have killed an unarmoured man. The second time, Bertram staggered back, but was able to get his blade up again before Ruprecht could come in for the kill. Both of them were bleeding from a number of wounds now: Bertram's left arm hung at his side, and Margerite could see the gleam of bone beneath the wash of blood from his open forearm, but Ruprecht's robe was sodden with blood from a cut to the thigh, and his right leg was beginning to buckle with each step.

O, Maria, Margerite prayed, clenching her fists tight. O, Maria...but she could go no farther.

Ruprecht landed another blow on his foe's helm, knocking the steel cap sideways on Bertram's head. Half-blinded, Bertram backed away, keeping his sword between them. Ruprecht lunged, his full strength behind the blade - and Kobolt suddenly rose up behind him, sinking all his claws into Ruprecht's calf with an earsplitting yowl.

Ruprecht did not stop, but the point of his sword wavered, skidding across an iron plate and cutting sideways into the leather, rather than piercing it straight-on. Bertram's return stroke was true, sinking in beneath Ruprecht's breastbone. Bertram did not try to pull the sword out, but let it fall with his foe. Margerite got shakily to her feet, hurrying across to them. Ruprecht was not quite dead yet: she could hear his breathing, bubbling and hoarse, and see the flicker of his lashes.

"I was betrayed," he whispered. "And you turned against me as well...But I did...I do...love you."

Margerite could not bring herself to grasp his cooling hand, nor did she want him to look upon her. Yet she would not move away from him as he died, for his words had struck more deeply into her breast than she could say, twisting her heart about them like a skein of ill-spun threads. She had thought that she no longer loved Ruprecht, had thought it often enough that she had come to believe it. And yet...and yet...

Father Etienne left Eva, coming over to kneel beside Ruprecht's fallen body with Margerite. "Ruprecht von Falkenstein," he said, his voice stern, "you are dying, but you are not yet dead. The mercy of Christ has given you one last chance: repent, receive absolution and Last Rites, and whatever your sins, you may still attain the Kingdom of Heaven."

Ruprecht almost laughed, a bubble of blood bursting at the corner of his mouth. "Ex Tenebrae, Lux," he answered. "Let the Lord of Knowledge receive me into His light: I shall not break my oaths and shame myself now." He closed his eyes.

"So be it," Father Etienne said. He stood up, his shape seeming inhumanly tall and dark to Margerite from where she crouched on the floor beside the dying man. "Ruprecht von Falkenstein, Graf of these lands, Archbishop of the Order of the Light-Bearers, as you have turned away from Christ's mercy, I hereby speak the sentence of Christ's wrath upon you, that your spirit may go forth to the place to which you have condemned yourself, and work no further harm upon God's earth. Thou servant of Lucifer and his Infernal Realm, thou shalt go forth, to burn forever in the lake of unquenchable fire..."

Margerite hardly knew what she was doing until she was actually standing, her hands grasping Father Etienne's upraised arm. The priest looked down at her in shock.

"Father, no!" Margerite said. Although the tears were flowing from her eyes, her voice was steady. "Please! Although he was...what he was, he was also a kind husband to me, as well as he could be, and he...may have been the father of my child." She quailed within, but could not take her words back.

"What would you have me do?" Father Etienne asked. "I cannot give him the Last Rites against his will, nor do I think they would help, when his last waking thought was to reject the Kingdom of Heaven."

"He did not want Heaven," Margerite answered. "He wanted..." She remembered then, the pain twisting sharp in her heart, how she had first seen Ruprecht, laughing within her father's hall; she remembered him riding through the green summer woods, caught up in the wild joy of his hunting; and the keen delight in his eyes as he gazed at the great eagle perched on his wrist. "Ruprecht said to me once that God could keep his heaven, so long as he could hunt in his woods. And his men," she added, "called him Lord of the Wood."

Etienne looked down at Ruprecht's body. Another bubble of blood burst at the corner of Ruprecht's mouth, the thin trickle of red trailing down over his pale cheek. The rise and fall of his rent chest was feebler; soon, perhaps within a few heartbeats, it would cease altogether.

Kobolt stalked over to Ruprecht, nuzzling the fallen man's cheek before he began to lick the blood from it. "Other gods," Father Etienne whispered, as if remembering something from long ago, "and other beings in the universe." He paused. "And his magician's circle would never have broken, if true love had not made two of his will. Not soon enough for Heaven, true, but perhaps a little too early for Hell..."

Father Etienne lifted his hand again. "Ruprecht von Falkenstein, called Lord of the Wood, hear your doom, as you spoke it yourself. As you hunted in your woods while living, so I condemn you now: hunt there until Judgement Day! In the name of Father and Son and Holy Ghost - so be it."

He brought his hand down. As if he had flung a door open to the storm, a great cold wind suddenly swept through the room, snuffing out Margerite's torch and all the candles in an instant. Margerite's womb panged within her, and she doubled over, falling to the floor. Yet through her pain, she could feel the snow beating against her body; something brushed across her face for an instant, like the tail of a rider's dark cloak in the wind, and it seemed to her that she heard the high silver sound of a hunting horn blowing the mote through the shrieking of the storm.

The gust died down as quickly as it had risen, leaving them in silent blackness. Margerite heard the sound of scrabbling, then the sharp strike of steel on flint, sparks leaping through the darkness. One caught, a little red eye glowing brighter through the darkness as its holder blew on it; then the flames curled up around the torch's stem again, lighting Father Etienne's face from beneath so that his brow-ridges jutted out grotesquely and his cheekbones shone bright above the dark hollows below.

Bertram's gasp was muffled as he looked down at what the torchlight revealed. "Where is he?" the Hauptmann whispered.

Below them, Margerite heard the soft sound of a door banging back and forth in the wind. Father Etienne ran from the room, and she followed, back into the guard tower and downwards on the spiral staircase. The oaken stairs were slippery with melting snow; the door at their base was open to the howling winds. Margerite and Etienne looked out into the whiteness whirling across the ravine's snow-cloaked crags.

"Could he have gone that way?" Margerite whispered. If Ruprecht had not been as badly wounded as he seemed...But the wild wind whipping the snow into their faces had hidden any tracks, any traces of blood that might have been there.

"I do not know," Father Etienne answered. "Do you think he could have made it down that path, wounded as he was?"

Slowly, Margerite shook her head. "We must see to Bertram and Eva," she said. "And if Paul is still alive..."

"Yes."

The fires in Ruprecht's alchemical laboratory had gone out as well. Etienne did not relight them, but he kindled all the candles again. Bertram was sitting propped against a wall, his right hand clenched over his left forearm to stanch the blood that still dribbled out between his fingers. Relieved beyond measure to have something she could do, Margerite drew her eating dagger and, after Father Etienne had nodded approval, cut strips from the hem of Eva's silken tunic to bandage Bertram's wounds with.

"I would have let him burn in Hell," Bertram whispered. When Margerite looked into his eyes, she could see that the left pupil was larger than the right: Ruprecht's blows to his head had not been without effect.

"I know," she whispered back. "But I could not."

Feebly, Bertram lifted his sword-hand to squeeze her fingers. "Maria bless your mercy," he said. "I have struck my blow." His eyelids drooped down.

"You must not sleep!" Margerite said. "Bertram, open your eyes. Your head was struck hard: you must stay awake, or I fear...I fear..." She could not make herself get out the last words: I fear you will die. "Stand up, for my sake if not your own."

Bertram grimaced, pushing hard against the wall behind him with his wounded hand. A gasp of pain hissed through his lips as he shoved himself upright. "What of Eva?" he asked.

"She lives, but she will sleep for some time yet," Father Etienne answered. "Ruprecht must have drugged her before the rite began: I suppose it was easier than binding her and hoping the bonds would not only hold, but keep her from moving about anddistracting him throughout a long ritual."

"Or perhaps it was to spare her fear and pain," said Margerite.

"If you wish to think so," the priest replied. "There is little more we can do here. I think cleansing this place will have to be left to Jochanan and his gunpowder." Etienne bent down over Eva once more, heaving her limp body up over his bony shoulder. Margerite moved to Bertram's side, helping him up the stairs to the chamber where Jochanan sat beside Paul.

The Bear raised his head feebly, and Margerite thought that his colour seemed a little better. "Did you do it?"

"We did it," Father Etienne replied. "Jochanan, help him up. We will need to get the wounded to bed and see to their hurts, and then I have another task for you."

Ruprecht's mastiffs were pacing restlessly about his chamber. Mark stood up with his paws on the windowsill, howling softly at the storm outside; when Margerite put her hand out to Brangæne, the gray hound lowered her muzzle, whimpering.

"Do you think they know?" Margerite murmured to Father Etienne.

"They may." Then something else caught Margerite's eye. The hunting horn that hung over Ruprecht's bed, the horn she had given him - it had fallen to the floor and cracked, breaking into two pieces along its length. Without warning, she found that she was starting to cry, her shoulders shaking in great sobs.

"Calm yourself, keep going," Etienne said breathlessly. "Our wounded cannot stand much longer."

Father Etienne deposited Eva on her pallet in Margerite's room; with Jochanan, Margerite and the priest supported Bertram and Paul down to Bertram's chamber. They laid Paul on the bed, but Bertram sat up in a chair by the window. Margerite ran back upstairs, banging on Gerhild's door until the midwife opened it.

"Yes?" Gerhild asked sleepily. She was dressed only in her shift, long hair down around her shoulders. "Is Eva all right?"

"She is. But you must gather your healer's tools, for we have two wounded for you to see to. And bring poultices against poison, as well."

When Gerhild looked at the two wounded men, Paul breathing hard on the bed and Bertram sitting unsteadily in the chair, she drew in her breath.

"What has happened?" she asked. "How did you two get into this state?"

"Uh, we were drunk," Paul said feebly. "I challenged Bertram to a few passes with weapons, and he took me up on it."

Gerhild put her hands on her narrow hips. The knife-score across Paul's chest gaped open, the lips of the wound already gone bluish-black. Though his right arm had only been lightly scratched, its flesh was swelling as though it had been rotting for days, and the same was true of Bertram's left hand, where Cundrîê's knife had grazed the knuckles.

"You expect me to believe that?" The midwife cast back the hood of her hastily donned cloak. "Lie still: this may hurt, but it is for your good, believe me. Frowe Gräfin, you may use the things in my bag to see to the Hauptmann, if you please."

As the two women tended their patients, Father Etienne spoke quietly to Jochanan. The gunner nodded, slipping out quietly.

"I believe I have stopped the spread of the poison," Gerhild said at last. "The Bear is a strong man; Christ willing, I think he will pull through. I should like very much, however, to know what weapon dealt those frightful wounds."

"What of Bertram?"

"Keep him awake for a full night and day. If the blow to the head has not hurt him too badly, and his wounds do not take fever, he should recover. That deep cut on his arm above the poisoned scratch may have helped to save the hand, for much of the poison seems to have drained out with his blood. I should like to know," she added pointedly once more, "how these men were so scathed."

"I need you to see to me, as well," Margerite said. "I had a sharp pain in my womb earlier this evening, and I wish to be sure I am not miscarrying."

The two women returned to Margerite's chamber. Eva had rolled over in her sleep and begun to snore slightly; Kriemhilt was curled purring by her cheek.

"Tell me about this pain you felt. Was it a single pang, or several? Did it feel like the cramping of your courses? Did you notice any blood or discharge?"

"I am not sure. It was just one twinge, but it was very strong. I did not look for blood."

"Hmm. Lie down and let me see."

The midwife examined Margerite thoroughly, her gentle fingers prodding the rounded curve of Margerite's belly. "All seems to be well, but you should rest easy for the next few days. Do not run, or even walk up and down the stairs too often: if you want something, send Eva to get it for you. I have..." Gerhild paused, scratching absently at her pointed chin as her wide gray eyes stared past Margerite. "It is not easy to explain, but often I have a feeling for babes in the womb. I can tell how they lie, sometimes what sex they are, and sometimes whether...whether they will need more care in bearing and birthing." Whether they will not come to term, or die in birthing, Margerite thought; but she would not have spoken those words to a woman with child either.

"And what of mine?" Margerite asked.

"I do not know," Gerhild confessed. "I know the child is there, and all the signs seem well, but when I touch it, my senses fail me. Therefore, I can only advise you to be as careful as you can, and take no risks with either yourself or the babe."

Margerite thought of the things that had just passed that night. Despite herself, though she tried to stifle it, she began to laugh, her laughter rising to a hysterical near-shriek that she could not stop.

"Frowe Gräfin!" Gerhild exclaimed. "Frowe Gräfin, calm yourself."

But Margerite could not. The tears were rolling down her cheeks now, so that she did not know whether she was laughing or sobbing. Gerhild grabbed her by the shoulders, shaking her, but it made no difference.

Finally the midwife pulled back her hand, slapping Margerite sharply across the face. Margerite gulped, the hysterical fit gone from her as quickly as it had come on. "Thank you," she said raggedly.

"You should go to sleep. Shall I brew you some chammomile tea?"

"No. I shall be all right."

When Gerhild had gone, Margerite crept back down to Bertram's room. Paul was asleep, snoring noisily; Bertram and Father Etienne were sitting up together, speaking quietly. The priest rose, gesturing Margerite to take his chair.

"You are the ruler of Burg Falkenstein now, Gräfin," Father Etienne said. "What is your pleasure in regards to Graf Heinrich and the siege - and what story do you mean to give out about the Graf's disappearance?"

Margerite rested her chin on her hand, thinking. "I suppose we must try to negotiate with Graf Heinrich. Now that Ruprecht is gone, he may be willing to treat reasonably with us, in spite of all he has suffered in the course of this siege. I will not give up Burg Falkenstein itself, but..."

"But there is your child to think of," Etienne said gently. "Yes, it may be that I can talk Heinrich into a settlement that leaves him something to inherit. But what of Ruprecht?"

"He took sick and died in the night. There are plenty of people who can swear honestly that he had been sickening for days, for he ate little and would not touch meat or wine. We buried him quickly, lest the sickness spread, and secretly, lest the men of Burg Falkenstein lose heart at their lord's death."

"That is well-thought." Father Etienne's narrow hand curled into a fist on the edge of the table. "I wish I knew what it was that Ruprecht was trying to do this night. There is little doubt that the Order of Light-Bearers will look more closely into this matter: the only question is how closely, and when? We must have a story ready for them, as well. The bodies are no problem, for Jochanan is down there even now with a quantity of gunpowder, which will serve better for destruction than fire." He stroked a fingertip along the edge of his close-cropped beard. "It were best," he went on slowly, "if someone could pretend to be a low-level initiate of the Order, who knew that Ruprecht was doing something great, but not what or why; who heard the explosion from the chambers above and came down to find Ruprecht destroyed and his servants' bodies broken and charred."

"I will do that," Bertram broke in.

"No. You are too well known as a mercenary servant to the Order; if you had the least talent for magic, or interest in it, you would have been initiated long since. It will have to be Margerite. If you will do this, Gräfin, I will teach you what I can of their knowledge, and any lapses in your learning can easily be explained by your pregnancy, for Ruprecht would have kept you from any high lore or strenuous rites to protect both you and his heir. Do not," Etienne warned, "underestimate the risk this poses to you. If the Order realizes that you are lying to them, they will take vengeance, and I do not think I need to go into the details of their punishments to frighten you more. Further, though much of their knowledge is of the simple practice of the arts arcane, not so different from what I do or even what Jochanan tries to do, much of it is also diabolical and blasphemous, and the simple learning of it is not without danger to the soul."

"Is there no way Margerite can be spared this?" Bertram appealed. His hazel eyes with their mismatched pupils shone unnaturally bright as he leaned across the table, wincing as the wood pressed on his bandaged forearm. "Surely we can find some other - perhaps Jochanan might..."

"They would know Jochanan for a Jew at once. Bungled as his Qabala may sometimes be, his style is still recognisable, just as the fighting style of a man trained from boyhood as a knight can be told from that of one who began a warrior's career as a brigand run away from a peasant village. And I might deceive an Order member of lower rank, as indeed I have done before, but those of the higher grades know my name too well. If any of us can do this, it is Margerite."

Margerite crossed her hands protectively over the child swelling in her womb. She knew that, if she accepted Father Etienne's advice, she would once more have to touch that dreadful power Ruprecht had wielded, the power she had felt in his hidden chambers, the same that had come to her the night of her child's conception...she shuddered. I would rather juggle adders in my bare hands, little Wolfram, she said silently to the babe within her. But I know no other way to keep you safe, if the Order should come looking for us.

"I will learn," Margerite said firmly. Bertram opened his mouth to speak again, but she silenced him by putting a finger across his lips. "No, do not argue. Each of us does what he can and takes the risks that it brings. For a man, fighting; for a woman...what she must do to protect her own."

It was a little before dawn when Father Etienne and Bertram finally forced Margerite to go to bed, sensibly pointing out that if she were to lead the negotiations with Graf Heinrich, she would need to be well-rested and clear-headed. Margerite had protested that she would never be able to sleep, but she found herself dropping off as soon as she had laid her head on the pillow, wondering with her last sleepy thoughts if Father Etienne had worked some charm upon her.

Chapter Nine

Margerite awoke the next morning to the blowing of trumpets from the gates outside. She sprang out of bed, flinging open the shutters and looking out an arrow-slit. The cold air bit crisply into her face, numbing her nose and bringing a tear to her eyes, but the storm had died down, leaving the courtyards and walls of Burg Falkenstein glittering white in the sunlight. Even the mass of peasant shelters in the outer bailey had been transformed into rolling hills of snow, their raw construction hidden beneath the thick white drifts. A man sat on horseback before the gates. He was too far for Margerite to see his face, but she recognised the banner he held at once, the three yellow horse-heads on a blue field: it was the banner of Graf Günther von Hohenfels.

Torn between hope and a dreadful shuddering terror, Margerite knelt down and shook Eva's shoulders until the girl opened her eyes. "Frowe Gräfin!" she said. "I had such an awful dream…"

"It is over now," Margerite told her comfortingly. "But rise now, for I must be dressed swiftly." She wondered how much Eva knew - what she had seen before Ruprecht's potion had wended her into her deep sleep, and what she might have sensed through her drugged dreams. But there was no time to ask her now.

Margerite was halfway down the stairs to the great hall when she met one of the guardsmen running upwards. "Frowe Gräfin, is the Graf in your chamber? We have searched everywhere else for him, and he must be found now."

"The Graf is indisposed," Margerite said. "Whatever matter has come up, I shall handle it."

"There is a messenger outside from Graf Günther von Hohenfels," the guard panted. "He says that Graf Günther has marched with an army to the relief of the siege, and would speak with Graf Ruprecht now."

"He cannot do that. But he may speak with me. Come." Margerite swept regally down the stairs, letting the guard go before her to tread a clear path for her through the snow when they got outside. She mounted to the top of the guard tower by the main gate, walking out onto the wall and hoping that none of Heinrich's archers would seize the opportunity to cut her down. The icy wind was stronger up here, the stone walkway between the crenellations slippery, but Margerite moved very carefully so that no misstep could diminish her dignity.

"I am Margerite, Gräfin von Falkenstein," she called down to the messenger. "You may tell me what you have to say."

The messenger looked up at her, his hood falling away from his clean-cut face. Margerite recognised him at once: he had brought the news of Ruprecht's arrival to Burg Hirschenberg.

"Greetings, Frowe Gräfin. It pleases me to see you well in your new home, but I must speak with Graf Ruprecht."

"You cannot. He is very ill, and until he has recovered, I am in command here. What news do you bear?"

"The army of Graf Günther von Hohenfels is less than an hour's march from Burg Falkenstein, for he has heard of your need and come to break the siege. Graf Heinrich has been made aware of this, and he has agreed to re-open negotiations with Graf Ruprecht which, he promises, will be more moderate than his previous offers. Does Graf Ruprecht wish to treat with him, or will he ready his troops for battle?"

"Take this word back to Graf Heinrich and Graf Günther: Burg Falkenstein will negotiate. We do not wish more bloodshed, unless it becomes necessary; but let Graf Heinrich know that if his terms are not acceptable, we will not hesitate to fight."

"Your message shall be delivered, Frowe Gräfin." The messenger made an elaborate half-bow, turning his horse and riding away.

Margerite returned at once to Bertram's chamber. Father Etienne had come back as well, or perhaps never left: the priest's face had the sallow cast of one who had been up all night, and his thick gray-shot hair looked disheveled and unwashed. Quickly she told her news to the two of them.

"So!" Father Etienne said. "The hour has come faster than I expected." He reached into the pouch at his belt, drawing out a silver ring, and gave it to Margerite. "This is your Order ring, the sign of initiation into the first rank."

Margerite turned the ring over in her fingers, looking at it with loathing. The silver circle, graven with the familiar motto EX TENEBRAE LUX, felt slick and cold to her touch. Reluctantly she slipped it onto her left forefinger. It was only a little too big; it must have been made for Father Etienne's slender hand.

"It will serve," Etienne told her. "It was once a genuine Order member's ring, and, though it will do you no harm to wear it now, enough of that with which it was first imbued lingers that Graf Günther will not become suspicious. Remember: if he addresses you as Priestess, that is the sign that he is speaking of Order business, and you in turn will address him as Prince."

Bertram frowned, but said nothing. He was looking better now than he had the night before: there was more colour in his face, and his pupils were closer to the same size.

"Bertram, are you able to dress yourself and sit so as to hide all your wounds?" Margerite asked. "I want you to be beside me when we carry out our negotiations with Graf Heinrich."

"I shall manage," he replied.

After several hours of messengers riding back and forth, carrying demands and written safe-conducts, six men at last approached the gates of Burg Falkenstein. Father Etienne, who had gone out to assure Graf Heinrich of the legitimacy of Margerite's offer, accompanied Heinrich, his eldest son, and one of his lieutenants back; by Graf Günther's side - Margerite almost wept to see the familiar grizzled beard beneath the battered old helm, the deep green cloak embroidered in light blue patterns along the hem - was Margerite's father, Ritter Martin.

"Open the gates for them," Margerite commanded. The gates swung open; the porticullis lifted, dropping again behind the riders.

When the men had all dismounted, Margerite's father grabbed her in a gentle hug about the shoulders. "It is good to see you again, my daughter. You are looking well - and I believe you are bearing a child! My congratulations, to both you and your good husband. When is it due?"

"Thank you," Margerite replied, dazed. "I should bear the babe at the beginning of May."

She could hardly believe that Ritter Martin was here, after all that had passed; but of course, not only was he - had been - Ruprecht's father-in-law, but he was Graf Günther's sworn man.

The others politely waited their turns to greet her. Margerite had never seen Graf Günther in person before, but she had formed an image of him as huge and burly, dark-haired and brooding. In truth, though tall, he was of rangy build, with grey-blond hair peaking sharply on his forehead and receding over his temples, a long, expressive face, and a pointed chin made sharper by a neat grey-blond goatee. Graf Günther smiled charmingly at Margerite as he lifted her left hand in his, brushing his lips half an inch above the Order ring. Margerite felt an unpleasant cold tingle through the silver, but she ignored it, smiling back at him. "Your help is timely arrived, good Graf," she said to him. "I am sorry that Ruprecht cannot see you to offer his greetings and thanks in person."

"There will be time," Graf Günther said. His blue eyes twinkled as if with merriment, but it seemed to Margerite that she could see the cold in their depths, his friendliness false as sunlight reflected from the ripples of thin ice.

"Greetings, Gräfin Margerite," Graf Heinrich boomed. He looked - as Margerite remembered him from the dream in which she had flown to Burg Fürstensee to overhear his plans: a big man, broad-built and heavy in the gut, with graying hair and beard, and a lumpy nose that looked to have been broken several times. The sharp daylight showed his age more clearly than the dream's candles, the deep spiderwebs at the corners of his eyes and the crevasses of his forehead above bushy gray eyebrows. "Where did you say Ruprecht is?"

"Indisposed," Margerite repeated. "But do not think that his illness will change the outcome of our talks in any way. I am the Gräfin of Burg Falkenstein, and I shall defend our rights as staunchly as my husband ever did, for I speak for him and the heir within my body as well as for myself."

"Bravely said, Frowe Gräfin," approved Graf Heinrich's son. Close to, Christoph looked much like a shorter, clean-shaven copy of his father, save that his nose was small and up-tilted at the end, and his eyes were a light shade of green-tinged gray.

Ruprecht had mentioned that Christoph was twenty-two years old, and still unmarried...Margerite caressed her stomach, thinking, Even when they find out that Ruprecht is dead, they cannot seek to marry me off so soon! Christoph went on smoothly, "You may be sure that we shall respect your position, and that we seek only redress for the wrongs your husband has done us, and a peaceable end to this war. But forgive me: I have not introduced myself as I should. I am Ritter Christoph, eldest son and heir to Graf Heinrich von Fürstensee." He bowed over her hand, his lips touching her fingers lightly. Margerite could not help comparing him to her memory of his brother Nikolaus, and was glad that Christoph was the eldest.

"Come into Burg Falkenstein, gentlemen, welcome guests all," Margerite said. "A meal will be served in the great hall shortly, and we will be more comfortable within than we are standing here in the snow." Margerite took her father's arm, allowing him to escort her into the castle and up the stairs, with the others trailing behind them as if they were part of a feast-day procession.

The great hall was warm, for Margerite had ordered the fires lit: one way or another, even though Graf Heinrich's army was still encamped outside, the siege of Burg Falkenstein was over. Although she had no fresh meat to work with, Berthe had done well with what she had: platters of smoked ham, smoked eel, and cheese were set out on the table, together with white bread and pitchers of wine, and savory odours were wafting in from the kitchen. Bertram was already seated in his place, for which Margerite was glad; if Bertram did not have to walk, it was less likely that anyone would notice his wounds.

"It seems that you have not been suffering too greatly from this siege," Graf Heinrich rumbled, settling himself across from Margerite and accepting a goblet of wine from Eva, which he drained in a single draught. "How much of this came from my villagers, I wonder?"

"Father!" Christoph protested. "We are here to speak of terms with the Gräfin, not rekindle our enmity."

Heinrich held his goblet out to be filled again. "To terms, then. Graf Günther, what brings you here?"

"Loyalty to Graf Ruprecht, an old friend who once served as Knappe in my court," Günther answered smoothly.

"Strong loyalty, to last that long," Graf Heinrich grunted. He cut a slab of smoked ham, slicing it neatly to pieces upon his bread trencher and eating as he talked, with scarcely a pause to chew between words. Although Christoph's manners were neater than his father's, he was eating just as voraciously, as though he had not seen a full meal for days. Margerite noted their hunger with secret satisfaction, guessing that they would be eager to come to a settlement and end the siege before their army starved around Burg Falkenstein's walls. "I shall return to the offer I first made upon shutting you up in here. Give up all claim to Burg Düsterstein; give us Burg Eichenwald and the land for half a day's ride around, and repay the damages Ruprecht's army did to my lands for the course of the war."

"That is not possible, and you know it," Margerite said calmly. "Make me a more reasonable offer, and I shall consider it. Elsewise, I shall bid you farewell, and our men shall do their debating with their swords."

Heinrich looked across the table at the other Graf. Günther grinned and raised a gray eyebrow, his pointed face sharpening with wolfish appreciation. "As Gräfin Margerite says. I shall not quail in the least to follow her lead, if she orders an attack." Martin nodded vigorously in support of his lord. Bertram only glared at Heinrich, and the gleam of his eyes between the wild black tangle of his hair and beard would have frightened Margerite if she did not know him.

"Well, then. Before I give you different terms, however, I must know this. Is Graf Ruprecht truly ailing, or is he dead?"

Margerite froze with her hands on the table, staring at Heinrich. The Graf looked back at her, his furrowed features expressionless. She had not discussed this with Etienne and Bertram, she had not...She did not even dare glance at either of them for a cue, lest one or the other of the men at the table notice and divine, by arcane means or simple logic, the nature of the conspiracy within Burg Falkenstein. But the truth would have to come out, sooner or later.

"He is dead," she said flatly. "He died of fever late last night. Bertram buried him swiftly, lest the sickness spread, and in secret, so that our folk within the castle would not lose heart by knowing of it."

Heinrich's lips curved beneath his beard. "And no doubt the good Father gave him the last rites?"

"I am as surprised by this news as any of you," Father Etienne declared. As mediator, he had seated himself at the foot of the table, between the two sides: he looked at the others with his pointed eyebrows raised in an expression of genuine curiosity.

Graf Günther was frowning, as if deliberating something within himself. A little time passed before he spoke. "If Graf Ruprecht is dead, then Burg Falkenstein and all its lands belong to Margerite. But if the child she bears is a son, then he will inherit, and he must have a guardian until he is of age. No doubt that will be his grandfather?"

But Martin was hardly listening to him. He covered Margerite's hand with his own, murmuring, "My daughter, I am sorry. You must be mourning: do you wish to go on with this later? I think," he added more loudly, "that there is nothing which must be settled today, if we may wait a while in respect for a widow's grief, and for the dead."

"No, Father. Although Ruprecht is gone, I cannot set aside my responsibilities so lightly. We should settle the matters between us as swiftly as we may."

"Brave girl," Martin said. The Ritter straightened his shoulders. "Well. If my grandchild needs a guardian, I shall be that for him, of course. But we must make sure that he can inherit in peace. Graf Heinrich, I believe you were preparing to make my daughter a second offer?"

"I had one in mind. But these tidings put a very different face on things. A woman alone is hardly in a position to command an army or rule a land. Since, for better or worse, we are already neighbors, I propose this. I am a widower these past six years: rather than deprive the Gräfin of any of her late husband's lands, I shall now offer to marry her, that the holdings of Burg Falkenstein and Burg Fürstensee be reconciled by our wedding. As for her child, if it lives, I shall give it a name and raise it as my own."

Margerite felt as though one of Jochanan's big guns had gone off on either side of her, stunning her senses and blasting all thought from her mind. Graf Günther's answer sounded dimly through the ringing in her ears. "It is too soon for the Gräfin to remarry, and I doubt - " his gaze slid swiftly to the side, meeting Margerite's for a moment - "that she is even of a mind to be betrothed again so swiftly. You are not, are you, Gräfin Margerite?"

"No." Margerite shook her head, as if to drive the echoing shock from her skull. "No, I am not." Against her will, her eyes sought Bertram's. He was looking at her, and it seemed to her that she could see the sudden mad hope springing beneath the careful mask of his features and the black tangle of his beard. O, if only...In law, Burg Falkenstein was hers. In law, as a widow, she could send Günther and Heinrich both away, marry Bertram, and hold it beside him for the rest of her life. But she knew that she would never be allowed to do that, for two armies waited outside her gates, and their leaders both had a high stake in this game: they would not withdraw to leave Margerite to her desire.

"We shall consider this further," Graf Heinrich said. "Christoph, the list of the damages we and our folk suffered?"

Christoph pulled a scroll from his belt, unrolled it, and began to read. Margerite let his words flow over her without notice, for she knew Heinrich and his son were only playing out a part. Soon they would return to the real issue: the question of her guardianship or remarriage, which would determine the shape of not only her future, but those of the folk of Burg Falkenstein and, perhaps, of Burg Fürstensee.

The discussions went on throughout the day: the midday dinner was eaten and cleared away, the evening supper brought in, and still they were unable to come to any conclusion. Graf Heinrich seemed set upon a marriage, to which Christoph eagerly assented; Graf Günther was just as adamant that Margerite's rights as widow, and her father's as guardian to her child, should be preserved.

Father Etienne held himself largely aloof from the discussion, observing only that Margerite should not be married until the prescribed period of mourning had passed, though a betrothal, if she were willing, might be acceptable. Margerite herself wanted only time to think, to clear her head of all the dark visions upon her - perhaps even to mourn for Ruprecht, or at least the man with whom she had fallen in love - but that, she felt more and more sure, would not be given her.

The talks were wearing hard on Bertram: she could see his face growing whiter as the evening wore on, the little lines standing out more clearly around his eyes. Beginning to fear for him, at last she rose to her feet.

"It is clear that we shall not come to a decision this night," Margerite said. "If you gentlemen agree, we shall resume our discussion tomorrow. For now, may I offer all of you the hospitality of Burg Falkenstein tonight? Chambers have already been prepared for you: please forgive us if they are not what you are accustomed to, but after all, we had scant notice of what would come to pass this day."

Graf Heinrich and Graf Christoph were bedded down in the second-floor chamber that Paul had been sleeping in, with Graf Günther in the room beside that, hastily converted back from a temporary armoury into a bedroom. Ruprecht's room could not be used, for his two mastiffs would not leave it.

When Margerite went in, it nearly broke her heart to see Brangæne whimpering upon Ruprecht's bed and Mark lying prone across the door to his hidden stairway, their brown eyes turned pleadingly up at her as if they thought she could bring Ruprecht back. The bowl of breadcrusts in beef broth which Eva had carried up to them early in the day was untouched, and their whines were weak and fever-dry.

"Poor hounds, poor darlings," Margerite said, scratching Brangæne behind the ears. "I wish you could reason like humans, to know that Ruprecht did not deserve such faithfulness from you. Or…" She sighed sadly. "Perhaps he did, for I know that he never did ill to you."

Mark rolled his head back, looking up at the door through which his master had disappeared, and let out a soft, scratchy-voiced howl.

"At least you shall be let mourn in peace, or as much as I can manage for you," Margerite told them. "Brave hounds, good hounds."

In the end, Gerhild had to be moved into Margerite's room so that Martin would have a chamber to sleep in. When the bedding had been cleared and changed, Martin invited his daughter in to sit with him. He had brought up several flasks of the light wine from the vineyards around Burg Hirschenberg. When Margerite tasted it, the delicate tart sweetness nearly brought tears to her eyes, for to her it was the taste of home, of the well-known woods around the little keep, and the Hirschenberg villagers greeting their May-Queen, the Ritter's daughter, with delight as she rode among them. And Gertrude…

"Where is Gertrude?" Martin asked, as if he had heard the thought forming in his daughter's mind. "Did she, too, fall sick?"

"She disappeared at the beginning of August," Margerite admitted. "She may have run away."

"That is sad news. I shall ask if anyone has heard of her, but I think they would have told me. Her parents were very proud of her, you know."

"I know," Margerite said sadly. She remembered Gertrude's parents vaguely: her mother, fat and cheerful with a cloud of curly brown hair around her head; her father, stooped and brown from his work in the fields, but always with a lively joke or word of advice for his daughter and her young mistress on those occasions when they had stopped by his house in the village. It was unlikely that she would ever see them again, and they would never know how their daughter had died in her service: Margerite felt deeply guilty for that, and at the same time, shamefully relieved that she would never have to face them and say how she had failed their trust.

Martin patted his daughter on the shoulder. "And I am very proud of you, Margerite. When I brought you here, I was afraid...you know how an old man can be, and you my only living child. I was afraid that you would be overwhelmed and frightened by Ruprecht's court, or have your sensible head turned by the excitement of suddenly being the Gräfin, for the higher one rises, the more perils there are to fear. But you have managed magnificently. Indeed, you have grown into the very image of your blessed mother, whom I think must be praying in Heaven on your behalf."

"I hope she is, for I need her prayers." Margerite gulped back a sob. "Father, what do you think I should do?"

"Graf Günther cannot stay here with his army forever, you know," Martin said gently. He shifted in his chair, pressing his knuckles into the small of his broad back: it had been a long ride in hard weather for a man of his age, Margerite knew. "You could come back with us, but if you leave Burg Falkenstein now, asserting your right to it, or your child's, will be a matter of appealing to Kaiser Karl in order to reclaim it from Graf Heinrich's hands. And the Kaiser will be most likely to marry you off to one of his own supporters, with or without your consent."

"That is true. But if I stay here…"

Martin tugged at his grizzled beard, thick eyebrows lowering in a frown. "Margerite, if you stay here, I see no way for you to be safe and hold to your lands other than marrying Graf Heinrich or, at least, one of his sons. I know Graf Heinrich is older than I am, but that boy Christoph seems a fine lad, courtly and well-spoken, and, God willing, he should succeed his father in time. You would hold Burg Falkenstein, and eventually be mistress of all Graf Heinrich's lands as well: would that be so bad? And if we are able to delay the marriage until after your child's birth, the child, if it is a son, will still be heir to Burg Falkenstein in his own right when he comes of age."

"I do not know. Heinrich would take my child's guardianship, or Christoph would."

"I am willing enough to give it up, if that will make sure that you are safe and happy. My daughter, that is my counsel. I know marriage must be the last thought on your mind, with your dear husband so lately in the ground, and I wish you did not have to face this now, but…Let the betrothal take place, and when the time for the marriage has come, perhaps at least the first sharpness of your grief will have faded. It does fade, or at least its edge will come to dull in time," he added softly. "I know."

"Father, I will think on it."

Margerite and her father talked on that, and other matters, for a time. It was late when she left his chamber at last. She did not notice the tall figure waiting in the shadows outside the door until she nearly bumped into him. "Graf Günther!" she exclaimed. "May I be of service?"

"You may indeed - Priestess."

A cold shock ran through Margerite's body. The Order ring on her left forefinger tingled, an uncomfortable prickle that made her want to tear it from her hand and fling it away. But her womb was shifting, the child within moving in his sleep, and that gave her the strength to reply, "What are your wishes, Prince?"

"Take me to Ruprecht's chambers, for I have private words for you."

Silently, trying to control the shaking of her limbs, Margerite led Günther down the corridor to Ruprecht's room. The mastiffs cowered away from him, Mark growling deep in his throat. Margerite mustered the best smile she could, looking at Günther as she would have looked at a village Meier reporting his hopes for a good harvest. She could think of nothing to say except the Order motto, and this she repeated slowly, hoping that the Order Prince would take it as meaning whatever he ought to hear. "Ex Tenebrae, Lux."

Günther smiled back at her, merriment twinkling in his blue eyes. "Ex Tenebrae, Lux, indeed. I shall not keep you standing here long, for you should be resting and strengthening yourself for your son's sake. But I should like to make plain to you what my position is on the situation here. I want you to come back with me, with your father to be appointed as guardian to your child. I would vastly prefer for you to be at my court from your time of birthing onward. Is that clear?"

"It is clear," Margerite replied, trying to hide her disheartenment. Her father would not, she was sure, go against the desires of his overlord; and how could she object, without showing herself unfaithful to her supposed oath to the Order of Light-Bearers? And where is the difference between being truly bound by an oath of fealty, and having to act just as if I were? Margerite knew that the question had been tormenting Bertram for years, throwing him into the profoundest doubt of his hope of Heaven: was she, then, to answer it in a night?

"And we must come to a resolution reasonably soon, for I need to be back in my own castle by the New Year. Thanks to Ruprecht's failure, the feast we hold will not be the victory feast we had hoped for, but all those who wear the amethyst and ruby rings will be gathered there: even he of the adamant may come from Avignon. It will be well for them to see you now."

"As you wish, Prince," Margerite answered, her heart quailing at the thought. Yet she had one hope of escape, the weapon Ruprecht had put into her hand even as he betrayed her trust. "Only remember that it will not be too long before my child is born. I must ask my midwife if it is safe for me to travel, for a long ride so late in my carrying could do harm to both of us."

Günther frowned, then nodded. "Ask, then. You are right in thinking that I wish, very much, to see that no harm comes to either of you. But this, too, you must keep in mind: do not speak of any of our plans with the priest, or listen to his advice. Did Ruprecht tell you who he is?"

"He only told me to keep away from him," Margerite lied. "I had never heard of Father Etienne before he forced his way in here. Ruprecht wanted him to leave, but then Father Hans died, and Etienne insisted that he would stay until the siege was over and we could find another priest for our villagers and castle folk."

"Hmm. Well, let it be enough for you to know that Father Etienne has often been at odds with us. If it were not that he has very powerful friends, we should have been rid of him long ago. In any case, be careful of him, and do not speak to him at all unless you must."

Back in her chamber, Margerite washed her hands in silence, until at last she had calmed herself enough to say casually to Gerhild, "Graf Günther thinks I should go back home with my father now. That is a long ride for a woman in my condition, is it not?"

"Frowe Gräfin, you must not do that," Gerhild said in alarm. "Your pregnancy is too far along. Even in a wagon, such a journey would be a great strain, certainly enough to risk your child."

"Thank you," Margerite sighed. "Will you tell that to Graf Günther, if he should want your word on it?"

"Frowe Gräfin, I should tell that to God Himself, if He asked me."

As Margerite had anticipated, the two sides had hardly sat down to break their fast in the morning when Graf Günther, looking sideways at her, said, "It seems to me that we have reached a point where Gräfin Margerite must tell us what she will do. Gräfin, do you wish to marry Graf Heinrich, or will you return to your father's castle under my protection?"

"Graf Günther, I thank you for your kind offer. If I had only myself to think of, or if my child were born already, I should certainly come back with you. However, I have spoken with my midwife, and she tells me that I must not risk any long journey before my birthing."

Margerite could see the little muscles jumping at the side of Graf Günther's slanted jaw. She clenched her right hand over the Order ring on her left, as if she were tightening a tourniquet to keep its poison from spreading out from it.

"I would speak with this midwife," Günther said.

"Eva, fetch Gerhild to us." Margerite's maid curtsied to her and ran from the room, returning only a few moments later. Gerhild was dressed as well as Eva's best efforts could make her, her long hair pulled severely back from her face and Margerite's own little gold cross hung about her neck.

"Graf Günther, Graf Heinrich, good gentlemen," she said, curtseying. "I understand that you wish to ask me about the Gräfin's health?"

"We do, indeed," Günther answered, eyeing her suspiciously. Gerhild did not seem daunted by his gaze, looking him straight in the eye.

"The Gräfin is young, and this is her first birth. She is not carrying as easily as some women, though there have been no signs of real danger thus far. However, she mentioned to me that she might wish to travel back to her homelands with you. Graf, I must tell you that if she does, she is likely to lose the child she bears."

"She can travel in a wagon," Graf Günther began, but Gerhild shook her head firmly, her long braid swishing from side to side.

"Even the jouncing of a wagon might well shake the babe loose within her. If you wish the Gräfin to bear safely - " Gerhild looked about at the men, fixing each of them with her eye in turn - "you will leave her here in peace until she and her child are both well out of any danger."

"Thank you, good woman," Günther said. "That will be all."

"Margerite," Martin murmured to his daughter, "have you thought on the matters we spoke about last night?"

"I have," Margerite whispered back, but Heinrich's voice was already booming over theirs.

"If we marry now, Gräfin, I will pledge to leave you safely here until your child is born. You need fear no ill-treatment from me."

Margerite looked at Heinrich, then at his son. She could not imagine lying with either of them, though Christoph was well-favoured in a rounded and cheery sort of way and Heinrich, large and imposing though he was, could not be called ugly. Again she thought on her father's advice.

A betrothal could last for a year, perhaps for several: and by the time it was up - who knew? And Heinrich was not young: if she let herself become betrothed to him, and he died in the interim, she might be free, or at least more free than she was now. And...Margerite could not deny the thought...she knew that she could not keep up the masquerade of being a member of the Order of Light-Bearers forever.

Sooner or later, she would have to break, and then she would need a strong protector. Christoph might be too young and inexperienced, might even be susceptible to the wiles of his younger brother, but Heinrich had not held his title and lands by being weak or naïve. Though he most likely had never heard of the Order, his stand as the Kaiser's true man made him their foe in deed if not knowledge, if only in their mundane dealings: she would be safe with him.

"It is too soon for me to give myself in marriage again," she said, doing her best to look sweetly at the big Graf. "But if we can agree on terms for a betrothal, terms that allow me a decent period to mourn for Ruprecht and recover from the birth of my child, then I am willing to become betrothed to you."

Heinrich's bearded face broke into a wide grin. He raised his heavy arms, and Margerite knew that if he had not been across the table from her, he would have clasped her in a bear-hug. "That is the most welcome news I have had since before this war began. You are wise as well as beautiful, Gräfin, and I shall be proud to take you to wife."

"And I shall be proud to have you as stepmother," Christoph said, bowing to her from his seat. Margerite blinked. She had not thought of what it would be like to have two stepsons older than herself. And Nikolaus as one of them, she thought sourly. But betrothal to Heinrich seemed the best choice: indeed, the only one left to her.

"Well, since your father is already here, let us talk betrothal terms," Heinrich went on. "For I am anxious to have this sealed and done as soon as I may. Ritter Martin, what of your daughter's dowry?"

Margerite sat silent for most of the day while the men talked, only looking down at Bertram whenever she dared, as if to give him strength and comfort with her eyes. Although he seemed to have recovered from the blows to his head at last, he was shifting uneasily in his chair, as if his other injuries pained him greatly. She knew that he should be in bed, for even with the fires burning, it was cold in the great hall, and the heavy clothing and thick cloak that hid his bandages would not be enough to keep a chill from settling into his wounds.

Unlike her, however, he could not plead weakness and retire. And, for all Bertram had said to her when they had talked of the matter earlier - though he would likely not have accepted marriage if she had proposed it to him, for all the good and sufficient reasons that had led her to accept betrothal to Heinrich - she knew that his heart must be breaking as he listened to Martin and Günther and Heinrich dicker over her marriage portions.

At last, to Margerite's relief, the contract was drawn up, written out in Father Etienne's elegant French hand and ready to be signed. The quill trembled in Margerite's hand as she wrote her name, the smooth curves of her letters marred by a spattering of ink, but then it was done. Heinrich signed it in turn, bearing down so hard that the point of the quill nearly broke beneath his hand; then Martin, Günther, Christoph, and Etienne witnessed it.

"Now we shall celebrate!" Heinrich boomed. "My betrothed, will you now open the gates of Burg Falkenstein, so that my poor frozen men may come in out of the stormy night?"

Margerite looked at her father. "Twelve months from now, they will be your men as well," Ritter Martin said.

"And there is now no cause to expect treachery - from either side," Father Etienne added. "For we are all amicably agreed, are we not?"

Each of the men about the table nodded in turn. Even Graf Günther did not seem too dismayed, although Margerite did not like the thoughtful look upon his long face: she had no doubt that he was thinking of new ways to turn the arrangement to his will.

"There is one more thing I should like to speak of before we are done," Christoph said. They all looked at the youth, but he went on confidently beneath their gazes. "My good warhorse was shot from beneath me in the battle at the gate, where I broke my shield-arm. The arm is healed well enough now, but it is not such an easy thing to replace a good horse. Now, if Graf Ruprecht's steed is still alive and well, I should like to have it. I will be willing enough to compensate you for it," he added quickly, as if realizing how rude he sounded. "But I have seldom seen so fine a steed, and it has been much in my thoughts these last months."

"Ruprecht's horse..." A vision of Ruprecht riding his gray-black steed, his golden hair flowing about his green-clad shoulders, came to Margerite's mind. As when she had given Gertrude's clothes to Eva, she found that the shock of her husband's death was only now coming home to her: if she saw Christoph riding the dark warhorse, it would be the final proof to her heart that Ruprecht was truly gone forever. "Bertram, what do you think? You are the Hauptmann of the guard here: should you not have our best steed?"

"I do not want it," Bertram answered. His voice sounded hollow, and he would not meet her eyes, sitting sunken in his chair near the end of the table. "And I would not advise another to risk his neck on that horse, either. Nor, I think, would any man in Burg Falkenstein, for Graf Ruprecht's beasts were always uncommonly loyal to him."

Margerite thought with a pang of Brangæne and Mark pining away in Ruprecht's empty bedroom, but Christoph was already on his feet. "If you let me, Gräfin, I shall take the risk. I have not yet met a horse that I could not sit."

Margerite shrugged, telling herself that she really did not care if Christoph could ride Ruprecht's horse or not. "If you wish him, you may have him."

"Thank you, Gräfin!" Christoph said enthusiastically.

It only remained to spread the news to the folk within Burg Falkenstein's walls. Although a light snow was falling again, Margerite had everyone assemble in the outer courtyard. She mounted to the top of a wall, where her voice would carry above the gathered throng, and seized a horn from the nearest sentry. Its blast rang mournfully over the courtyard; she spoke through the silence that fell as its echoes were dying away.

"My people," she called. "It is my sorrow to tell you that your Graf, Ruprecht von Falkenstein, died of fever two nights ago. The siege of Burg Falkenstein is over: I am betrothed to Graf Heinrich von Fürstensee. You folk of Tiefensee may gather your belongings and families and go back to your village; as for the rest of you, I shall receive your oaths on behalf of myself and the child I bear, the heir to Falkenstein and all its lands, within the great hall this night. Soldiers, you may open the gates, for Graf Heinrich's men are no longer our foes, but our allies."

A few people cheered; the rest only stood there, their faces grayed by the drifting veil of snowflakes, as if they feared that Margerite might take any sign of happiness or relief as showing that they were rejoicing at Ruprecht's death. Margerite descended through the guard tower and out into the yard; the castle folk and villagers moved out of her path.

"Well, Christoph," she said. "The light is beginning to fail. Do you wish to try the horse's paces today, or will you wait until tomorrow and see if the weather is better?"

"I shall try him today, if I may."

"Ready Graf Ruprecht's horse, and bring him from the stables," Margerite commanded one of the guardsmen.

Ruprecht's gray-black steed pulled restively on his lead-rope as the guardsman brought him out into the courtyard. Christoph walked up to him with no sign of fear, stroking his snow-starred neck. "Soft, soft," he murmured. "Your master is dead; will you serve me now?"

The horse stood still as Heinrich's son placed his hands on the saddle, vaulting up onto his back. Then he exploded into action, rearing, snorting, and kicking as he galloped through to the outer bailey. Christoph's boast had not been idle, for he clung tenaciously to the saddle, not fighting against the wild horse, but shifting his weight and his grip on the reins to match his mount's movements. For a breathless moment, Margerite thought he might have a chance of mastering the steed.

But then the horse's dark body seemed to twist in midair, and Christoph arched from his back. A loud crack echoed through the courtyard as the youth thumped face-down into the snow beside the castle gates. Ruprecht's horse stood panting for a moment, eyes rolling and sweat dripping from his black mane. Then, before anyone could move to catch him, he reared again, neighing loudly, and plunged forward, galloping through the gates and out.

"Christoph!" Heinrich called, running through the outer courtyard to go to his knees in the snow beside his fallen son. Christoph rolled over with a moan. His shield-arm was badly broken, the bone above the elbow jutting at an unnatural angle beneath the thick light wool of his cloak, and Margerite could see the purple lump already rising on his forehead, but she thought he was lucky to be alive: if the snow had not been thick where he landed, he might well have broken his neck.

"The same place," he groaned. "Just when the arm had healed, too." His head dropped back into the snow.

The betrothal feast that night was scantier than it might have been, for Margerite was unwilling to use up too much food with the prospect of such a hard winter still ahead of them, and very subdued. Christoph had come around twice since falling unconscious in the courtyard, and was likely to live, but he had taken a serious blow.

"Christoph must stay here until he is recovered," Graf Heinrich declared. "As for the rest of us, we may as well start home tomorrow. Is that well enough with you, Margerite?"

"It is well enough."

In fact, Heinrich stayed three days more, until it was certain that Christoph would live and had lost none of his wits. Ruprecht's mastiffs still would not eat, and Mark died on the evening of Heinrich's departure, Brangæne within a day of her mate. Margerite had them buried in the herber, beneath the linden: in the spring she would plant two rosebushes over their graves, in memory of their faithfulness. Thinking on that, and looking at the two sad dark mounds and the earth scattered black through the snow around them, Margerite realized that she had one last duty remaining to Ruprecht.

As Margerite entered the mews and hailed Johann, she realized that she was uncommonly lucky to find him there. The falconer had been out on every clear day since the siege had ended, trying to get the castle's long-confined birds back into hunting shape. But he had clearly met with some success: the long body of a hare draped limp and gutted across the back of his chair, and he was crooning to Enid as if to a long-lost lover.

"Frowe Gräfin! Will you go out hawking this afternoon?" Johann asked eagerly. "If you do not expect too much of them yet, the birds are much in need of exercise."

"I will go out with them, but not to hunt. Johann, I made a promise to Ruprecht once that, if he should die first, I would set his eagles free. Will you come with me to do that?"

"Frowe Gräfin!" the falconer exclaimed. "You cannot mean that. Who else has eagles trained to bring down roedeer? I know no other falconer - I do not lie - who has taught the great birds so well. They are the pride and joy of Burg Falkenstein."

"They were Graf Ruprecht's pride and joy," Margerite corrected gently. "I do not have the strength to hunt with them. And...Ruprecht's horse is gone, and his hounds are gone. I would send his hawks after him, as he wished."

Johann sighed, and Margerite thought that she saw the glimmer of a tear in the little man's eye, but he turned to the eagles. "Come Ginovêr, come Artûs," he said in a low voice. "You have flown well for me; now, I suppose, you must fly for yourselves."

Though Ginovêr's weight quickly began to ache in the muscle of Margerite's left shoulder, she bore the bird without complaint, riding up the snowy mountain path beside Johann. "We must let them go from a high place," the falconer instructed. "The days without flight have worn badly on them, for they are fat and soft. It would be better to keep them until spring, even summer... no? Well, then, we shall let them get the best start they can."

Although the sky was clear, the light breeze scattered snow down from the branches of the pines onto their heavy cloaks. Ginovêr hunched her shoulders against the shower of damp flakes, puffing her feathers up and glaring about her. "Soon," Margerite promised, shrugging her shoulder as unobtrusively as she could to relieve the shooting pains in it.

Margerite and Johann stopped at the top of the mountain, looking down across the ravine and to the castle on the other side. "This will do, I think," the falconer said. He drew his belt-knife, delicately slicing the jesses and bells from the eagles' feet. "Now?"

She nodded. Together they cast the eagles off. The great birds dropped over the ravine; then their wings caught the air, and they soared slowly upwards, circling the mountain until they had passed out of sight.

Margerite would have liked to ride further, to go on to the shrine and pray out all that was in her heart. But the shifting weight of the child within her reminded her that she had taken enough of a risk by riding up the mountainside, and should not compound it further. "That is Ruprecht's wish fulfilled," she said. "Thank you, Johann. I know that did not come easily to you."

"I am yours to command, Frowe Gräfin," Johann responded, his voice flat and unhappy.

"This summer, if all goes well, we shall get some fine birds to replace them."

"That is very kind, Frowe Gräfin."

Margerite did not press him further, but let him grieve for his loss in silence as they rode back. She had enough thoughts of her own to trouble her.

Bertram was in his chamber in the guard-tower above the chapel, deep in concentration among several sheets of parchment with names and figures neatly lettered upon them. Although he was well-wrapped in blankets, with a charcoal brazier burning at his feet, his face was very white, and the quill shook in his hand.

"You should not be at work yet," Margerite scolded. "The fighting is over, and if there are accounts to be done, they may be left to myself and Kai."

"Perhaps so," Bertram answered softly. "Yet I must have something to fill my mind."

"Rest," Margerite said, taking the quill pen from him. Bertram's rough fingers were very cold beneath her hands, and she held them until they were warm.

"Bertram," she said finally, "I must know this, for it has been tearing at my heart. Will you come with me to Burg Fürstensee when the time comes?"

"What would I do there? No doubt Graf Heinrich has his own Hauptmann of the guard, and they will hardly need another."

"I will need you. Father Etienne has promised to follow me there for a little while, as soon as he has found a priest for Burg Falkenstein and Tiefensee, but he has much to do and will soon be away again. Nor will I be safe by myself in Burg Fürstensee, for the Order already has its man there."

"Nikolaus," Bertram breathed, as if the name were a curse. "Yes."

"And I would not be without you, for I love you."

Bertram straightened his back as if to hide a wince of pain. "I love you as well, Margerite. And yet you will be married to Graf Heinrich - no, there is no doubt that it was the only way to keep you safe, and I thank Mother Maria that Heinrich will be able to protect you, as I cannot. Yet would it be wise for us to be so close together?"

"Perhaps not," Margerite answered. "But I would have you by me, whatever befalls. Will you come to Burg Fürstensee with me?"

"I should not," Bertram said softly. He stared down at the parchments, as though some answer lay in the black letters he had carefully shaped - his beautiful handwriting as much a betrayal of his origins as his skill in fighting on horseback, Margerite thought. She wanted to weep, for the harsh choice that had been given her, the fetters of her marriage to Heinrich that would chafe herself and Bertram equally - but was not being together in shackles, though they were kept from each other's arms by every power of law and custom, better than being free and apart?

Then Bertram looked up at her again, the flecks of green in his eyes shining clear through the shadowed brown, before he closed them for a moment. "I should not," he said again, his voice hoarse as if with tears. "But I will."

to be continued in Book Two

This book takes place in Germany of 1365, four years after the return of the Black Death. The Landgraf's realm (and the bishopric) of Niederwald are, like those of Fürstensee and Falkenstein, fictional, though Bernhardt's neighbors, the Markgraf of Meissen in Saxony and Landgraf Friedrich of Thuringia, are both historical. In this period, the Holy Roman Empire was highly fragmented, so that any number of smaller counties like the above could easily have existed without obvious historical impact.

The Order of Lightbearers is likewise fictional, though well-suited to the background of the fourteenth century, which was both a time of great heresies and the beginning of the Renaissance. The Order is chiefly based on a combination of ideas of the time concerning heretical beliefs and conspiracies, such as those expressed in the trials of the Templars in the early part of the century, and conspiracies of a later date, such as the Bavarian Illuminati. Had a proto-

Glossary

aventail - a throat-protector of chain-mail worn with a
bascinet.

bascinet - an open-faced helmet with a conical top,
sometimes worn under a greathelm.

Frowe - Lady. The masculine equivalent, fro, had
probably been lost before the conversion of the
Germanic peoples; hence the modern Frau and Herr
(the latter from the Old High German herro, implying
age and wisdom). Herr is used here roughly as "lord".

fustian - a type of relatively inexpensive fabric, usually
wool, with a raised nap, similar to velveteen.

Graf - specifically, "Count", but in practise, a Graf could
be anything from a local lord with three knights to the
prince of a very large area. Ruprecht and Heinrich are on
the lower end of the title's implications.

Gräfin - the feminine equivalent to Graf.

greathelm - the typical knight's helmet of the Middle
Ages, covering head and neck. It offered better
protection than the open-faced bascinet, but also
restricted the vision, head-movement, and breathing
of the wearer. Modern re-enactors have been known to
refer to helmets of this type as "sweat-buckets", and for
good reason.

Landgraf/gräfin - a title similar to Graf, but suggesting a
realm of very significant size.

Knappe - squire. Young men of noble birth would be squired to a knight, and would expect to be knighted either on the battlefield after a significant deed, or in the general course of proper service.

Ritter - knight. "Ritter Gottfried" would be equivalent to the English "Sir Gottfried".

Óðinn - the Old Norse name of the god also known as Wodan or Wotan in Germany. He is the Germanic god who is most often associated with magic, particularly the magic of runes and incantations.

panache - a crest of feathers, most popular in eastern Europe at this time.

rondel - a flat circle.

Verjuice - a sharp flavouring made from unripe grapes or sometimes crabapples, used in much the same way as lemon juice is commonly used nowadays.

Melodi Lammond-Grundy grew up in California and went to college at the University of Southern Mississippi. She spent some years in Colorado, then moved to San Francisco, where she was, for a time, a member of the well-known household and writers' community. She has been in the pagan/heathen community since the 1990s and has degrees in both history and anthropology.

In her spiritual life, she has studied spae-craft, a form of trance-based native Germanic divination. A spákona is the diviner, not the art of divination. which she learned from Diana Paxson.

She still practices divination and psychic readings to this day, lending herself to speak about current events. Her writing skills were first shown in several online publications, followed by co-authoring the Falcon Dream Trilogy. Melodi was one of the first authors to come on-board at Three Little Sisters, and we are pleased to be able to present both her non-fiction work and her upcoming Atlantis novel.

From his humble beginnings, Stephan Grundy/Kveldulf Gundarsson would make his mark on the world by writing on the rarest and obscure myths breathing new life into them, for a new generation of readers. His fictional works written under Stephan Grundy focused on mythology and history and were met with international success. Along with his fictional works, under the pen name Kveldulf Gundarsson he stamped his mark on Germanic Paganism (also known as heathenry) and Germanic Culture.

He is an Elder in the organization The Troth where he has dedicated a majority of his life influencing major changes in the organization, including the development of anti-racist and anti-sexist ideals. He has fought for equality in transgendered communities, as well as fighting for the acceptance of Loki. Gundarsson has shaped heathenry through his numerous academic and fictional works as well as his extensive articles, thesis papers, and his creation and sustainment of the lore program within The Troth. His hobbies included wood-working, jewelry making, and gardening as well as historical re-enactment. He is currently attending medical school in Ireland supported by his loving wife Melodi where they maintain a local hof called The Tribe of Thor

The Three Little Sisters

The Three Little Sisters is an indie publisher that puts authors first. We specalize in the strange and unusual. From titles about pagan and heathen spirituality to traditional fiction and non-fiction we bring books to life.

https://the3littlesisters.com